To
FREE
A
SPY

To

FREE

A

SPY

NICK B. GANAWAY

Cover artwork by Karri Klawiter

Published by Greyhart Press

ISBN: 978-1484885734
Also available in eBook editions.

Greyhart
Press

www.greyhartpress.com

For my beloved Lee, without whose love, patience
and encouragement this book would not exist.

CONTENTS

PROLOGUE

Sarov, Nizhny Novgorod Oblast, Russia

BORIS PETREVICH LOOKED AT his hands as he held them in front of him. No tremor. Better than his insides as he watched the seconds tick down on his digital watch, which was synchronized precisely with another digital timepiece three thousand feet from there. No matter his months of preparation, his maplike brainshot of the Sarov compound, his familiarity with the security safeguards, his encyclopedic knowledge of bomb-grade nuclear materials—all of those factors combined held no guarantee that his plan that night and the following days would succeed. He'd weighed whether the stakes were worth the risk but there was no turning back now.

To the extent possible Petrevich had calculated the risks his plan for that night presented. The first would occur when time zero arrived minutes from now. There'd be no problem moving around within Sarov but the guards manning the checkpoint inspected every car leaving the sealed city for radiation. Petrevich had used the most emission-secure travel container available to him in the nuclear lab but the lab's Geiger-counter still reported miniscule leakage. He shielded the radiation exposure within his car as much as he could with the only remaining lead-lined blanket to be found. While there was no assurance he would get past this first hurdle unscathed he was not totally unprepared. Stuck under his belt in the small of his back was the World War II-vintage Russian TT-33 7.62 mm semi-automatic pistol he'd been issued years ago. The model had its flaws, such as no safety latch, but it was what he had. He had not fired it in years, saving up his ration of ammunition, and had never had the occasion to use it in a hostile situation. His once-fine shooting skills would certainly have waned but any use of the pistol required at the Sarov checkpoint would be at close range. Later could be another story: He still had to cross the borders into Georgia and Turkey, then into Iraq—the most worrisome of all. Seth had said certain connections in his network guaranteed Petrevich's safe passage into Iraq at the Habur checkpoint

Seth. Petrevich was putting a lot of faith in this man he'd communicated with only by way of a go-between courier. And he wouldn't see a penny of the money Seth was to pay him until they rendezvoused in Baghdad—if Petrevich made it there with the contraband. It was then that he would collect more money than he'd ever dreamed existed—and that was just the down payment. The rest of it would be paid upon completion of his mission, which was yet to be revealed by Seth. Petrevich knew only that it was a one-year project. He'd demanded payment in United States cash dollars and trusted no one, certainly not some Arab he'd never seen before, and he would be prepared for that meeting in Baghdad; he would find a place to stash the uranium until he was paid to avoid any subterfuge Seth might be planning. But for now he was focused on the present moment.

Sarov, known as *Arzamas-16* during the Cold War and later *Kremlyov*, was Russia's answer to the U.S.'s Los Alamos, the respective nerve centers of nuclear weapons design during the decades of psychological belligerence between the two world powers. Petrevich had been the chief nuclear scientist, officially the "Scientific Director," at Arzamas-16, and ruled his scientists with an iron will.

When the Soviet Union collapsed, so too had Petrevich's political armor that had once enabled him to thumb his nose at the generals and even party under-officials. The little people had taken control and decided they had no need of Petrevich, throwing him out of his relatively luxurious suite. It wasn't that he had been targeted for revenge. Far worse, the former Scientific Director had been ignored as an irrelevance.

Now for the last time Petrevich looked around the meager flat assigned to him and got down to his car to wait as the final seconds ticked off. His aged black Volvo was packed with the few personal items he was taking, along with the case containing the uranium. Exactly when expected, the flash from the blast lit up the sky and three seconds later the sound reached his ears. The ground trembled momentarily under the car. He waited the ten minutes it would take for authorities to be awakened and to realize that the explosion was at the old monastery where the nuclear material was secured. Not that the three-hundred-year-old monastery still held any religious sentiment. They would be worried about containing the nuclear hazard. Every military, fire and hazmat operative in the city would be needed at the site, and even the checkpoint security was sure to be in disarray, with too little time to regroup. Petrevich's life depended on that and his timing was critical.

He pulled into the street and took the route through the dark city that he knew would be the less traveled during the minutes after the explosion. It would take him four minutes to reach the checkpoint and by then fourteen or fifteen minutes would have elapsed since the explosion. The remaining checkpoint guards would be focused on the blast with their radios and phones. Boris Petrevich in his old Volvo would be the least of their worries.

Petrevich approached the halogen-flooded checkpoint that was framed by the reinforced-concrete archway and columns that had always reminded him of Berlin's Brandenburg Gate. Gone were the machine-gun emplacements but the tangle of concertina wire topping the parallel concrete walls bordering Sarov's four square miles remained. Flight from this top-secret military-industrial complex where he'd devoted his life to his country's global security was mere seconds away. *If only it were that simple*, Petrevich thought. There were no other vehicles at this the only remaining checkpoint in Sarov and Petrevich felt a moment of relief when he saw only two guards rather than the usual eight or so. A single alert German Shepherd stood watch inside the kiosk with one of them as the other officer approached the Volvo. "What's going on?" Petrevich said to the officer.

"We are not sure, sir. The first report was of an explosion at the monastery, where I've heard nuclear materials are stored. They've called for every available guard to report there." He held the Geiger-counter at his side and walked around the car, as Petrevich knew he'd done a thousand times before. The guard returned to the driver-side window and stuck the hand-held instrument inside the car, where it began its signature ticking that was so familiar to Petrevich. "Do you know of any reason your car might be hot, sir?"

Petrevich's pulse quickened but he maintained an unconcerned look. "My work is inside the monastery. I go there daily." He shrugged. "That's likely the problem."

"Let's be sure." The guard said it without a hint of suspicion. "You don't want any extra exposure. Why don't you step out of the car so that I can check inside more thoroughly? And I will need to see your credentials." Petrevich had hoped to avoid these intrusions.

He got out of the car and reached behind his back as if to retrieve his papers. The officer did not see the T-33 before the 7.62 mm round destroyed the left side of his head. The other guard, who had been paying only casual attention, became alert and took aim at Petrevich but not soon enough. At least one of Petrevich's four rounds struck him, entering his right

13

eye socket and exiting the back of his head along with fragments of skull and brain tissue. Still, he had managed to activate a piercing general alarm before being shot but Petrevich knew it would be only one of the many to which overloaded authorities were busy responding. Petrevich fired a round at the guard dog, who did not die immediately but was incapacitated and yelping in pain. He had studied the video security system at the lab and knew how to delete all images at the checkpoint kiosk. With that done there was nothing to give the authorities any information to track him with. They would figure it out eventually, of course, but there were ninety-thousand residents in Sarov and a budding nuclear disaster to deal with. It would take some time. By then Petrevich would be far away, perhaps even all the way to Georgia, whose cooperation with Russia was in shambles. Soon after that, Turkey, but his trail would be cold by then. His final border crossing, at Habur, into Iraq, was nineteen-hundred miles south—three days driving, with luck. Once in Iraq it would no longer be the authorities he'd be worried about. It would be Seth.

Petrevich soon reached the P180 highway and turned south. He drove through the night and well into the next gloomy afternoon, stopping only for fuel and food and eating at the wheel. He kept an eye on his rearview mirror where the occasional car, following for too long, raised his awareness but in every case it sooner or later turned off on another route or went past him. Nevertheless he'd survived this far by being paranoid and he wasn't going to relax his senses now. By nightfall he found an obscure spot to park the car and slept for an hour.

Petrevich felt himself tensing up as he drew closer to the checkpoint at the Georgia border but he was waved through with hardly any delay. The drive through the small country was short. The mountainous Turkey terrain slowed him down but he didn't mind. He was far from Sarov.

The road sign said the Iraq border was one mile ahead. Petrevich pulled off the road at the first fuel station he'd seen in hours, thinking it might be the last one before he entered Iraq. Seth had promised Habur would be an uneventful checkpoint. Petrevich would soon find out.

* * *

Back in Sarov, a young Russian Army officer walked into the office of her commanding general. "Sir, we have a possible motive for the murder of the two guards at the checkpoint four days ago. A significant amount of nuclear material is missing from the secure area."

Washington D.C.

President Garrison Cross finished a White House meeting with House and Senate leaders from both sides of the aisle, including those from the intelligence committees, and now nurtured a blinding headache both literally and figuratively. *How could so many lawmakers in Congress believe that attacks stemming from 9/11 were in America's rear-view mirror now?* He'd made little progress that morning in convincing them to act on his demand for the list of aggressive new security measures he'd proposed. But Cross had the advantage, *or was it the disadvantage*, he thought, of the intel briefings, classified as Sensitive Compartmented Information, brought to him every morning at eight o'clock by a top-level officer of the Central Intelligence Agency.

It wasn't enough for Cross to scan the reports or to have them summarized for him. He read through them while rapid-firing questions at the CIA officer, who had long ago learned to come prepared. The reports had become increasingly ominous in recent months, in part due to ever-advancing detection capabilities but Cross knew the Al-Qaeda mentality had proliferated among independent operators. The looming consensus of those in Cross's intelligence team was that a major nuclear event on the mainland was a good bet within the next year. It was no secret that the terrorist groups were just one buy of bomb-ready nuclear material away from such an attempt. Acquiring enough for a "dirty" bomb—something to cause local destruction, however devastating—was no longer their aim: They wanted a world-class disaster, something on the order of the bombings that ended the war with Japan more than six decades ago. It was not only Al-Qaeda he worried about. Many other rogue states and movements frequently made statements to remind the United States and its friends of their hate-filled intentions. Still, Congress wouldn't budge, citing constituency opposition.

But there had been two signal events that ultimately brought President Cross to the decision he was about to implement. Russia recently announced that it would no longer cooperate with the United States and other Western nations to secure and effectively manage the former Soviet nuclear stockpile, saying that Russia could manage it alone. Cross and his national security apparatus were dubious of the claim and believed that opened the door for dramatic expansion of the black market for weapons-grade nuclear materials, for which there certainly were customers. The second factor was the recent apprehension of one Harvey Joplan, an officer of the Central Intelligence Agency, believed to be a mole on the inside of the secretive organization playing against American interests. And Cross knew from his own term at the CIA that the Agency maintained a database not only of locations where the old Soviet nuke stockpile was secured but also the names of actors believed to pose a risk of smuggling nuclear materials out of Russia. U.S. intelligence knew that many of the nuclear scientists at Kremlyov were essentially abandoned by the broken system and even now remained unemployed—some of them likely ripe for using their privileged knowledge and access for illicit purposes. Kremlyov was the former secret government compound where Russian nuclear war systems were designed and manufactured—and still stored. All of this added up to potential for the most dire of outcomes. The identity of the Russian scientists was among the CIA's carefully guarded secrets.

Cross had been CIA Director before winning the White House, and ensuring the safety of the American people had been his signature presidential campaign theme. It was unknown at this point whether the mole had already delivered compromising intelligence to Iran or other supporters of terrorism but it was irresponsible to assume otherwise. Although the CIA and the FBI had scored many successes in the war on terror, Cross knew the U.S. was fighting with one hand behind its back because of bureaucratic hoops and counterproductive laws and regulations—not to mention the press and the ACLU—that often made necessary security measures impossible. And now the *Washington Post* had reported the deliberate exposure by NSA contractor Edward Snowden of a highly secretive National Security Agency operation known as PRISM. Cross knew the leak rendered the program, which the FBI had said prevented numerous terrorist operations, a liability rather than an effective prevention tool

Now it was time for Cross to find a way to do what Congress wouldn't do and the intel agencies couldn't do.

The Pentagon delivered Cameron Warfield's military records to the Oval Office and President Garrison Cross spent the next forty minutes going through them. Once finished, he told his secretary that he was not to be disturbed, leaned back in his chair, and propped his feet on the corner of the grand *Resolute* desk that had served a number of presidents before him.

Cross gazed out into the Rose Garden thinking over his plan one more time, then thumped Warfield's thick folder, confirmed in his belief that Warfield was the choice candidate for the job he was about to throw at him. If not Cam Warfield for this job, *then who?*

Cross frankly was skeptical that Warfield would accept the assignment. For one thing, Warfield was dedicated to Lone Elm, the counterterrorism camp he built from scratch as an army officer and later took over as a private contractor. Warfield conceived the Lone Elm Counterintelligence Center when he was a full colonel in the army, and sold the idea up the chain of command. He received support for its creation from the secretary of defense, and Congress approved the facility following secret hearings in which Warfield's successful record in counterespionage carried weight. But it had been a fight. The CIA and FBI opposed it, which Cross knew was simple rivalry.

Warfield could make it from Lone Elm to the White House in an hour except during rush hours. He would just as soon never cross the Potomac River into the city again but curiosity about the meeting with Cross occupied his mind now. Paula Newnan, the president's personal assistant, had called him the day before to set up the meeting but if she knew what it was about she wouldn't say. Warfield liked Garrison Cross from the time they first met several years ago at Lone Elm. Cross was just getting his feet wet as Director of Central Intelligence, his only government job before winning the presidency, when he called Warfield and invited himself to spend a few days at Lone Elm for orientation.

Warfield knew of Cross even before then. He had been a business leader in the news often during a three-year battle to save Berington Pacific, a Fortune 100 company, from bankruptcy and his name had become a household word. The president had grown up on a farm, gone to Yale and then to Harvard Law where he graduated third in his class.

Warfield cleared security at the White House compound's Northwest Appointment Gate and inside was escorted to a waiting area where Paula Newnan soon appeared. "Knew you couldn't wait any longer to see me," she said. Warfield had learned he could rely on Paula. She'd cut through bureaucratic red tape for him more than once but always gave President Cross the credit. "The boss says I am to always accommodate you. Otherwise, you wouldn't get the time of day from me, *Cameo*," she said, laughing. Warfield had her birthday in a reminder file and always called her. They had lunch or a beer now and then and she had enough self-confidence to rag him any time she found an opportunity.

She parked Warfield in a small office in the basement that she said was rarely used.

Cross walked in a few minutes later carrying a thin leather folder and stuck out his hand. At six-foot-one he was about an inch taller than Warfield and maybe ten pounds heavier. Warfield hadn't seen him for a few months except on TV. He still had an athletic build, a full head of hair that matched the silver-gray suit he wore and an easy smile.

"Glad you could come, Cam." The president's handshake was rock solid.

"Mr. President."

Cross gestured toward a pair of leather chairs separated by a corner table. An aide brought in coffee and pastries and closed the door when she left.

Cross said, "You're looking well, Cam. Fleming DeGrande must be taking good care of you."

Even though Cross and Fleming had met on a few occasions, Cross always referred to her by her first and last names.

"As always. But she's as busy as I am. We meet up on weekends."

"Marryin' that girl, Cam?"

"Not sure she'd have me. And how's the first lady?"

Cross smiled as he took a croissant off the tray. "I'll tell her you asked. She's fine. She never dreamed it would be like this, the public life. Handles it okay I guess, after two years."

"And her husband?"

Cross laughed. "Ah, her husband. That's another question. I can't say I was ready either, but I asked for it. Truth is, I like the action. I think my blood pressure optimizes when things are hovering around the edges of chaos. Which brings me to the reason I invited you here, Cam." Cross paused and locked onto Warfield's eyes. "There's a mole. He's locked up— at least for now. CIA operator named Joplan, Harvey Joplan."

Warfield nodded, wondering how he fit into this picture.

"I need you back in, Cam. For awhile."

So that was it. It had been a long time since Warfield worked in the field. At Lone Elm, he taught others how to do it—at least the mechanics and theory of it. But the art of intelligence and counterintelligence was something like having a talent for the violin. Either the candidates who come to Lone Elm have something on the ball or they achieve mediocrity.

Warfield loved action but Lone Elm was his life now. He was responsible to the people who came there for training, to the army and to his employees, but he owed the president the courtesy of listening. He waited for Cross to continue.

Cross briefed Warfield on the FBI's investigation of Joplan. They had been trying for months to get enough evidence to convict him before they arrested him but ten days ago he was boarding a flight to Paris and they had to pick him up before they wanted to. Joplan was not cooperating and the FBI director, Earl Fullwood, couldn't give Cross any assurance that he ever would. Of course the most urgent problem was to find out who Joplan's present contact was. Then they would determine the damage he'd done within the CIA and attempt to mitigate it.

The FBI had filed an affidavit in federal court detailing what it had on Joplan so far, in order to persuade the judge to allow the Bureau to search his house, office, cars and computer hard drives. The judge was reluctant based on the slender evidence but agreed to the searches with the condition that Joplan would be released in seven days unless substantial new evidence was uncovered.

With that said, Cross paused and looked at Warfield.

Warfield still wasn't clear on why Cross needed him. The Bureau understood the requirements and had the people to press the investigation. That was what the Bureau did, wasn't it?

"So what did you have in mind for me, Mr. President?"

"Take Joplan over."

Warfield was stunned.

He didn't think highly of FBI chief Earl Fullwood but the Bureau had its resources. And unlike in the old days, the CIA cooperated with the FBI in the investigation when either agency had a security problem like Joplan.

Warfield stood up and ambled around the room for a minute as he gathered his thoughts. "Don't see how it would work, Mr. President. You've got the FBI, the CIA. They're not bad at what they do. I can tell you they wouldn't hang out any yellow ribbons for me to come in and claim the prey they just brought down. They opposed Lone Elm, as you remember. And I'm not too hot to work with them, either, to tell you the truth. All that rigmarole they have to go through. The bureaucracy, the press. Criminal rights to the point of absurdity. I'm more into the kind of work where we don't have so many rules. Even made my own a time or two," Warfield said.

Cross nodded. "That's why this case needs you, Cam. You'd take Joplan out of their hands for awhile. Work on your own, from this room we're sitting in. Whatever staff you need is here." He threw his hands out to indicate the vastness of the resources available.

"With all respect, sir, I don't see how it would be any different with me. Somebody here goes to the john and the newspapers write a front-page story about it. ACLU or some other group files a lawsuit. We fill up all the file cabinets with denials, rebuttals, explanations. Everything moves an inch per millennium. Pretty soon I'd be as bogged down as the FBI or any other outfit here in Washington."

Cross nodded. "That's just it, Cam. Only a handful here will know what you're doing. No reporters coming around. Your name won't be on anybody's list. You need red tape cut, some rules bent, that kind of thing, you call me. You already have all the security clearance anyone can get. No one will be checking to see where you are. You'll report to me, maybe through Paula at times—she knows how to get around the roadblocks. Lot of autonomy to act on your own judgment, and a phone number that'll reach me anywhere in a couple of minutes when you need me."

Warfield had to admit it made some sense. His existence wouldn't be known outside of a small circle—Fullwood from FBI, CIA's Quinn, the secretary of state, the national security advisor. And even they wouldn't have to know much if Cross wanted it that way.

Warfield sat down and finished the last of his coffee. "What's the Joplan investigation turned up so far?"

Cross pushed the Joplan file over to him. The FBI summary inside told what they had learned about Joplan's bank accounts, spending habits, social contacts, family relationships, cars, clothes and house mortgage. Phone taps and the trash recovered from Joplan's garbage cans revealed almost nothing. Cross said the FBI didn't expect to find much more, even with the warrant. Joplan had covered his tracks.

Warfield scanned the file. "It's obvious why they can't hold him with what they have here."

"And the clock's ticking."

"What have you told Fullwood and Quinn?"

"Nothing. If you take the job, I'll get them in here for a little kickoff meeting. I'll bring in Stern, too." Otto Stern was the national security advisor.

"Where is Joplan being held?"

"The Bureau has him across the river in Virginia. Alexandria Detention Center."

Warfield thought about it for a moment, then said, "Here's what's holding me back, Mr. President. I would have to run the show—Joplan all to myself. No interference from CIA or FBI, any other agencies. You're not going to want to grant me that."

Cross stood and Warfield followed. Cross's hands capped Warfield's shoulders as the president seemed to weigh the moment with due gravity. "I'll give you Joplan exclusively, Cam. But with that comes all of the responsibility that a president can transfer to you. A lot of our intel brains think something big is in the works now. You're the one man I trust with this job and it's not just national security. The very essence of American culture is at stake. You have seven days to find out who Joplan's contact is. That will lead you to the nukes that walked out of Kremlyov, which if not stopped … well, only God can help us."

PART ONE
Karly Amarson

CHAPTER 1

KARLY AMARSON WINCED AT the tremor in her fingers as she punched the *Washington Post* telephone number into the phone next to her bed. When the line began to ring she replaced the receiver in its cradle and laid out the jewelry she'd chosen to complement the dress she was going to wear before jumping into the shower. Thoughts of the evening, now just an hour away, raised goose bumps on her soft skin even as the steaming water drenched her body. Never in the eight years she'd entertained Atlantic City's high-end clientele had there been so much to gain as tonight. Or so much to lose. A smile crossed her lips as something reminded her of the times as a little girl when she lured Tommy Scott who lived next door into some scheme she'd dreamed up that never turned out well for him.

Karly stepped out of the shower, pulled a body towel around her shoulders and bent closer to the mirror, focusing on the micro wrinkles around her eyes as she'd done with increasing frequency over the past few months. *What do you want, confirmation you're getting old? That you're doing the right thing?* She traced one of the threadlike lines with a fingernail until the water drops winding their way down her neck turned her attention to her body. *Not so bad,* she told herself, her breasts were still high, her buttocks firm, stomach hard and flat, and the attention shown her by her regulars had never waned. But twenty-nine in her line of work approached retirement age. The quality of life curve for high-end ladies of the evening nosedived after thirty. Maintaining her assets in spin classes, in the pool, on the strength machines…that all took more and more time, and inevitably at some point would quit producing the results she required. Surgery was the usual fix after botox, laser, Sculptra, and the like no longer did the trick, but even that was simply delaying the inevitable. *Go in for a remake every couple of years? Pass!* She'd invested some of her money but not nearly enough to provide the lifestyle she had become accustomed to—and intended to enjoy for the rest of her life.

Frank Gallardi had offered her a job, any job she wanted, there in his Golden Touch Casino & Hotel if she decided to get out of the business, but Atlantic City no longer excited her as it once did. No. It was time to advance to a better life. For the last year, she had dreamed of a new place away from the hotel. Away from casinos, away from Atlantic City. Maybe New York. She loved the city the times she'd been there with Jag, and if her plan she called the 401-Karly went well tonight, her dream could come true.

Karly had done okay in Atlantic City but it had not always been like that. Looking back at the beginning of her career now, she could only smile at her naivety at that time. That was, what, ten years ago? She'd dropped out of the Monahan Finishing College in Des Moines and headed straight to New Orleans. Her street-smarts were nil and the education she received there were painfully expensive. Karly landed a job her first day in the Crescent City and she grimaced now as she remembered the serpentine copper-top bar on which she danced and taunted Bourbon Street revelers with her charms. Dominick, who owned the place—the *Cajun Palace*, it was called, *a misnomer if there ever was one*—had followed through on his promise to give Karly's poster top billing on the Bourbon Street marquee and the money was good, but soon Dominick was renting her out. She resisted at first but the other young dancers seemed okay with their lives and encouraged her. *It's only while you're getting started*, they'd said.

Dominick had served himself as well to her wares when he felt like it and the greasy bastard's scent still haunted Karly's olfactory memory. Like those professional fragrance experts she'd read about who could identify a perfume he or she had last sniffed twenty years earlier. And then there was Richard, her next encounter, who put her in the hospital twice. She shivered now as she recalled how close she'd walked to the edge, how desperately homicidal she was after that, how she'd acted on her impulse. Except for the murder detective who hated slimebags like Richard she'd be in prison now, she knew, instead of a luxurious hotel suite where she'd worked out an arrangement with Frank Gallardi, a man who represented the other end of the decency spectrum.

As Karly started her makeup now she thought of a couple of girls who'd made it big in Atlantic City, but most of them stayed with a pimp until they were too old and wound up with second-rate clients for awhile, then dancing for garter cash in one of the strip dives a block off the Boardwalk.

Half of them ended up dying of violence or AIDS before they hit forty. It was an unthinkable end, but what was the next act if they had lived?

Karly knew she still had what it takes. She'd learned she could make one of the politicians from Washington want her more than he wanted his political campaign fund. And she had lost count of the men who would pay her to undress and simply lie there while he looked at her. Somehow that, of all things, made her uncomfortable. They would talk about her milk-white skin and golden strands of hair and perfect legs and green eyes and never lay a hand on her. Some sobbed. She wasn't about to believe all the things men said to her, but she knew she was different.

Her favorite clients were the power brokers from the nation's capitol who came to Atlantic City on weekends. Seeing them on TV, she'd laugh at the swaggering speeches they made about drugs or honor or children, and then she'd get one of them in her bed and let her blond mane fall over his face and whisper to him. "What'll it be, now, cowboy? Those family values you talk about, or Karly's values?" After she had satiated them they would go back to Washington to run the government. The world, to hear them tell it.

She had experimented with some of them with a well-timed whisper. "When can you come back? I don't wanna spend any more time than I have to with someone else," she would say half-jokingly. "If I do, it'll just be to pay the rent until you return." Some actually fell for it: "How much d'you need to get by on until I can get back a couple of weeks from now?" and they'd add a few more crumpled bills to the wad in her hand. Never examine it in their presence, Karly had learned. But she'd count it the instant they were out the door and seldom was she disappointed as she showered and powdered and made herself ready for her next rendezvous.

Tonight she would put to work all the street smarts and charm she could muster. *Like a final exam*, she thought. If it worked, hard days would be over. Several of her Washington regulars had wanted to see her tonight and that had provided her the opportunity to play the supply and demand game. "Oh, I wish you'd called sooner," she'd said, but she had no one other than Jag on her mind and he'd called that morning. Just as she knew he would.

"Oh, Jag, you're my fave," she'd breathed into the phone. "But you've called so late. I'll have to see if I can get out of anoth—"

"Work it out!"

"I'll try, Jag," she'd said. He was powerful in Washington and according to her research, rich. That was the main thing. And he was hooked on her. He was the right man for her plan, and he'd taken the bait, right down to the last hour.

Frank Gallardi, the developer, owner and operator of the Golden Touch, widely considered the top casino and hotel on Atlantic City's legendary Boardwalk, was going over the words he would deliver that evening downstairs in the Austin Quinn Ballroom, the largest and grandest of all those in the Golden Touch. He'd agreed to emcee the Quinn celebration that was to take place in the room named after Austin Quinn himself. Gallardi saw politics as an evil to be tolerated, but Quinn was due a lot of credit for the reality of casino gambling in the state. Gallardi had managed the industry side of the legalization process and fed Quinn, then a state senator, the technical knowledge he needed in his political negotiations and the eventual crafting of the legislation in Trenton. It took eight years in all. Gallardi was awarded the first casino license issued in New Jersey and Quinn's reward was election to the United States Senate. Gallardi named the walnut-paneled ballroom after Quinn as a tribute to him by the industry and an eighteen-karat gold plaque signed by all the original casino owners on the Boardwalk adorned the entrance to the Austin Quinn Ballroom.

Gallardi expected to see a lot of his Washington regulars at the Quinn party. At least a dozen of them had called today to say hello. Some of them were rarely seen or heard, and others frequently made the Business & Finance pages of the *Wall Street Journal*, but all of them were powerful and wealthy. They liked being at his place, and Gallardi knew they wanted him to know they were there.

Even President McNabb might make an appearance at Quinn's roast. The Secret Service was busy putting their security in place but told Gallardi that McNabb's appearance was iffy due to a developing incident with North Korea. It was great publicity to have the president visit the Golden Touch but the last time he was there his security network caused a ripple through the casino.

The hotel was full tonight and the game rooms reserved for members of its private Trophy Club were jammed. The Precious Metal, the Tiger's Tail and every other casino on the Boardwalk also had its own VIP club with private elevators and secluded gambling rooms for high-stakes gamblers who wanted separation from weekenders and honeymooners, even the usual run of professional gamblers, but none was as successful as Gallardi's Trophy Club. Frank knew from the start it would take more than showgirls and glitz to attract the icons of politics and entertainment he wanted in his place. They would come for luxury-class treatment, plenty of action and the chance to leave their identity at the door for a change. No damning front-page photo in tomorrow's paper after a night letting their hair down.

He sent that promise along with complimentary Trophy Club membership to every man and woman in the U.S. House and Senate, to all the president's cabinet members and to U.S. ambassadors to fifty countries. To the governor of every state, field-grade officers in the military, and to appointed top officials in all three branches of government. To well-known high-stakes gamblers, and even the heads of all the other Boardwalk casinos. To his friends in the business world and hundreds in the entertainment field. The promotion alone cost five million dollars up front but now the Trophy Club's game rooms and other reserved areas bustled with the people Gallardi wanted in them. Most of the casinos on the Boardwalk were owned by large corporations with unlimited budgets and were twice the size of the Golden Touch, but Gallardi didn't care about size. He'd built the Golden Touch for close to a billion dollars and by now had paid off his loans and owned it outright, and the Trophy Club's success had earned him the respect—and envy—of the other casino owners.

On the twelfth floor, the man Karly Amarson called *Jag* stood at his window overlooking the Atlantic in what could pass for reverence for the power of the sea as wave after wave slammed against the shore. The cold December rain had stopped for now and the few who ventured out onto the Boardwalk, perhaps to seek better fortune at another casino, were shapeless figures, changing from dim to dimmer and back to dim in the sea mist as they passed from one lamppost to the next. Hostile ocean waves like the ones below had always held a strange appeal for Jag. Despite their might, or maybe because of it, he felt in control. He could taunt them with his closeness, yet with all their fury they could do him no harm.

He nodded unnoticeably at the thought of seeing Karly tonight, and wondered, as he'd done since meeting her three years earlier, what was so different about her. Women before her had been plentiful but his interest in them was usually measured in hours. Karly was mysterious. Smart. Not too available. Never to be taken for granted. In a dream one night, he could never get a clear look at her because of a whorl of smoke between them. He could see her tempting smile, the suggestion of her perfect body through a sheer covering, and hear her call out to him, but when he tried to approach her she turned her face to him and flashed her long eyelashes tauntingly as she disappeared into the mist.

Karly had known he'd be in town tonight but told him on the phone this morning she was busy. She would try to work it out. He tolerated her bullshit games, but the other side of the coin was that she demanded nothing of him. No visits to the boutiques or restaurants downstairs and no guilt-trip lectures even if he didn't call or show up for weeks. Just the wad of hundreds he put into her hand when he would leave her, which he could afford. And liked. It was a small price for the freedom to appear and to leave when he wanted to, to not be expected to account for his whereabouts. For anything. A mutually-rewarding relationship that existed on weekends, when he'd leave the government and his wife and head for Atlantic City. There he could dismiss his personal armor whose week-long job it had been to defend against all the official intrusions on his limited time and allow his hormones that had been pushed aside all week to take their inalienable role. That's when he would become *Jag*, as Karly had branded him the first time they met. But that tag was between them and he intended for it to stay that way.

He downed his second Glenfiddich 18 and checked to be sure he had all the parts to his tux. He'd bought a red bow tie with gold stripes to wear this time. There needed to be some distinction between the servers and the served. As he shaved, he thought about the party. He still had time to see Karly before it started if she called, but if not he'd see her afterwards and spend the night in her suite upstairs, as usual when he was in Atlantic City.

The phone rang as he was about to hit the shower. He couldn't deny his thin smile as she breathed how she had managed to get free for the evening. "All for you, Jag." Did she think he fell for her obvious manipulations, he wondered, but it didn't matter. The party downstairs did matter. He was a politician and seeing and being seen by the right people was life blood. But as he showered, his thoughts were on Karly—her scent, her smoothness, the silky hair, her voice rasping her *where-the-hell've-you-been- I've-needed-you* fodder, her sculpted calves and thighs that would wrap him in a prison of soft yarn…and those green eyes. He knew the thinness of her adoration and figured she knew that he knew. Just part of the charade they would continue this weekend.

He checked the time again. Less than two hours until he was downstairs among the Who's Who of Washington, and here he was thinking of Karly. He had sworn off of her once but didn't remember why just now. It sure wasn't because of the marriage vows he'd taken. He doubted now if he loved his wife even years ago when maybe he thought he had. Now their marriage, beyond hostile, worn-out, wasted away like property values in a D.C. ghetto.

But there was no way out of the marital union. His father-in-law was a retired United States Senator from Jag's own state who liked Jag from the beginning and catapulted him into politics. Now, more than twenty years later, the old man, a national icon, still wielded enormous power: An advisor to presidents and a favorite of television news types who went to him and others like Henry Kissinger for a weighty utterance on the international crisis *du jour*. If Jag feared any man, it was his father-in-law. He could doom his son-in-law's political future, including his fertile hopes for the White House that lived in the back of Jag's mind, with no more effort than required to pick up the phone. And it looked like the old Washington warrior was going to live forever.

But Jag didn't worry much about his wife stirring things up for him. She had her own reasons for hanging onto their marriage. She never seemed to mind being seen with him at high-profile Washington balls or finding her picture on the society pages. He wondered for a moment whether she was involved with someone, but rolled his eyes at the thought: *That would involve sex.*

He'd fantasized about a future without his wife but knew Karly Amarson would have no place in it. There'd be no need for the secrecy she offered. And even if she was the most beautiful woman he'd ever seen, the most uninhibited lover, she was still who she was, simply a high-priced whore. But she was convenient now. He could fly her to meet him in New York for plays and museums and shopping at Saks and Tiffany's and dinner at Fiorio's on West Fifty-Second where he wouldn't be recognized and the music was seductive and they could dance and then go to their hotel suite and make love and sleep it all off, and he'd go back to Washington and she'd return to the Golden Touch Casino & Hotel and a life he never allowed himself to think about.

But today he was in Atlantic City and he'd see Karly for the first time in two weeks, or was it three, and distancing himself from her was not in his immediate plans. She was an elevator ride away, his ambivalence was banished, and for the weekend Karly Amarson was everything he wanted.

Karly finished dressing, poured herself another drink and leaned back in a leather chair in the living room, taking a minute to survey her place. It hadn't been that hard to swing, actually. She had proposed the deal to a reluctant Frank Gallardi one morning after he'd had a blockbuster month in the casino. "Frank, I can bring my clients to the Golden Touch or I can take 'em somewhere else. They don't give a damn where my bed is. Before and after they're through with me they're gonna play the tables downstairs or in the Trophy Club. Give you their money. You know it's true, and all you have to do is give me a furnished suite. One I can live in. Like an apartment. No checking in and out at the front desk. And I want maids when I call them. No knocking on the door, '…Sorry, just checking your room, Ma'am….' That's a fatal interruption if my customer's about ready to buy me a new ring—one, I might add, I can help him pick out in one of your nifty jewelry shops downstairs."

Frank had suppressed a smile when she playfully ended her proposal with a modified curtsey that day and lifted her skirt to reveal much of her legs. He walked to the window of his office and looked out at the ocean for a couple of minutes before returning to her.

"Okay, I'll do it, Karly, but it's strictly business. I'm not into sport sex and I run a business here. I ever get the idea it's not paying off for me in dollars, that'll end it. There won't be any discussion. Understood?" Then he walked over to where she was standing and enveloped her with his arms. Secretly, Frank loved her like the daughter he never had.

That was three years ago, and Frank put everything into her suite she had asked for. He threw in an allowance for room-service meals and gave her access to old Doc Ricardo, the house physician who'd been with Frank since Day One. Gallardi didn't go out of his way to promote sex, but he wasn't naïve either. It was going to happen with or without Karly Amarson, with or without the Golden Touch, and with or without Frank Gallardi.

Karly and Doc Ricardo had become close friends. He never judged her and he frequently examined her in his small office on the third floor to be sure she was still healthy. He never hit on her but they would often have dinner together at a good restaurant at one of the other casinos. They were possibly Frank Gallardi's most loyal business associates within the hotel and casino. Karly knew that Doc, who had no specific duties other than an occasional guest or patron emergency, kept his eyes and ears alert for anything business or personal that might be harmful to Frank or the casino or hotel. Like Karly, he lived in the hotel and she felt like she could call on him for anything at any time.

She had selected the furniture and artwork for her suite, the kitchen appliances, designer cookware *(as if I'm going to cook!)* and the finishes for the walls and floors. She insisted on the precise shades of rust and cream in the rugs to complement the Italian marble and now she thought how well they looked together.

Karly walked over to the bookcases that framed the fireplace, where a blown-glass vase in a swirl of sunrise reds pointed to the sky and occupied its own shelf. Leather-bound books lined other shelves and Karly pulled down *The Portrait of a Lady*, by Henry James. The book fell open, allowing a bookmark to flutter to the floor. She sat on the sofa and read a couple of passages to remind herself what was happening when she last put it down. *There'll be plenty of time for reading after tonight.* She took in her place once again and thought how different her life was now compared to the two years she spent in New Orleans a decade ago. Yet another phase would begin tonight!

As she was finishing her drink Jag's signature rat-a-tat-tat on her apartment door broke the silence. She made a final mirror check. Everything she had on, he'd given her. Like the diamond necklace and earrings, which she figured were fake. They might be CZs but she didn't mind: The rocks were big and no one could tell cubic zirconium from diamonds anyway. But the diamond ring was real for sure. She was with Jag at Tiffany's in Manhattan when he bought it for her. She had asked for their initials to be engraved inside the ring's gold band and he had agreed to "KA & JAG".

She touched the rim of the blue bottle of perfume he'd bought for her in New York. It was called "Angel" and he'd said it was named just for her.

That New York evening at dinner he had told her the gifts were for never expecting anything of him. That was when she knew Jag had big bucks and would shell them out. Who besides a fool would spend that much money on a hooker unless he had a ton of it? Jag sure wasn't some backwater on his first trip to the city who'd get caught up in the glamour atmosphere of beautiful girls and fast-flowing whiskey and max out his American Express card. What she didn't like so much was having his security detail, usually just one man, follow them around when they went out of Atlantic City. He was always out of sight, but she felt his presence nonetheless. Jag told her the shadow was a necessary fixture in his life in government. She wondered if that was a fact. She was adjusting an earring when he knocked again. "Just a minute," she sang, downing a second Valium for insurance, which Doc Ricardo supplied to her.

She scanned the living room and dimmed the lighting another notch. As she stood by the door, she mentally ran through her lines that she would use later in the evening and nodded to herself. *Game time.* She cracked the door and gave Jag a mischievous look until he pushed it open wide and took her into his arms. At that very, most inopportune, moment, Maria Sanchez walked by in the hallway. The hotel's head of housekeeping flashed Karly an embarrassed grin and picked up her pace. Karly had gone out of her way to make friends with Maria soon after occupying the apartment. Her housekeeping staff could be an ally or they could be a nuisance, and Karly often sent small gifts and flowers to Maria. They had become friends and Karly had called Maria for lunch many times over the years to unload her problems on her. Even The Bad need a shoulder to cry on sometimes, Karly told herself. But there was something in it for Maria, too, Karly knew: Straight-laced Maria was able to glimpse a world that was forbidden to her.

"Don't you look great!" Karly chirped after Maria passed, clinging to Jag's neck. "Sorry I kept you waiting, Big Guy."

Jag had drawn away. "Who was that?" he said, peering down the hallway.

"Nobody important," she whispered, pulling him into the room.

"Who was it?" he said, wanting to know who'd seen him there.

"*Jaaag*, come on. It was only Maria, the executive housekeeper."

"The maid in the blazer! Always nosing around."

He was over it now. He smiled as he pulled Karly close and craned around her shoulder to get a better look at the back of her. The bottom of the cocktail dress revealed her thighs, and her tiptoeing made her calves so very appealing. She was wearing nothing under the dress, and he felt the familiar excitement as he caressed her neck.

"How much time do you have?" she asked.

"Hour or so. It's downstairs at seven, then back here little later." He followed her to the sofa near the window overlooking the ocean. "I could use a drink."

"Great, and I've got your stuff, of course," she said, prancing over to the stereo. She was more playful than usual.

She put on a CD and said she'd do the drinks. "You can take the cheese into the bedroom. I mean, if the bedroom's okay with you," she said teasingly.

Jag liked the idea of having a drink or two, lying in bed with her, lights low, touching her skin, and it was okay with him if they put off lovemaking until later. For one thing, time was not unlimited now, and he'd have something to anticipate during the roast downstairs. After it was over, they'd have all night. All weekend.

Karly set their drinks on the bar and disappeared into the bathroom. Jag put them with the cheese on the bedside lamp table, sliced off a sliver, popped it into his mouth and drowned it with Scotch. Pepper cheese, it was. His favorite. He lowered the lamp, undressed and was propped up in the bed when Karly came out of the bathroom. Joe Cocker's *You Are So Beautiful* wafted through the dim light. Jag recognized the black silk wraparound he'd picked out the last time he saw Karly. She let it drop to the floor and stood before him for a moment, the fair skin of perfect breasts blushing softly in the muted light. He wondered whether there could possibly be another woman as desirable as Karly. So much for putting sex off until later.

"Thought this moment would never come," she whispered as she slid between the silk sheets. She ran her fingers through the hair on his chest and slowly let them work their way down to his sex. "Such a man, Jag, you're such a man. I love looking at you." She cooed it in a soft way he could almost believe. He always listened for sincerity on the many times Karly had told him he was the best of all of her lovers, how great his body was, how good he looked. No matter the level of a man's self-confidence, he'd told himself, he doesn't mind hearing those things. After they made love they lay quietly in each other's arms for a few minutes before he handed her drink to her and sliced off more cheese. They chatted about tonight's party and their plans for later. Life didn't get any better than this. Karly drained her glass and lay silently for maybe a minute.

He didn't give it much thought at first, but sensed she'd withdrawn a bit. He leaned back against his pillow and let another slug of the Scotch work. "You okay?"

After a slight pause, "*Pretty* well." Her courage was waning.

Code words, he thought. "So what's wrong?" He looked at Karly, thinking how quickly the moment had changed. Her face was pale.

The Valium and alcohol had failed her and Karly knew she had to reveal her plan before she was ready. She hesitated for several seconds. "Okay, since you asked." She said it with the release of a deep breath, and swallowed hard. "Pretty soon, Jag…, I, uh, I will be too old for this work. I need you to help me with my, my retirement." Her voice was a little hoarse now.

He sat up and leaned on his elbow. "Why in hell are you bringing this up now, Karly?" He was amused and annoyed at the same time.

She started to speak but Jag went on: "Anyway, you need to talk to a financial man about that kind of question, not me." He settled back to the bed.

"No. No. Wait." She put a finger to his lips. "Twenty-nine is ancient in this business, Jag. I need…" She paused when her voice broke.

"Say it."

"Okay, look, Honey, I need a couple million dollars." She delivered it in a little-girl voice.

He stared at her, not understanding.

"Now, Jag," she sang. "I know all about this. If I invest it now I can have five, six maybe even eight million when I'm old."

"Well, then, that settles it," he said with sarcasm. "If you have the money to invest you're all set." He threw the sheet back and started to get out of bed, in no mood for her now.

More serious now, Karly grabbed his arm. "I don't, but you do."

"*What?*"

"*You* have it. You *are* my retirement," She said, trying to maintain calm.

He quaked inside. "*You…you're serious? What're you talking about?*"

She looked at him with resolve: "You're gonna give me the two million."

Jag was dumbfounded. "You've gone crazy! It's idiotic to think I'd do that, Karly, or that I have that kind of money."

"Oh, you've got it, all right. I read the papers. Multi-millionaire, everyone knows."

He'd seen that, too, and only wished it were true. But that was not the issue here.

Sitting upright now, he said, "This is insane! You've gone off the deep end, Karly." Fury reflected in his face.

Karly regained her voice. "I don't think so," she shot back. She was sitting up too. "I know *you*, and you don't want every voter in America to know the kind of slime pit you are, sleeping with your whore for years while you're making high-sounding promises to your dumb-ass voters. A little three-month affair, that's one thing, and even sleeping with the same woman for years while you're married may or may not matter to many these days. But taking money from whoever believes in you and then laughing at their stupidity when you're with me, buying me clothes and diamonds with the money they give you? That'll get some attention. I can tell 'em lots of stuff about you, Jag. You're nothing but a whore yourself. At least I admit it. I may not be as smart as you but I see through you like a piece of glass. And that big-deal father-in-law of yours? I bet he'd like to know what kind of man his daughter's husband really is."

Jag jumped out of the bed and grabbed his undershorts, but then on impulse leaned over the bed close to her face. He was trembling from adrenaline. In dramatic whisper, he said, "You know, Karly, you're rotten right down to the core. I've been good to you, never jerked you around. And now you decide you can blackmail me with all that shit you think you know about me." He had given up trying to pull his shorts on. "Open your eyes. People are used to it. They don't *care*. *Nobody* cares. And who would believe a casino hooker anyway?" He was shouting now.

"Well, let's just find out if anybody cares!" The flash from Karly's eyes said she had something in mind that would trump everything.

She pressed the redial button on the bedside phone while she was yelling, and the live voice on the speakerphone startled Jag: "*Washington*

Post. May I help you?" Momentarily confused, Jag glared at the phone and stiffened against the torrent of blood that surged through his veins as his hopes for his future flashed through his mind. *This belly-crawling two-faced morally bankrupt societal parasite has decided she can take what she wants from me.* Blind now with rage he lunged across the bed for the phone, but his feet caught in the covers and he fell against the lamp table, knocking everything to the floor. He felt a sharp pain in his right hand, which had landed on the cheese knife and was bleeding badly. He flew to his feet grasping the knife.

"May I direct your call? Hello? You've reached the Washington Post!"

Those were the last words Karly Amarson heard. The knife wasn't large, but Jag, enraged now, plunged it into her chest. Her eyes widened in stark fear. Jag watched for a moment as blood slowly covered the discreet starburst tattoo on her belly and strangely thought of the parlor in New York where she got it on their last visit there as the reality of what he'd just done sank in.

Frank Gallardi had donned his tux and was about to leave the office when one of his private lines rang—the one for Trophy Club members. He was running late but picked it up.

"Frank! Oh thank God you're there!" Gallardi didn't recognize the hoarse voice for a moment. Its owner was shouting. "You alone?"

Gallardi moved the receiver away to protect his ear. "Yeah, leaving to go downstairs. What's the matter?"

"Don't say my name for Chrissake. S'body'll hear you. Just listen—"

"What the hell is it?"

"I don't know, it's…uh…I've…I mean Karly, she's…uh…I—"

"Get hold of yourself. Make some sense."

"Karly…she's dead, Frank, I think she's dead."

"Is this some kind of joke? What the hell—"

"No, it's not a joke! I need your help. Listen to me: No police. None of your security. I mean nobody," he demanded, still shouting.

"Are you drunk, man? Calm down! Calm down! What's this about?"

"Listen to me, Frank!" He instructed Gallardi to send someone he trusted from outside the hotel up to Karly's apartment to remove her body and anything that pointed to violence, like the bloody carpet and sheets. It should look like Karly just moved out—nothing so unusual about that.

Frank must know someone he could trust to do it and keep it quiet. Things *just happen* in hotels.

Gallardi, in a daze, was through listening. "That's enough! Stop running off at the mouth. This is a respectable place, *it's my place,* and you're screwing with my reputation. What the hell have you done, anyway?"

"Frank, look. Karly was going to blackmail me. There was an argument. It ended up bad, and I swear, if anything goes wrong—ever—I'll cover you. I'll say I forced you to help me. This gets out I'm dead anyway."

"You realize what you're asking me to do? We'll both end up in prison."

"This can't get out. I'll be ruined. Listen, I'll put it all out on the table here. It's terrible and I wish it hadn't happened. I'd change it if I could. But Karly, Frank, face it, she was a prostitute. Prostitutes disappear. They vanish sometimes. Nobody expects them at home for dinner or at some PTA meeting. They're *always* unaccounted for. Nobody's going to start looking around for Karly and causing trouble. If anything ever comes up, I'll pull some strings. I'll handle it! But right now you gotta help me!"

Gallardi thought about the trap *he* was in. If he did nothing and waited for someone to find her body, there would be police all over the hotel and casino, non-stop TV coverage, stories in all the papers. He'd have to risk telling the police he knew nothing about it, or tell the truth and destroy this man he considered a friend, a course contrary to his personal code. "I'll think about what I'm going to do," he said.

He slammed the phone onto its cradle and paced around his office for a moment before staring out at the few souls on the Boardwalk below, for whom life went on as if nothing had happened. Frank Gallardi was faithful to a framework of his own principles when making decisions, but now the principles that involved integrity and those having to do with loyalty sat staring at him from opposite corners. This was a problem that had no solution. Even all his wealth couldn't make it disappear. Whatever his decision now, it would affect the rest of his life. He sat at his desk, hypnotized by the raindrops trailing down the window, reflecting the light from the flashing sign on the Precious Metal Casino next door. He felt sick in his stomach. Maybe he would sit this one out and let the chips fall where they fall, he thought. But the questions wouldn't go away. *When do you pull up stakes on a friend? Fingers get dirty? So what.*

It wasn't like violence was alien to Gallardi. He had straddled the fence between his friends in the mafia and the law for years. Both sides used him for a sounding board, so he always knew what was going on in town. The mob had never pressured him. He wasn't sure why. Respect, he wanted to think. He had made it this far on his own and didn't like the idea of calling on them now. If he did, he knew the rule: Ask for help and you get it, and when asked you give back, *whatever* it is. It's that simple.

Gallardi swung around to his credenza, looked up a number and dialed.

"Yeah." The voice was coarse, almost threatening.

"This Matty Figueriano?"

After a moment, "Who wants ta know?"

"It's Frank Gallardi."

Matty's tone changed immediately. "Aw, Frankieee! Long time, my man. How you been doin'? I was in the casino last week. Didn't see ya 'round."

Any other time those words would have struck fear in Gallardi. An underworld character in a casino brought on more scrutiny from the regulators, but there was no time to worry about that now. "Look, I need a favor."

"All you gotta do is name it, Frankie. You know that."

"How soon can you be here?"

"For you, Frankie, immediately. Seven minutes flat."

"Use the back elevator."

Gallardi hung up and took a moment to wonder about his own sanity, then dialed his frantic friend.

"That…that you, Frank?"

"It's taken care of."

"Frank. How can I—"

Gallardi answered quietly. "Now you get this: You let this ever touch me, I'll kill you."

Gallardi told Matty Figueriano to *clean up* the designated room. More specificity was not necessary, as a man of Matty's ilk understood its full meaning. Gallardi then hurried back through his office toward the executive elevator. He was certainly in no mood for the party downstairs but he was the emcee. And if this mess ever came up it might look suspicious that he hadn't been there. As he rounded the corner outside his office, the voice of Lenny Magliacci chilled him.

"Night, Frank."

Gallardi stopped dead in his tracks in front of Lenny's office, which was within earshot of Frank's. He'd never liked his sister's son before, but now he had contempt for him. "What the hell you doing here this late, Lenny?"

"Couple important matters to wrap up."

Gallardi thought: *Important matters?* No one in the office ever gave Lenny anything important to work on. Gallardi considered the situation for a second and decided not to pursue it. Lenny was too dumb and lazy to have caught any of what happened, and Matty Fig had come in and departed through the back entrance to Frank's office, where Lenny wouldn't have seen him from his own space. As Gallardi hurried on, he cursed himself for ever letting his sister Molly wheedle him into hiring Lenny. He had done it more to stop her whining than out of any feeling of family obligation. As far as Gallardi was concerned, her worthless son had his chance and blew it long ago. As the elevator opened, he wondered how many times like tonight he'd regretted hiring the loser. He made a mental note to have Lenny's office moved to another floor. Close to Maintenance, in the basement.

When Frank Gallardi reached the Quinn ballroom the din of chatter rose a notch as his guests noticed him. A few clapped. Gallardi was not a natural gladhander but made the rounds with a word or two or a body hug for these people who knew and loved him.

Three hours later, Lenny Magliacci blended himself into the casino crowd near the entrance to the Austin Quinn ballroom. The dense carpet covering the casino floor absorbed only a fraction of the noise from the slots, tables and revelers.

Seldom had he seen as much security. He was asked for I.D. by two men in black suits. President McNabb was surrounded by his Secret Service entourage. Magliacci wondered whether the mystery caller his uncle had threatened from the phone in his office earlier in the evening was here in the ballroom.

CHAPTER 2

Six Years Later

ANYONE WATCHING WOULD HAVE thought Frank Gallardi was daydreaming as he sat in his office and gazed out at the crowd on the Boardwalk and the ocean beyond, but far from that, he was thinking over the call he'd received minutes earlier from Sean O'Malley, an Atlantic City police detective who had once worked weekend security for a couple of years in the Trophy Club. When O'Malley was promoted to city detective he gave up the part-time job at the casino, but Frank saw O'Malley as a pipeline to the police and invited him to drop in on him once in a while. They talked about the M.O.'s of the latest rip-off artists to hit the casinos and of other cases O'Malley had inside information on, but it was unusual for the detective to call for an appointment. "Something interesting," he had said.

O'Malley sat across from Gallardi and pulled a plastic evidence bag out of his pocket. "Still advertising with this kind of pen?" he asked. As Gallardi examined the pen, O'Malley told him a local house builder putting in a foundation out on the west side of town had dug up what at first appeared to be trash, but called the police when a rolled-up rug was stained with blood. Rolled up in the rug was a writing pen bearing the Golden Touch Casino & Hotel logo, and some cocktail glasses that had remained intact. Finally, there was a bloody framed photo.

"Recognize this woman, Frank?"

It was a picture of Karly sitting at a table with Gallardi in what he recognized as the small secluded bar in the Trophy Club.

"Of course, I know as well as you do! Karly Amarson."

"Yeah, and we found a man's gold bracelet there with the name of an underworld character we keep an eye on engraved on it."

"What's the name?" Gallardi asked.

"Figueriano. Matty Figueriano. Know him?"

Gallardi leaned forward in his chair. "Everybody knows Matty," he uttered. "So where are you going with this?"

"Haven't found a body yet! Just all the stuff I told you about. But we believe there is one. You seen Karly lately, Frank?" It was a rhetorical question.

"Yeah, yeah, she's been gone from here a long time. Just disappeared. You think it's her?"

"One of the blood samples matches Karly's DNA. The amount of blood makes the M.E. sure she's dead."

Gallardi looked stressed but said nothing.

O'Malley continued. "Matty Fig, or whoever buried that stuff, may have been told what to do, and may not know what had happened to the body, or he may have disposed of it elsewhere to separate it from other evidence. There is a body, though. You can bet on that."

O'Malley left and Gallardi closed his office door behind him. He was in an uncomfortable quandary. *What the hell would Figueriano have done with the body?* It was an unexpected, and unacceptable, loose end.

He picked up the phone and dialed a number in Washington, one that would bypass all bureaucrats, secretaries and assistants. "Yes," a man's voice answered.

"We need to talk."

"Okay. Shoot."

"In person."

"Wish I had the time, Frank. Phone'll have to do."

"Uh-uh."

The man in Washington chuckled. "Hell, this is the most secure line in the world. What's it about, anyway?"

"Not on the phone," Gallardi asserted. "When can you meet me?"

Frank Gallardi stood at the corner window of a D.C. hotel suite taking in the White House and further away the Capitol, both gleaming in the darkness. Their symbolism was never lost on him but he didn't need to live in Washington to appreciate them. When the door rattled, he opened it and saw his expected guest standing between two men wearing dark suits and no smiles. One of them started to enter the room, but the visitor nodded for him to wait.

Gallardi turned the dead bolt lock in the door and the two shook hands. "Ever get tired of the shadows?"

"Rest of 'em stayed down in the lobby. Guess they trust you."

"I'm touched. Drink?" he said, gesturing toward the mini-bar.

"Glenfiddich, neat. What's on your mind, Frank?"

Gallardi set his drink on the bar. "Some builder in Atlantic City dug up items the cops believe is from Karly's apartment."

The man took a moment to let it sink in. "Tell me about it."

"This construction crew digs up something suspicious and calls the police. They come out and take a look, bring in the medical examiner, the crime scene stuff, yellow tape and all that. There was crusted blood on a rug that was rolled up. Drink glasses and other shit inside it, including a writing pen that's got the Golden Touch logo on it. The cops had Karly's DNA in their database. I'm sure you've already figured out that it matches some of the blood on the rug. They also found blood that belonged to Matty Figueriano and a gold bracelet with his name engraved on it. They figure it came off while he was burying the stuff and he didn't notice it until afterward, when it was too risky for him to go back and dig it up. And there's a third blood sample. No match in the database."

The visitor stood in thought for several seconds. "You didn't mention a body."

"Not there, but there was a body, right? Are you positive?"

The visitor was clearly uncomfortable with this question. After a minute he said, "Yes, there's a body, Frank!" And then, "Who else knows about any of this?"

"Figueriano. Matty Figueriano."

"And he's the guy you had take care of this?"

"Yes."

"*You used that gutter mop?* I expected a clean job."

Gallardi reacted angrily. "Yeah, I had a lot of time to screen applications that night!"

The visitor thought for a few seconds, and slowly shook his head. "They've got nothing that points to me as her killer, Frank!"

"Don't be too sure. There's still someone else's blood on the rug. It's pretty easy for me to figure out who that blood belongs to."

Jag looked down at the floor for a moment. "They won't find me in the criminal database, Frank!" After a pause, he said, "Anyone else know anything about this?"

Gallardi took a deep breath. He'd always wondered whether his worthless nephew, Lenny Magliacci, overheard his phone calls on the evening of Karly's murder. Lenny was nearby in his office that night when Frank had called Matty to clean up the mess but had never given Gallardi any indication that he overheard his call. Besides, the listless bastard was too lazy to cause trouble. He practiced law for awhile but couldn't make it and got into some trouble. No sense mentioning him, Gallardi decided.

"No," Frank replied.

"What about Matty Figueriano?"

O'Malley had kept Gallardi up to date on the investigation, which was moving fast. "Here's what I know so far," Gallardi said. Matty Figueriano had become high-profile in recent years, squabbling with Atlantic City mob boss Joey Domino over drugs and for bringing a lot of attention down on him. Joey Domino, who turned thumbs down on the drug business after his own son died from a cocaine overdose, found out Matty was running a drug op on the quiet. Joey Domino had no use for Matty Fig anyway because he was with Joey's son when his son O.D.'d and died, and wanted to kill him as soon as he found out. The feds and local cops were watching too closely and Joey decided to wait, but now this discovery of Matty Fig's DNA and gold bracelet in a burial pit with a dead woman's belongings was the last straw for Joey. Joey knew the feds would try to connect him to the girl's murder because of his known association with Matty Figueriano. With this new evidence, they were likely to trace it to Karly. So Joey Domino sent Matty a message to take the rap all by himself—not for that suspected murder alone, but also for two others they'd been trying to pin on *Joey*. Matty denied everything but Joey's messengers told Matty that life without parole, even the death sentence, would be better than the consequences of not bailing Joey out, and Matty Fig had no reason to doubt that was true. "That's all I know," Gallardi said.

Jag had stood at the window overlooking the city as Gallardi talked. "They find anything besides the gold bracelet?"

"That's about it, but it all points to my place."

"She *lived* at your hotel. So what?"

"Loose ends. I don't like it."

The man shook his head. "Where do you get all this information, Frank?"

"Never mind where I get it. I get it."

They stared at each other for a moment. Finally the visitor said, "Worried aren't you, Frank?"

"I don't worry but it's a problem to deal with," Gallardi said. "If Figueriano confesses to Karly's disappearance and those two murders as well, he can get himself off the hook with Joey Domino."

"And go to prison for life? You don't have to worry about that. He'll take his chances with Domino. Tough guys think they're invincible."

Gallardi looked at the man in disbelief. "You know damn well it won't turn out like that. Figueriano's afraid of Joey. He'll confess to those three hits and get off the hook with Joey Domino. Then he'll plea-bargain with the feds to stay out of jail."

"*Plea bargain!* With what?"

"*You're looking at him!*" Gallardi said, jabbing his thumb into his own chest. "That D.A. in Atlantic City's trying to make a name for himself. Hates gambling. Blames everything that happens on the casinos. You think he wouldn't give his left nut to see me hanging from that flagpole on top of the Golden Touch? He'd trade Matty Figueriano for me in a heartbeat."

The Washington man nodded and turned back to the window. A minute later he said, "Thought about how you'd defend yourself, Frank?"

Gallardi went over to the man, who was several inches taller than he, and spun him around. The blood vessels in Gallardi's neck bulged as he spoke. "Listen to me! I saved your ass that night! Put my own reputation on the line! You keep me out of this like you said you'd do, and I don't care how you do it. But you better hope nobody comes to me about this."

"How do you expect me to deal with it now, Frank? I'm too visible and you know it."

"That's *your* problem. My name comes up in this, the chips fall where they fall. I warned you six years ago. You remember that, don't you?" Gallardi was an inch from Jag's nose now, his prominent chest bumping the visitor's.

Jag studied Frank for a moment and then put his hands on the casino man's shoulders and forced a smile. "Frank, you're tough as ever. I like that."

Gallardi pushed him away, in no mood to be mollified. "You'll do well to remember that!"

The man nodded. "Forget it, Frank. Don't worry. You knew I'd take care of it."

Jag scrolled down his list of contacts and selected a number as his driver navigated the SUV through D.C. traffic.

The line answered after one ring. "What're you doin' out so late?"

"Little problem has come up. Meet in 30 minutes."

CHAPTER 3

ANA KORONIS THOUGHT IT must be the fiftieth time she rolled into a new sleeping position that night, and it had been like that for the last month. Today was Sunday and she had planned to sleep in, but the combination of sleeplessness and the impending end of her relationship with Austin Quinn seemed to pull her down more each day. Her productivity at the law firm was lagging and one of her partners had brought it up at lunch on Friday. "Not yourself these days, Ana." He had ignored her denial. "Why don't you take some time off and get it together?"

It was more than a casual comment: Her personal life was impacting the law firm. The partner's admonition had edged her over the threshold and now she was waiting for the right time to talk to Quinn. Couldn't just let him come home to his place in Georgetown one day and find she had moved back across the river to her own townhouse in Alexandria, even though he too had to know it was over. He wasn't blind.

She was dozing again when Quinn's official line rang. The glowing red numbers on the digital clock said it was ten past five. Had to be Langley, as she was sure no one except his lieutenants at CIA had this number. Quinn fumbled for the speakerphone button in the darkness.

"Yeah?"

"Director Quinn?"

"Yes."

"Hold for Mr. Lloyd Tracey."

The White House! Tracey was President Garrison Cross's chief of staff and Ana was curious. Her handling of legal matters for the State Department often gave her the kinds of official details she was interested in, but since moving in with Quinn, the amount of knowledge she had accumulated tripled. It had taken Quinn a long time to begin confiding in her about operational goings on at the CIA, but then, as if his trust in her suddenly bloomed, he opened up. Ana knew Quinn enjoyed dealing out intriguing details of some ongoing clandestine operation like cards in a poker hand, causing her to sweat them one at a time. Ana would remember every nuance until she could get back to her office the next morning and dictate it all into a flash drive. She stored the drive in a small floor safe under her desk, to which only she had the combination. But Quinn had not been saying much in recent weeks, and it was clear she had gotten about all the spy scoop she was going to get from him. She had liked Quinn for himself at one time. His CIA stories were a bonus. But she was glad the relationship outlasted them.

"Hold on," Quinn said to the speakerphone. He left the bedroom and walked to his study down the hall. When he picked up the call there, Ana continued to hear both men's voices on the speakerphone. The CIA director had neglected to put the line on Hold.

"You there, Lloyd?" she heard him say.

"Sorry, Austin. It's about Frank Gallardi."

"Gallardi!"

"Shot dead couple hours ago. Got his security man, too. Professional hit according to the police. That's all I've got right now."

Quinn was silent for a moment. "Why are you calling me?"

"President wanted me to notify you and Stern. Oh, and General Scrubb at the Pentagon. Mostly as a matter of courtesy, I think." Ana knew Stern was the president's national security advisor.

"How'd you get it?"

"The Bureau."

Ana had met Gallardi a few years earlier at the celebration and roast for Quinn at Gallardi's casino in Atlantic City, and knew he had lofty connections in the government, but his murder was not of more than general interest to her. When Quinn hung up, Ana got out of bed, took a hot shower and got dressed. She heard the phone ring again while she was showering, but she'd turned off the speaker. She put on a robe and sauntered down to the study where Quinn was scanning the morning reports on the Langley computer terminal he'd ordered installed in his home.

"I heard Tracey's call, Austin. You left the speaker on. What do you make of Gallardi?"

Quinn glanced at her peripherally. "Doubt if it's anything as sinister as Tracey implied."

"You knew him well?"

"We worked on the New Jersey casino bill together years ago. Pretty much a business relationship."

Ana was leaning nonchalantly against the door, arms folded and ankles crossed. "Gallardi involved in the mafia?"

Quinn still hadn't looked up from the monitor. He grunted and shook his head. "Stayed out of it."

"Anything for you to do?"

Quinn shrugged. "Met his wife couple of times. She'll expect me to do something."

Ana knew there was little Quinn could do. The CIA had no investigative powers inside the U.S. That was the FBI's bailiwick. Quinn would promise Mrs. Gallardi he would make some phone calls to encourage the FBI and state authorities to take special interest, but given Gallardi's high profile in gambling, that would happen without Quinn's input. And Quinn wasn't one to demand a Congressional investigation every time a squirrel scampered across a street somewhere in Washington.

The next morning, Monday, Ana Koronis was in her office at the law firm at eight-thirty with *The Washington Post*. The paper said there were no suspects, no murder weapon and no clues in the Gallardi case. The story credited the wealthy casino owner, working with then state-senator Austin Quinn, for the state laws and regulations that enabled casino gambling in New Jersey. Gallardi had been rewarded with the first casino license, and Quinn with election to the U.S. Senate. This set him up for his subsequent appointment by President Cross to his present post as Director of Central Intelligence.

The paper referred to Gallardi's high-profile clientele as the envy of the other Boardwalk casinos.

The article said police also were investigating the murder of known underworld figure Matthew Figueriano, killed on the same night as Gallardi. Police didn't think the murders were related since Gallardi was not believed to have been involved with the mob. Power struggles between mob boss Joey Domino and Figueriano were legendary.

Ana leaned back in the chair and looked up at the ceiling. Her talk with Quinn about ending their relationship would have to wait a while longer.

It was a quarter past seven Monday morning when President Cross got Austin Quinn on the phone.

"Too bad about Gallardi."

Quinn was sitting in the middle rear seat of his black SUV. "For sure."

"Where are you?"

"Heading to Langley."

"Looks like a hit, but I just talked to Fullwood at the Bureau. He says Frank wasn't involved with the mafia."

"Could be anybody. You know, big loser at the tables. Somebody Gallardi fired," Quinn said.

"They'll look at that."

"Right."

"Listen, Austin, hate to ask this but someone needs to represent me at Gallardi's service. He did a lot for me, others in the party. You being from Jersey—"

Quinn interrupted. "Be glad to, Garrison."

The CIA's Security Protective Service met Quinn at the Atlantic City airport with three cars and a dozen security officers for the trip to the chapel. Even though going to a memorial service in Quinn's home state didn't seem to be particularly risky, Quinn didn't mind the highly visible security. He was a career politician and to be seen surrounded by men whose job it was to protect his life with theirs did nothing to detract from an image of power. Especially in his home state, thought Washington newspaper reporter Tommy Phelps, usually soft on Quinn in his articles, who was ushered into Quinn's vehicle for the ride to the memorial.

The tree-lined boulevard curved in a way that afforded a view of the Gothic architecture of The Cathedral of the Good Shepherd several blocks before they got there. Quinn instructed that the government cars were to wait in a remote corner of the parking area to leave space for others to park closer to the building.

The bright, sunny day with birds chirping all around seemed determined to belie the occasion, Phelps thought. Reverent mourners in black, some blotting their eyes, crossed the exquisitely manicured church grounds in silence as they approached the tall stone entrance. Even the city streets were empty, as if the citizens of Atlantic City took time from daily routines to pay their respects to Frank Gallardi, a home-town boy who grew up poor, pulled himself up by sheer determination and will, fought a long but not universally popular battle to bring in casinos, risked everything he had before it bore fruit, and then returned so much of it to the people: New symphony center, children's hospital, the new park, endless funding for the homeless shelter, and the list went on. Even casino critics could find nothing negative to say about Frank Gallardi.

The live acoustics inside the old church were excellent for music but the echoing words of the speakers lost the glue that held them together before reaching straining ears. Gallardi's widow Rose, their grown children, and Frank's sister Molly sat in the first row. Molly's son and Frank Gallardi's nephew Lenny Magliacci sat in the second with other family members, and Quinn was escorted to the reserved third row. Phelps noticed two or three U.S. Congressmen, several military officers in uniform and a few show business personalities he recognized. Not present was Ana Koronis.

After the service, Quinn spoke with Rose Gallardi and told her the president sent his personal condolences. They hugged each other before Quinn moved on.

Quinn stopped along the way to his car to shake hands with a few of the dozens of supporters who had gathered. Minutes later he was ready to return to the airport.

Leonard Antonio Magliacci had tuned out the eulogies and prayers and remained in his seat when the service was over as his mother Molly, Rose Gallardi and the others emptied out. In the days since Gallardi's murder Magliacci had dwelled on a phone conversation that took place in Frank's office one early evening several years ago and now possibly held some potential for Magliacci. Magliacci had been in his cubicle near Gallardi's office that night and heard Frank get upset with a caller. A few minutes later, Frank had summoned someone to his office. When he came, Lenny couldn't hear what was said even though he had moved as close as he dared risk.

All of this came back to Lenny when he read the newspaper account of Gallardi's murder. The story said an underworld character named Matty Figueriano was killed across town on the same night as Frank. Police said there was no known connection between Gallardi and the gangster known as Matty Fig, or their deaths.

Lenny Magliacci wasn't so sure.

He walked out of the chapel and looked for his mother. Some of his cousins who were talking with her finished their conversations and left as he approached. He had grown up with them, played on the same little-league teams at Kimble Park, but all that was long ago and Lenny felt he and his cousins had little in common now. Lenny had gone to law school and none of his cousins made it through college.

Magliacci skipped the family gathering at the Gallardi home and drove to the Golden Touch. Frank had moved him downstairs years earlier but he had kept a key to the executive elevator. He got off at the third floor where the executive offices were located and walked through the empty, large reception area where Gallardi's collection of art was displayed, past the windowless room Lenny once occupied and on to Gallardi's office suite. He half-expected the area to still be sealed off and was glad to see that the police and FBI had released it. He'd never had the courage to venture into Gallardi's private office before, but Frank was dead now and the executive offices were officially closed for the day. So Lenny was surprised that the feelings of apprehension that had kept him away reappeared now.

He stood in front of Gallardi's huge desk and thought of the first and only time he sat there across from Gallardi. There had been no small talk or family news to start the meeting off, even though the two men hadn't seen each other in months. Gallardi had opened a tan folder that held Lenny's papers and frowned as he studied it, a deep vertical crease appearing between Gallardi's thick brows as he spoke.

"Molly tells me you got into a little trouble," Gallardi said that day. Lenny remembered Gallardi's chilling voice as he sat forward in the big leather chair and formed a steeple with his hands as they lay on the desk. Lenny understood that it was time to grovel.

There was no doubt in Lenny Magliacci's mind that Gallardi already knew every detail of his nephew's problems—a malpractice case that cost him his license to practice law and put him into bankruptcy—but he wanted them extracted through Lenny's pores in small pieces with sharp edges. Magliacci was flat broke and had no alternative to the offer Gallardi made him that day sitting at the desk he now stood in front of. Lenny's mother Molly said she had forced her brother's *generosity*, but the way Lenny saw it he had been made to pay the price by once again humiliating himself before the high-and-mighty family patriarch.

On the rare occasions when Frank spoke to Magliacci after that, he would stand at the door to Lenny's office, never quite entering, and deliver a reprimand over something Frank couldn't blame on someone else. That was the way Lenny saw it. Never any small talk. The work assignments Frank's legal staff gave him weren't even worthy of a beginning paralegal, and over time they grew into mountains of paper seldom asked for. Once a month or so, Lenny trashed them.

Lenny wandered around the large room now, taking in the luxury. Gallardi had selected exotic leathers and rare woods for the furnishings. One wall was all glass and took in the Boardwalk and the Atlantic Ocean. Magliacci watched the waves lap the Boardwalk below for a minute, tried Gallardi's chair for size and then moved to one of the walls covered with photos. There were more than a hundred of them on the tall wall, Lenny estimated, showing his uncle with entertainers, government officials including President Cross, former President McNabb, Austin Quinn, numerous New Jersey politicos, local charity officials, several military officers, and members of his family. Noticeably absent to Lenny was even a single photo of himself.

In the center of the cluster was a portrait of the Gallardi estate, the mansion framed by brick pillars in the foreground that guarded the entrance to the property, from which the driveway curved to the right and ran beside verdant gardens anchored by towering oaks before reaching the grand mansion in the distance. This photo was as close as Lenny had ever been to Frank's home.

Molly never missed a chance to hold Gallardi up to him with stories of her brother's rise from kid dishwasher in the restaurant of the old Staffordshire Hotel on the Boardwalk, long before the casinos were even thought of. Gallardi had attended law school at night while supporting himself selling real estate, and years later *bought* the Staffordshire. "If you did something besides eat and watch television all the time, you could go out there like Frankie did and make yourself rich," Molly would say. Lenny thought she had always placed her brother above him, *her very son,* but that might be about to change. Once he uncovered all the facts of that mysterious night of a few years back, perhaps his mother would see her brother in a different light. Her son, too. Perhaps there would be a *new* patriarch.

As Lenny continued to explore Gallardi's office now, he ventured into a closet that turned out to not be a closet at all. A fierce-eyed eagle logo peered down from above the door of a bank-like vault that had an ancient combination knob in the center of its door. The cold steel door wouldn't budge and Lenny went through the retro Rolodex on Frank's credenza (he wondered why the investigators had not taken the Rolodex) and any drawer he could open hoping to find something resembling a combination. After twenty minutes searching he found a tiny sliver of paper bearing a set of numbers taped to the top edge of a door and was trying to make the combination work when he heard the back elevator start up. He closed the closet door, looked around to be sure nothing was out of place, turned out the lights and went back down on the executive elevator.

Next day at work, Lenny thought about nothing but the vault and the opportunities that might arise from a Gallardi and Matty Figueriano connection. After work, he went home and settled on the sofa in front of the television and watched *The Simpsons.* He set an alarm clock to go off at ten p.m. in case he fell asleep.

Lenny Magliacci was sure no one noticed when he got on the executive elevator at ten-thirty that night. The red exit directionals on the executive level afforded enough visibility for him to get through the familiar reception area and around the corner to Gallardi's office, where the Boardwalk lighting reflected off the office ceiling and cast a soft glow on the walls and furniture. The Ferris wheel out on Steel Pier stood out against the black ocean like a giant roulette.

This time he succeeded with the vault combination on the first try and pulled open the heavy door and stood at the threshold for a minute or so taking it in. The vault was tall enough for Magliacci to stand up in, about eight feet deep and just wide enough for his 350-pound frame to squeeze between the boxes lining the shelves on the side walls. A single fluorescent light overhead lit the top shelf but left those below in shadows. He rummaged through the contents of the boxes for close to an hour before conceding they contained nothing more important than yellowed bank statements, political correspondence and real estate files dating back to the beginnings of the Golden Touch. The vault was nothing more than dead storage. Magliacci's hopes took a dive.

Standing at the vault door taking a final doleful look, he spotted a small black bag he hadn't noticed before, stuffed behind a box on the bottom shelf in the front corner of the vault. His heart raced as he emptied the contents out on the carpet. In it were a pair of earrings, a gold chain, a colored gemstone ring, a small serrated kitchen knife, a ring with a large stone that looked like a diamond, a tiny black dress he thought was silk, and a phone number someone had penned on a Golden Touch memo pad. All of the items were crusted over or at least spattered with a dark substance Lenny thought was blood. He sat looking at all of this, considering the possibilities. After a few minutes he put everything back into the nylon bag, closed the vault and left with the bag in hand.

By the time he reached his car, he had held his excitement as long as he could. He kicked the rusted rear bumper of the Lincoln. *"You are one smart dude, Lenny Magliacci. One smart dude!"*

CHAPTER 4

MAGLIACCI'S USUAL ROUTINE WAS to show up at the office around nine. After moving papers around his desk all day he would go to Harry's High Hat Lounge, whose clientele and worn furnishings betrayed its name, four blocks from the Golden Touch where Eve the bartender had a pitcher of beer and frosted mug waiting. Several beers and a M*A*S*H rerun later he'd wander over to his apartment, find something in the refrigerator and turn on the TV. Some nights Eve would come over after work and they would nuke some frozen pizzas. It was always around two when he rolled into bed, and waking up to go to work was hard. His supervisor over at the Golden Touch warned him several times about his appearance and work habits, which led to snipes back and forth about Lenny's attitude.

That was before Frank Gallardi's death. Tonight he went straight to his apartment and dumped the bag out on the kitchen counter. He scrutinized each item one at a time and kept going back to the diamond ring.

Next morning, he woke up before the alarm clock went off—first time he could remember that happening—and got to the office at seven-thirty. He closed the door and pulled the Golden Touch memo sheet from the bag. It was the kind of pad the hotel placed by the phone in guest rooms. Brownish-black stain dotted the page but the scribbled word *Post* and a phone number were legible. Lenny dialed the number and got a recorded message that said the area code had been changed. When he redialed using the area code the recording gave him, a voice said he had reached *The Washington Post*. He hung up.

As he lined through the newspaper's old area code on the memo sheet and wrote in the new one, he noticed that the Golden Touch's area code beneath the logo also was no longer current. Both the Washington and the Atlantic City area codes had changed since the blood stained pad was printed.

At lunch Lenny walked over to Pacific Avenue a block off the Boardwalk where unlucky gamblers traded their remaining possessions for a last, desperate chance to reverse their losses. He stopped at a door that said *Barella's*. A red neon sign in the window read *Cash for Gold*. Halogen light beamed down on the gold jewelry and diamonds that sparkled on black velvet. The elderly shopkeeper kept one hand in his pocket as Lenny walked in.

"Tony Barella?" Lenny said.

"That'd be me." The man was expressionless.

"Leonard Magliacci. *Junior*."

A smile began to develop on the man's wrinkled face. "I'll be damned." He removed his hand from his pocket and shook Lenny's. "You were knee-high last time I saw you. How's your mother, son?"

"Fine, good. I, uh, need—"

Barella reached across the display case and grasped Lenny's big shoulder. "Your dad and me, pretty good buddies. Yeah, soon's we got back from Germany after the war, I made that wedding ring of your mother's for him. I bet you didn't know that!"

Magliacci nodded and started to speak, but Barella continued.

"Say, too bad about your uncle Frank. Your mother's younger brother, right? Couldn't believe it."

"Yeah, yeah, bad day for us," Lenny said, looking at his watch. "Look, I need a—"

"So did I hear you're a lawyer?"

Lenny nodded and forced a faint smile. "Need a favor." He pulled the diamond ring he'd found in Gallardi's safe out of his pocket and placed it on the glass top of the case. "Bought this off a guy who needed some cash. Wanna be sure I didn't get stuck."

Barella considered Lenny for a long moment as his enthusiasm disappeared. "I see." He louped the stone and measured it. "Well, some of these shops along here, they'd give you maybe three or four grand for it. Worth more but you know how it works. Guess you know, it's a Tiffany."

Lenny was surprised.

"Yeah, they'd get thirty for it today. Find the right buyer, you might get eight, ten grand." Barella looked at the inside of the ring under the loupe. "Got some initials in it. Here. Take a look." He handed the ring and magnifying glass to Lenny. Magliacci moved the loupe around until he could see the tiny inscription: "KA & JAG."

His mind raced as he headed back to the casino. He could forget about this whole affair right now, sell the ring on the spot, and put a small fortune in his pocket. God knows he could use it. But he had a feeling the names associated with those initials were worth more to him than that. A *lot* more. He was going to gamble on it.

Lenny stayed at Harry's High Hat until midnight that evening before returning to Gallardi's private office suite. It looked the same as always. Magliacci knew the family had pleaded with the authorities to leave it intact for the time being: Frank was still there with them as long as his office looked the same. Lenny himself didn't go for that kind of bullshit thinking. Some of that bunch were still crying and people like them made Lenny sick, but it had worked in his favor. The outmoded Rolodex Gallardi had maintained his phone contacts in was still sitting there on his credenza.

Lenny sat in Gallardi's chair and turned the directory to *K*. Frank had entered first names and very few last names but within minutes Lenny narrowed the possibilities for *KA* down to someone named *Kent* or a *Karly*. He copied both numbers. The Rolodex yielded no clues to JAG's identity.

The next morning he dialed the number for Kent. The woman who answered said Kent wouldn't be home until after high-school baseball practice, around six. There was no other Kent there and never had been. She'd had the number for seventeen years. Lenny hung up. He guessed Kent was a player on one of the little league teams Gallardi sponsored.

The Rolodex number for Karly now belonged to someone who'd moved to Atlantic City a year ago and didn't know anyone named Karly, and the phone company told Magliacci it never revealed information about the prior owners of a phone number for any reason short of a court order.

That night at home, Magliacci decided to leave for New York the next morning. He got up early and left a message on his supervisor's phone that he was sick today and would try to make it in tomorrow. He threw his best sport coat in the back seat of the Lincoln and headed north on the Garden State Parkway. Lenny knew Tiffany's had a store in Atlantic City but that was not an option. Too many people in Atlantic City knew him, and any notice of his activities with this ring, unique because of its inscription, had the potential to cause him trouble.

He parked off Fifth Avenue near Tiffany's and smoothed his hair in the car mirror. The beard needed a trim but it was too late for that. When he tried to button his jacket he realized how long he'd had it, and thought of the promises he'd made to Molly to lose some weight. He took another look at the diamond ring, holding it in the sun to get the full spectrum of colors, and stuck it back into his pants. He patted his pocket several times for reassurance the ring was still there as he walked the two blocks to the corner of Fifth Avenue and 37th. He knew it was a tell to pickpockets but he couldn't help himself. He looked at the Tiffany's sign, shined the tops of his shoes on the back of his trouser legs and walked into the store. He looked around at the lights and displays and thought of the contrast between there and old man Barella's shop.

A floor manager met him at the door. "How may I help you, sir?"

Magliacci fished the ring from his pocket. "Uh, I inherited this ring. I think it came from here."

"Oh, wonderful!" said the manager with a congratulatory smile. "How can we help?"

"Well, I want information about it. You know, details."

The man led him to a small paneled room. Lenny sank into a leather chair and moments later a woman came in and introduced herself as Laura Lerner and asked how she could help.

He gave her the diamond ring and addressed her as he might a subordinate. "Laura, I represent the estate of the deceased who left this ring. We'd like to know something about it."

She left with the ring, returned with it two minutes later and punched something into her computer. She confirmed that it had been bought at Tiffany's, gave him technical details about the stone and confirmed Barella's thirty-thousand-dollar estimate for a new similar stone.

Lenny suppressed his excitement as he pressed on. "And can you determine who you sold the ring to from the initials on the inside?"

She looked at him apologetically. "That would require a great deal of documentation from you."

Lenny thanked Lerner and left. The trip wasn't a waste. She had confirmed what old man Barella said about value but, more important, Magliacci gleaned from a peek at the computer monitor the exact date the ring was purchased.

Driving back to Atlantic City, Magliacci racked his brain for a way to identify *KA* and *JAG*. The purchase date of the ring was a little more than seven years ago. Someone at the GT besides Gallardi must have known KA or JAG, probably both of them. Lenny thought of a handful who had worked there for a long time and scribbled their names on a legal pad as he drove. Of the seven he came up with, five were top Golden Touch executives, close allies of Gallardi's who wouldn't throw a bucket of water on Lenny if he were on fire, and the sixth was dead. He might have a chance with the seventh, a woman whose office was not located on the executive level with the others.

Before she became the Golden Touch's first executive housekeeper, Maria Sanchez held the same position at a small four-star hotel in New York. She had bided her time for years waiting for the right opportunity to get out of the city. Maybe this new hotel and casino in Atlantic City was it, she told her husband when the headhunter contacted her. In prior years, they had driven down on vacation twice and loved the Boardwalk, the ocean air and the less frenetic pace. After clearing three preliminary interviews with some of the hotel executive staff, Maria met with Frank Gallardi himself for final approval. She knew within minutes he was a man she could work for all out. Everything about him—the people he surrounded himself with, the fact that he made eye contact when he talked to her, his straightforward manner—felt right. She figured Gallardi was impressed as well because he hired her on the spot. That same day, she and her husband found a house they liked within walking distance to both the Golden Touch complex and a Catholic church.

Maria had spoken to Gallardi's widow soon after he died and offered her services in any way that might make things easier. Rose Gallardi thanked Maria and told her how much her husband thought of her, but of course there was nothing she or anyone else could do. She would not hesitate to call.

Since joining the Golden Touch Maria had been approached by headhunters representing almost every hotel in Atlantic City. Although her housekeeping department and its army of workers was not a profit center for the hotel, it contributed to the Golden Touch's success. Every day, thousands of sheets and towels had to be laundered and hundreds of rooms cleaned and restocked—and all before three p.m. How efficiently it was done made an impression on the guests, and how economically it was carried out affected the hotel's operating cost. Frank had told her more than once that the Golden Touch outperformed the other Boardwalk hotels in those areas and always gave Maria the credit. Which of course made her work all the harder for this man she loved like a brother and respected so much. Frank's murder would not change that for Maria.

It was nine-fifteen when Maria's phone rang for the hundredth time that morning. She picked it up without taking her eyes off of her computer monitor that listed checkouts.

"Leonard Magliacci. Need a few minutes."

Maria took a deep breath. The hotel had been packed for a week and she didn't have time to talk to anyone. The last person she wanted to see was Big Lenny, as those in her department referred to him. Although she had few direct dealings with him, she'd heard the occasional idle chatter among other managers that Frank had hired him as a favor to his sister and that he was nothing but a drain on Gallardi. To some, Big Lenny was laughing stock but Maria disliked his reputation too much to waste her own time even thinking about him.

"Very busy." She spoke with a slight accent.

"Since it's about my uncle's estate I'd say it's more important than whatever you're doing."

Maria restrained herself. "Go ahead then."

"Not on the phone. Be there in a minute."

Maria went to the ladies' room to check her starched white blouse and green blazer. She was fifty-seven now, and even though she didn't care what Leonard Magliacci thought about anything, she took as much pride in her personal appearance as in her work. When she returned to her office Magliacci was seated behind her desk in her chair, which was too small for him. She wasn't pleased about that, and she wondered if he would be able to get out of it.

"What can I do for you, Mr. Magliacci?" She stood in front of her own desk, arms crossed behind her back.

Lenny looked at some papers he'd brought, and Maria wondered if they were her employment records. "You been here since the hotel opened, right?"

"Since day one. Yes."

He nodded toward another chair beside her desk. "You can sit down."

"I'll stand. I'm sure you can see how busy we are," she said, forcing a smile that was polite at best.

He nodded. "Came across the name *Karly* in some of my uncle's things. She was probably around the hotel several years ago. I think her last name was spelled with an *A*. Know her?"

Maria looked away. Know her? Oh my God! I was all but a mother to the girl. *Honey, when you gonna get outta this business?...Just a little longer, Maria, don't worry...But I do worry. So many things can happen....* And those nights when Karly would call her late. *Maria, I hurt so much. Could you come up here for a few minutes?...Oh, Dear God, it's happened again. What've they done to you this time? I'll be right there, Honey....* And that apartment deal with Frank! *Karly, don't be afraid to ask. Frank's a businessman. He may give it to you. But, oh God, listen to me now. Here I am helping you do something I don't even approve of... Oh, Maria, God knows where your heart is. He's not going to punish you, too....* And those times when Karly wanted to talk. *Maria, listen to what happened with this dude last night... Oh, Honey, I shouldn't! But I guess it's okay to listen to part of it....* And there was that Washington Big Shot she was seeing. *Honey, that man's trouble and you're seeing too much of him... Oh, Maria, Jag's the best thing I got going... Yeah, but he's too powerful. Something tells me you should leave him alone... You sound like my grandmother, sometimes, Maria. Stop worrying so much....* And then there was Karly's retirement plan, *that 401-Karly, or something like that. It's not right, Honey, and besides that you're playing with fire. You know how I worry about you with that man, anyway....* All that had been—what was it now?—six or seven years ago.

She made a sign of the cross in her mind as she answered Magliacci. "May have heard of a Karly. That was a long time ago."

"You know she was murdered?" Magliacci said.

Murdered! Maria had her suspicions but had never been sure. When she had asked Gallardi about her, he said he figured she moved on, like girls of her trade do. No ties to anyone. Those hookers, they lead a helter-skelter life, he'd said. Maria had never mentioned to anyone, not even to Frank, that she had seen that high-powered boyfriend of Karly's entering her apartment that day, that last day she occupied it. What good would it do? She couldn't prove anything. Besides that, Frank didn't miss much. He knew it when anything was wrong, and she wasn't about to question what he decided to do or not do about it. Besides, the big-shot boyfriend was someone she was sure Gallardi knew. So Maria decided then to keep her mouth shut.

"*Murdered?*" she said.

"Looks like Frank, uh, knew her pretty well."

"I wouldn't know about that, Mr. Magliacci."

"How else could he have gotten the things she was wearing when she died."

Maria erupted. "If you're saying Mr. Frank had something to do with Karly Amarson's dea—?" Maria swore at herself, realizing what she had done.

"*Amarson!* Thank you for her name, Ms. Sanchez."

His sarcasm on top of her own blunder was more than Maria could take. Job or no job, she wasn't putting up with this ass. "*Go now. Get out of here you disrespectful pig!*"

Magliacci tried to stand up but realized he was stuck and started wiggling himself out of the chair as he spoke. "You've been very helpful, Ms. Sanchez, giving me Karly's name, but you've done nothing to convince me that my uncle didn't kill her." He'd ignored her insult.

"*Mr. Frank didn't kill her!*" Maria said in near hysteria. Her employees in the outer room looked around to see what was going on.

Lenny was standing now with his hands resting on his hips. "Well then, if you're so sure, you must know who did, Ms. Sanchez? You can help me clear my uncle's name!" His voice was becoming more and more intimidating.

Maria buried her face in her hands. Frank Gallardi hadn't killed Karly, but what if Big Lenny had found something that made it *look* like he did? A dead man couldn't defend himself and she didn't believe for a second that Lenny was trying to clear Frank. If Karly was murdered, the killer had to be the man Maria saw at Karly's door on the day she disappeared—the pompous bigwig Maria had warned her about. *Jag,* Karly called him, but Maria knew his real name. And if he didn't do it, well, he'd have to take care of himself now. But she wasn't about to let Big Lenny drag Frank Gallardi's name through the sewer. When she looked up she was sobbing, but calm. "I will talk to you."

* * *

Alicia Fraser knew it was going to be another unusual call. It had been a zoo around her office all week. The girl who usually took the boss's calls was on vacation and Alicia was covering for her as well as trying to corral her own out of control cubicle. Alicia was reprimanded for mishandling calls once before and uncertain what to do with this one. She put the caller on Hold and pressed the intercom.

"Sir, I have a man on the line who insists you will want to speak with him. His name is, is…Magliacci."

"Don't you know how to handle my calls?" he demanded. "I don't know any damn Magliacci. How'd he get through?"

"Sir, it sounds like he convinced the central operator you'd want to know about some person named Karly. Karly Amarson, I think he said."

He closed his eyes briefly in reflection, then told Alicia to put the caller on Hold and walked over to the window. He suddenly realized how hot it was in his office and loosened his necktie. Millions of unwelcome memories flashed across his brain in the two minutes that passed before he went back to the phone.

"Put him through."

He flipped on the voice recorder and picked up the flashing line. "Mr. Magliacci?"

The caller cleared his throat and said, "I'll get right to the point. I have some things that may have belonged to Karly Amarson. I was hoping you could help me identify them."

"Amarson?"

"Karly Amarson. You knew her, didn't you? And *Jag*?"

There was a pause, then, "Come to my office tomorrow at ten."

Magliacci was surprised how easy it was the next day. The guards checking his I.D. at the security points called him *Mr. Magliacci*, and if he was self-conscious about his old car, no one else seemed to pay it any attention. The young man who escorted him inside the building called someone to announce his arrival and showed him to a room where he was to wait for

67

another escort to take him to his host. He declined the offer for coffee and flipped through the pages of a *Time* to keep his mind off his anxiety.

He wondered if he had made a mistake by agreeing to meet here. He could have named the place. Any place. After all, he *was* in control, or would have been elsewhere. He thought casinos had pretty good security but this place put them to shame. Maybe he should've handled it another way—sent a note demanding what he wanted without identifying himself. But he had taken steps to protect himself and now he had no choice but to trust in them.

A woman in her twenties showed Magliacci into a large office and he was standing at the window when his host walked in a few minutes later. He shook Magliacci's hand and spoke with a sunny smile. "Leonard, I'm glad you're here. It's great to see you. Sit anywhere you like. They offer you something to drink? Pastries?"

Magliacci glanced around the room as if to see whether anyone could overhear him, although he knew that what he was going to say would never be heard by anyone outside this room even if it was taped. He took a long breath.

"Let's just do our business. You do know Karly Amarson?"

"Heard of her, yes. Disappeared, didn't she, few years back?"

"Yeah, but now they dug up some things that belonged to her at a building site in Atlantic City. DNA shows it's her blood on them. Maybe you saw it in the newspaper."

"Had no idea!"

"Yeah. Few weeks ago."

The man looked silently at Magliacci for a moment, then said, "Is this what you wanted to tell me?"

"Well, it's related. See, Frank Gallardi was my uncle. I went over to his office after the funeral. I found some things that might have belonged to Karly in his vault. Also found your name."

The host tried a laugh. "My name shows up in a lot of places."

Magliacci glanced at his own hands and was surprised they were holding steady. "Exactly my point. Unfortunately, things have this way of getting in the newspapers when big names like yours are involved. Inadvertently, you know. And I'm sure you don't want that to happen."

"So where did you find it? My name."

"The vault, indirectly."

The man hesitated for a moment. "I don't know where you're going with this, Leonard. Could you get to the point." It wasn't a question.

Magliacci leaned forward. "Okay, I…I've got some financial problems. That's why I'm here."

The man studied him.

Magliacci went on. "I can make sure none of the information I found ever gets to the press, FBI, that sort of thing."

The man looked at Magliacci for several seconds, then said, "Look, Leonard, I hardly knew Karly Amarson, certainly have nothing to hide. But if you need some money…well, Frank and I, we go way back, and you're his nephew. How big are your money problems?"

"The price is five million dollars."

The man's face went pale. The seconds seemed to Magliacci like an hour before he responded. "Mr. Magliacci, I'm afraid you don't know what you're getting yourself into."

"Well, let's talk about that." Magliacci described what he had found in the vault: The Tiffany ring with initials inscribed; the bloody knife; the black dress; and the phone pad bearing the Golden Touch logo and the *Washington Post* phone number. Then he talked about the time frame for the murder: Karly Amarson had to have been murdered somewhere between the day the ring was bought at Tiffany's and the date the new area code for Atlantic City went into effect, a date Magliacci got from the phone company, because it was logical to assume that was when the hotel would have replaced the old note pads with fresh ones that showed the new area code. That was a 146-day window.

Those facts alone didn't prove anything on this man Magliacci knew to be JAG but Magliacci was sure it would convince him of the kind of detail he was up against.

The man seemed to be in thought for a minute, then stood up as a clear indication the meeting was over. "Mr. Magliacci, there's nothing there that concerns me. I have another appointment now, so if you'll excuse me I'll call someone to escort—"

Magliacci knew if the conversation ended there his remaining life would be very short. He remained seated and leaned forward.

"Maria Sanchez. Know her?"

"It makes no difference, but no, I don't."

"She knows you. Knew Karly too. Executive housekeeper at the Golden Touch. Very loyal to Frank. I'm finding out Karly talked to Maria about everything. You know how women are bad to talk like that."

"And how does this Maria fit in?" The man was gripping the back of the chair he was holding so hard that his knuckles turned white.

"The ring. At first, you see, I was lookin' for someone with the initials J-A-G, but when Maria told me Karly's nickname for you was Jag, well, it sorta cleared that up."

Magliacci watched the man's eyes narrow as he looked at the floor, then back at Magliacci.

"Nobody ever called me that in my entire life."

Magliacci nodded. "Karly confided in Maria at times, and Maria warned her to stay away from you. Then Maria saw you entering Karly's apartment on the very day she disappeared. Said Karly was, like, draped all over you."

Jag shook his head. "If she knew anything about Karly's death she would have taken it to the police a long time ago. How did you dream up this frame, Magliacci?"

"Yeah! I wondered the same thing, I mean, why *didn't* she go to the police then? So I asked her. And you know what? She had the perfect answer, given the kind of person she is. Maria was worried about Frank's reputation. She thought you were a friend of Frank's and knew it would look bad for him if you were associated with a murder there in his hotel. But then when Frank was murdered, she looked me up. Couldn't hold it any longer. I'm the only person she trusts now that Frank's gone. I've got her under control for now, no FBI or anything, but of course if she ever starts to think you might have been involved in Frank Gallardi's death too—"

Jag slammed the chair he was leaning on into the coffee table, causing a surface crack in the glass top. He looked like he was about to move on Magliacci when Magliacci thrust a sheet of paper before his face.

"Better read this first. It's Maria's statement."

Magliacci gave him a minute to digest the photocopy of the hand-written letter he had dictated to Maria Sanchez and said, "I can make all of this go away for you and keep Maria quiet. That's what you're buying."

The man uprighted the chair and sat back down. Nothing was left of his eyes but twin dark beads. He was hoarse and breathed rapidly. "Leonard, you seem like a bright man but you've made a mistake here. A very big mistake. First, in thinking I have that kind of money, but most of all for taking me on. Take a look at where you are, this room you're sitting in, who you're talking to, all the security you saw out there, the resources I control. If I had anything to do with Karly Amarson's death or was worried about you or this toilet scrubber Maria, has it not occurred to you that I could wrap all this up nice and quiet? You would not walk out of here if I was the man you say I am. You sane enough to understand that?"

Magliacci nodded. "That worried me some. So I planned for it."

Jag sneered. "Not something you can plan for. That sort of thing is over when it happens."

"Now you're insulting me. You're too wise to not assume I have planned for every contingency. Everything is in a safe-deposit box at the bank. That may seem like an old Edward G. Robinson movie trick to you but everything's in there. Sanchez's affidavit. The knife. Karly's black dress, and the blood stains on it. Maybe all of the blood's hers, maybe some of it came from the person who killed her. I don't know, but the cops can figure all that out. With DNA and all. Anything happens to me or Sanchez, the police get a letter from my attorney directing them to the safe deposit box. When I get the money, the letter goes away and you get the keys to the box."

With that, Magliacci lifted himself off the sofa. "Look, I know it can take some time to raise five million, so don't worry about that. I can keep everything like it is for a few days. I'll be in touch."

PART TWO
Cam Warfield

CHAPTER 5

AFTER WINDING UP THEIR Joplan discussion Cross and Warfield took two steps at a time up the wide stairs to the executive level where they stopped and shook hands, wordlessly looking at each other, cementing the charge given to and accepted by Warfield. If he'd ever before signed on for a mission filled with greater potential for widespread disaster, social upheaval and political consequence he could not think of it.

Warfield emerged from the White House compound and drove across the Potomac River into Virginia then south to the Alexandria Detention Center—no more than a twenty-minute trip. A deputy sheriff checked his I.D. at the visitor kiosk and Warfield parked in the shadow of the seven-story jail.

The four-hundred inmate capacity lockup was a county facility but the ADC housed federal prisoners awaiting trial in the Eastern District of Virginia under a contract with the U.S. Marshals Service. The ADC had hosted some interesting inmates. The FBI spy Robert Hanssen and CIA turncoat Rick Ames were held there for a while. A few Al-Qaeda types had landed there—Zacarias Moussaoui, the American John Walker Lindh and others accused of being part of the Osama bin Laden network were guests in the famous jail for a time. The detention center's upscale architecture and the manicured gardens that graced the grounds did little to offset the chilling effect of the razor wire, concrete barriers and shotgun-toting deputies at the guard station.

Warfield parked under an oak and spent a few minutes reading the FBI file before going inside. A deputy keyed-in the information Warfield gave him. "I'll get the lieutenant. Hold one."

Warfield puttered around the vintage motorcycles in the lobby and looked at the black-and-white photographs of a simpler police department of half a century earlier. Before he left Cross, the president had called Paula and instructed her to make the necessary arrangements. The jail would require approval from someone in the justice department, and even though the request came from Cross the filtration down to jail level would take some time. Justice wasn't going to turn its catch over to an outsider without some ado— especially not if the request went to a United States attorney who recognized Warfield's name.

Warfield was checking his watch again as a young officer came into the lobby rolling his eyes. He apologized for the delay.

"Cameron Warfield, right? I'm Aubrey Holden, a lieutenant in the Security Division here. Been on the phone with that bunch for most of an hour. First there was clearance and then they called back and said no deal. Now it's on again. Photo I.D. Let's get you in before there's another change."

Warfield signed a form that listed twenty-seven visitor regulations. Holden told him he was on Joplan's approved list and there would be no delay next time.

Warfield thought about the man he was about to see. The limited methods and procedures the FBI could get away with were not going to do the trick with someone stonewalling, as Joplan was doing. The FBI knew Joplan was dirty but he and his lawyer knew the FBI hadn't yet accumulated enough hard evidence to hold him. The prospect of his being freed seven days hence worked on Warfield.

Three armed deputies stood near the door to the private interview room Warfield had requested, and the security camera above the door recorded anyone entering or leaving. When Warfield started in, Lieutenant Holden stopped him. "Sir, if you don't mind a personal comment—it's about my brother. He went through Lone Elm few years back. Tom Holden. Navy sent him there after he completed SEAL training. He has great respect for you and Lone Elm."

Warfield nodded, but he didn't remember every student that passed through Lone Elm. "Still in the Navy?"

"FBI now. He'll want to know I met you."

Warfield nodded. "Give him my regards."

The orange jumpsuit didn't hide Joplan's muscular build but heavy lines in his forehead aged him beyond his years. A sharp, slightly bent nose gave him a severe appearance. He sat with his right arm draped over the chair back and cocked his head to the side as he sized up Warfield.

Both men were silent as Warfield took in Joplan for a moment. Here was a man whose sworn duty it had been to recruit foreign sources of intelligence to benefit the United States. Now he had turned. His motivation was contained somewhere in the acronym MICE: Money, ideology, compromise and ego. For Americans who crossed over, it was not often ideology; few believed there was a better system than America's, even with all its flaws. Rick Ames did it for money. Robert Hanssen was an enigma: He was driven by childhood fantasy, ego, and money combined. Others put themselves in a position to be blackmailed: A well- placed U.S. government official with damning personal secrets or indiscretions to hide—even one who may have never had a disloyal thought—was easy prey for enemy intelligence. But the most common reason for betrayal was money.

"Well, well, it's you they've sent now," said Joplan.

"So we've met before."

"Lone Elm. Few years back. I actually thought you were okay."

"Should've paid attention in class."

Joplan almost smiled.

"Treating you okay?" Warfield asked. He realized the hollowness of his question and regretted asking it. This wasn't a social call and Joplan knew it.

"Don't condescend to me, Warfield."

Warfield looked straight at him. "Why'd you do it, Joplan?"

Joplan got up and walked to the back of the small room. "FBI had their little play-cops following me for months. The Fidelity, Bravery and Integrity boys! Got nothing my lawyer can't explain away. Neither will you. So, do I look stupid enough to hand you a noose to hang me with?"

Warfield walked over to the narrow vertical slit in the concrete wall that served as a window to the outside. It was too narrow for even the smallest prisoner to use for escape. A hundred yards away, drivers zipped along the Capital Beltway with free will most took for granted. Standing on the inside looking out brought to mind the preciousness of freedom to come and go wherever one pleases.

"They'll track you and track you and one day they'll have enough. You'll need a nursing home, Joplan, if you ever get out of prison."

Joplan sneered. "But you're gonna help now, right? You got some kind of special deal for me if I bare my soul to you. Well, hold your breath, Warfield. I'm out of here in a week."

If there'd been any thoughts in Warfield's mind that Joplan might not be the man the FBI thought he was, they were gone now. Joplan had not even tried to profess innocence.

Warfield thought about his days in the field as he drove away from the jail. Training people for this kind of work was fine but there was a layer of fluff between training others, and being out there in the world where theory became nerves and will, skills and some measure of smarts. It changed you forever. Carry out a clandestine operation that redirects the course of history and you never go back to any normal existence. The withdrawal symptoms don't go away. Remission, maybe, but the only fix is to go back.

Warfield called Paula Newnan and said he needed a plane to pick him up at Lone Elm at nine o'clock sharp that night. Las Vegas, round trip.

When he got to Lone Elm, he walked over to Macc Macclenny's desk where he was typing into a computer. "How busy are you?"

Macc was the operations manager at Lone Elm and a man who had Warfield's respect and confidence. He pushed his Arizona Diamondbacks baseball cap to the back of his head. "Oh, not at all. Just doing the daily log on fifty trainees, filing an accident report, ordering two cars with armor plate, planning tomorrow's activities, reading resumes for a mechanic I'm trying to hire, ordering fourteen kinds of ammo…meaningless odds and ends like that. Then I'm gonna eat my lunch. It'll be about sundown by then. I sure hope you had a nice day at the White House."

Warfield ignored the sarcasm. "Just came from ADC."

"The jail? President lock you up, or what?"

"Offered me a job. Better get used to doing without me out here."

Macc shook his head. "Yeah, like you're leaving Lone Elm."

"In and out. We'll talk about that later. Right now, there's something else."

"Shoot."

"Your pal in Las Vegas. Funny name."

"Uh, LaRez Sanazaro? But I wouldn't tell him it's funny if I were you."

"Need to see him. Tonight. You and me."

Macc issued a stunned look. "Oh, that should be easy. 'LaRez, cancel all plans for the evening. The great Cam Warfield wants to see you!' He's only got a casino to run, Cam. He hasn't retired yet. Of course I've got nothing to do here, either."

"Do it on the plane."

"Cam, I—"

Warfield cut him off. "It'll be here at nine. Check the runway."

Warfield sifted through the Department of the Army correspondence on Macclenny's desk.

"What the hell do I tell LaRez?" Macc asked.

"Tell him it's been awhile. You want to drop by tonight and say hello. That I'm tagging along. Around ten at Nellis."

Macc reached LaRez and after the two caught up on the course of their lives Macclenny explained what he wanted and said it was important. "Tell them at the guard post that you're there to meet Cameron Warfield's plane. They'll escort you."

The plane arrived at Lone Elm at eight-forty-five. The Gulfstream G650 was a sixty-five-million-dollar civilian plane the military frequently used for flying government officials around. Warfield thought of the power the president had at his fingertips. Make a phone call, a plane appears just like that, complete with crew. Macc gave last minute instructions to the Lone Elm cadre and boarded with Warfield. Warfield razzed the Air Force officers in the cockpit for a few minutes about working the graveyard shift and sat down across the aisle from Macc. When they were airborne Warfield told Macc what had transpired earlier at the White House and with Joplan at ADC. "Joplan's lawyer gets him out of jail, we don't know who's got the nukes taken from Kremlyov, what's coming down."

"Where's LaRez come in?"

"Fill me in. Didn't you save his kid's life, something like that?"

Macc chuckled. "LaRez thinks I did. Probably would've worked out okay without me. The boy panicked a little. I was swamping on my old man's boat. Happened to be there on leave one summer when LaRez chartered the boat for his family for a six-day ride down the Colorado through the Grand Canyon. We stopped all along the way to let them explore some of the beauty. You know, fossils, Indian ruins, waterfalls in the side canyons.

"One day LaRez and his wife and two brats and me, we took a hike up into one of the canyons, a mile or so along trails that climb gradually. The older kid, he's about ten or eleven then, he runs ahead and gets to this narrow ledge that serves as a pass to where we were heading. People navigate it every day but it can be a little unnerving. Anyway, LaRez is hollering at the kid to stay with us, and I shout something to rein him in a little because I know the trail narrows just ahead. So the kid gets to this sheer vertical stone wall that borders the trail—it goes straight up to the sky on his left, and on the right it's a couple hundred foot drop to car-size boulders in the canyon. So he's on this little ledge between the wall on one side and nothing but air on the other. Where he stands is about this wide." Macc held his two hands about twelve inches apart. "And he's clinging to roots and twigs sticking out of the rock wall to keep his balance. That's when he makes his mistake. He looks down at the rocks in the canyon below and freezes. We couldn't coax the boy back to our side or get him to go on to the other side. Crying his ass off. And the mother, she's screaming like a banshee. LaRez talked to the boy while I went back down to the boat as fast as I could for some equipment, and then maneuvered back up above the kid on the canyon wall. I was able to rappel down and grab him."

"Surprised LaRez didn't put out a contract on you."

Macc laughed and removed some paperwork from his briefcase. "Ever been in the Canyon?"

Warfield reclined his seat. "One of those sightseeing planes."

"You ain't seen nothin'. Gotta take you sometime."

"How long's your dad been doing it?"

"River guide? Since I was three. Forty years. Hung it up last year. I swamped for him summers until the army. It was hard leaving. Could've had a boat of my own, will someday. What a life, there on the river, most beautiful sights in the world, Cam. You're down there, two-hundred miles of river between walls that go high as you can see. You know there's a God."

"Tell me about LaRez."

"Helluva guy. Nice family. Had me down to Vegas after all that, treated me like a son. I went to his kid's high-school graduation last year. Now LaRez, you know he's the underworld. No saint, him. I met some of his people. They wear coats and ties but you don't have to wonder what business they're in. I get the impression LaRez is pretty straight now. It's the good life, doesn't want to screw it up. He ragged me some on the phone tonight, but he didn't have any problem with meeting us. He's heard of you."

"Uh-oh."

"I've told him a few stories—some of the things we've done—without giving away the farm. He's a fierce American patriot. Likes spy stories. Doesn't care much for disloyalty."

Warfield had the pilot radio ahead to Nellis Air Force Base and arrange for them to escort Sanazaro to their plane when it landed.

The Gulfstream was being refueled when a midnight blue Mercedes SL600 rolled up and LaRez stepped out, his red silk shirt filling out in the breeze, a bank of white hair on the temples, the perfect tan. Except for the bushy eyebrows, he was immaculately groomed. Warfield followed Macc to the bottom of the steps where LaRez and Macc bear-hugged each other before Macc introduced his two friends. Warfield asked the flight crew for privacy and they exited the plane.

Warfield, Macc and LaRez Sanazaro sat at a table in the plane and briefly made polite conversation, allowing Warfield and LaRez a little time to become comfortable with each other. Warfield asked LaRez to respect the sensitive and confidential nature of their discussion and gave him a ten-minute snapshot of the Joplan situation, emphasizing the critical timing. When he was finished, Sanazaro leaned in and folded his arms on the table.

"So what you need is for this man Joplan to talk, and you think I can convince him it's the thing to do."

Warfield nodded. "Assuming you've got friends in the right place." LaRez's eyes were partially obscured by wild untrimmed eyebrows. Warfield figured it was intentional. Hard to read a man if you can't see his eyes.

"Not the kind of favor I specialize in," LaRez said.

Warfield felt himself wince but quickly stood up. He had come to ask. He had failed. He understood. This was clearly not a man who bluffed. Warfield needed to move on to another solution and there was no time to waste.

LaRez motioned for him to sit down and continued. "But I have no patience with people who are disloyal—whether it be to their family or their country. And America has been good to me. Where is your man Joplan?"

"Alexandria Detention Center, in D.C."

LaRez stared out of the plane's window at another aircraft landing in the distance. "If you could get him transferred to Atlanta, that federal pen there…that possible?"

Warfield said it was.

"Cosmo Terracina is the man there who will help you. Can you believe life without parole, and what he did was nothing if you think of the damage a traitor like your Joplan can do, or those Islamic terrorists." LaRez shook his head in disgust. "I'd be proud to have Cosmo sit at my table again. He's an honorable man."

Warfield and Macc looked at each other and at LaRez. He wasn't offering any more information about this operator named Cosmo and they didn't ask.

"Tell me the requirements," LaRez said.

"Well, first, you already know it has to be fast," Warfield said. "Cosmo's job is to convince Joplan of the joys of confession. I mean rock-bottom bare-it-all download. But Cosmo's gotta be careful. Joplan's no good to me with his brain kicked out. I have to find out what's in it. When he's ready to talk, I'll send somebody in."

"Cosmo has a way of influencing people to see things his way."

LaRez shook hands with both men and held up his hand in protest when Warfield tried to thank him. "It is my country, too. Besides that," he said, glancing at Macc, "you are a friend of my friend."

CHAPTER 6

"THREE THINGS…THREE THINGS," Cosmo Terracina said. "Better have 'em all if you plan stayin' alive." His stagewhisper voice was cavernous and raspy from years spent in smoky game rooms and lounges. "Number one is *instinct*. That bellyful of guts you got, well that don't count for much if you don't feel it in your bones when something's coming down. Number two is they gotta *fear* you, shake some on the inside when they see you. I mean because they know you don't take no shit off nobody. *Nothin'*. They don't know how the hell you gonna react. You may whack 'em over a nickel. And *luck*. That's number three what I'm telling you. You ain't lucky, then fear and instinct, they don't mean nothin' either, Doyle. But in your heart here," Cosmo Terracina had said to Doyle Riley years ago in Boston as he fisted his own massive chest, "in your heart you gotta be fair. You treat people fair as long as they show you respect. They don't show you respect, then you gotta deal with it."

Riley had seen Cosmo's philosophy work for him in prison as well as it had worked on the streets of Boston.

For the power-hungry and impatient, eliminating an established boss like Cosmo was a tempting shortcut to power. For some who tried, it had been an early trip to hell.

In prison as in business, there are leaders and there are followers. When Cosmo arrived at the United States Penitentiary in Atlanta three years ago, it didn't take long for the prison population to learn who he was. The tenures of former members of the organized crime community in the *Big A* were always a topic of conversation among new inmates, as if it were an honor to occupy the same prison that once held Al Capone and Vito Genovese, so the appearance of a modern day crime boss caused a stir: In some, fear, and in others that notion of opportunity. The century-old USP Atlanta was one of the toughest facilities in the Federal Bureau of Prisons and housed hard-core criminals. And because of its age and open inside design, security among inmates was difficult to achieve making it one of the most dangerous.

Cosmo Terracina entered USP Atlanta with the presumption of power and became the most feared man in the prison. He had respect and power and the loyalty of an inner circle capable of handling any threats to his position. But the last year had been so peaceful that he worried his men might lose their edge.

Cosmo never spoke to anyone other than Doyle Riley. Men who studied Cosmo didn't risk eye contact and anyone wishing to communicate with him went through Riley. Unlike other power brokers, Cosmo didn't dehumanize men unless he had to, but any perceived disrespect toward him would result in a warning from Doyle Riley at a minimum. Cosmo had created the same power for himself here that he had enjoyed on the outside. Even in prison, life for Cosmo Terracina was good.

Cosmo's continuing activities in Boston required reliable communication, and all messages to and from the outside went through Riley, who as a lawyer had worked for Cosmo in Boston for years and then got into cocaine and became too incapacitated to function. When he was charged with obstruction of justice, perjury and a book full of other offenses, he refused to plea bargain and ended up in the Atlanta prison with Cosmo, who got him off drugs and put him to work as his lawyer again. Cosmo depended on him to handle details, and Riley, not much of a physical specimen, relied on Cosmo to keep him safe. It was an unspoken arrangement both men benefited from. It was family.

"Word from LaRez Sanazaro," Riley said now. They were eating lunch at a stainless steel table that rested on the bare concrete floor of the mess hall. They always sat in the noisy southeast corner where they could talk business without being overheard.

"LaRez?" Cosmo was surprised.

"Sending us a little job."

Cosmo had never forgotten he owed LaRez. Years ago when one of Cosmo's associates faced tax evasion charges, the spotlight was so hot on Cosmo and his men that when it was time for the trial they still hadn't found a safe way to silence a family accountant who had agreed to testify for the feds and entered the witness protection program. LaRez sent his personal representative, a man unknown to the feds, from Las Vegas to visit the accountant's mother on the day before he was to testify. The accountant developed a sudden case of amnesia on the witness stand and the case was dismissed then and there.

"What's on his mind?" Cosmo asked.

"There's this CIA spook that's been playing footsies with the other side. He's coming here. LaRez wants him to open up to the feds."

"To the *feds?* Maybe LaRez would like us to call a little meeting, get 'em in the conference room together. Have some tea. What's he done, anyway?"

Riley shrugged. "Some international thing."

"Wha' *kind* of international thing?"

"Something overseas. I…, hell, Cosmo, you think LaRez sent me a book about all of this? I should have studied cryptic codes instead of law. You wouldn't believe some of the messages I get." Doyle Riley was the only man alive who could be that direct with Cosmo. "Something about nukes."

Nukes. Cosmo understood. It was a big business. Brokers who can get them are selling nuke parts Russia made during the Cold War to anybody who wants them.

Next day at lunch, Cosmo filled his lunch tray and sat down across from the new man who fit the description Riley had given him. Cosmo had his complaints about some of the laws in this country, but no hard feelings. The U.S. had welcomed his grandparents off a boat from Italy and not only had Cosmo himself done okay here, America provided his children with legitimate opportunities, and they, now grown, had stayed away from crime. Cosmo got into it before he knew what he was doing and then it was too late. The money wasn't all that bad even in the beginning, and then one thing led to another and soon he was into loans, protection and drugs, the thing he regretted most. But betray America? Cosmo had no tolerance for someone like this Joplan.

Per Cosmo's instructions, "Brows" Brickley seated himself at Cosmo's table. "Make the face so you will remember him," Riley had said, and Brows had asked if that meant a follow-up job later on. Cosmo knew of Brows back in Boston, doing various jobs for the mafia. When Brows was convicted of dismembering a local night club comic who had made the mistake of sleeping with an underboss's girlfriend, the family arranged through government contacts to have Brows serve his time in the Big A.

"Listen to this, Cosmo," Doyle Riley had told Cosmo then. "Brows is gonna join us here. The boys want us to look after him."

When Brows arrived at the Big A, Cosmo was amused. "You never told me he was Frankenstein," he grunted to Riley. "Seen that cliff over his eyes?"

"Steroids."

Cosmo saw what he needed to see of Joplan for now. He rose from the table holding his tray and stepped behind the bench seat with his left foot. As he lifted his right foot over, another inmate rammed him from behind. Cosmo windmilled to maintain his balance but couldn't recover and fell to the concrete floor. Food scraps and utensils pelted down on him like hail in a thunderstorm. He looked up to see a man with stringy red hair and a face to match bent over him. He was laughing. Loudly. Cosmo was agile for a big man but when he scrambled to get up the red man dumped his own tray on him—just in case anyone thought this had been an accident. By then, the floor was so slippery that Cosmo could get no traction. In one last try, his arms slid out from under him and his chest popped the floor. His humiliation was indescribable.

The man who'd knocked him down put his foot in the middle of Cosmo's back. "You've met Red Russell, old man. I heard you was tough, but now *look* at you down there, in all that slop and all." Red slapped his own knees in uncontrolled derision. "You know, that's the way we used to feed them hogs back home," Russell whined from the top of his voice, like a TV sports announcer might call an exciting play.

Brows was standing behind Russell waiting for some sort of signal from Cosmo. He deflated when Cosmo shook his head, the corners of Brows's mouth turning down in a pout. As Red walked away, he looked down at Cosmo again and said, "You have a Red Russell day now, ya heah!"

The hush in the room left no doubt that every man there saw Red's power play. A new man had made his move and right then he looked pretty strong. It had all happened in a matter of seconds and the first guard didn't arrive until Cosmo was back on his feet. Then two-dozen more in full riot gear stormed in and locked down the place.

"Banana peel," Cosmo grunted, waving a hand at the mess on the floor when the first guard got to him.

"Don't give me that, Terracina, I know what happened."

"Clumsy in my old age." He knew the guard didn't believe that, but that made no difference to Cosmo. After a few minutes the guards backed off but every eye in the room was on Cosmo. A low murmur replaced the hush that occupied the room minutes earlier.

Harvey Joplan, still wondering why the hell they suddenly transferred him here with only days until his release, sat in the seat across from Cosmo and watched this Red Russell thug make his move. Joplan was no stranger to peril but realized he was in a world that had its own hazards.

Red Russell couldn't manage a straight face as he walked out of the chow hall. The feds had transferred him to Atlanta from the federal prison in Lewisburg, Pennsylvania, so they could break up a gang he'd organized back there. They didn't say that was the reason, of course, but he knew. And he loved it. He would soon be in no less of a power position in Atlanta than he was in Lewisburg, and the drug dealers he controlled in Chicago would keep on making him money. Not a month in the Big A and he had made his move. The legendary Cosmo Terracina was laughing stock now and would have trouble maintaining respect among his own men, not to mention the general population there.

Red couldn't wait to see Rudy. Rudy Snow had warned him against going after Cosmo. "He ain't easy, that Cosmo, he dangerous as a snake with two heads, man." But that made Cosmo an even more appealing target to Red. If today's little introduction didn't work, force would. Cosmo could stay alive if he was smart but if he resisted, well, Red would be as happy to do it the hard way. Besides, killing Cosmo Terracina would make the others fear Red more. *Fear.* That was control.

In the yard later, Rudy smiled. "You looked good, man, *real* good. Everybody seen what you done. But sleep with your eyes open. Ain't over 'til it's over. Cosmo, he's mafia, man."

"He's finished, that old bastard. I've dealt with them mafias before. They don't wanna die no more'n anybody else does."

Later that day in the yard Cosmo described his plan to Doyle Riley in the fewest words possible. Riley had been in on Cosmo's planning of hundreds of operations in Boston and there in Atlanta, and their simplicity always surprised him. This one had the interesting potential to fix two problems. It could settle the matter with Red Russell, and with a little luck it might fill LaRez's order regarding Joplan at the same time. Riley liked the plan and went off to find Joplan at the next yard time.

"Cosmo Terracina invites you to join him for dinner tonight," he said to Joplan.

Joplan was standing alone and continued staring at nothing. "Who's Cosmo Terracina?" he said, showing no interest.

"You'll get to know him. Has a proposition he thinks you'll find interesting. He'll be sitting with me, southeast corner of the chow hall," Riley said.

Cosmo and Riley were seated when Joplan arrived. "This your man?" Joplan asked Riley, making no eye contact with either man.

"Meet Cosmo. Cosmo, Joplan."

"Saw him at lunch," Joplan said, with a smirk.

Neither Riley nor Cosmo showed any reaction.

"Look, you got any idea why you're here? In the Big A, I mean?" Riley asked.

Joplan stared.

"The reason you're here is because Cosmo's here. They wanted you to meet him. Cosmo feels bad about that because otherwise you would be in some nice new place instead of this rat trap."

"*They?*" Joplan seemed amused at this story.

"His friends, business associates on the outside. You know how it works."

"So what is it *they* want?"

"This is where it gets a little sticky," Riley said, leaning closer to Joplan and lowering his voice. "They want you to, like, cooperate with the feds."

It was the first time Joplan showed any reaction at all. He shook his head as if to clear it. "*Cooperate?*" He looked at Cosmo, who didn't bother to look up from the fries he was eating, and then at Riley.

Riley nodded. "Completely."

Joplan's eyes narrowed. "Now this is cozy. What are you two in for, bustin' parking meters? I must be missing something. I'll be on the street in a few days while the two of you go on rotting here."

Riley nodded that he understood Joplan's confusion. "It's like this. My client here feels a debt of gratitude to this country. He has reason to believe you've betrayed it. Now although he has an appreciation for men who keep their secrets to themselves, he requests that you come clean. Tell the feds everything. In return, Cosmo will see that no harm comes to you while you're here."

Joplan almost laughed. *"He's going to protect me?* From who? That Red Russell redneck that walked all over him today?"

Riley put his fork down. He spoke in the level tones he had used in the paneled conference rooms in Boston when bargaining with one or another government attorney over the fate of one of his mob clients. "It's considerate of you to worry about my client, but you might be surprised to know that he and Mr. Russell think very much alike. Cosmo holds no grudge toward him at all. It's the way things work. You know the old saying, survival of the fittest. Same rules here as he lived under on the outside, Mr. Joplan."

Joplan stood up to leave.

Riley said, "My client understands a man likes to sleep on a proposal before making up his mind. He'll wait until tomorrow morning for your decision."

"He'll be waiting when hell freezes over," Joplan said. "Don't come near me, either of you. You see me, you go another direction. My style is different than Russell's, and more conclusive."

As Joplan walked away, Cosmo looked at him for the first time, and then at Riley. "Give this Joplan the consolation prize," he mumbled, as he dumped more ketchup on the fries.

CHAPTER 7

RED RUSSELL FELT LIKE a million dollars as he walked to the showers that evening. Cosmo was sitting alone in the rec room staring at nothing. It was all over for the old man now, since Red made a public spectacle of him in the chow hall. You could see it in his eyes. And Red was going to make Rudy Snow his number one man. Someone to watch his back, deliver orders to his other men. As Red entered the showers another inmate high-fived him and a couple averted their eyes. Their new respect for him was evident. Predictable. Fear was king. That was why all of them cleared out when he came in—fear and respect. And to give him privacy. Red Russell liked the Big A as well as he could like any prison.

He got under the shower, made it as hot as he could take and backed up under it. This was something of a celebration and since no one else was in the room, he risked closing his eyes for a moment. He didn't have to see the rusty pipes and crumbling plaster walls. Even the stainless steel sinks were rusty. As the water did its relaxation trick Red imagined the gold shower head in the mansion he built for himself in Chicago, the white marble floor, the inch-thick glass shower partition on which he paid an artist to etch a silhouette of Elyse. He felt Elyse's gleaming wet skin as she sidled into the shower with him. As the steam rose from his back he wondered if everything would be the same when he got back to the Windy City. No, it'd be better! He would be stronger with a tougher rep! Meanwhile, he would enjoy life as a man to be respected. He wouldn't allow prison to change his standing among others.

The reverie was replaced by the shock of the metal bucket that slammed against his forehead! Several men—he couldn't tell how many—were all over him now. They whirled him around like a top and kicked his legs out from under him. The ringing in his ears was almost as loud as the shouts of the attackers. He could see only straight down because of the bucket. He was on his back, and four or five pairs of hands scrambled to bind nylon ropes to his ankles and wrists. *Hadn't he learned anything? Never should have closed his eyes, not for one blink. And if he had signed Rudy on today he would have been there in the room with him and this would never have happened.*

Another kick to the bucket. Everyone was shouting, but Red knew the noise would attract no help. There was new pain where his limbs were attached to his body as the goons stretched him into a double Y and tied his ankles and wrists to the old cast iron plumbing pipes that ran along the walls. His torso lay on the cold concrete floor. *Everything went black. He was back in the youth prison in southern Illinois. It was warm. The kid that snitched, laughing, looking down at him now, holding his very own quivering bloody arm that Red had ripped from its socket… The Roman candle. July Fourth. And then, that black bastard. The pleading, the screams, the smoke, the threat of death to the man and his family if he ever told what Red did to him with that Roman candle. The laughs at supper that night as he and his brothers told their old man. Both of his victims looking at him now, refusing to help, laughing as he cried out.*

The bucket. Someone kicked it again. The towel in his mouth muffled the screams. He couldn't breathe. His eyes were ready to pop out. Were the droplets streaming down his face tears or were they blood?

He struggled to maintain consciousness and thought of other tight situations he had been in from which he emerged more powerful. A few broken bones but bones always grew back. There were scars, but he liked scars: They had an impact on anyone who might be thinking of challenging him. His eyes opened to the sight of a large cockroach on the wall beyond his feet. It began to climb and then as quick as it had appeared darted into a crack in the concrete. Thousands came back out, all running down the wall to the floor and toward him. Then another kick—to the ribs this time. In the sliver of consciousness that had returned to him, he heard the others laugh. At the same time another voice said, "Don't do that no more, man. Cosmo wants him 'live." Another answered, "He gon' *wish* he dead in a minute."

His eyes struggled open again and tried to focus on the inside of the bucket. All the voices were gone now. How long had he been unconscious? Beyond the rim of the bucket was the blurred shape of another man checking the knots in the rope that bound him. As his eyes focused, Red Russell knew he had seen this man before. *Today. Chow hall. Sitting with that Cosmo dude! Brows, was it?*

Maybe it wasn't too late to make some kind of deal. Offer *him* the Main Man job instead of Rudy. Everyone had a price. He couldn't speak because of the gag in his mouth but he made nasal sounds and flexed every muscle in his body to get the big man's attention. His wide-open eyes tried to convey the message that he wanted to talk. His focus improved to the point that he could see the knife blade in the man's thick hand. Brows Brickley walked around to his side, kicked the bucket away from his head and jerked the muffler out of his mouth. "Red Russell?"

Red talked fast. "Look, man, you and me, we can run this joint, man. You won't be no flunky no more. You'll be *somebody*. You can have all the power Terracina's got. Tell me what you want and I'll get it for you. Anything!"

Brows gave no indication he even heard Russell. "You Red Russell, right?"

Russell couldn't resist being himself any longer. "Yeah, man, untie me and I'll show you my name tattooed on my ass. You can kiss it while you're checkin' the spelling."

Brows again seemed not to notice. He positioned himself on his knees between Red's splayed legs and looked into his eyes. "Cosmo, he ain't got no hard feelin's 'bout that little accident at lunch today. Knows it wasn't nothin' personal."

Red's attitude continued to prevail over his present circumstances. He cleared his throat and with every ounce of wind he could muster, blew the collection into Brows's face. Brows hesitated for a moment, took a damp towel from the floor and wiped it off, held up the rusty knife blade for Russell to see and exhibited what might pass for a smile. Russell watched the serrated edge until the big man moved it to some place between Russell's spread legs where Russell couldn't see. He now understood why Brows had knelt there, but had little time to think about it before his body quickened. A sting at first, then pressure, then pain like nothing he could ever have imagined as the blade jerked and sawed through tender tissue and nerve endings, and pulled on other parts that were connected somewhere deep inside him. He heard himself crying. All the colors in the world flashed before him. He was hotter and more tired than he'd ever been in his life. He felt his bowels release. In less than a minute the screams died out and the bright colors faded away. What seemed like hours since he stood under the shower thinking about Elyse, about the power he held, about how he had replaced Cosmo Terracina as top dog, had been a little more than four minutes.

Next morning, Harvey Joplan walked over to Riley in the exercise yard. "You're Neanderthals," he said, his eyes bloodshot. "Not even human."

Riley didn't try to hide his amusement. "Problem?"

"You oughta live in the jungle."

"This *is* the jungle, Joplan. But smaller than you're used to. In the spy jungle, you deal in information that affects thousands of innocent lives, millions maybe. Here in my jungle, Cosmo's jungle, the problems are much simpler. They involve one life at a time. No innocent victims. They always earn it. And there are no newspapers, no political spin, no lawyers, no appeals, no long waits. It's sudden, decisive justice."

"I understand about Red Russell. Politics. Ran for higher office and lost. But why the focus on me?" Joplan asked.

"Cosmo's got a sense of right and wrong."

"According to whose rules?"

"Whoever's got the power to enforce them. In your case, it's Cosmo."

Joplan thought for a moment. "What does he want, Riley?"

"Tell the feds everything you know. Answer every question truthfully, even questions they *don't* ask. Answer them too. That's it. Any holding back or lying, Cosmo will wonder if you missed the little hint he gave you. He might decide he needs to be more direct with you next time."

Warfield was in his car when Macc Macclenny called. "Got the word from LaRez. It's all set."

"Joplan?"

"Yep. Ready to talk. And you're not gonna believe how it happened." Macc told Warfield the story.

Warfield shuddered. "So Joplan caved after hearing about Russell's misfortune."

"Well, Joplan didn't exactly *hear* about it. Woke up the next morning and found Russell's testicles in his cell—scrotum and all—wrapped up in a bloody towel."

"God!" Warfield shuddered. "Russell alive?"

"He'll live. Warden's got him on suicide watch, though."

CHAPTER 8

WARFIELD WONDERED WHO ELSE would be present at the meeting with Cross as he waited for the guard at the Northwest Appointment Gate to let him enter the White House compound. Today was sort of an official turnover of Joplan back to the FBI. After Macc called him, Warfield wanted to get the ball rolling as soon as he could. Instead of flying to Atlanta to meet with Joplan yesterday, he had asked the warden to put Joplan in a private room and arrange a phone call between him and Warfield. All Warfield wanted from the conversation was to satisfy himself that Joplan was indeed going to talk. It was the FBI's job to download him before the seven days expired and get the judge to approve continuation of his incarceration.

The phone conversation with Joplan yesterday afternoon satisfied Warfield and he'd called Cross with the news. Cross wasted no time arranging this morning's meeting. Warfield thought the president was making too big a deal of it, however, and suggested instead that he get FBI chief Fullwood on the phone and tell him Joplan had had a conversion. Cross blew that idea off without even thinking about it. He wanted Otto Stern and Austin Quinn to attend the meeting along with Fullwood.

Warfield went to a reception area near the Oval Office where Paula Newnan was talking with Earl Fullwood. He didn't know the FBI Director well but had met him on a couple of occasions, the most recent being a National Security Council meeting months earlier. The FBI Director was not an official member of the NSC, but, like Warfield and others, was invited when his input at a meeting was needed. Warfield's first thought on seeing Fullwood now was of the scent of the black cigars he chewed on. Warfield remembered that the last time he saw Fullwood on a TV newscast he would have sworn he smelled cigar smoke.

Paula saw Warfield and walked over to greet him. She had the rare ability to maintain a sense of who she was *before* the White House, even in the midst of all the egos and pressures there. Warfield had seen too many others get caught up in the thin air of apartness that too often infected those who existed in the shadows of power. Warfield was having a laugh with Paula when he noticed Fullwood standing across the room eyeing the two of them as if he had just spotted two of his Most Wanted. A minute later Warfield walked over to Fullwood. Brown-stained teeth greeted him.

" 'lo Warfield. What's goin' on at that little camp of yours—*Lone Elm* is it?" Fullwood had headed up his home state's crime investigation agency before his present appointment. To Warfield, Fullwood neither looked the part of FBI Director nor acted it. Polyester suits. Thin, grayed shirts. Scuffed wing-tips. Forty pounds overweight. A seemingly-fixed scowl on his face. Warfield noticed once at a meeting that Fullwood's socks incredibly didn't match. Fullwood must have had some terribly damning information on the former President, John McNabb, who'd appointed him, Warfield mused. He thought Cross would ease him out and knew that could not come soon enough for the troops a few blocks down Pennsylvania Avenue at the FBI headquarters.

"It's Mr. FBI himself," Warfield responded. "How's crime, Earl?" Warfield knew the Bureau's reported stats showed a turn for the better in the last year, but an investigative reporter at *The Washington Post* was looking into allegations the Bureau had played with the numbers. It was a sensitive subject for the FBI.

Fullwood's bushy eyebrows moved closer together but he hardly made eye contact with Warfield. "You've seen the numbers, Warfield. It's *down*." He crammed the cigar back between his teeth and went to the coffee pot.

Otto Stern joined Warfield. As broker and filter for information that reached the president, the national security advisor had the greatest degree of access to the president of all his inner circle.

"Otto. How goes it?"

"Warfield." Stern said flatly. He was a solemn man with a calm, strong, monotonic voice. Warfield thought it all fit, including his name. Stern had been CIA deputy director for operations at the time the CIA mole Aldrich Ames was spying for Russia. In the Ames aftermath, Stern resigned. It had happened on his shift. The investigation cleared him but there were leaks that some members of the investigative panel were not one-hundred percent satisfied Stern should be absolved of responsibility. Stern went on to join a Washington think tank and Cross later brought him into the White House. Warfield had wondered whether that was a wise move by the president, because even a hint of impropriety by such a high-profile figure as the former director of the Central Intelligence Agency was never really forgotten, but gave Cross credit for having the courage of his convictions.

The conversations stopped. Cross had walked in and as usual started working the room with greetings and personal comments. He smiled when he got to Warfield. "Fleming DeGrande still happy?"

Warfield deadpanned, "Still has *me*." Cross always bantered with Fleming at the times they'd been together. One night as Warfield and Fleming drove home from a function at the White House she'd laughed and called Cross a *hunk*. Warfield feigned jealousy and cried that Cross was too old for her and, by the way, *he's married*.

Austin Quinn arrived and migrated to Cross after shaking hands all around. When he had gotten to Warfield he smiled and said, "Colonel, good to see you. You know, every time I hear your name mentioned at Langley it's on a good note." It occurred to Warfield that Quinn was always Gentlemen's Quarterly perfect. Warfield was particular enough about his own appearance, whether in camo's or a sport jacket, but Quinn was a male fashion plate with the addition of an infectious smile that exhibited perfect teeth. Warfield had never seen him even remove the jacket to his suit. Always wore cufflinks that peeked out beyond his coat sleeve. Never without a pocket square. Every hair in place. He must not ever sit down because there's never a single wrinkle in his clothes. Appeared on Best Dressed lists every year. Shoes that looked spit-shined. None of this, however, diminished his image as a man's man who was well-liked by his colleagues inside the beltway as well as the folks in his home state of New Jersey.

Warfield had first met Quinn at a roast in his honor in Atlantic City more than six years ago and his power and influence had ratcheted upward since then. As a U.S. senator he sat on the intelligence committee and became a frequent guest on Sunday morning TV news shows. He campaigned for Cross, and when Cross was elected president he named Quinn to be Director of Central Intelligence. Cross's critics yelled cronyism but Quinn had since received good marks at CIA.

Quinn was informal with Cross. "Can we get started, Garrison," he said, looking at his watch. They were old friends—football teammates at Yale— but Warfield was unimpressed with Quinn's lack of decorum. Warfield felt that unless you were alone with the president, you addressed him as *Mr.*

President even if he was your own brother. There are invisible lines you don't cross. And you don't tell the president when to start a meeting. All in all, nevertheless, Warfield had a favorable opinion of CIA Director Austin Quinn.

Cross smiled over at Stern, on whom Warfield figured it was wasted, and dealt with it perfectly. "My pal Austin here, he comes down out of the Langley mystery tower and wants to take over the White House." The president tapped Quinn on the shoulder and laughed, but that was a reminder to Quinn that the president was the president. A man like Quinn had to be shown the boundaries now and then. And Warfield knew there was more truth than banter in Cross's remark about Quinn's desire to take over the White House. Quinn's yearning for the presidency had long been a point of speculation by Washington observers and Warfield figured he'd run when Cross's tenure ended, along with many others.

Paula and Warfield trailed behind the others en route to the Oval Office. "You didn't tell me this was a summit conference," he mumbled.

She looked up at him with mock irritation. "Had to rearrange his appointments with two senators because of this meeting. They don't like that, Cameo, and they get mad at me, not him. It's your fault, so you owe me one."

"If it's any consolation to you, I don't expect to win the popularity contest here this morning."

Warfield followed the others into the president's office. He'd been there quite a few times over the years but it never failed to inspire him. The history of the room, the men who had sat behind that desk and made decisions that to one degree or another changed the world—for better or worse. He walked around the presidential seal in the heavy carpet and joined the other four and Paula, whom Cross had invited to stay, at a round-top, polished maple table. Cross kicked it off. "You're all aware I asked Cam Warfield to take over the Joplan investigation. All I want to do this morning is bring you up to date on—"

The FBI Director Earl Fullwood interrupted. "Mr. Pres'dent," he drawled, waving his cigar in the air. It had never been lit but the end was gnarled. "Now look here. No disrespect to Kunnel Warfield here, but I just do not understand your motivation in bringin' him into this. We arrested

Joplan without any help. Used every trick in the Bureau's book for two weeks to open him up. You think somebody else is gonna do a better job than the Bureau? Now, we only got a couple days left before Joplan's lawyer gets him out. Judge already warned us. Lack of evidence. You have an obligation, Mr. Pres'dent, to give Joplan back to the Bureau. It's in the best interest of national security, and it's the law," Fullwood gambled, and shot a scowl at Warfield as he finished.

Warfield anticipated this. If Cross had handled it differently it would have deprived Fullwood of his pulpit.

Cross fired back. "We're here Earl to get a current update on Joplan, not to debate what my responsibilities are, but since you brought it up I will say this: Warfield knows terrorists. Immune to bureaucracy, hidden from reporters. No headlines in the papers every time he doesn't dot some *i*. You didn't have enough on Joplan to hold him. Our objective is what is best for the country—not to massage the FBI. Now let's move on."

It went downhill from there. Fullwood spouted obscenities, chewed on his cigar and stalked around the Oval Office—a level of behavior Warfield thought inappropriate by anyone in the Oval Office. "You want to stick it in the Bureau's face, Warfield, that it? You'll get nothing out of Joplan but you'll make up somethin' won't you? Put on a little show for the pres'dent."

"I didn't call this meeting, Earl, but the fact is that Joplan's agreed to cooperate," Warfield said.

Agreed to cooperate! Fullwood was caught off guard. He reeled for a moment but quickly turned offensive.

"Well then, I commend you, Kunnel," his eyes all but shut. "Now if you'll tell us how you accomplished this, maybe we can all learn from it," he said sardonically. "Could it be that you stepped over the line? The law sets limits, you know, on physical force, threats. Or maybe you offered a plea bargain you can't deliver. And I'm sure you Miranda'd him. This is not like what you're used to, where they's no courts and defense lawyers, no rights groups looking. I'll believe Joplan is cooperatin' when I see it, but if I'm gonna sit here and get my ass chewed out by the pres'dent while you take credit, I want him to know exactly how you did it."

Fullwood's face reflected anger as he drummed the table and stared out the window. Warfield was amused. He waited. So did Cross. Everyone in the room was silent.

After an awkward pause, Fullwood more calmly said, "Pres'dent Cross, you bringin' Warfield here into this matter sends a clear message to me— and to the nation if it gets out—that you've lost confidence in the FBI. It'll put the Bureau at a terrible disadvantage 'round the world."

Cross turned to Warfield, dismissive of Fullwood. "What was Joplan up to?"

"Joplan's contact wanted the CIA's list of Russian scientists who are considered security risks. Joplan retrieved the names from a CIA database but destroyed them when he realized the FBI was onto him. The bad news is that his contact is still there, and money seems to be no object."

"Anything else?" Cross asked.

"That's the essence of it. I only spoke with Joplan long enough to be satisfied he's ready to cooperate."

Cross turned to Fullwood. "Earl, he's in your court. Can I count on you to deal with it?"

"We'll begin the debriefing tomorrow morning," he replied curtly.

Warfield was in his office the next morning when the prison warden in Atlanta called. "Bad news Mr. Warfield. Your boy Joplan got it last night."

"*Got it?*"

"He's dead."

The news didn't particularly stagger Warfield. Anything could happen in a prison like Atlanta. It was outdated and wide open, and as dangerous as any in the system, but Warfield knew Joplan's death was no ordinary prison killing. There were several possibilities related to his case: If it had leaked that Joplan was arrested, his contact would want him dead to prevent Joplan from exposing him; also, any other mole operating in the U.S. intel community could worry that Joplan knew of him through Joplan's own foreign contacts and might give him up in a bargain with the FBI; still a third possibility was that Joplan was working in tandem with another agent like himself, who'd be worried that Joplan would take him down with him and might've had Joplan killed. Warfield discounted that possibility. Joplan was too much of a loner for that.

"Any details?" Warfield asked the warden.

"Last time anyone saw him alive was around eight last night in a workout room. Guards found his body behind a weight machine about nine. Somebody pulled a piano wire from his Adam's apple all the way through to his spine. Pretty much decapitated him. Not a pretty image."

"Who visited him in the last few days?"

"Checked that of course. You're the only visitor he had here."

The only registered visitor, Warfield mumbled. He kicked himself for not going to Atlanta to meet with Joplan in person after he agreed to cooperate. At least he would have learned who his contact was.

When Warfield told Cross about Joplan's demise, the president was furious that the opportunity was lost. He said he would order Fullwood to investigate the murder, but Warfield knew the killer would never be found. Prison murders were as easy to come by as snow at the North Pole and if anyone knew too much, he'd end up like Joplan.

Warfield spent the next two hours driving without purpose through the Virginia countryside. At one point he pulled off the road and sat on a creek bank, picking up small stones around him and tossing them into the stream. Joplan was a scumbag, a traitor. And except for the obvious reason, Warfield didn't care that he was dead. Saved taxpayers' time and money. But the practical effect, the real problem now, was that Fullwood's people would never know what Joplan could have told them that might stop an ongoing operation, or learn what damage he had done in the past.

That afternoon Warfield called Fleming DeGrande at her office. "How many more basket cases you got wringing their hands in the waiting room?"

"If all I did was basket cases, as you call them, you'd occupy most of my time."

"You could close the office then. Treat me at my place."

"You can't afford me. What's on your mind now? Got people waiting. You know, people who actually *pay* to see me."

"I feel like riding. I need some country air."

"Meet you at Hardscrabble at four."

Warfield had the horses saddled when Fleming got to Hardscrabble Ranch. She left her car in the driveway next to Warfield's and ran in to change.

Minutes later she strode across the manicured lawn toward Warfield, who was leaning against his horse, Spotlight. It was sunny and seventy degrees, perfect for riding: Fleming on Freud, Warfield riding Spotlight. Fleming walked up and put her arms around Warfield's neck. She wore jeans and a white cotton blouse in which she looked excellent. He mockingly checked her out as if he were deciding whether to accept her, and nodded.

Fleming pushed back to arm's length. "You act like some prince contemplating an addition to his harem."

"Worry not! I've decided to accept you."

They followed the path around the perimeter of the stables and corral. Half of the ranch was covered with hardwoods, and they pointed the horses along a trail leading into the trees and let them find their own pace as they rode side by side. Unlike many in northern Virginia, Warfield and Fleming rode Western style, which to Warfield, who grew up on a horse in Texas, was the only way to ride.

Warfield was quiet after a few minutes and Fleming noticed.

"You okay, War Man?" He'd told her about his meeting at the White House, including Fullwood's fit.

Before Warfield answered, Fleming went on about Fullwood. "I can tell when I see the old boy on TV that he's got a problem. Worried about losing his job?"

"Cross can't fire him, that's the problem."

"Who else was there? Anyone interesting?"

"Guess I should tell you the president asked about you."

Fleming laughed. "That's very flattering. Thank you. The President of the United States!"

"Stern, Quinn…"

"Your alter ego."

"Quinn? Hardly. But the position he holds ain't bad."

"Head of CIA! Like to have it, wouldn't you?"

Warfield thought about that for a moment. "Have to admit I wouldn't mind having my finger in all those pies, but I'd be too involved in the nuts and bolts. Quinn, he's not a technician but he's smart and he's a leader, and that's what it takes to run an outfit like that. It's mammoth, Fleming."

"CIA?"

"The intel community's made up of numerous organizations but CIA is the flagship. If I was going for one, it would be CIA."

The woods thickened as they rode along. The trail became so narrow that Fleming dropped behind and the crackle of the brush and leaves beneath the horses' hoofs became the only sounds. Sun rays sneaked through the dense trees and Joplan moved further from Warfield's consciousness by the minute. Squirrels in the branches froze in their tracks as the horses went by. A hawk circled lazily far above.

Fleming rode as if she grew up on a horse, although she didn't. She was raised in the city, the daughter of a surgeon, and became a doctor herself, a psychiatrist. She met her husband, Tom, at a horse auction and they lived on his Hardscrabble Ranch, an hour or so west of Washington.

Twenty minutes later they came upon a cluster of boulders in a clearing, and just beyond that a rushing stream. As they came closer the furious sound of the water spilling over the rocks drowned out all other. The creek banks were solid rock, exposed over the centuries as the water chiseled through. Fern and other plants grew wild and some of the roots of the towering trees were exposed above ground. Giant moss-covered boulders rested near the edge of the creek. Leaves rustled in the breeze. Warfield had never seen this part of the ranch.

He loosened the horses' saddles as they drank from the stream. The late afternoon sun poised over the water upstream found its way through the trees and splotched the landscape. Warfield climbed onto a rock the size of a car to absorb it all.

He'd become preoccupied with Fullwood. There was more to his little tantrum than Warfield understood in the meeting. He thought how the whole episode had been rendered a waste of time by Joplan's death, and began to think of Joplan again.

Fleming retrieved the blankets from their saddles and climbed onto the rock with him as he told her about Joplan's fate. They discussed it for awhile and then sat without talking. Fleming ran her fingers through his hair and rubbed his shoulders. Even the worst of worries lost some of their edge in such a place as this, and he stopped dwelling on Fullwood and Joplan and yielded to drowsiness. It seemed like no more than ten minutes later when he awoke. Fleming was under the blanket with him and had removed her clothes

"There's this particular therapy I recommend for you," she said, nuzzling his neck.

He pulled back and admired her. No woman was more beautiful to him than Fleming DeGrande. He was captured when he looked at her, but it wasn't only her fine bones, her sharp jaw line. She was honest. Loving. Caring. Sexy. Easy to be with. And her eyes, the brim-full windows to the curiosity and excitement and intelligence that lay within. They had enough things in common. She put up with him, filled in where he fell short. She could out-think him half the time. He was at peace with her. That is, when he could put work aside.

Fleming was the soft part of his life. He never thought of himself as unhappy before her, but he wasn't in any hurry to try life again without her. She massaged something in his soul he didn't know existed before.

Now her full length of bare skin fused with his own. They lay still except for the little finger of Fleming's right hand that traced out something on his face. With her lips almost touching his, she whispered something and smiled.

"You're asking for trouble, you know!" he said, as she rolled over on top of him. As he pulled her close she threw her head back to clear the hair from her face. They fell asleep on the rock after making love.

Warfield was the first to quicken. One of the horses had neighed but that wasn't what startled him. It was the distinctive crackle of twigs breaking beneath a two-footed being, but he couldn't see anything because the blanket covered his head. In the instant he was weighing his options he felt the unmistakable sensation of a gun muzzle pressed into his back.

"Just be right still now. Got this gun onya. Don't you move none or you won't never get outta this crick bottom alive."

The mountain characters in the movie Deliverance crossed Warfield's mind. He calculated the movement he would have to make in order to disarm the gunman in a single continuous thrust. Since he was lying on his right arm, he had to rotate 180 degrees before he could make contact. The blanket would slow him down. It was risky, but Warfield decided it was the lesser of risks. He figured this man to be a farmer or rancher, who likely would hesitate before shooting another human being, but Fleming in her nakedness would be tempting to any perpetrator. He cursed himself for getting into such a compromising position. No weapon, completely undressed even. And out in the open. The only thing he had going for him was surprise, if he moved quickly enough.

He gave Fleming a silent shush in the muted light that filtered through the blanket and waited for the gun barrel to touch him again for position, in case the gunman had moved. It had been no more than five seconds since the gunman first spoke when the gun poked Warfield again in the same spot. His muscles flexed into the ready position.

"That somebody in there with you?"

That was Warfield's cue He spun and catapulted himself sideways to the position he calculated the gunman occupied. His arm caught and deflected a long gun barrel and he kicked the man, who reeled backwards. First thing he saw was the shotgun hitting the ground, then the startled gunman a few feet away—on his back and scrambling to reach it. Warfield beat him to it and rammed the gun against the gunman's throat.

It was only then that Warfield realized he was an old man, perhaps in his eighties. He wore overalls and a baseball cap bearing a Skoal logo.

Before Warfield could say anything he heard Fleming's voice from the rock behind him. "*Mr. Whitney? Oh my God! Is that you, Mr. Whitney?*"

Whitney had wasted no time leaving the area but Warfield was disgusted with himself for getting into such a vulnerable position. He finished dressing and looked at Fleming.

"What the hell's he doing here, Fleming?"

Despite her embarrassment Fleming hadn't stopped laughing and was still fastening the last snap on her shirt. "He used to own this land. Nine hundred acres in all. My husband bought most of it from him before we married, but Mr. Whitney still has his home and a few acres across the creek. Since Tom died, Mr. Whitney sort of takes it on himself to investigate any unusual happenings on my property that he sees."

Warfield grudgingly smiled. "So he thinks that's unusual—you naked on that flat rock?"

"*Au contraire,* colonel. I think it was you dressed out in nothing but socks that turned him on."

A few days later Warfield's cell phone rang as he exited the parking lot at the Pentagon. He had met with Lieutenant General Robert T. Hendricks, the army's principal military advisor to Lone Elm. One of Hendricks' responsibilities was to keep Lone Elm stocked with a ready supply of people to train, which meant his staff had to track and maintain the files of the recruits designated for Lone Elm training as they processed through State Department and other filters up the line. Hendricks had approved the required number of candidates for the next Lone Elm class, which would begin in a month, and invited Warfield in to review them. They discussed the latest military scuttlebutt for an hour over lunch and spent the rest of the afternoon going through the files. Warfield got fidgety at long lunches, but such was the lubricant that kept the machines working.

It was Macc Macclenny calling from Lone Elm. "Got a recruit here says he works for a general over in Russia you're supposed to know. General Antonov? Sent you a message."

"Speak English?"

"With an accent!"

"Maybe because he's Russian, Macc! Put him on."

"It's a letter. Says his orders are to deliver it personally."

As Warfield drove west toward Lone Elm he thought of the nuclear assessment conference in Moscow where he'd met Antonov. It was one of many meetings with the goal of containing former Soviet nukes during the years that followed the collapse of the Soviet Union, and most of the Western nations were represented there. The U.S. team included a CIA rep, someone from State, and military brass including Warfield, a young officer with high hopes at the time.

At an official dinner, Warfield happened to be seated next to Aleksei Antonov, a Russian general in his early forties. At first there was no serious conversation but toward the end of the evening Antonov, speaking quietly in English amid loud toasts, cigar smoke and war stories all around, told Warfield he'd heard of him in KGB briefings before the breakup. The general was concerned about the nuclear material stashed around the Soviet Union. It was an easy target. Russia had too many pressing problems to focus on any one of them in particular, even nukes, and they had lost control of the other Soviet bloc nations who also had nuclear stockpiles. None of that was news to Warfield even twenty years ago, but he had a gut feeling

Antonov had more than the official bureaucratic interest in the problem. It was personal.

"Retiring one of these years," Antonov had told Warfield, "and then I will be in a better position to work on this problem. I can be more effective than the clumsy politicians and *apparatchiks*."

Warfield had let it drop that night. He had no authority to pursue anything like that off the record but he invited Antonov to notify him of any development the general thought he should know about. Warfield discussed it with his army superiors as they flew back to the U.S. but they dismissed it as the voice of Russian vodka. Nothing more had come of it since that night years ago.

When Warfield got to Lone Elm, the Russian—tall, blond, about twenty-eight—stood tall and stiff as he shoved a giant hand out to the American. "Lieutenant Aleksandr Nosenko, sir."

"Lieutenant."

"General Aleksei Antonov sends you this message. He had it delivered to me at the airport in Moscow before I boarded my flight."

Warfield took the gray envelope from Nosenko. "You work with the general?" He peeled open the envelope as he spoke and looked for some sign of authenticity on the stationery.

"Indirectly."

"He sent you here?"

"The general is retired from the military but his opinion is given much weight. It was his request to the army that I come here for training."

"So you didn't want to come?"

"Excuse me, sir?"

Warfield smiled and elbowed his shoulder. "You'll like it at Lone Elm, Lieutenant. Sergeant Macclenny here will see to that."

Warfield took the letter to his office. It was hand-written in English on expensive-looking paper. He closed the door and read it standing by the window.

It was dated yesterday. "Colonel Warfield. I have learned one of our physicists has been recruited to transfer quantity of bomb-grade uranium to foreign agents in the Middle East. If my source is accurate, as I suspect, the quantity of uranium exceeds that used in the Hiroshima bomb. This physicist has not been identified, but is believed to have worked at

Kremlyov. I am quite sure the Russian authorities will not deal with this quickly enough. Will inform you as the situation develops." Antonov's signature and email address followed.

Kremlyov! Warfield had studied the ultra-secretive Soviet installation formerly known as *Arzamas-16* during the Cold War. It was the Russians' first and most important nuclear design center, built in 1946 on the site of a 200-year-old monastery in the city of Sarov, which then disappeared from all official maps. It was Arzamas-60 in the beginning, which by Russian postal designation meant it was sixty kilometers from the city of Arzamas. In their demand for secrecy the Russians changed its designation to Arzamas–16. They sent their top physics graduates there to work.

Traffic was monitored twenty-five miles out from the center. Sensors warned of unauthorized visitors anywhere near the compound, and multiple walls and fences patrolled by armed guards and dogs protected the buildings that housed the nuclear materials.

Kremlyov was self-sustaining. Residents' clothing and food were produced within. Staff members were not often permitted to leave the city even for vacations. Now, years after the end of the Cold War, despite being given back its original name of Sarov, security remained high because of the sensitive materials stored there.

When the Cold War ended, fifty-thousand weapons specialists from Kremlyov and other nuclear cities went overnight from the status of Russian elite to unemployed and forgotten. Workers who hadn't been paid in months demonstrated in the streets. A joint effort by the European Union, Japan, Russia and the U.S. helped create peacetime projects to employ them, with some success. Still, there was real concern some scientists would be lured into the lucrative black market that existed for their skills. In recent times, under Vladimir Putin, Russia had downplayed the importance of the project.

The nuclear materials remained under tight security and the scientists' travels were monitored and limited. Any who might be tempted to sell out had to consider the possibility that their customer might kill them to protect their secret when their services were no longer needed. Yet Warfield knew there were those who would do it for the right money. Even with all the fences and dogs and elaborate security systems, some of them had the right keys and combinations to get to the nuclear material. A small package of weapons-grade uranium went a long way. The quantity equivalent to the Hiroshima bomb that killed four-hundred-thousand people would fit inside a business briefcase with room to spare.

Warfield read Antonov's note again and thought about Joplan. Warfield now thought it not unreasonable to connect him with the smuggling from the Soviet nuke stockpile General Antonov informed him of. But with Joplan dead he would never know.

After situating Lieutenant Nosenko, Macc caught Warfield in the Lone Elm parking lot as he was leaving. "How 'bout a beer?" He nodded in the direction of the It'll Do Lounge, across the highway from the Lone Elm entrance.

Warfield looked at his watch. Fleming was expecting him on this rare occasion that he could get home at a decent hour, and he also had to make a phone call, but the It'll Do was tempting. For a long time Warfield was a regular at the place—country music, cold beer, Toni the sexy bartender who always had a trivia question floating around, good dance floor, single women there to meet the regulars as well as the trainees from Lone Elm— but his frequency dropped off after he met Fleming and started going to Hardscrabble after work instead of hanging out. Sometime later he reluctantly admitted to himself that the It'll Do had become a destructive daily routine for him. Over a period of time the evenings grew into early mornings. A couple of beers grew into six or eight. Jack Daniels on the rocks replaced the beers. More than once he had woken up with a girl whose name he couldn't remember. His daily five-mile run became hit-or-miss. Now when he looked back on those days he thanked God he pulled out of it before it ruined him. And Fleming. She didn't cause his change—change comes from within—but in her he saw a dimension of life he had almost lost.

"Can't go," he told Macc.

Macc gave him a smile of pity and flapped his arms like a crowing rooster.

As Warfield drove away, he saw Macc in the rear-view mirror still laughing at his boss, whom he was classifying as henpecked.

On the drive to Hardscrabble he left a message for Earl Fullwood at the FBI to call him. Soon after he arrived at Fleming's, FBI Deputy Director

Rachel Gilbert returned his call, without explaining why Fullwood himself didn't call. Warfield knew of her but they had never met. Gilbert said she knew who he was as well.

Warfield gave her the gist of Antonov's letter and explained how he knew the general.

"I'm familiar with this intelligence," Gilbert said. "It came in today."

Warfield was impressed. "And?"

"We're considering it."

"What does that mean?"

"Whether it warrants any action at this time, for instance."

Warfield paused for a moment. "Help me out here. Do you mean you're trying to decide whether the intelligence is valid, or that you believe the intelligence but don't know what to do about it?"

Gilbert paused. Warfield could hear her breathing pattern on the phone and knew she was not pleased. He had dared question the deputy director of the Federal Bureau of Investigation.

"Colonel Warfield, the Bureau has this intelligence and we're quite capable of determining the best course of action. And maybe you aren't aware that, uh…is this a secure phone?"

"It is."

"Maybe you don't realize this is a dry run we're talking about."

"By that you mean that you believe the Russian will travel the route without the nukes, and if nobody seems to notice, he'll do it again with the real stuff?"

"Something like that, yes."

"Well, if I'm a nuke smuggler that's what I want the FBI to think."

"Don't you think this Russian believes he can figure out what we will do, and adjust his activities accordingly?" she said.

"I think he's smart enough to convince you of what he wants you to believe."

Gilbert seemed to think about that for a while and said, "Colonel Warfield, I'm not going to discuss this with you. I understand you have—you *had*—a job to do for the president, but Director Fullwood…" She stopped mid-sentence.

"Fullwood…?"

"Sorry. Nothing."

"What about Fullwood, Ms. Gilbert?"

She paused, then said, "He's made it clear we will have no communication with you."

Warfield mulled over the conversation for a moment and went into the den where Fleming was catching up on medical journals. He knew she had held dinner for two hours.

"Sorry, Babe, about dinner."

"Still warm." She studied him. "Couldn't avoid hearing the tone of that call. Something to drink first?"

Warfield nodded. Fleming poured herself a glass of wine and opened a bottle of Sam Adams for him. She set out chips and a "spinach thing" she had made and sat down next to him on the sofa.

"Something coming down?"

Warfield was never careless with sensitive information even if it didn't have a security classification, but it wasn't unusual for him to confide in Fleming. She knew the critical nature of secrecy. He told her about the note from Antonov and the conversation with Rachel Gilbert and then changed the subject. It wasn't worth talking about, at least not until the situation developed more.

After eating dinner in virtual silence they watched TV for awhile, then at eleven-fifteen Fleming announced she was going to turn in. She kissed him on the lips. "Wake me when you come to bed."

Warfield lowered the lights in the den and sat in silence for the next half hour. He'd spent many good evenings at the old ranch house with Fleming. Always outside in the warm months, but there had been plenty of roaring fires in the huge fireplace on snowy nights. He reclined on the sofa and looked up at the rough-hewn beams supporting the roof and wondered how many others had done the same in the lifetime of the grand old house.

He opened another beer, looked up Abbas Mozedah in his laptop and dialed the number in Paris. Abbas operated a consulting engineering firm as a front but his zeal was for fighting terrorism and plotting against the ruling regime in Iran. Warfield had had several occasions to share information with Mozedah over the past few years and had a high degree of confidence in the Iranian.

"Cameron Warfield!" Mozedah's voice was deep, foghorn quality.

"Probably woke you. What is it there? Six in the morning?"

"You know I never sleep, Cameron. No time for that, but tell me, how are things at that summer camp of yours?"

Warfield chuckled although he was not in the mood for it, and managed to return the volley. "Calling to see if you're still playing hide-and-seek."

They small-talked for a minute and Warfield got to business. "Remember the Russian army general I told you about? Aleksei Antonov?"

A moment's pause, then, "Years ago."

"Received a message from him. He retired but I guess he has intelligence sources there. Says there's going to be a movement of bomb-grade uranium out of Russia."

"Surprise, surprise. In what quantity?"

"Six, eight kilos if Antonov is right."

"To where, Cameron?"

"Middle East, Antonov says. Nothing more specific."

"Who is doing this?"

"Supposedly a Russian physicist who used to make their nukes at Arzamas-16."

"You doing anything—officially I mean?"

"Contacted the FBI. They knew about it from one of their own sources. They say the Russian will be making a practice run to see if anybody's watching."

Abbas groaned.

"Yeah, that's the problem. Try to confirm."

"I will do what I can, Cameron."

"Hurry."

Abbas called back late the following afternoon, catching Warfield in his office at Lone Elm. "You are on to something here, Cameron. Looks like Antonov is correct about the uranium shipment."

"Talk to me," Warfield said, sitting up in his chair.

"Seth is behind it."

Warfield whistled. "Seth again," he mumbled, thinking about the legendary broker of death and destruction. The terrorist known as Seth was believed to be protected by Iran. He was an independent broker, arranging deals for terrorist groups with their own agenda. He didn't often carry out terrorism himself but his name was associated with high-profile bombings against Americans and U.S. interests abroad and at home, including the failed Christmas Day *underwear* bomber over Detroit. His work to date was nothing of the magnitude of 9/11 but by concentrating on less ambitious projects he managed to often stay below the radar. Still, his notoriety gave him access to large cash reserves with which he could buy American spies. Harvey Joplan crossed Warfield's mind again. "Who's Seth selling the stuff to?"

"Not sure yet, but we do know this Russian's name: It is Boris Petrevich. He will go from Russia through Georgia, cross into Turkey at the border gate at Sarp, and then cross from Turkey into Iraq at the Habur border gate where two of the guards on the Iraqi side of the border have been recruited for this operation. We do not know where he will go from there."

"Anything else?"

"When the Russian moves, he will have the uranium. No dry run."

"You're sure of your source?"

"That would be Hassan, the brother-in-law of Seth. And yes."

Warfield shook his head. *C'mon Abbas!*

"I know, I know what you are thinking, Cameron, but listen to this first. Hassan's sister was murdered—this I know. Hassan believes it was Seth who had her killed. She was Seth's wife. Hassan is appearing to go along with Seth's claim that he was not involved so he can stay close to him. Wants to be sure nothing happens to Seth until he has proof. Then Hassan wants him all for himself. Seth is a hero to the world of terrorism, but as a human being he's despised even among his closest allies."

"If you're satisfied, Abbas, I buy it."

"No need for worry, Cameron."

"When will it happen? The uranium movement."

"An answer I do not have yet, but I will find out. I have sources close to this, Cameron."

"Close?"

"Inside Russia. Yes. We are making progress there."

"Find out everything you can." Warfield wished he could recapture those words. It was a stupid thing to say to someone like Abbas.

"Of course, *Colonel Warfield.*"

"Sorry, Abbas."

Abbas feigned irritation with a deep groan, then said, "Not to worry, Cameron. I am the same way. I will call you when I have something."

Warfield punched in Fullwood's number and got a receptionist who demanded a lot of details. He was surprised when Rachel Gilbert came on the line.

"Colonel Warfield. Again."

"Okay Rachel. I don't give up easily. For what it's worth to the Bureau, I've got confirmation the uranium is traveling on the Russian's first trip. It will not be a dry run."

"Colonel Warfield, I don't mean to be rude but I have orders."

"Look, Rachel, nobody benefits from this kind of standoff. You're the deputy director over there, second in command, which must count for *something*. This is intelligence I will stake my own reputation on in the intel community. You going to stand behind the stupid decree Fullwood made because he doesn't like me?"

Gilbert took a deep breath. "You don't know the director very well if you think I could change the plan on this operation without his knowledge. He's all over it. And I think he has done some well-poisoning."

Warfield now understood. Not only were Rachel Gilbert's hands tied, Fullwood was preparing others within the intelligence community in case Warfield went to them. Warfield was still thinking about this when Gilbert continued.

"I think it will be better if you don't call here again, Colonel Warfield."

Warfield told the receptionist to hold his calls and spent the next hour weighing his options. If it came to a showdown, Fullwood had the cards stacked in his favor. Warfield could go to the president but that would put him on the spot and there would be only losers in the ensuing battle of egos, while the Russian Boris Petrevich carried out his nuke-smuggling mission unimpeded.

Warfield leaned back and surveyed the goings-on outside his window. Half a mile away Macc and a couple of his men were giving instructions on evasive driving. A cloud of dust rose from a pair of Abidingos in the distance, the new vehicle that replaced the Humvee. He felt like saying to hell with it and joining them.

Next morning, Warfield was back on the phone to Abbas. "I'd like you to put someone on the smuggler every step of the way."

"How do you want this carried out?"

"You said he will make the trip on the ground. Tail him with a Geiger. If he's carrying uranium there'll be leakage. Might show up on his clothes, car, if you can get close enough."

"FBI. Will we run into them?"

"Hope they don't figure out what you're doing but I'm not going to worry about that. If Petrevich is hot, stop him before he crosses into Iraq. But wait until the last second, in case the FBI decides to take him on their own. If they do—and I hope to God they do—we're home free and your men are out of the picture."

"Of course. And if they do not?"

"In that case, and if you know Petrevich has the stuff on him, it's your baby. Do what you're comfortable with. You know the risks. You okay with that?"

"You can sleep tonight, Cameron. I know what to do. And we want to stop this operation as much as you do."

Jalil flipped through the stack of colorful Turkish blankets, pulled one off the shelf, studied it for a minute and dropped it into his shopping caddy. The store was crammed full of Turkish products from jars of olives to photographs of the country's landscapes to woven straw baskets. In the time Jalil had been there he'd looked at everything at least once and worried that if Boris Petrevich did not show up soon, the store personnel were going to become suspicious. The Russian must have made another stop along the way. The thought occurred to Jalil that he and his two partners sent by Abbas Mozedah may have miscalculated: Petrevich may not stop at this border store at all, and it was the last one before the Habur crossing point. This was their first and last chance to confirm that Petrevich was transporting nukes.

Zayed's resonant, calm voice broke the silence in Jalil's radio headset. "He's approaching the store now."

Jalil glanced out the window and saw the black Volvo he and Zayed and Salim had followed since it exited Russia. Petrevich had wasted no time forging southward across the bleak Russian landscape, through the city of Volgograd and on to the border with Georgia. Abbas's Russian contacts had tracked him that far—using three different cars in an effort to prevent Petrevich from becoming suspicious. Salim, Jalil and Zayed picked up the Volvo there and shadowed it through Georgia and Turkey to the fuel stop and retail store where Jalil now stood as Petrevich fueled-up.

When Petrevich entered the store Jalil worked his way over to where he stood at a news rack. The Geiger-counter inside Jalil's back pack was set at maximum sensitivity and as he walked past the Russian, the headphones began to click. It was the sound he had heard at the university where Abbas Mozedah had sent the three of them to learn about the Geiger-counter from his contact there. When the Russian went to the restroom Jalil signaled Zayed to check his car.

"The car is hot," Zayed said into Jalil's earphones a minute later. "I will tell Salim."

Salim stood on the narrow concrete island to the side of one of the checkpoint kiosks at the Habur border gate on the northern Iraqi border and held his AK-47 at the ready. As cars and trucks took their turn through customs Salim wondered how much time he had before one of the other guards realized he wasn't one of them. He had edged into the more prominent position at the border gate a minute ago when Zayed signaled that the Volvo was on its way and confirmed that the Russian was to be stopped. Salim knew it would have been safer to take out the smuggler somewhere else, but because they had to give the American authorities the opportunity until the very last second to do the job, that course of action was not possible.

The black Volvo was now the fifth vehicle back in the lane to Salim's left, practically lost among the sea of trucks backed up at the border gate. Unless the FBI were there somewhere and took their own action he would do the job Abbas sent him to do before the Russian was inside Iraq and out of their reach. If Petrevich made it across the border safely, the Iraqi

118

insurgents would be protecting their new assets: The Russian physicist Petrevich and his uranium, the critical component for a deliverable weapon of mass destruction. If the Russian had to be killed, it had to be on the Turkey side where the Iraqi border guards could not take possession of the uranium.

Salim thought of his two young sons and hoped they would live long enough to enjoy peace. He believed in what Abbas was doing and wanted to work with him as long as he could hold a gun. Today would not be the first time he killed, if it came to that. People from his part of the world learned killing when they were young. Maybe what he was about to do would at least *slow* the accumulation of nuclear materials by terrorists in the Middle East.

Salim tried to appear normal. A Turkish guard wearing a lieutenant's uniform and dark glasses seemed to be paying him a lot of attention but turned away when Salim looked at him. Salim ran through his escape plan one last time and glanced at the Iraqi guards, who were said to be working in tandem with Petrevich, a few meters beyond the first checkpoint. They too would be watching for the black Volvo and would try to take possession of its precious cargo. That would mean taking out Salim, too, when they realized who he was—but by then he would have disappeared behind a kiosk and the approaching vehicles. Salim knew there was no promise of safety today, but then no such promise ever existed in the fight against forces who would destroy the world to accomplish their own objectives. He tried as hard as he could to steady the trembling in his hands.

Petrevich was now second in line to show his credentials to the guard inside the kiosk a few meters from Salim. There was no mistaking the car. He would wait until the Russian was cleared and about to drive away through the checkpoint. If the FBI were there, they would have acted by then. If not, then Salim would spray the windshield of the Volvo as he counted off the seconds—one...two...three. Then in the ensuing pandemonium he would escape to safety using backed-up cars and trucks for cover. His work there would be complete.

Salim's eyes narrowed as the memory of the blood-covered body of his younger brother in an earlier operation flashed through his mind. Seconds to go. The trembling calmed. The Russian pulled into position. Moments now, unless the guards decided to do a thorough search on the Volvo. No, they waved him on! It was time. Salim was the final barrier.

Salim had stood with his weapon cradled in his arm so he would not have to attract attention by raising it before firing. Now he placed his finger against the trigger. Before he squeezed it the nightmare he had not planned for became reality. Someone in the lane to his right recognized him.

"Salim! What are you doing there? In that uniform?"

Salim had little time to wonder who had recognized him and the guard wearing the dark glasses didn't wait for an explanation. He opened fire and Salim's head fragmented. He flew backwards, his arms and legs dancing to the automatic rifle's deadly tune, onto the hood of a car in the other lane. All of the guards were distracted for a moment before the hydraulic barricades in each lane had been opened, and by then the Volvo was safely inside Iraq.

Minutes later Abbas received the sorry news that the mission had failed. Jalil and Zayed escaped but his long-time friend and fellow-warrior Salim was dead. He fought the tears that welled up in his eyes as he looked out onto the Paris street in front of his office. Terrorists had won the battle but they had not won the war.

Earl Fullwood sat in his corner office on the seventh floor of the J. Edgar Hoover Building and read the report delivered to him minutes earlier. The crossing took place at Habur as expected. A Bureau operative got caught in the crossfire and was killed but the imposter guard who tried to shoot the Russian got it too. When he finished reading, he pulled out a new cigar and stuck it between his teeth. A trace of a smile hit his lips.

Fullwood dialed Paula Newnan's number. Newnan could get him in to see Cross on short notice. Now, by God, he had a case to take to the president, and Cross had no choice but to back him. Fullwood couldn't prove anything on Warfield, but he didn't need to. After all, he *was* Earl Fullwood, the director of the Federal Bureau of Investigation, the greatest investigative organization in the world, and it was time to reclaim the prominence he'd lost at the hand of Cameron Warfield.

CHAPTER 9

THE OTHERS WERE STANDING around in the Oval Office chatting with Cross when Warfield arrived at seven-forty-five that morning. Earl Fullwood looked away when he saw Warfield enter, so, as Warfield thought when Paula had called, the meeting was about the Habur border incident. Fullwood no doubt had asked the president for the meeting and it was about Warfield.

The only man in the room whom Warfield didn't know walked over and introduced himself as Bill Reynolds. "I work for Quinn," he said.

"Cam Warfield."

"I've wanted to meet you. Guess I never thought it would be in the Oval Office."

"Good to see you, Bill. Quinn coming?"

Reynolds shook his head. "Out of town."

President Cross looked at his watch and everyone took the cue. Otto Stern, Fullwood, Bill Reynolds, the president and Warfield seated themselves around Cross's maple table. Warfield ended up directly across from Fullwood.

Cross kicked it off. "Okay, Earl, let's get it going. What is this national security crisis?"

Fullwood looked straight at Warfield. "Well, Mr. Pres'dent, since the Kunnel is here, I'll let him tell you. Seems like he's maintainin' his good record of interferin' in the Bureau's business."

How in hell did this guy ever become head of the FBI? Warfield thought. His fantasy was to grab Fullwood by his fat neck and choke the bastard until his eyes popped out, but some degree of civility was required in the presence of the president and anyway Fullwood wasn't worth it. Why waste time and energy with that kind of ignorance and arrogance?

Warfield indicated that he wasn't going to respond to Fullwood, and President Cross told the FBI chief to move on. Fullwood told his version of the Turkey/Iraq border incident from the day the Bureau first knew of it up to the Habur shooting incident. The Bureau had the Russian under their watch all the way from Russia, through Turkey right to the Iraqi border. Even had a man there at the border gate posing as a Turkish lieutenant. The Bureau was gathering data on the Russian so they could pick him off on his *next* run, when, according to their intelligence, he would be in possession of the stolen uranium. The John Wayne shootout, as Fullwood called it, rendered that future operation impossible. Fullwood was in full stride. He talked louder and louder, paused for drama and resumed with a quiet, "Thanks to Kunnel Warfield here, the Russian has been alerted."

"And the consequences are…?" Cross asked.

"He'll find another way to get that uranium to wherever it's going in the Middle East! Forget about catchin' him doin' it next trip, Mr. Pres'dent. It's a done deal for their side. It's over."

Warfield saw the trap Fullwood had set. Whether or not Fullwood believed the dry run story was not important: His objective was to put Warfield in a scenario that would force Cross to get rid of him. Petrevich, to Fullwood, was incidental by comparison.

Cross said to Fullwood, "Why did you think there would be no transfer on the Russian's first trip, Earl?"

"Initial intelligence that this would be a dry run came from CIA. And as to Kunnel Warfield's involvement, my own men dug up that information."

Dug up was a good way to put it, Warfield thought.

"Tell me about the CIA intelligence," Cross said.

Fullwood twisted in his chair. "Okay, well I, uh, I don't have all those details with me at the moment."

Cross turned to Bill Reynolds, who told the president he'd received late notice to attend this meeting and wasn't familiar with the details of the case. He'd research it and get back to him.

Cross looked at Warfield. "Okay, Cam. What about Habur gate."

Warfield took a moment to decide how much to tell. Habur had been no different than the other times he'd taken life and death matters into his own hands. Sometimes you were the hero for it and sometimes the goat. Decisions like this one weren't often so clear-cut—reliable intelligence that weapons-grade uranium was destined for a region where terrorists were supported by government and revered by zealots; deaf ears at the FBI. But the president had not authorized that specific action and Warfield wondered if he himself could land in court over it if Fullwood and Justice pushed it. That would be disastrous for Cross. So there was but one course for Warfield now. "I'm flattered the director thinks I could set up such an operation."

"You denyin' you were behind it?" Fullwood said.

Warfield displayed only mild irritation. "Russians could've set it up. How about the CIA? But whoever it was, you said your people were there at Habur that day. I informed Rachel Gilbert it was not going to be a trial run. You could have stopped it but you ignored the information I gave her. You instructed her to have no more communication with me and now you're trying to dodge the blame." Then Warfield looked directly into Fullwood's eyes and dropped a bomb: "Mr. Director, it would be easy to believe you knowingly let the Russian go through with the uranium so you could serve some other agenda of yours."

Fullwood was speechless for a moment, as his face turned crimson. Finally he said, "Last time I checked the rules, the Bureau was not takin' orders from retired army kunnels. Who the hell are you Warfield to tell the Federal Bureau of Investigation how to run its affairs? I've never seen the likes of your audac'ty. But let me get this straight. You actually disputin' our initial intelligence from CIA?"

"I am."

Fullwood pressed. "And if you're flatly statin' that the uranium crossed the Iraqi border with the Russian, I suppose you got some evidence to support that."

Glancing at his watch, Cross brought it to a halt before Warfield could answer.

Warfield was saved. He wasn't about to reveal his collaboration with Abbas, or any other part of his involvement, but he didn't want to lie to Cross.

"We're getting nowhere," Cross said. "I've got a press conference in a few minutes. We'll meet here again at noon tomorrow for fifteen minutes and get to the bottom of this. I want your sources, Earl. Same for Warfield and CIA. I expect everyone to be prepared. And, Earl, I'm spending more time on your problems than on the rest of the country."

Fullwood crammed his papers into his attaché case and left without saying anything. Stern and Reynolds, more amiable, followed. Cross cornered Warfield in the hallway. "Listen Cam, we're in a tough spot here, you and me."

Warfield nodded.

"I probably don't want to know the answer to this question," Cross said, putting his hand on Warfield's shoulder, "but I have to ask—"

"About the attack at Habur crossing."

"Exactly."

Cross had saved him from answering that question in the meeting, but now he wanted to know, and Warfield wouldn't mislead him. Not that he couldn't lie. In the dirty business of espionage, lies, deceit and betrayal were the essence of the job. CIA and other intelligence operatives had to guard against letting this professional behavior become their personal baseline and they often failed, but Warfield had kept that part of his life—the set of skills he used to deal with the enemy—in a separate compartment from his personal values and conduct. When he answered the President's question now, he was factual.

"I authorized it on certain conditions. Those conditions were met. The operation was carried out accordingly. Now you have to tell me if you want to know more."

Cross understood the protection from knowledge Warfield was offering but said, "I do. Go ahead."

"I may have gone too far, sir, but to let the Russian cross into Iraq was a risk the United States couldn't afford, in my judgment. Given the intelligence we had—*I* had—the operation at the Habur border gate should have been almost routine—and carried out by the FBI."

"And you notified the FBI in advance."

"Yep, twice, and they didn't want it."

"But you didn't talk to Fullwood?"

"Asked for him. He put Gilbert on me both times."

"What did she say?"

"That they had their own sources. I think it's possible she gave some credibility to my information but doesn't have the balls to defend it to Fullwood. So I set up a safety net to stop the smuggler if and only if the FBI didn't stop him before he entered Iraq."

"You were certain there was uranium in that car?"

"There were radioactive emissions from the car and from the Russian himself when he was out of the car. I'm absolutely sure of that."

"How did Fullwood know you were involved?"

"He's bluffing. *Couldn't* know." Warfield was that certain Abbas didn't leak it. No one else knew—except Fleming.

"What about Earl's story that CIA was the source for the trial-run intelligence?"

"If it's true, could mean another mole. Maybe in the CIA. Or the FBI."

"That's a jump, Cam. Could just be bad intelligence. It's not a perfect world, you know."

"If they got the dry run story from the CIA, their intel was wrong and mine was right, if you believe the Geiger-counter. So one possibility that has to be considered is that the dry run report was engineered."

"And it couldn't have been our boy Joplan." Cross was thinking out loud.

"Right. It was long after Joplan's arrest that the FBI said they received the intel from CIA. Me too."

"What about your source?"

Warfield nodded. "I'd bet my life on him. Fact is, I have, more than once." He told Cross of Abbas's return to his own Iran after he graduated from MIT, and his eventual escape to Paris with his family and most of their wealth just before the religious regime took over Iran in the seventies; of his engineering firm in Paris that was a front for his operation to undermine terrorists and rogue regimes; and that Warfield and Abbas had cooperated in several operations over the years.

"CIA know him? Abbas, I mean."

"He worked with CIA twenty years ago."

Cross thought it over for a minute. "Look, don't worry about this. I'll handle Earl when we meet tomorrow. Keep your nose clean 'til then." He patted Warfield on the back and left him standing there.

Warfield stayed over at Fleming's that night and when he stepped out of the shower the next morning his cell phone was ringing. He grabbed the phone next to the bed as Fleming, now waking, rolled over, revealing the whiteness of her breasts in the tangle of sheets.

"Yeah," he answered, somewhat preoccupied. Fleming was teasing him.

"Garrison here. Read this morning's *Post* yet?"

Warfield was caught off guard. Cross didn't place his own calls.

"Uh…no, sir."

"Call me when you've read it."

The front page showed a ten-year-old 2x3 photo of Warfield in uniform, and the headline, "Cross Assistant Foils FBI Operation in Turkey". The story quoted "most-reliable unnamed" sources as saying Cross recruited Warfield to work behind the scenes, and that had led to Warfield's interference in an FBI operation that compromised national security. Cross and Warfield may have operated in violation of federal law, according to the sources. Warfield was described as a forced-out army colonel who was handed a lucrative government contract to run a small training center subsidized by Congress. It went on to describe the border incident with details that could have come only from someone present at yesterday's Oval Office meeting.

Fleming was reading over his shoulder. "Know who leaked it?"

Warfield couldn't rule out Otto Stern or Bill Reynolds, but he put his money on Fullwood.

"Fullwood. Welcome to politics," Warfield muttered.

Now the President would take plenty of heat, and any retaliation by Cross against Fullwood would give credibility to the story. Warfield knew he couldn't so much as empty the president's wastebasket now without it showing up in the news, leaving one avenue for him: He had to resign the White House post, and there was even a chance Lone Elm could be in political jeopardy if the story lingered on.

Later that morning in the Oval Office, Cross told Warfield, "I've put you in a lousy position. You could've gone into politics if you wanted this kind of harassment."

"It's my own doing."

"You mean Habur? I hope I would have had the guts to do what you did."

"I'm a liability to you now, Mr. President. If I disappear, so will the story. And you can get back to work. You hired me to handle this but you're having to spend time on it."

Cross weighed that for a moment. "Let's hang in there, Cam. Years ago, I was naïve to think I could get into politics and stay above this part of it, but now that I'm in, I can play the game."

Warfield shook his head. "It's no good. The advantages I held for you—my anonymity, independence—that's gone now. And the longer this lives, the worse it'll get. Congressional hearings, investigations, special prosecutors. There'd be no time left for me to do what you hired me for. I leave, the problem goes away."

Cross thought it over. "Tell you what, Cam, don't jump yet. Spend your time at Lone Elm instead of this office, but keep working on this. It'll be unofficial. We'll say you've resigned the post here at the White House. I'll keep the followup meet with Fullwood and Reynolds at noon and see what they have to say about their sources."

Paula Newnan sat with Warfield while he packed up the personal items he'd brought to the White House. She cursed Fullwood. Warfield put the boxes in his car and headed to Lone Elm.

Cross called Warfield after his noon meeting with Fullwood and Reynolds.

"Told them you decided to go back to Lone Elm."

"Made Fullwood a happy man."

"Looks like the CIA source came through Quinn himself via a former KGB officer he met in Russia when he was in the Senate. Quinn doesn't want to identify his source—a commitment he made to him."

"This was direct from the KGB officer to Quinn?"

"So it seems."

Warfield thought about that. It sounded too much like his own relationship with Antonov. An incredible coincidence. What about Antonov? Could he be Quinn's source also, playing both ends against the middle? Could Quinn, *the CIA director*, be lying? Not possible.

"You there?" Cross said after a few seconds.

"Just thinking. Now what about Fullwood's claim that I set up Habur? He tell you how he got that?"

"Nope. He chewed on that cigar and tried to explain but he's shooting in the dark."

"What about the *Post* story?"

"Fullwood knows that I think he leaked it," Cross said.

Warfield was putting his Lone Elm office in order the next day when Abbas Mozedah called. "This may or may not be important, Cameron, but very interesting. Our friend Seth has a sister in America—right there in Washington."

"Yeah? Seth, the terrorist?"

"Name is Ana Koronis."

"Koronis." Warfield knew the name. "Married to—"

"Spiro Koronis. *Was.* As you know, he is dead now."

The former U.S. Ambassador to Greece! Warfield was stunned. Not only was Seth's sister the widow of the ambassador, *she had been the constant companion of Austin Quinn for some time!* Also a prominent lawyer and high-profile Washington socialite, Ms. Koronis was often in the news.

This woman was the sister of a Middle East terrorist?

"Abbas, you sure about that?"

"It is from Hassan. And what he has told us to now has proved true."

Hassan again. "What does he have to say about her?"

"He does not know of any communication between Seth and his sister now, but he says she lived with Seth in Iran for six or seven months, then moved back to Washington. That was a few years ago, after her family was killed, but Seth was the same outlaw then."

"So you're confident about this."

"I am, Cameron," said Abbas in his baritone voice.

Warfield hung up knowing he had a decision to make. Ana Koronis couldn't be condemned simply because her brother was a terrorist, but it would be flat-out irresponsible to ignore the connection. He searched the Internet for "Ana Koronis" and came up with three-hundred-ninety-eight hits, not an extraordinary number for a person of notoriety, many of which were newspaper and magazine references that included everything he knew of her and much more.

None of the information he found was in-itself damaging but the irony was too great. Talking to the FBI was not an option but he remembered a United States attorney he'd met on a case a couple of years ago and trusted. He dialed Joe Morgan and reintroduced himself.

"Sure," Morgan said. "The Rattarree case. Been a while. How's it goin' Warfield?"

They met at Louie's Blue Plate in Tyson's Corner, Virginia, outside the Washington Beltway. It was a retro joint with plastic laminated table tops and chrome chairs, and its reputation for vegetables and chicken fried steak was legendary. Earth Angel by the Penguins was playing on the juke box when they arrived. It was loud enough to assure a private conversation.

Warfield told Morgan what he'd learned from Abbas and the Internet about Ana Koronis. Her life resembled a Greek tragedy as much as it did a spy case. During her courtship with Spiro Koronis, society magazines pictured a beautiful, olive-skinned Ana along with the ambassador week after week, referring to him as one of the most eligible men in the world and describing Ana as a charming, brilliant young attorney who grew up in Chicago and moved to Washington to practice law. It happened that her law firm had ties to the State department, where she met the ambassador.

People photographers had found a way into the palace in Greece where the couple married. They had a child soon, and Ana left her law practice so she and son Nikko could be with the ambassador in Athens.

The press coverage was no less frenetic during the three years after their marriage. There were photos of them aboard their yacht, at the embassy in Athens, on Santorini with friends and always with beloved Nikko, who never failed to favor the cameras with a happy smile. They became America's Couple. But the fairy tale was cut far too short by a terrorist incident at the airport in Athens. Spiro and little Nikko were taken hostage inside an airport restroom and dragged onto a hijacked passenger jet as the other armed terrorists covered them. The other passengers had been ordered off the plane.

A pair of U.S. warplanes sandwiched the hijacked plane as it crossed the Mediterranean but despite military communications that reached all the way to the Pentagon—and to the White House, some later said—the airliner crossed into Syrian air space before the F-15 Air Force pilots were given authorization to take any action. The U.S. fighter jets impotently turned back at the border.

Months later, after the U.S. had refused to meet the abductors' demands, photos were released to the international press showing the slain bodies of Spiro and Nikko Koronis. It was never clear what the Air Force fighter pilots could have done even if authorized, but the American press blasted the Pentagon and the White House for allowing the ambassador and little Nikko to be taken to their deaths with impunity.

Warfield found no record of any negative public statements attributed to Ana, but the *New York Times* reported that she had privately expressed bitterness, even to the extent of threatening to find a way to set things straight with the U.S. Government for standing around with their hands in their pockets while her loved ones were taken to their eventual deaths. Ana had denied the story.

In the aftermath, it was revealed that the ambassador had lived beyond his financial means for years and had nothing but debts to leave Ana after his death.

Morgan looked through the magazine and Internet articles Warfield had printed out and made notes while he talked. It was a sensitive matter given Ana Koronis's high standing in the Washington community but Morgan left the meeting saying he would look into it.

They were out in the parking lot, about to get into their cars to leave when Morgan said, "See much of Stern when you're at the White House? He's the national security advisor now, right?"

"In a meeting now and then. You know Stern, though. Doesn't say a lot."

"Little surprised Cross put him in the sensitive job he's in."

"Never thought much about it. He was cleared after the Ames case," Warfield said.

Morgan looked as if he wanted to say something, but didn't.

"Anything I should know about Stern?"

Morgan opened his car door. "Nah. That case is closed."

Warfield hadn't seen Fleming since the morning before, when *The Washington Post* carried the story about Cross and him, and they hadn't been out to dinner in a week. He parked in the turnaround at Hardscrabble and let himself in through the garage. Fleming was standing in front of her bedroom mirror adjusting the straps on her dress when he walked in. The ivory dress accented her tan and her hair was cut above her shoulders the way he liked it best. Fleming's look was always fresh, a little different, never routine—even when he was with her every day. His concerns about Fullwood and Ana Koronis and Boris Petrevich moved for the moment to an obscure fold in his brain.

She gave him a light kiss. "That's all you get," she said, patting him on the cheek. "I'm all dressed."

Warfield showered and put on a pair of tan slacks and a Tommy Bahama knit shirt. He was ready in ten minutes.

He put the top down on Fleming's convertible when they got to the end of the gravel driveway. The orange ball hovering above the western horizon cast long shadows on the winding rural roads as they drove toward Middleburg. Warfield often contrasted the Virginia countryside with the plains of his West Texas heritage—where there were no stone fences and you could drive for hours and never even see a stream. They called them *runs* here in Virginia and you couldn't go a mile without crossing one. Weathered stone fences still defined what once were thousand-acre estates, but high-paid Washington officials and business types willing and able to pay the asking price for this respite from the Beltway swarmed to Hunt Country with dreams of looking out from their verandas at pastures full of grazing horses. Laser-straight four-board wood fences bordered the new fifteen- or twenty-acre mini-farms.

Some of the newcomers were horse people who knew what they were getting into, but most of them were not. Traditionalists whose families had lived there forever didn't like the newcomers destroying their once-tranquil countryside but no one could deny the positive economic impact on the area. Blacksmiths got hundreds of dollars to shoe horses, and plumbers, electricians and stonemasons had more work than they could keep up with. It took a trainer a year to get a rider and horse ready for the steeplechases and foxhunts, and this brought on new stables and more jobs for trainers. It was a thriving free-market economy.

Loudoun County had taken on most of the growth in the area and the little town of Middleburg was bursting at the seams. Art galleries, boutiques, quaint restaurants and historic inns lined the town's few streets, and on weekends when city-dwellers drove out Highway 50 from Washington to see what it was all about, the merchants couldn't keep the smiles off their faces.

"So what world are you in, Warfield?" Fleming asked after a mile of silence.

"Horses. Land. All the things you natives do around here."

"I'm not exactly considered a blue-blood since I was raised in Charlottesville. I blend in okay, though, don't you think?"

"You sit a saddle the right way."

"Western. I just never got into the hunts."

"All they do is *chase* the fox. They don't even want to catch it. Back home we'd consider that a waste of a bunch of good dogs and horses."

Fleming shook her head and laughed. "No couth, War Man."

Fleming had called ahead and reserved their favorite table at Ticcio's, a small Italian place at the edge of town that got most of its business from locals. Fleming and Warfield went there a couple of times a month for a few laid-back minutes and some pretty good food. Fleming once told Warfield that if she ever left him it would be for Ticcio, the restaurant's owner. His resonant voice and European accent put her in the mood to remove her clothes. Ticcio led them past the bar to a corner table overlooking a courtyard outside the window and took their drink order. A family of ducks played Follow Me in a fountain pool in the garden.

Warfield settled into his drink. Fleming's charm and beauty, the open-air ride through the country and the serenity outside the window had mellowed him. It was rare. Every second of his life was crammed full and he wouldn't change it if he could, but he knew he needed to stop for a breather once in a while. Fleming had not been too far off with the couth bit. He'd grown up in Texas on a dairy farm. In time, he came to the realization his family was poor, but poor was a relative thing and no one he knew then was any different. Besides, his family had had what they needed: Clean clothes, a warm house and plenty to eat. Dairy farming wasn't easy but he never thought much about that either. Milk cows knew no holiday and every day started at four-thirty in the morning. Put feed in the stalls, hook up the milking machines to the cows, save the milk, clean the floor, and do it over and over again until every cow was cycled through. Then he'd prepare the milk for pickup and get ready for school. Repeat the whole thing that evening. Summers meant working in the fields, putting up the hay that would be needed for winter.

Warfield's father Raymond was a hard driver with no patience for extracurricular diversions that took Warfield away from the farm, but young Cam bargained with him so he could play football and baseball: He would take over the entire milking responsibilities all to himself in return for the time he wanted for sports and the library, which meant he had to get up even earlier for the morning milking, and do the afternoon chores after practice or games.

Warfield's love for the military began in the ninth grade. After learning in a World War II history class about the Enigma cipher machine used by the German U-boats to communicate with Berlin, and the allies' successes that came from breaking the code, he was hooked. For the next three years he spent any time not required by the farm or sports at the library. By the end of his senior year he'd read everything there was in the school and county libraries about cryptography and the role of codes and code breaking from the first world war to the present. His interest expanded to war in general. He memorized the conditions for the use of spies written by a Chinese philosopher named Sun Tzu in a book titled The Art of War two centuries earlier. Every life decision Warfield made after that was in pursuit of a career in military intelligence.

Warfield went to the army recruiting center the day he graduated from high school and told the recruitment officer what he wanted to do: Sign up for as long as the army would allow on the condition that he could go to OCS and be assigned to military intelligence. "Forget it, son," the officer said, when he stopped laughing. Only a few qualified for officer candidate school, and the folks in military intelligence do the inviting—not the other way around. "Besides, why would you want to, boy? Those people out there in Fort Huachuca are a little creepy."

Armed with the name Fort Huachuca, Warfield went to the library in Wichita Falls and found out what else he needed to know. He went home and typed up a letter to Major General Thomas K. Feranzo, Chief, Military Intelligence, Fort Huachuca, Arizona, specifying what he wished to do. He also typed and enclosed his own nineteen-page analysis of Sun Tzu's principles of spying, a copy of his high school transcript that showed he graduated with honors, and letters from his principal and his football coach that said he worked hard and was a boy of good character.

Eleven days after he mailed the package off to General Feranzo he received a large tan envelope from Feranzo's office. All the documents he'd sent, including his original letter to the general, were inside. A list of army recruiting stations was enclosed. That was it.

Later that day, Warfield told his father he was leaving home. He had prepared his parents for this day so it was no surprise. He loaded everything he owned into his nine-year-old Ford pickup, and Raymond and Cam talked for a few minutes and hugged each other. As Cam was about to drive off, Raymond pulled a Ka Bar pocket knife out of his jeans and handed it to him. He wanted Cam to have it.

Two days later Cam pulled up to the gate at Fort Huachuca. When the MP at the gate required documentation before he could enter the base, an apprehensive Cameron Warfield fumbled through his papers and found the envelope that had General Feranzo's name and return address on it.

"It's all in here," he told the military police officer and flashed the envelope in front of him. Bluffing wasn't much different than faking, and he had learned how to fake in football. Sun Tzu would approve of it too. The MP glanced at the return address and instead of examining the contents as he should have, nodded and gave Warfield directions to the military intelligence command center. Warfield finally breathed again as he drove away from the guard station.

The MI headquarters building was a one-story cream-colored building that was built out of wood—a long time ago, Warfield decided. "Here to see General Feranzo," he said when he got inside.

The corporal sitting at the wood desk looked up at him. Warfield thought he seemed not more than two or three years older than he. "You want to see the general?"

"Yes sir."

"You in the army?"

"No sir."

"Didn't think so. You don't say *sir* to a corporal, buddy."

Warfield knew that. "Can I see him now?"

The corporal suppressed a smile. "No way. *You can't just walk in and see a general!* Gotta go through people and you need an appointment to do that around here. Where you from anyway?"

"Rawlings, Texas."

"What do you want to see Feranzo about?"

"Nothing that concerns you. How do I get to see him?"

The corporal looked Warfield over, chewed on his lip for a moment, glanced around the room and got up from behind the desk. "Come with me."

He led Warfield out the door he had entered and they stood on the porch. The corporal pulled out a pack of Camels, tapped the top against his finger until a tight-wrapped cylinder popped out, and offered it to Warfield.

Warfield shook his head.

The corporal lit up, took a deep drag and exhaled parallel streams of smoke through his nostrils as he studied the Texan. "Look, I don't know why but I like you. You got some balls walking in there like that. But you don't know what the hell you're doing! Either that or you're stupid. Now tell me what it is you want. Maybe I can help you out."

Warfield looked at the name plate on the soldier's uniform. Macclenny, it said. "So, Corporal Macclenny?"

"That's right. Actually you can just call me Macc. I'm pretty much a peon around here."

"Didn't mean to be rude, but I'm gonna see that general." He told Macc of his two contacts that got him nowhere and showed him the package that had been returned to him. "I want to make a deal with the army and it looks like only some big shot can do it."

Macclenny laughed. "You *are* determined," he said. "Tell you what. I sort the Old Man's mail when it comes in. Some of it goes in the trash and the rest goes to the other brass on the general's staff in there. They decide what he sees, and I can tell you it *ain't* much. The major back there, he's the one who collects the winning pieces and puts 'em in a neat little stack on General Feranzo's desk every morning."

Warfield's hopes stirred. "So what can you do?"

"Okay, you give me what it is you want Feranzo to see. I'm in and out of his office all the time. Phone messages and stuff. I'll put yours on top of his stack."

Warfield cracked a smile. This was good. "What do I owe you for this?"

"Nothing. But the way I figure it you're gonna be a general someday yourself. Remember me then."

The rest was history. Officer candidate school graduation at the top of the class, a degree in international studies from the University of Arizona compliments of the army, graduation from the military's famous National War College, years of intelligence training and hundreds of undercover operations. These were now part of Warfield's military innards. As was Macc Macclenny.

Warfield looked at Fleming. Smiling now, she said, "Wherever you were the last couple of minutes, you were having a good time. Better not be because of the redhead dancing out there."

He chuckled. "The redhead would've been more exciting."

The one-man band across the room included a keyboard, accordion and synthesizer. The voice behind it was doing his best to sound like Dean Martin and had filled the small dance floor. Fleming pulled Warfield onto the dance floor.

"Good as the It'll Do, War Man?"

Fleming often teased him about his life before her. He'd given her piecemeal glimpses of those days and when she brought them up he accused her of using his own bullets against him. Now and then he still went to the It'll Do with Macc for a beer and they'd laugh about the women they'd known and dragons they'd slain, but that lifestyle was behind him now.

Being with Fleming like this made him think about the important things he always put aside. Like kids, for one. Not that he was too old for them, but he hadn't even decided to marry yet. And was marriage *for* him? Never would he find a better lover and more loyal companion than Fleming, and maybe she came along at a time when he needed something to latch onto besides chasing spies and barflies. But get married? He'd always packed light. A wife and kid or two would slow him down. Kids ought to be raised on a farm or in a small town with a drug store and soda fountain where you could still get a strawberry shake after football practice and talk to your high school sweetheart and go home to a mom who always had dinner for you and a dad who couldn't wait for your game Friday night and was not preoccupied with catching some terrorist who might be planning to blow up the world. There were men like that. They should be the fathers.

Cameron Warfield had followed his passions. He cared about Fleming, maybe loved her even, if he understood what loving a woman meant, and he hoped she felt okay about him pretty much as-is, because he couldn't change course right now. Maybe someday, but he couldn't expect her to wait around for that.

Dean Martin shifted into Everybody Loves Somebody, and Fleming DeGrande snuggled her head under Warfield's chin. "You're pensive tonight, Warfield."

After dinner they meandered out to the car and drifted back to Hardscrabble Ranch. The road was deserted and the CD played loud enough to overcome the sounds of the road. It was still warm out and Fleming stood up in the seat of the convertible and folded her arms on top of the windshield. Her hair was blowing straight back when Warfield looked up at her, and she had removed the straps from her dress and let it fall away, exposing her breasts to the moonlight and balmy evening air. He thought how beautiful she was, how much confidence she had in herself. Twenty minutes later he pulled the Beamer into the garage at Hardscrabble and hit the button that rolled the door down. Fleming smiled. He'd be staying over.

Next morning, Warfield woke up before the alarm and mapped out his day as he went through his morning routine in Fleming's weight room. After a shower he said goodbye to her and grabbed a yesterday's bagel on the way to his car. The sun peeking above the horizon glistened in the dew that covered the Lone Elm Mercedes. At the instant he put the key into the ignition switch, he noticed that the grass next to the driveway was matted down by recent foot traffic. In the millisecond it took his brain to register that he should not turn the ignition key, it was too late.

The windows in Fleming's bathroom crashed in from the shock wave. She looked out at the smoke and dust and ran down the stairs with her half-on robe flying behind her. She figured the explosives were taped to the frame beneath the driver's seat, because the Mercedes came to rest on its right side. Warfield dangled from the seat belt harness, his lower body and legs hanging down to the right-side door, which now lay against the ground.

Fleming desperately looked for some sign of life. She cupped her hands around her face as she looked through the crazed windshield and saw blood trickling from Warfield's nose, mouth and ears. She scrambled up to the driver side of the car and tried the doors without success. Even if they weren't locked or wracked by the explosion, the weight of their steel armor plate made opening them impossible. She banged and screamed but Warfield didn't respond. Two drivers who heard the blast had driven halfway from the main road to the house. One changed his mind and left and Fleming shouted at the other to call 911.

Fleming felt the helplessness she'd experienced a few times with a patient whose condition was beyond help, but this time it was personal. This was the man she loved. A small crowd of curious and concerned gathered as Fleming sat on top of the car like a guardian angel. Debris covered the driveway. The pungent smell of explosives lingered in the air. The armor plating had protected the fuel tank and at least there was no fire. Some tried frantically to get inside the Mercedes but failed. Finally, emergency crews and a life flight helicopter arrived, and Macc got there at about the same time. Warfield was alive but unconscious when the life flight crew hooked him up to support systems and lifted away.

CHAPTER 10

CROSS INVITED QUINN AND Fullwood to the Oval Office on the morning the Ana Koronis trial started. He didn't want to be blindsided by any embarrassing testimony, and wanted a fresh read on his friend Austin Quinn who as the head of the CIA had been under pressure since the Koronis story broke. It was bad enough that a federal grand jury indicted Ana on charges of spying at the same time she was sleeping with Quinn but ever since the day Otto Stern told Cross she was a suspect, Cross knew the mess would infect not only himself personally, but the CIA and even Cross's presidency. Over the months, cable news programs made household names of Austin Quinn and Ana Koronis and never missed an opportunity to remind that her parents were Iranian. In the process, it evolved from gossip to speculation to sacred truth that Ana despised the United States for killing her husband and son.

The contrast that morning between Quinn and Fullwood was striking. Fullwood's straining shirt collar cut into his neck and the cigars had left a permanent mark on his teeth. By contrast Austin Quinn could have stepped out of a TV ad for men's clothing. Cross wondered if Quinn still ordered eight new suits every year. His shirts and ties alone cost more than most men spent on entire wardrobes. There were new wrinkles in his face but the strain hadn't changed his style.

"Anything I need to know about the trial?" Cross asked. Neither man had much to offer that Cross didn't already know, and, as Cross expected, Quinn was subdued. His ex-lover was on trial, along with his credibility. Cross needed assurance the testimony wouldn't contain any surprises. Enough damage had been done. Each man said it wouldn't.

Through the U.S. attorney Joe Morgan, Warfield had kept up with the pretrial proceedings during his recovery from the explosion. The Justice Department spent most of a year collecting and analyzing information about Ana Koronis before deciding to go with it. They wanted to proceed because she was a high-profile Washington insider, a potential feather in the Justice's cap if she were convicted, but that sword had two edges: There would be a lot of negative press if they blew this one.

The paneled courtroom in the E. Barrett Prettyman Courthouse in Washington, the same from which a federal grand jury investigated former president Bill Clinton in his Monica Lewinsky scandal, was packed. Ana had no living relatives in the United States and her law firm associates and socialite friends kept their distance like cats from water. The only person in the courtroom who might have been in Ana's corner was a woman who showed up for the trial daily and seemed to nod approval when testimony favored Ana. Warfield found out through Morgan that she was a State Department employee named Tot Templeton. She worked with Ana's law firm before Ana married Spiro Koronis. Ana's only other friends there, and in all of the country it seemed, were her attorneys, led by Manny Upson. But these were *paid* friends.

Warfield knew Ana had two strikes against her before the trial started. Americans hadn't forgotten the four-hundred-forty-four-day Iranian hostage crisis that began in 1979, and the anti-American demonstrations and rhetoric had rekindled if anything in recent years; Iran continued to be an international pariah to this day. Ana Koronis was a living, breathing, present target for Americans' anger toward and mistrust of her native country even though her parents had moved from Iran to the U.S. a few months before she was even born. The second strike: She was the sister of the notorious terrorist, Seth, who was hated by the peoples of the earth who respected human life. Judge Millard Leaf and the defense team weeded out prospective jurors who couldn't hide their prejudice, but an impartial jury of her peers in all probability didn't exist.

There was no TV in the courtroom but the media hype soared once the trial started: Countless daily updates on all the cable and broadcast networks; endless Ana-bashing on radio and TV talk shows; cover stories in all the national magazines; front page newspaper articles; even editorials. All anti-Ana. Terrorism incarnate on trial, right there in Washington. Conviction of Ana Koronis, it seemed, would mean everything despised in America would be locked away with her in some remote prison cell. A ceremony to mark the end of terrorism and the beginning of world peace and universal love. Just like that. Period.

There was discussion among the prosecutors before the trial about calling Warfield to testify. Joe Morgan had told him they wouldn't get a conviction—wouldn't even go to trial—without Warfield testifying that Petrevich smuggled the uranium into Iraq, thus establishing the thread from Ana, whom they charged found the names of Russian security risks in Quinn's computer; to her brother Seth, the terrorist; and, as the prosecutors hoped to convince the jury, on to the Russian Petrevich. Warfield's testimony about the Habur crossing incident would go a long way. Neither Warfield nor the president wanted Warfield's involvement aired, and he told Morgan he would claim amnesia if put on the stand. The government caved on its demand that he testify.

The explosion of Warfield's car a year earlier resulted in two burst cardrums, a brain concussion, damage to internal organs, and ceaseless ringing in his ears the doctors said might never go away. He was mostly recovered after months of rehabilitation but probably could have gotten away with claiming amnesia to Morgan.

The prosecution's first witness was Austin Quinn. He spent an hour describing how he and Ana met, what their relationship was like and the absolute trust he'd had in her. Then federal prosecutor L.A. Harriman warmed up.

"Director Quinn, if you weren't a responsible man," L.A. said, "you wouldn't be in the high-level position you're in. Now it puzzles me that a man like yourself, entrusted with so much responsibility for the security of this country, would be caught off guard. Anything like that ever happen before at the CIA? I mean any security breaches on your part?"

Quinn smiled faintly. "No it did not."

"When you were in the United States Senate? State politics?"

"Certainly not."

"Would you say it's your nature to be pretty careful with sensitive information?"

"I would say *very* careful, yes."

"So while you are careful with sensitive matters, it's still possible Ana Koronis used the CIA computer terminal in your home. Is that right?"

Regret showed on Quinn's face. "Well, I can't say absolutely that it's *not* possible."

"Even though Ms. Koronis had a laptop computer of her own that she used when she was in your home. Right?"

"That's right."

"But aren't there codes and passwords required to get into the CIA files?"

"Of course."

"Then how could she have accessed any CIA files?"

Quinn paused for a moment. "The passwords, I—"

"You wrote them down on a piece of paper there by the Langley computer terminal you have at home, because you knew you wouldn't remember those passwords. Is that right, Director Quinn?"

Quinn nodded. "Yes."

"Now would you say the reason for your carelessness boils down to your trust in Ana Koronis?"

Quinn wasn't on trial in the matter—at least not yet, though he could be—but if the prosecutor was trying to give him cover for all the criticism he'd received, he couldn't have done a better job. If Quinn had made a mistake, at least it was one that every American citizen and every newspaper reporter could identify with: Who among them hadn't misplaced their trust in someone along the way? Or been careless with a password?

"Yes, I suppose it does," Quinn said.

"Well, then, Director Quinn, would you say the defendant, Ms. Koronis, went out of her way, perhaps used her ample charm, to build your trust in her so she could steal CIA secrets and give them to her brother, the known terrorist Seth?"

The defense attorney jumped to his feet. "Speculation!" Judge Leaf sustained his objection, had the question stricken from the record and instructed the jury to disregard it, for whatever value that had.

L.A. continued. "Director Quinn, given your testimony that Ms. Koronis was an experienced computer user and that she had access to the CIA terminal in your home and all the passwords she needed, would it have been possible for her to access CIA records and databases?"

Quinn could not say that was not possible.

So, Harriman went on, once inside the CIA computer system, wasn't it possible Ms. Koronis could determine the names of the Russian nuclear scientists the CIA considered security risks? Names a terrorist could use in search of nuclear material? The defense objected again, but not before the jury heard Quinn acknowledge it was possible.

Then it was time for Harriman's brief but by far most damaging witness against Ana. Helen Swope was Quinn's housekeeper during the time Ana lived there. She testified she'd seen Ana sitting at Quinn's computer making notes. "Just once, Mrs. Swope?" "No sir. Lotsa times."

On the day of closing arguments, Cam Warfield took his usual seat on the first row behind the prosecutors' table, which overflowed with charts, files and briefcases. Ana Koronis, several feet away, huddled with her lawyers.

Earl Fullwood arrived in the same rumpled suit and bleach-starved shirt he seemed to always wear, cigar-in-hand, to hear the final arguments and sat in the same row as Warfield, but separated by two other men. Warfield thought of that Oval Office meeting when Fullwood accused him of interference at the Iraqi border and denied the Russian was carrying uranium. The irony was that in testimony for Ana's trial, the FBI reversed itself and backed the government's contention that the Russian was carrying uranium at Habur when he crossed into Iraq. Warfield wondered whether the Bureau had actually come around to that belief or adopted that position to bolster the government's case against Koronis. Either way, it made Fullwood look like a fool to anyone who'd been in the Oval Office that day.

L.A. Harriman stood before the jury box. It was now or never. Public sentiment was on his side but, taking nothing for granted, he rehashed all the evidence presented against Ana during her trial. He talked about the terrorist abduction of Spiro Koronis and the defendant's two-year-old son, Nikko, at Athens International Airport, where Spiro and Nicholas waited to board a flight to Washington. Spiro and Nikko were in the restroom when six men with assault guns came out of nowhere. Their plan was to take Spiro and his son to Syria and hold them until their political demands were met. They jerked Nikko out of Spiro's grasp, pushed Spiro in front of them, and rushed through the gate and onto the plane as Ana and the other screaming passengers watched the horror helplessly from the gate area. Soon after the plane was airborne, two U.S. Air Force F-15's flown by Lt. Colonel Jerry Schmidt and another pilot overtook it and flew alongside, but the airliner flew into Syrian air space without interference from the American planes. Ana put her head down on the table as L.A. laid out the scene. The

United States refused to negotiate with the abductors, and a few months later photos appeared showing the beheaded remains of Spiro Koronis and son Nikko.

Harriman conceded Ana Koronis was a loving mother and wife grieving over the tragic loss of her family. *Who wouldn't?* Her husband and child were mercilessly slaughtered after their country failed to save them. L.A. described again Ana's stay with her brother in Iran after the incident. He was all the poor woman had left.

"Yes, Ana Koronis's reactions seem normal and innocent to us at first, ladies and gentlemen, but then…," L.A. said, holding up a cautionary finger as his voice rose, "…then, then, we find out her brother is one of the most notorious, malicious, hate-mongering terrorists in the world!" Seth and his reputation were already well-known objects of hatred in the United States, but L.A. pounded home his role in terrorism anyway and pointed out that he worked for hire to the highest bidder, his guiding principle being that any operation that could bring harm to the United States was worth any cost.

L.A. placed his hands on the polished wood rail in front of the jury box and leaned in to the front row, spoke in a low, raspy voice and let his disgust be seen. He said he wanted the jurors to understand that Ana Koronis did not storm out of her brother's place the moment she learned about his mission as the defense claimed, but instead bought into her brother's propaganda that her husband and son were victims of America's policies. That men like those who hijacked the plane in Athens that day were fighting for peace. *Because America was evil!*

Warfield was watching juror sixty-seven, a special forces veteran of Afghanistan, who was showing signs of stress. L.A. Harriman must have noticed, as well. Looking straight at him, Harriman rammed his fist high into the air as his voice regained volume. *"Terrorists? Fighting for peace?"* he wailed, and shook his head, simply too angry to say more. L.A. pulled a handkerchief out of his pocket and wiped his forehead of perspiration. "Not my kind of peace. Not yours either, ladies and gentlemen. *But the defendant's terrorist brother convinced her he was fighting for peace in their homeland."*

Sixty-seven's veins bulged. Tears stained the cheeks of some of the women jurors. L.A. went on. He told the jury Seth indoctrinated his sister with his rhetoric for months and then told her to return to Washington, to keep her eyes and ears open, to position herself well, and one day he'd call on her. It wouldn't destroy her career or ruin her friendships because no one would ever know what she had done. All he would ask from her was a little information. No big deal. After all, it was for their parents' homeland, for their people, for Allah, for justice. For peace. So Ana Koronis did as she was told, and one day gave Seth better news than he could have dreamed of. She had worked her way into the bedroom—and computer terminal—of the top man at America's central intelligence agency. The computer was linked to CIA headquarters. How could she help?

How she could help was to find the names of the Russian scientists the CIA considered security risks. They had the knowledge and the materials Seth needed. "And the result of that, ladies and gentlemen? The result was that one of these Russian scientists smuggled uranium into the Middle East. God only knows what will become of it."

L.A. conceded that perhaps Ana was in a vulnerable state of mind that allowed her brother to brainwash her. "She is human, after all. But, for heaven's sake, by the time she gave those CIA secrets to Seth, she'd had plenty of time to think it over, to return to her senses. So why didn't she stand up to her brother and tell him she wouldn't think of doing anything that would harm the United States? *This* was *her* homeland, and one single act by her government, flawed or not, could not destroy her loyalty. Why didn't she say those words?"

L.A. walked around for a moment, allowing the jury to again see what a state this whole thing had brought him to. When he returned to face them he spoke in hushed tones. "She could've told her brother she wanted no part of his cowardly ways. That's what you would have done, my friends, and that's what I would have done." L.A. walked over to the defense table and stood in front of Ana. "But that is not what Ana Koronis did," he said, wagging a finger at her. "She did just what her brother asked. She betrayed the United States! She betrayed you and me, my fellow countrymen. She sold us out to terrorists."

L.A. reminded the jurors Ana Koronis was a Washington insider and lawyer who knew her way around government. She found it easy to develop high-profile social connections where she would be visible to Mr. Quinn, a ripe divorcee who would be attracted by her charm, beauty and social position. She was well-suited for a man of his stature. And Director Quinn's failure? He fell in love with her, put his trust in her.

L.A. acknowledged there was no direct, iron-clad proof the Petrevich operation resulted from Ana Koronis's treason, but showed that the timing was right. The circumstances were ideal. The principal characters were in place. Was Ana Koronis guilty? Could it be mere coincidence that the terrorist behind it all had a sister who had access to the innermost records of the CIA? A sister who was bitter against the United States for killing her son and her husband? A sister named Ana Koronis?

Harriman thanked the jurors for their attention and returned to the prosecution table.

Warfield looked over at Ana. Except when Harriman described the hostage scene, she had shown no emotion throughout the trial. Now she locked her black eyes on the jurors, one by one. Warfield thought she did herself no favor. She looked menacing enough to convince any fence-sitters on the jury that society needed to be protected from Ana Koronis.

Warfield had been certain it was Harvey Joplan who'd provided the terrorists with the names of the questionable Russian nuclear scientists. Now he wasn't so sure.

In the course of the thirty-three years United States Senator Ferguson Luke Abercrombie had been in the Senate, his office became an antiques showplace, thanks to Bernice Abercrombie's insatiable habit of shopping for antiques with the taxpayers' money. Bernice made regular stops at antique shops in northern Virginia and Maryland, and Ferguson Luke and Bernice sashayed across Europe or Asia or Africa every year to pick up a few more prime specimens. When Abercrombie's office could hold no more of the government's select purchases, Bernice began to keep the overflow in their Washington condominium or at home back in Taylorville.

Angie, the Senator's primary assistant, stuck her head inside his office as he was hanging up the phone. "FBI director's here, Ferguson Luke."

"So, anything seem unusual? He appear to be upset?"

"The director? Well, he never sat down the whole ten minutes he was waiting, going from one of your art pieces to another. Picked up a few things and scrutinized them. Took some pictures."

"Pictures!"

"With his cell phone. Is he a little creepy, or is that just the FBI in him?"

"Creepy, honey."

"Security video was on all the time. He didn't seem to notice it."

"Show him in."

Abercrombie took in Angie's tanned legs as she walked away. He knew his colleagues suspected Angie was more to him than an assistant and he enjoyed the oblique remarks they made after walking behind her down to his office. He would smile at them. When Bernice would complain about the way Angie dressed he explained that he didn't much like it either but couldn't afford to lose her—depended on her too much. If his wife thought there was more to it than that, she let it go, but then they had little time for conversation anyway, he with his committees and other official obligations and Bernice with her bridge and antiquing.

Earl Fullwood jumped as if he'd been caught stealing and almost dropped the ebony chimp he was holding when Angie greeted him with a touch on the sleeve. "The senator asked me to apologize to you in advance for not having as much time as he would like. Has to be on the Senate floor for a vote in a few minutes. If you'd like to follow me, Director Fullwood."

"It's aw'right, little lady. That'll be fine."

Abercrombie saw and heard it all via the ubiquitous security cameras piped into his computer monitor. The irony of snooping on the FBI chief amused him. He turned it off as Angie and Fullwood entered. Fullwood scanned the furnishings and accessories. Abercrombie knew he was envious. No FBI office was like this. Certainly not Fullwood's.

"Welcome, Earl, glad you came by! Coffee, Coke? Little cocktail, maybe? Angie can get whatever you'd like."

Fullwood was looking out the window at the Capitol, right across the street. "Nothing, thanks."

"How're things in the crime business?"

Fullwood didn't seem to know how to make small talk. "You...you've seen the numbers, crime is down."

"Earl, Earl, Bureau's doing a superb job!" Abercrombie said, waving the question away. "No doubt about that." Abercrombie leaned back in his leather executive chair and propped his feet on the corner of his desk. "This a business call, or social, Earl?"

Abercrombie almost laughed at his own question. Fullwood had never made a social call in his life. He was there looking for a pay-back of some kind. No doubt about that. Abercrombie had called on Fullwood to assist in a committee hearing a year ago. The senator himself was not a member of that committee but the future of one of his big contributors, a statewide banking company, rode on the outcome of the hearing. He suggested to the committee chairman, a crony of his, that he take testimony from the FBI in the matter. A large national banking firm was attempting to break into Abercrombie's state and Abercrombie needed the Bureau to present the banking firm in a bad light in order to keep them out.

"That Cloudland Banking outfit will run our established banks out of business if we let 'em in," Abercrombie had told Fullwood. "I'm sure there's something in all those files you got over there at the J. Edgar Hoover Building you can use to discredit Cloudland."

When Fullwood's assigned agents came up with nothing, Abercrombie called Fullwood and made it clear he expected better cooperation. "Appropriations is looking into ways to reduce budgets, Earl. As it stands now, I'll have to do battle to preserve even the Bureau's current funding level. Don't want you to have to cut back," he'd said.

A month later at the committee hearing, a young FBI Agent testified his investigation determined Cloudland Banking had on at least one previous occasion used "unethical and marginal legal practices" to overrun smaller banks in its path. The committee chairman then said a full investigation would be required before the committee could go further. Next day, Cloudland's attorneys read the tea leaves and withdrew their application to move into Abercrombie's state. That had been the end of it.

Fullwood pulled the worn-out cigar out of his mouth. Abercrombie's Persian rug caught his eye as he composed his opener. "It's about that counterterrorism camp at Lone Elm, Fuggason. It's a army operation and—"

Abercrombie guessed where Fullwood was going. "Yeah. I'm familiar with Lone Elm. Cam Warfield runs Lone Elm more or less as a service to the army. Heard good things about it, too. Always liked Warfield." He knew that was the last thing Fullwood wanted to hear.

"Well, Fuggason, maybe you're not familiar with some of the recent activities of Cameron Warfield. The Pres'dent brought Warfield in like

150

some kind of private detective to work for him out of the White House and Warfield ended up interferin' with one of the Bureau's operations, pretty near blew it. Had to do with a Russian tryin' to cross into I-raq. Think it was a real embarrassment to the Pres'dent."

"Yeah, something about that came out in that Koronis trial couple weeks ago. In the papers, too. I didn't connect Warfield with that operation."

"Then you already know about it. The kunnel left the White House after that border screw-up, but who the hell knows what he's doin' out there at that army-subsidized Lone Elm of his. My guess is that he's doin' the same thing the CIA and the Bureau do at our trainin' centers. Pure and simple duplication. Waste of the taxpayers' money, Fuggason! The place is nothin' but a retirement program for that would-be-hero Warfield, and he needs to be put outta binness before he does some real harm to our country here." Fullwood punctuated his rhetoric by banging his fist on the lamp table next to his chair.

Abercrombie thought for a minute. How bad did the director want Warfield out? He looked at Fullwood over the top of his glasses. "Well, Earl, I see what you mean, but there might be a small problem. It'll be impossible for my committee or the whole Senate to take any direct action about Warfield since he's more or less a contractor to the army. Pentagon would accuse us of micro-managing one of the military services, you see. The army has a history of a certain amount of autonomy. You know that, Earl. Besides, a lot of people in the Senate are right fond of Warfield."

Fullwood slumped in his chair.

Senator Ferguson Luke Abercrombie hadn't been in Washington for thirty-three years without learning a few bargaining skills. After Fullwood had a minute to dwell on his failed mission, the senator stoked the embers again, shaking his head this time. "I just don't see how I could pull it off, Earl. I'd have to call in a few favors from some other senators to even have a chance, and that's a mighty big price to pay. Been saving up those favors they owe me—you know how that goes. Pretty soon one of my big contributors will need a highway to his farm or a new airport close to his factory and the only way I'll get it through Congress is by calling those favors due. Now if I use them all up to help you out with Warfield, you see where that leaves me."

Fullwood, still staring at his shoes, nodded slightly that he understood.

After a minute of dead silence, Abercrombie appeared to have a new idea. "You know, Earl, I just thought of one possibility, but it's slim. There's this office building back home that, well, it belongs to one of my good constituents."

Fullwood perked up.

"Don't want to bore you with details. Let's say my constituent relied on the income from the office building after his business got into some trouble. Now his tenant has moved out of the building and he's looking at bankruptcy. I been wondering what I can do to help him out. His poor mother's about to die and he has to stay home with her so much it's affecting his ability to make a living. Now if the Bureau could use that space for a field office…"

Fullwood nodded. "Well, yeah, I see where you're going, but one problem I see, Fuggason, is the GSA. You know how they look at everything."

"Don't worry about the General Services Administration. Fellow I know over there owes me a favor or two. Get your people to write up a requisition for office space in Taylorville and send it to me. Fifty-thousand square feet. Forty bucks a square foot a year."

Fullwood looked worried. "Sounds a little risky, Fugga—"

"Treasury spills more than that on the way to the bank! Get me that requisition. Meantime, I'll go to work on your problem."

As soon as Fullwood left, Senator Abercrombie dialed his sister who handled his personal business back home in Taylorville. "Barb, it's me."

"What is it Ferguson Luke? I'm busy!"

"The Oak Street building? Got a tenant for it."

"No jokes today, Ferguson Luke. I can't laugh. You don't have enough to pay your mortgages again this month."

"No, Barb. This is real."

"Listen, Ferguson Luke, I've about had it with your problems. By the time you get a lease written and rent coming in, the banks will own those dilapidated buildings of yours. There's going to be foreclosures! They don't give a damn anymore that you're a senator. That held them off for awhile, but now it wouldn't matter if you were Abe Lincoln. They want their money."

The state had been in a recession for three years. Many businesses in Taylorville had layoffs and scaled down or closed their offices and plants, leaving a glut of vacant space and jobless workers. Senator Abercrombie, who had bought the four-story office building and various other real estate over the years, no longer had rent income from his properties to pay the taxes and mortgages and was sinking deeper in financial quicksand by the day. If it went on much longer, he'd have to sell his home in Taylorville and everyone in the state would hear he was broke. Then he would lose his Senate seat. His opponent in the next election would say to the voters that if Abercrombie couldn't manage his own affairs, how could they trust him with the nation's business?

"Listen, Barb. It's as good as rented. All 50,000 feet."

"I'll believe it when I see the first rent check. How much?"

"Forty a foot. To the FBI."

Barbara was silent for a moment. "You're not serious. Best rent I've heard in this burg was ten a foot! The old Madison Building."

"Yep. Two million bucks a year!"

There was silence again before Barbara chuckled, then laughed hard. That triggered the senator and he began laughing too, and for most of a minute both of them laughed and giggled without ever saying a word, pouring out the tension built up in each of them for so long.

"Congratulations," Barbara said, regaining her composure. "God knows you need it, Ferg, and so do I. Too much pressure for me."

They chatted for another minute before Abercrombie excused himself. "Gotta go, Barb. Little committee business I gotta take care of."

CHAPTER 11

ANA KORONIS WAS FOUND guilty. If she were, what about Harvey Joplan? Warfield knew that was a question to which he might never know the answer even though the government made a compelling case against Ana Koronis. Nevertheless, the mole hunt that President Cross had assigned to him was over, at least for now, but undisputed was the fact that Boris Petrevich had moved nuclear material into Iraq at the Habur border crossing, and undiminished was Warfield's determination to find him and the nuclear material before—he hoped—it was put to use. It wasn't enough to identify and bring to justice any American involved: The unlimited potentially disastrous consequences of nuclear material in the hands of the wrong people remained. President Cross yielded to Warfield's request to be allowed to execute the case to the end without interference from Fullwood but cautioned him about covering his tracks. There was only so much Cross could do to help if he went too far over the line.

Early the following Friday morning, the receptionist at Lone Elm told Warfield General Hendricks was there to see him. Bob Hendricks was the Pentagon advisor to Warfield regarding Lone Elm matters. They came up through the ranks together and both had come up for promotion to general at the same time. Warfield retired instead to take over Lone Elm and Hendricks was now a two-star and worked for the chairman of the Joint Chiefs of Staff at the Pentagon. It was a position that provided a lot of visibility of goings-on.

"Come on in Hendricks," Warfield hollered to the outer room. "Must be raining on the golf course today."

"Trying to be more like you—work all the time."

"What's up, Bobby?" They talked about nothing for a few minutes but Warfield could tell Hendricks had something on his mind.

Hendricks took a deep breath. "Senate Armed Services Committee, they're gonna hold hearings about Lone Elm, Cam."

"Lone Elm? You mean for Lone Elm only?" Lone Elm wasn't up for funding this year, and even if it was, there wouldn't be a separate hearing about it—unless there was a problem.

"That Senator Abercrombie's going to say it's about something else, but it'll be about Lone Elm. I wanted you to know."

Warfield looked into his friend's eyes for the rest of the story. "Doesn't sound good, Bobby."

"It's not."

Warfield shook his head. "You sure about this? Abercrombie's always been an ally. Last I heard, he praised Lone Elm from the Senate floor. Always fought to fund us, even in times when military budgets were going south."

Hendricks nodded. "There's something behind it, Cam, but I don't know yet what it is. May not know until the hearings start. But you'll know then as well as I do."

A month later, Senator Ferguson Luke Abercrombie opened hearings to investigate the Iraqi border incident at Habur. Was this what Hendricks was referring to? Warfield looked for reasons to be optimistic. If the committee got into it, maybe they'd find the truth, which wouldn't hurt Warfield, but then he wondered why he wasn't notified he'd be called to testify.

Warfield got the picture when Senator Abercrombie called the first witness. *Earl Fullwood!* Through questioning, Abercrombie led the director to a point where he would almost seem negligent if he failed to discuss Warfield. In a two-day tirade broadcast live on C-Span and played later by the TV networks, Fullwood left no facet of Cameron Warfield unscathed, and ended by alleging Warfield interfered in an FBI operation. After other witnesses, hand-picked by Fullwood and Abercrombie, left Warfield looking even worse, the senator did a made-for-TV display of disappointment in the retired colonel, "who in the past has done some pretty good work." In the end, the committee recommended the army close Lone Elm as soon as practical.

General Hendricks called Warfield when it ended. The army would have gone to bat for him but Abercrombie made it clear that it would be wise for them to follow the committee's recommendation without any fuss. "Army's hands are tied, Cam. You know how it works."

Warfield did know. The army depended on Congress not only for its *needs* but for its *wants* as well. "Lone Elm is history," he said. "Politics never loses out to practicality."

The two were silent as it soaked in. After a moment, Hendricks said, "Any idea why Abercrombie turned against you?"

"Fullwood got to him somehow." He told Hendricks about Fullwood's assaults in the White House meetings and the story of the border crossing. "No surprise about Fullwood, but Senator Abercrombie, I never would've thought it of him."

Lone Elm was in the middle of a training rotation when the announcement came, so it was almost two months before it closed and then another few weeks before everything was cleared out. Warfield, Fleming and Macc spent the following week in their favorite restaurants and hangouts before Macc packed up and went back to Arizona to look into running a boat on the Colorado. On the last night, they vowed to see each other soon. After all Warfield and Macc had been through together, *goodbye* wasn't an option.

The next day Warfield made a final check of the vacated buildings at Lone Elm and loaded up the last boxes containing his files and mementos. The army worked out a deal with the FBI, which was taking Lone Elm over for its own use and would begin occupying it tomorrow. He went into the locker room for what would be his last shower there. As the hot water poured over him, thoughts of getting back into the game began to take over. The Russian. The uranium. The car bomber. All were there to be found but time was the enemy. Eighteen months had passed since Habur, and over time clues disappeared like morning dew. As the shower stall filled with steam Warfield renewed his commitment. With Lone Elm closed, he could devote himself to it.

He made a final trip around the cluster of Lone Elm buildings, drove down the six-thousand foot runway and made a swing around the perimeter of the thousand-acre facility. He'd been there since the day the army purchased the land. When he got back to the main entrance off the highway he stopped, got out and stood with his arms folded on top of the car. As he surveyed the vast complex that had defined his existence in recent years, he thought of the many other lives that had been affected as well.

His drive to his condo took him past the It'll Do Lounge a short distance from the stone pillars that marked the entrance to Lone Elm. He looked over at the familiar hangout and began to dwell on the times he'd had there. The many friends he'd drunk with, the trainees, the brass…the women. He wondered aimlessly how many hours he'd lingered there, how many thousands of dollars he'd burned, how many trips across the dance floor there'd been. How many late nights he was unaccounted for.

Two miles later he wheeled around and drove back to the road house, almost hesitantly walked in, and picked a place at the bar where he'd sat so many times with Macc and some of the Lone Elm crew. Always a few willing beauties around, back then. They'd learned the It'll Do was a place where booze and money and loud music and good times were plentiful. Where were all those people now, he wondered. Even if someone from the past recognized him, they'd probably steer clear of him if they'd seen any of the Fullwood/Abercrombie circus on television. He was a marked man.

Everything there was the same. No new carpet or furniture, same old rubbed-smooth dance floor, even the dusty ceiling fan over the bar still squeaked. After a couple of beers and a trip to the men's room, he sat thoughtfully at the bar as he fingered the hair on his temples. He'd glanced at himself in the mirror in the low light of the restroom and decided his hairline had pushed back a notch. "Another Sam, then I gotta go," he told the attractive young girl tending bar. He swiveled around on the barstool and looked over at the dance floor he'd shined a few times and wondered if a floor like that ever wore through. There were three couples dancing to George Jones, holding tight, eyes closed, as if they'd never see each other again.

Three beers later he was back on the road. He opened all the windows in his car, hoping the wind noise would cover up the ringing in his ears. It was louder than usual.

Next morning Warfield was awake at five a.m. as always but remembered there was no Lone Elm or White House office to go to and went back to sleep. Most nights he would have stayed at Fleming's but having the last load of his things from Lone Elm in his car last night he had decided to go to his condo after leaving the It'll Do.

Later that morning the phone awoke him. "Lo," he said clearing the night out of his throat.

"You still asleep?" Fleming sounded surprised.

"Time 'sit?"

"Ten. I'm between clients. Thought I'd better check on you. You okay?"

"Ummh," he said, his eyes still closed. "Sorry…last night…"

"Don't sound like yourself, War Man."

"I'm okay, Fleming."

"Call me when you're awake."

It was another half-hour before he pulled himself out of bed. He ate half the corn flakes he poured and went to his SUV in a pair of cutoff jeans to bring in some of the boxes. The spare bedroom was already full and he'd planned to sort everything out today and make the room into an office, but got a beer from the fridge and sat down with it in front of the TV. He switched between CNN and Fox News for a few minutes and then flipped through the channels until he came upon an old Edward G. Robinson with Humphrey Bogart flick in black and white. He stayed tuned in for awhile but fell asleep before it was over.

He was dreaming about Lone Elm when he awoke. It was a dream in which the closing of Lone Elm was itself a dream. He wanted to go back to sleep and continue it.

He stood at the window and looked out. He had not often seen the afternoon sun from the condo. He thought about bringing in the newspaper, but instead got another beer and sat down in front of the TV. When he woke up that evening it was eight-thirty. He didn't understand where the day had gone. Tomorrow he had to set up his office and plow into the hunt for Petrevich. The president had invited him to set up his office again in the White House. There were no deadlines, no reporting, but there was understood responsibility and accountability—first to himself and of course to Cross. The problem now was that he was starving. Finding nothing he wanted in the fridge, he opened another beer and stood in the door of the bedroom where the boxes waited. It was time to get the rest of them out of the car and start unpacking, but he had to eat. That meant a trip to the store to pick up some things. After that he would call Fleming and get to the boxes.

The car radio almost blew him out of the car. Had it been blaring that loud when he drove home last night? An old Garth Brooks song took him back to the It'll Do. He had an unidentifiable but uneasy feeling about last night. Maybe that was because there were no familiar faces there anymore. When he got to the stop sign two blocks from the condo, he hesitated for a moment. The store was to the left but he turned right and headed for the It'll Do. He could grab a sandwich there and have a beer, and maybe get rid of the odd feeling he had.

He finished an It'll Do hoagie and ordered another beer. Someone behind him said, "What, no Jack Daniels on the rocks?" Even before he looked around he knew the sexy voice belonged to Toni, the bartender who'd served him so many drinks on those long, now dim nights back in another life.

He gave her a big hug and she held him close. "You must own the place by now?" he said half-joking.

"Matter of fact…"

"You deserve it, kid"

Slow, impossible-to-ignore eyes were part of Toni's charm. "Where you been, Honey? Long time. Oh, heard they closed Lone Elm. That stuff on televis—. Oops, sorry, Cam."

"Don't worry about it. Life goes on."

"Anyone who knows you won't—"

Warfield shook his head. "Thanks, Toni, but it's not worth discussing."

"Macc, he came by few days ago. Said you were like married to this girl."

For a moment he stared at her. He'd forgotten how the right side of her mouth kinked up at the corner enough to catch the eye. He didn't remember she was so good looking. "Good to see you, Toni" he said, ignoring her comment.

Warfield caught himself staring at her as they talked, and soon became aware of a sensation in his groin. They joked and chatted for half an hour and Warfield stood up. "Gotta be somewhere."

"Cam?" she said as he rose to leave.

He turned around. Her head was cocked to one side. Her lips were pouty. The silk blouse she wore draped softly over well-defined breasts.

"Don't stay away so long."

Next morning he was up at eight. He'd picked up more beer last night but there was still no food in the place. He went into the spare bedroom to set up his computer. Fleming called before he got started.

"Hey stranger, how 'bout some lunch? Brought some extra soup and salad to the office this morning."

"I, well, maybe I better not, Fleming."

"Pretty busy getting settled, huh?"

"All these boxes from Lone Elm."

"Coming to Hardscrabble tonight? Love to see ya, War Man."

"Let me, uh, wait 'til I see how things go here today. I'll call."

He finished his beer and lay back on the sofa. When he awoke, his hands covered his ears. Somehow he had to stop the ringing. He opened a new beer, hoping for some relief. He went back to the boxes but felt tired. The kind of tired rest didn't cure. He couldn't remember when he had so little energy. After a trip to a neighborhood grocery around five, he ate a bowl of cereal and went back to bed and slept until noon the next day.

His beard almost scared him when he looked in the bathroom mirror. It occurred to him it had been, what, two days, or was it three, since he'd showered and shaved. That was on the list but he grabbed a beer first. That seemed to help the ringing. Three beers later, he slept again.

When he woke up he wasn't sure how many days he'd lost. Fleming had called and left a couple of messages but he didn't remember hearing the phone. He thought about a run. He'd skipped his daily five-milers and workouts for the first time in years except while he was recovering from the car blast. But there was no food. No beer. He had to take care of that, and clean the condo, do the laundry. The Lone Elm boxes still waited on him. He needed to call Fleming. He wondered how he would ever get everything done. The ringing was worse. Maybe that's what caused the headache. He poured a slug of Jack Daniels over some ice cubes.

Warfield awoke startled. *What's going on with me?* Was all this because of Fullwood? Lone Elm? He had to bounce back. He'd never had any patience with men who wallowed around in their problems—perceived or real. He poured himself a Jack Daniels and turned on the TV. Fox News was running a piece on terrorists. He flipped through the channels and found a tennis match. As he sat there trying to motivate himself into the shower, the phone rang and he let the answering machine get it. It was Fleming. She was leaving the hospital late and wanted to swing by his place. Maybe they could have dinner together.

He couldn't let her see the condition everything was in. Besides, he was tired. He called to explain.

"Uhh, look, Fleming, I, I was gonna call you. Been a little under the weather. I better stay in tonight."

"What's going on with you, Cam?"

"Nothing, babe. I'm fine. Just busy right now."

Fleming hesitated. He'd missed her point, or ignored it. "It's been weeks, and I don't know what you're doing to yourself. This is not the Cam Warfield I know." She was angry.

The weeks became months and Warfield lost all sense of time. Exercise was non-existent and he seldom felt like going to the trouble of getting into the shower. When he thought about it he'd flip through his mail and pull out the bills that had to be paid, but late notices began to arrive. He existed on corn flakes and milk—and booze to tame the noise in his ears. The employees at the 7-Eleven and the bottle shop knew him by name.

He woke up one night thinking of Fleming. He'd dreamed about her and wanted to see her. He tried all the next day to call but had no luck reaching her at the office or Hardscrabble. That evening he decided to drive to Ticcio's where they had dinner so many times. He could continue trying to call her from there and maybe she could meet him. He felt an urgent need to make amends but where would he start? For almost three months he'd ignored her calls and the emails she wrote and after a while told her to back off. He'd call when he felt like it. It wasn't that he cared less for her. It was too painful to face her, even though she usually managed to be upbeat.

He always ended the conversation when she suggested he needed to get help. He was responding to his own guilt, but couldn't pull himself out of this inexplicable abyss he was in. The simplest decisions were monumental, and the weight of it all made him want to sleep. When his head was clear— as clear as it got these days—he tried to carry out his good intentions but he'd hit the bottle again while thinking about it and back into that pit he would go. Today had been a little different. He wondered if being out of booze had anything to do with it. He showered, pulled a starched, French blue button down shirt out of the closet, and squeezed into a pair of chinos that used to fit.

He'd gotten into the habit of walking to the stores around the corner and couldn't remember how long it had been since he drove a car. It had collected a layer of dust in his garage and he had to clean the windshield before taking it out. Ticcio's was about half way between his place and Hardscrabble and as he pulled into the familiar parking lot it hit him how much he'd missed Fleming. How much he'd missed life. How could he have let this happen to himself?

"Nobody respects you if you don't respect yourself," he had said to men in his command many times, and now he had fallen far below his own bar. His condo was stacked up with dirty clothes, unwashed dishes and the unpacked Lone Elm boxes, and although he had eaten little more than beer and chips and now and then a bowl of cereal during all that lost time, he'd gained twenty pounds. His muscles turned to mush. His hair was shaggy and for the first time in his life he had a beard, not according to any plan but by neglect. As he sat in Ticcio's parking lot, he felt the excess meat around his belly and stared at himself in the visor mirror. *Warfield, you slob. Why the hell didn't you at least shave?*

Ticcio was not there that night. Warfield sat at the bar and tried Fleming again. Still no answer but this time he left a message on her voicemail and at Hardscrabble that he was at Ticcio's now and hoped she would join him. He watched the couples on the dance floor snuggle to the Dean Martin impersonator and kept an eye on the entrance for Fleming.

After half an hour she walked in. He knew she would show, but seeing her was still a shock. His heart raced. Adrenaline rocked his nerves into high gear. He couldn't wait to wrap his arms around her and tell her how much she meant to him and ask what it would take for them to get back to where they were a few months ago. He felt her skin against his once again. Heard her warm voice. Sensed her fingers running through his hair. How he had missed her. The sheer white cotton outfit she wore emphasized her tan, and her hair swept her shoulders now. He despised what he had done.

As Warfield stood up to greet her, Fleming turned to the man entering the door behind her and laughed at something he said. She walked within inches of Warfield as the maitre d' led the couple through the bar to their table but if she saw him she didn't show it.

Aleksei Antonov walked up from the orchestra and as he lit a Cuban cigar a look of satisfaction graced his face. At least that was one thing the Russians had over the Americans. The smoke took on shades of maroon and gray as it curled upward to the lights. Captain Aleksandr Nosenko rounded the corner from the mezzanine where he was seated for the concert and lit a cigarette off the end of the general's cigar. Antonov was pleased with Nosenko. Not every young officer he'd selected to personally groom rose to his expectations, not to the degree Nosenko had. And like Antonov, Nosenko worried about the easy availability of the sea of nuclear resources left over after the Soviet Union fell apart. The captain contacted General Antonov with any news worth disturbing his mentor for in order to arrange a clandestine meeting. Tonight he informed Antonov that Boris Petrevich was in Tokyo. That was certain now. Antonov decided against telling Nosenko that he'd already learned about Petrevich from an old comrade.

There was no law or rule against Captain Nosenko's collaboration with General Antonov but it seemed to both of the men that privacy of communication was nonetheless in order. After all, Antonov and to some degree Nosenko were products of the old ultra-secretive Soviet culture. But it wasn't like the captain was hiding the information from his superiors: They had the same direct access to it he did. The difference was that Antonov in his retirement had not only the determination but also the time and financial resources to do something with it.

"So what will you do now?" Captain Nosenko asked after giving Antonov the news.

The house lights signaled the first call to return to the theater. The general studied the thick maroon carpet for a moment before answering.

"Tokyo."

"I will accompany you."

"*Nyet.*"

"You will go alone?"

"Initially, yes, until I have specific information about Boris Petrevich. Then I will invite the American, Warfield, to meet me there."

Nosenko looked away. "Just as I thought."

"You do not agree with that course of action, Captain?"

"You trusted Colonel Warfield to stop Petrevich once before."

"It was not Warfield's failure. Your own intelligence sources determined it was his FBI." Antonov said it in a tone intended to end the matter.

Nosenko persisted. "And that will not happen again in Japan? This may be the last opportunity to neutralize Boris Petrevich and recover the uranium he controls."

Antonov squinted at his protégé's tone. "Warfield is no less determined than you or me, Captain, to keep our nuclear arsenal out of irresponsible hands. And he is known to take personal risk when his objective requires it, so I suspect he will not involve his FBI in this matter again."

"May I remind my general that Colonel Warfield no longer enjoys the support of his own government? Perhaps determination is not the only important criterion in choosing an ally."

Antonov flared. He wasn't accustomed to being questioned by a captain, even Nosenko. "Be reminded yourself, captain, that Warfield consistently succeeded against us when he was our enemy. I am aware that was before your time, but I fear that your studies of military and KGB operational history have failed you in this regard."

The young officer glanced around to see how many others witnessed the reprimand.

Antonov looked directly into Nosenko's eyes. "Will that be all, captain?"

Nosenko nodded. "What would you have me do, sir?"

Intermission was over. Antonov knew Nosenko's motives were pure, and cooled off. Nosenko had been with the general so long and gone through so much with him that now he must feel shut out. And in favor of an American. Antonov put his hand on the captain's shoulder. "Without you here in Moscow, in the army," he said, "we lose our primary source of intelligence, which is crucial to our cause. Otherwise, you would accompany me to Tokyo."

Antonov arrived back at his dacha after midnight and poured himself a brandy. It went well with Cubans. He leaned back in the leather chair he called his thinking chair and stared at the ceiling, processing what he knew.

Before the cigar was gone, the six-foot-three general moved from the cracked and wrinkled leather of the old chair to his computer where he scheduled a flight to Tokyo the next day, then e-mailed a note to Warfield. It was almost three a.m. when he turned the lights out.

Warfield felt like someone had kicked him in the stomach. He couldn't bear to stay at Ticcio's any longer, that close to Fleming with another man. Before leaving, he went to the men's room where he got a shot of himself in the mirror. Was it possible she didn't recognize him? She hadn't looked right at him but she did seem to be aware of her surroundings. She had glided past him so near that he smelled the perfume he had given her. No way she would have missed seeing him before he...before he became so different.

The beard. That was it, that and the weight and his hair that had grown shaggy. What had he done to himself? To Fleming? Here she was with another man, no doubt having given up on him while he let himself and everything important to him disintegrate. He was enraged at his own doings. As he turned to leave the restroom he kicked the full-length mirror dead center, sending it to the floor in a million pieces.

He sat in the parking lot for several minutes to get himself together. When he got back to the condo there was a red, tan and black envelope taped to his front door. It was from his mortgage lender, who said his condo was in the process of foreclosure for non-payment of his loan. They had sent all the required notices about missed payments and, having received no response from him, regretted to tell him his home was now in foreclosure proceedings. He could expect the local sheriff to serve him with the legal documents. He read the letter three times under the porch light before going inside. He stood in the living room and looked around at the place for a minute, tossed the notice on the table and went back to his car.

The ringing was back. He opened all the windows in the car hoping to make it go away. When he reached ninety most of it did. He sat at the It'll Do bar and ordered a double Jack on the rocks. He swiveled around to the softly-lighted dance floor, much larger and louder than the one at Ticcio's, and watched over-heated lovers who might be having their first dance together melt into unity as Patsy Cline delivered I Fall to Pieces. He tilted his glass to the juke box. "Know what you mean," he mumbled.

Something surged through him when Toni walked up and rested her arm on his shoulder. "Out in the wilderness for awhile, huh Cam?"

Her question would've been painful except for the Jack. "Hi, Toni."

166

"Hey, I like the beard on you," she said, tugging at it. "Weight's not bad either. I like a man with some meat on his bones."

Toni's eyelids gently waved up and down like the wings of a July butterfly. The lovers on the dance floor caught Warfield's eye. "Workin' tonight?" he asked.

"Depends on who wants to know?" She smiled.

"Forgot. You own the place now."

"Thought it was about time you'd be back. Didn't wanna miss you."

"Dance?" he asked, as Celine Dion began to sing My Heart Will Go On.

She lowered her huge eyes for a moment as if she was thinking it over and then looked at him again. "Not here," she whispered. "My place."

A few hours after General Antonov and Captain Nosenko met in the Moscow theater, Fleming arrived at Hardscrabble to hear her phone ringing. It was Macc Macclenny returning her call. "How's my favorite shrink?"

"Macc, you bum! How's life on the Colorado?"

"Rough out here! Really rough! Thank that Senator what's-his-name for closing Lone Elm. Hope you're calling to tell me you and Warfield are headed my way."

She wished that, too. But she'd called Macc for another reason. Now she had to tell Warfield's best and oldest friend he'd stumbled.

Warfield had a constitution of steel, the stainless kind that came with a warranty. The internal fires, the passion, the grit that made him what he was couldn't be bought or created or turned on inside someone who didn't have them. You couldn't simply will yourself to be that kind of man: You either were or you were not. Macc would find it hard to understand that these hallmarks of Warfield had failed him.

He sobered after hearing her explanation. "The guy's never been depressed a day in his life, Fleming. If it wasn't coming from you I wouldn't believe it."

"Strong men like Warfield aren't immune."

"What's he doing?"

"You mean what's he *not* doing. He's a recluse. I've tried to rescue him to the point of badgering. He never initiates contact. God only knows what else is falling through the cracks."

"You mean you haven't seen him?"

"Hardly at all since you left. Couple nights ago he called from Ticcio's, left me a message to meet him there but I didn't get it until the next day. Tried to call him but his voice-mailbox was full and wouldn't accept any more messages. My e-mails go unanswered. The times I've gone by his condo all the blinds are closed. I don't know if he's there or not. I let myself in once and couldn't believe the condition it was in."

Macc groaned.

"Funny thing was," Fleming continued, "I was at Ticcio's that night when he called. My brother was here from Germany and I took him there for dinner. I'd have seen the War Man if he'd been there."

"How long does this stuff last? This depression."

"Varies case to case. Not easy to deal with. Sometimes it's a life sentence. I don't think that applies to Cam."

"Hell no, not for Warfield, it's not. I'll keep calling 'til I reach him and then I'll get him down here on the river and work his ass off. He won't have time to be depressed. He'll get over it in no time, Fleming; you wait and see."

Macc ran his hand across his pate as the twin-prop De Havilland 8 came to a stop and cut its engines at the Flagstaff-Pulliam Airport. His hairline had moved further and further back year by year and he'd begun shaving his head a few months before he left Lone Elm. The stubble reminded him he had neglected to use the razor on it this morning.

He wondered what his old boss would be like. Fleming had described him in a way Macc could not envision, but when he called him to invite him to Arizona he had a better understanding.

The Cameron Warfield he had known since that day at Fort Huachuca so many years ago was a guy who didn't even have bad *days*, not to mention bad months. It hadn't been easy to get him to make the trip, but to Macc a few days inside the Grand Canyon was better than any medicine a doctor could prescribe. The Grand Canyon and Colorado River had their own way of healing a man's mind and body and soul.

Macc was stunned when he saw Warfield. Long shaggy hair. Extra weight. Black eyes. Worst of all, the vacant look. Macc wasn't sure how he'd greet this stranger but when they were close enough Macc threw his arms around him in a bear hug and was surprised Warfield held on to him so long. It was a good start, Macc thought, but as they made their way out of the terminal little was said beyond Warfield's comment on his flight. He'd had to change planes in Denver and Phoenix.

The north rim of the Canyon, minutes south of the Utah state line, was a three-hour drive up U.S. 89 from Flagstaff and Macc knew it'd be a long, quiet trip the way things were going. Talk between them was stilted like a first date of teenagers, not like the two buddies they were. An hour north of Flagstaff, Macc pulled off the highway at an old wood frame structure with a stained metal roof. The building had been painted sky blue by someone who by now would be too old to work, and the paint was peeling. The thick layer of dust paste on the pickups in the parking lot told how long it'd been since it rained. Even the lone cactus standing at the right end of the building looked bedraggled. The faded sign out front said this was the Blue Penny Saloon.

Macc knew alcohol wasn't quite the prescription for depression, but he wasn't going to coddle Warfield, and besides that they wouldn't be at the Blue Penny long enough for a lot of drinking.

"It's about the only place between here and Utah," he said.

A blast of heat clipped them as they stepped out of Macc's white pickup, and Warfield muttered something about Saudi Arabia.

"One-eighteen today, twenty-percent humidity," Macc said. As they entered the dark roadhouse, four or five cowboys with leather faces and big hats sitting at a long bar turned to see who it was. The jukebox was loud. A layer of sawdust covered the plank floor and a pool table in need of new felt stood idle on the other side of a dance floor. The cool breeze from the swamp cooler provided a welcome hint of moisture in the air.

"Help you boys?" The barmaid wore tight shorts and a tank top. She smiled tan teeth but Macc figured it didn't matter. The tank top probably kept most eyes to the south.

"Draft." Warfield said, looking around the place. Dusty beams sitting on wood columns provided the support for the roof. The Budweiser mirror behind the bar had lost much of its silvering and now yielded gray, rippled images. A lone woman who looked like she belonged to the place sat at a table next to the dance floor. Three cowboys smoking at a nearby table appeared to be interested, but she didn't.

"Like the ol' days, Cam. Bar full of horny men, one or two wimmen. Numbers never did seem to work in our favor."

"We always beat the odds," Warfield said with a brief smile. It was the first one Macc had seen. A start.

After a couple of beers, Macc glanced at the lone woman. She probably wasn't bad in her prime but the Arizona sun and dry air had claimed some of their due. "I reckon she'd like to dance with me," he told Warfield. "No use in makin' her wait any longer."

Warfield glanced over his shoulder at her. He took a swig out of his glass and swiped the back of his hand across his mouth. "Tell you what, Macclenny. Give me the first dance with her and then she's yours if you can get her to leave me."

"She does, you're buyin' the beer."

"Deal." The next song to come up turned out to be Ray Charles wailing Together Again. It had the slow beat Warfield liked for dancing. He and then Macc danced a couple of times with the woman, who called herself Cherokee, as the cowboys at the table looked at them. Cherokee seemed to like joking around with Warfield and Macc as they danced. Warfield was at the bar watching Macc and Cherokee sway to the music when one of the cowboys left the table and tapped Macc on the shoulder.

"My time, Son. You can move on now."

Macc turned to look at the cowboy wearing a sweat-stained western straw hat and cowboy boots, and then at Cherokee. She shook her head.

"Looks like she's happy right now, partner," Macc said, and returned to Cherokee and Waylon Jennings. But the cowboy wedged in between the two. He and Macc exchanged a few words before the other two wranglers got up from the table and took a place on either side of Macc. Cherokee said something to the men and Straw Hat elbowed her aside.

"Sit down, Cherokee. This's between us and this skinhead. You keep your mouth shut."

Macc had stepped back to try to keep the three men in front of him when Warfield walked up. "Let it go," he said to Macc, and then to the three cowboys, "Relax, boys. Sit back down. Everything's cool."

Warfield saw it coming in time to pull back out of Straw Hat's range. He waited the split instant for the momentum of the man's roundhouse swing to pull him forward and chopped the back of the cowboy's neck with the edge of his hand as he went by. Straw Hat hit the dance floor nose first and didn't move.

Macc was ducking the big end of a pool cue that the second cowboy whirled in a large arc, but recovered his balance in time to land a punch deep into the cowboy's beer belly and an uppercut to his chin. One of the cowboy's teeth scuttled across the dance floor and blood ran down both sides of his mouth as he landed on the sawdust, but he wasn't through, and reached for Warfield's ankle. Macc planted his foot in the cowboy's stomach, this time causing the man to lose the beer and barbecue he'd eaten.

Macc heard the snick of a switch blade locking in place but Warfield caught the cowboy who wielded it in the chest with a kick that sent him reeling across the floor into the end of the bar. His rib cage took the blow. He fell to the floor and began signaling he couldn't breathe. Warfield kicked the knife away, listened to his breathing for a few seconds and felt his ribs. At least one was broken. "Lung's punctured, Cowboy. Take care of the good one...might wanna see a doctor."

Straw Hat still hadn't moved. Macc put his toe under his shoulder and flipped him over. He looked up at Macc and Warfield and shook his head. He wanted no more.

The drinkers at the bar sat still. "We got no problem with you boys," one of them said. Macc pulled out some bills but the bartender gave him a nervous smile and said the drinks were on the house. "Sorry 'bout the trouble," she said.

Macc told the barmaid to call an emergency crew and dropped a hundred dollar bill on the bar, and he and Warfield walked out into the heat and blinding sunlight and got back on Highway 89. After miles of red dirt and cactus and unrelenting sun, dusk was approaching when they pulled in at the Canyon Cliffs Lodge, an old one-story motel with frontier-town stone walls that formed a snaggle-toothed facade against the red cliffs behind it.

Next morning at the Cliffs Cantina a Jack Palance double served them a huge platter of scrambled eggs, sausage, hot biscuits and syrup. It was the most Warfield had eaten in months. From there it was a short hop down to Lee's Ferry where Macc's boat waited for them.

"You call that a *raft?*" Warfield said, when Macc pointed it out.

It took an hour to board the dozen passengers and all their camping gear. The thirty-five-foot raft was built in two sections hinged together in the middle to allow it to take the rapids. Bullet-shaped pontoons on each side provided a riding place for anyone who wanted to straddle them. Food, ice and other supplies were packed in the center of the front section of the raft along with the campers' gear. Macc and Warfield occupied the aft part of the boat. Warfield was the swamper. It was hard work and the days were long. The temperature routinely rose above the century mark but he learned fast and tried to do more than his share of work. Macc pointed out places and objects of historical and geological interest to everyone and a couple of times a day stopped for hiking trips into a side canyon. The hikes were optional and some campers sat them out on the boat for the two or three hours the others were away.

Warfield always made the side trips and was never disappointed in the reward. He thought he'd already seen most of what the earth had to offer, but the waterfalls and rock formations and drop-offs he saw in the Grand Canyon set new standards. On one of the hiking tours far above the river, Macc showed Warfield the ledge the Sanazaro kid froze-up on years earlier, and the bluff above from which Macc rappelled down and plucked him off.

Everyone on the boat got to know each other. Late afternoons, they cooled off in the river, some fished and others scouted around the campsite for a good place to put down their sleeping gear—preferably not too close to one of the boulders that through the night radiated the heat it had stored during the long day. Around six they gathered around for a few beers in celebration of the wonders they'd experienced that day, while Macc created a meal on par with the fare in the best restaurants anywhere.

Warfield wouldn't have believed it was possible. One night they charbroiled two-inch thick angus filets to order, with asparagus and twice-baked potato sides. That was Warfield's favorite. Lunch was sandwiches. Never the same meal twice. The huge Styrofoam ice chest on the boat even though not refrigerated kept the block-ice solid for the entire trip.

Everyone turned in soon after dark, too drained to go any longer. The heat and the trails took it out of them. The rush of the river serenaded them to sleep. Warfield and Macc got up in time to serve eggs and pancakes, sausage and biscuits at seven. By around eight-thirty, all the camping gear was stowed on the raft and everyone was set to experience another day of grandeur.

If Warfield's travels and experiences had diminished his capacity for awe, the *Grand,* as Macc called it, was a revival. Could there be 200 miles of such indescribable beauty in the world? Five million years of Colorado River flow had carved straight down through a mile of rock, revealing 2.5 billion years' worth of unmatched artwork created by volcanoes, erosion and an ocean that covered the area five-hundred-million years ago. The names of the features along their route were as beautiful as the places themselves. Marble Canyon. Deer Creek. Chevaya Falls. Toroweap Point.

At night Warfield made a bed close to the river under bright stars and dreamed about the pink castles that lined the canyon walls, or the picturesque streams and waterfalls he'd cooled off in that day, or the bighorn sheep that roamed the rugged slopes, or the Anasazi Indians who lived there a thousand years ago and the foundations of their primitive home sites that were still identifiable. Nothing Macc had told him about the Grand Canyon and Colorado River flowing through it over the years came close to describing the wonders he was seeing. And time flew. In contrast to his endless days and nights over the last few months, the hours on the Colorado slipped by much too fast.

Adventure trips through the Grand Canyon began at a landing called Lee's Ferry below the Utah border in northern Arizona. Everything below Lee's Ferry was referenced by distance from that starting point. The notorious Lava Falls at Mile 179 came on the sixth day and had been a thread of conversation sewn by Macc among the campers all week. The river narrowed there and fed into a thirty-five foot drop. Macc said Lava was the largest navigable falls in North America.

Some of the other boatmen didn't risk taking riders through the Lava rapids. They put them ashore upstream and from there the passengers walked around the falls and met the raft downstream. Not Macc. He drifted down near the falls to give everyone a sobering preview of the churning waters they had in store before he turned back upstream a hundred yards to begin his approach.

When the raft entered the falls, the rushing water arced over the bow and sucked the boat straight down into a black vortex. It was more than Warfield expected and he wondered if he would ever breathe air again. As soon as the chance came to gulp a breath, the boat went back under the relentless slamming and receding and plunging and backing of the fifty-five-degree water. It felt to Warfield like it lasted for five minutes and he didn't think the boat would survive it. Finally past the rapids, Macc brought the raft about so everyone could see what they had lived through. Or to thank God, Warfield decided. It was a ride to remember.

On the final morning they devoured another lumberjack breakfast and floated the few last miles to a sandy beach where helicopters waited to take the campers to a nearby airstrip for a plane ride back to Lee's Ferry. New friends had been made and some exchanged contact information. After everyone was lifted out, Macc and Warfield took the raft downriver a few miles to a landing where they loaded the raft onto a waiting truck for a ride back to the adventure company's headquarters to be restocked for its next trip. Macc had a few days off and drove Warfield back to Flagstaff.

They ate Mexican at Carlos's the night before Warfield was to return to Washington. Next morning Warfield awoke before the alarm, looked at the red numbers on the clock and decided to get up anyway. He trimmed the beard as short as he could with scissors and shaved the rest. When he was done, he watched the razor stubble swirl down the drain and knew this dark period in his life washed away with it. He looked at himself in the mirror and ran a hand across his new face. He had a good feeling about himself. About life. It had been a while.

At the airport Macc and Warfield looked at each other for a moment with mutual appreciation. "Owe you one, Macc."

Fleming watched as Warfield walked through the gate at Washington National. As he drew closer she saw the spark in his eyes, the old purposefulness in his stride. The crooked smile that always told her things were all right. They held each other for a long time, and she was glad because it gave her time to dry her tears before he could see them. He was back.

PART THREE
Fumio Yoshida

CHAPTER 12

FUMIO YOSHIDA EXITED THE elevator in the lobby of the Civil Aviation Bureau and stalked through Reception, checked his wrist watch with the atomic wall clock and headed to his office without so much as a glance at his employees. Most kept their heads down as he passed by their work area but Mrs. Nakamura, his long-time administrative assistant, signaled him to say that Minister Saito had called for Yoshida twice while he was out.

Yoshida nodded and went to his own office, sat down at his desk and swiveled around to his window that overlooked Tokyo's Narita Airport, less than a mile away. The queue of planes waited in turn for takeoff and when a 747 with its signature hump taxied to the end of the runway Yoshida stood up and moved closer to the window. His look softened as the 747 began its takeoff roll, and he turned away only after the plane was airborne.

He checked his voicemail messages and after listening to the one from his superior a second time he sat for a moment with his arms folded on top of his polished wood desk, barren except for the white legal pad centered in front of him as usual. It wasn't often that the Japan Minister of Transport called—the routine reports and executive meetings Yoshida hated so much were sufficient to cover everything—and when he did, it wasn't to tell him how good a job he was doing or talk about baseball.

Minister Saito worked nonstop and expected Yoshida and his other vice-ministers to do the same. Weekdays, weekends, evenings, holidays and lunch hours were all the same to Saito if there was unfinished work. Fumio Yoshida handled his own responsibilities but his priorities were different than Saito's. And there was never any conversation between them that didn't involve Ministry of Transport business.

He dialed the Minister. "Yoshida returning your call."

"*Hai!* Yoshida. Must meet immediately. My office, ten minutes."

Yoshida's heart picked up a beat. This was no time for Saito to start asking questions. His mind raced. Maybe someone under him had noticed something unusual and planted a seed with Saito. No way could it be related to his job performance. Gold plaques annually proclaiming Yoshida's Civil Aviation Bureau the best division of the Ministry of Transport lined the walls. The government auditors sent not only their glowing official report to Saito every year, but often attached personal notes of praise for Yoshida's precision operation. Yoshida knew his employees liked the recognition and he also knew that a substantial number of the same eleven-thousand-nine-hundred-sixty-four workers in the CAB hated his guts, but that mattered little to him. What mattered at the moment was the reason for Saito's call.

Following the stiff manner in which he and his boss always spoke, Yoshida said, "I have commitments today, Minister. Perhaps tomorrow morning?"

"Rearrange commitments!" Saito said in his usual staccato speaking style.

Yoshida spoke humbly. "To do so would reflect poorly on the Ministry. However, I am at your command."

The Minister of Transport took a deep breath. "No, then. Eight tomorrow morning."

"Hai!" Then, as if an afterthought Fumio Yoshida said, "If you wish to tell me the matter we are going to discuss I will be well-prepared when we meet."

"Hangar 23 refurbishment costs!" Yoshida heard Saito flipping through the pages of the cost report that was ever-present on his desk. "Also, the security. Much money has been spent on refurbishment and security, Yoshida. I did not authorize budget overruns!"

Yoshida, his heart speeding up, looked toward the airport again. He could make out Hangar 23 at the far left end. "You will be satisfied with my explanation, Minister."

When Fumio Yoshida arrived at his home that evening his younger brother padded across the small house to greet him, like he had done for as long as Fumio could remember. Jotaro's wide smile and childish giggles that belied his age meant he was ready to play. He loved the water and reveled in his brother's attention so much that Fumio Yoshida rarely allowed anything to stand in the way of their time together. But today he wished he could. His mind was far too occupied by tomorrow's meeting with Minister Saito to downshift into the ritual at the bath house.

On the walk back home with Jotaro after an hour at the Tomodachi *Sento,* Fumio Yoshida found himself a little less tense than at any time since his conversation with Saito. The water was refreshing and he'd even splashed around in the bath with Jotaro. The air was less humid than usual for mid-summer in Tokyo and the neighborhood residents, most of them Fumio's generation, sat on porches or in their small yards and took advantage of the pleasant evening air. Hydrangeas, morning glories, and the ever-present camellias filled garden plots that covered much of the lots they occupied. There were few children in Yoshida's neighborhood these days, as most younger people settled in newer developments where the homes had baths and other modern comforts. Bath houses were hard to find there but in areas like Yoshida's the sentos still facilitated a tradition indispensable to the older Japanese.

It was after ten when Fumio got Jotaro to bed but he had one other job before he could prepare for Saito. He booted up an aging desktop PC, logged onto the Internet and went to the website he'd visited hundreds of times before, if not thousands. The Internet was a gift from the gods for Fumio, making it easier for him to get the latest research from the Radiation Effects Research Foundation, where he had long hoped to find some breakthrough research that would mean a better life for Jotaro. He'd read multitudes of RERF reports and by now accepted what he had known deep down long ago—that all the research in the world could never help Jotaro. So when Yoshida visited the website these days it was for a different reason: To read the morbid statistics that nourished the hungry, organic hatred that grew inside him.

After twenty minutes at the RERF website he leaned back in the chair, closed his eyes and visited the familiar place in his mind where the essence of all the RERF reports was preserved, where the damnable reality of Jotaro had festered for so long, beginning with mere resentment in the earlier years when Fumio first began to comprehend what had happened—that by some fateful roll of the dice on the day Hiroshima was bombed, his mother was at the exact distance from ground zero and at the precise stage in her pregnancy that meant her fetus would survive to become Jotaro but that his mind would never be normal.

How could all those stars have lined up against his mother and his brother? In all of Hiroshima and Nagasaki close to half a million people died from the Americans' atomic bombs, but little Jotaro in the sanctuary of his mother's womb was much less fortunate than they were, Fumio felt, left with a mind too undeveloped to wonder or to imagine or to serve its own body.

And the guilt. How was it that he, Fumio, happened to be in Sapporo, far to the north with his aging grandmother when the bomb came, safe from any harm? He should have been there with his mother so that perhaps he could have died from radiation like she did soon after delivering Jotaro. But, no, that would have left Jotaro alone. Their father had placed his loyalty to Japan above everything else—including his family and his very life—and died a kamikaze in the second world war, and Fumio had come to understand his father. Over the years, Fumio Yoshida's resentment for Americans turned to blackest hate and consumed his soul. Like hate always does.

Fumio shut down the computer and took a folder labeled *Jotaro* out of his desk, removed the rubber band and looked at the last notation he'd made. His eyes narrowed as he read once again his own distillation of Japan's surrender to end World War II. It was not the first time he'd returned to his short manifesto in the two years since he'd written it: "The Emperor in surrender did not speak for Fumio and Jotaro Yoshida, to whom the only acceptable alternative to victory is a fight to death. The instruments are being put into place to achieve a modicum of justice for Jotaro and for other Japanese lives destroyed by the Americans."

After that entry, there had been no more analyzing or researching or rationalizing to write about. He had started a new file that night, a file he labeled *Harvest*. It was time to focus on the execution of his plan. Yoshida nodded as he closed the file, reaffirmed by his own writing. *This is what it is all about, Minister Saito. You will understand soon, but not tomorrow.*

Fumio replaced the thick Jotaro file, retrieved the one labeled Harvest and spent the next hour going over his notes and numbers inside. He compared them with printouts he brought home from the CAB, checked a few totals with a small calculator, and scribbled several notations on a legal pad. He wondered if it were the politicians who were behind Saito's inquiry. They were always snooping around in areas they didn't understand, but it didn't matter. He'd been careful. And he could give Saito all the explanation he needed for the politicians. His plan for Jotaro had cost more than he expected but he had succeeded in hiding the costs up to this point and could explain them away. And this would be the last time he'd have to do it. Of that he was certain.

It was almost midnight when he put the Harvest file back in the desk and slipped the notes he'd made into his notebook. He turned out the lights and went to bed but as happened too often he couldn't sleep. As his plan neared reality, excitement replaced the constant tiredness he'd felt for so many years.

Fumio walked into his office at seven-twenty-eight the next morning, zoomed through the paperwork his assistant left for him, cleared everything off his desk and walked up the single flight of stairs to the top floor where the Minister of Transport's office was located. He stood at Saito's outer door and counted down the seconds until exactly eight o'clock and entered carrying a thin vinyl notebook. "Ahh, good morning Minister Saito," Fumio said, with a traditional bow.

Saito's eyes bulleted in on the folds of green printer paper on his desk as the downward corners of his mouth reflected what Yoshida had figured were the result of a lifetime of negativism. Yoshida did not judge this harshly, however, as that was the condition his own life had brought him to. "Yoshida," Saito said with his usual bombast, "I have been called to a meeting with the Diet budget oversight committee this morning! I will be expected to explain this five million dollars for security systems at Hangar 23," he said, rigidly stabbing the printout with a stubby finger, "and this six-point-six million for Hangar 23 renovations. The committee demands an accounting for these expenditures, as do I! Why was I was not informed of these costs?" he said, his voice continuing to rise.

Fumio watched for any hint Saito suspected wrongdoing. He had hoped this accounting was only for Saito's preparation to meet with the politicians in the national legislature and not because of any suspicions he might have.

Saito had not invited Yoshida to sit and he stood straight with his arms at his sides. "Hai! I am preparing Hangar 23 to accommodate the Oberon."

Saito's face became a pretzel. *"Oberon!"* he said as he stiffened in his chair. "Impossible, Yoshida. You think I am a fool? The supersonic Oberon has three bases, just like the Concorde had before it was discontinued: Paris, London and New York. We do not even have the accommodations required to establish a base here, Yoshida! It will be years before it lands here, you imbecile, if ever." Saito was incredulous.

"The Oberon is much closer than you may be aware, Minister." Fumio nodded an apologetic gesture for daring to disagree. "I am in touch with my counterparts in London and Paris, who speak very encouragingly. It is currently most secretive, but Tokyo will have it, right here at Narita. In-progress design modifications to the Oberon will increase its range. I have been in negotiations for a Tokyo route for several months."

"Why have I not been told of this? And what imposters are you negotiating with, Yoshida?"

Yoshida looked down. "I am at fault for not better informing you, Minister Saito. The talks are rather general at this point, with officials beneath your level of authority. I elected not to burden you until decisions worthy of your time and position are required. As to the expenditures, I believed we would have much better opportunity to get the Oberon if we are able to demonstrate preparedness. I am aware that twelve million dollars is a very large sum, but to the total Ministry of Transport budget, it is like comparing the toy airplane of a child to a Boeing 747. Perhaps after consideration you will agree that it is a prudent expenditure. However, if not, I will accept full responsibility for my extreme foolishness and immediately resign my post as head of the Civil Aviation Bureau." Yoshida knew he was taking a great chance with that statement.

The gray-haired minister leveled an uncertain stare at Yoshida. Fumio knew the tyrannical egomaniac Saito had never liked him much and would be grateful for a reason to boot him to another area within the MOT so he wouldn't have to deal with him on a one-on-one basis, or even force him to retire, but for the Oberon he might tolerate him a while longer. Saito's face softened ever so slightly as he said, "You will not resign, Yoshida. I have rarely had cause to question your judgment so I must assume you have acted appropriately. In fact," he said after hesitating for a moment, "when it is time to tell this news to the legislative group I will acknowledge that we planned it together. The politicians will find value in any reasonable expenditures that may be expected to secure an Oberon base."

Walking back to his office, Fumio Yoshida had no regret for the lies he was forced to tell. Until he needed the money to carry out his plan, he'd never taken so much as one illegal yen from the Ministry of Transport, but now through obscure billing and payment procedures he'd managed to pay the down payment to the Russian and full payment to the broker named Seth who demanded all of his millions in advance.

Seth had made the arrangement with Petrevich for the procurement and transport of the uranium from Russia by way of Iraq. This was an intentionally deceptive route; the U.S. authorities were unlikely to even imagine Tokyo to be the final destination, while Iraq was easily believable. Yoshida was committed to make this final payment to Petrevich upon his completion of the project. Now his reconfiguration of the Boeing 747 aircraft to accommodate the deadly payload would be the final step. When the deception was discovered perhaps all of Japan—at least those who had suffered as he and Jotaro had—would approve after they have learned the whole truth. Yoshida's only concern now was that Minister Saito or someone higher up would decide to visit Hangar 23 to see all the non-existent improvements, but he could stall them for a few days and then it wouldn't matter—at least not to Yoshida. He almost smiled as he thought of the trap Saito was going to set for himself by claiming part credit for the Oberon idea at the highest levels of the Japanese government.

That night at the bath house Fumio caught himself staring at his brother as he splashed around in the water. He wished he could explain to him what he was doing. And why. But Fumio had no doubt Jotaro would approve. He was a Japanese first, and then a Yoshida. They would stick together no matter what, like after the bomb when they were placed in the government orphanage, and later when Fumio returned from the university and the military where he'd been a pilot like his father. After that, Fumio had applied to the Ministry of Transport for a job that would allow him to remain close to aviation. Jotaro was nineteen then and Fumio moved them into a private apartment over the strong protests of the orphanage officials. Impossible, they said. Unfair to both of them. But Fumio persisted. Jotaro was his brother and he would take care of him for as long as he lived. For as long as *we* live, Fumio thought to himself now as he stood in the edge of the water.

Early on at the CAB, Fumio Yoshida was recognized as one of the most capable and dedicated, and by the time he was forty he'd been singled out from the pack by his superiors. Making good money then, he bought a traditional Japanese home in an older section of Tokyo and went about

Jotaro-proofing it as he had done in their tiny apartment, removing anything his brother might harm himself with. After that he left Jotaro at home with the television and his toys while he was away at the CAB. And he bought a dog to keep Jotaro company.

Mrs. Tanaka, the old widow next door, had tried to get acquainted with the Yoshidas but Fumio didn't reciprocate. Even so, once she knew about Jotaro's condition her motherly instinct took over and she kept an eye on the Yoshida house during the day. Fumio Yoshida knew that. She intercepted Jotaro twice when he ventured out of the house but she'd never been so bold as to go inside.

As Fumio Yoshida climbed through the ranks to the top of the CAB he kept everyone at arm's length, more than fulfilling his duties but doing little to ingratiate himself to anyone. It had not been particularly difficult for him to get special approval to work beyond the standard retirement age, partly, he thought, because of his exemplary accomplishments in the Civil Aviation Bureau. If he took care of his family and did whatever was required to progress in his work at CAB, which was critical to his plan, nothing else should be necessary. He had never socialized with the others after work. There was no time for it. He had his brother to take care of, and the anger inside sapped his drives and desires.

When they returned home from the bath house that night, Jotaro and his dog Yuki-Yuki got into a wrestling bout on the floor and Fumio went to his own room and opened the Harvest file. He could recite every detail of the plan from memory, but holding the file in his hands made it more real. Things were falling into place now. It was true that he'd come to despise the Russian Boris Petrevich, but if he completed his project on time Yoshida would pay him the second half of the fee they'd agreed on.

Fumio had paid Seth his ten million upon his delivery of Petrevich and the uranium, but, still, he had no stomach for whores like Seth who sold their services to the highest bidder. Seth was a man with no values, no morals. Pay a man like him enough money and he would sneak up behind his own mother in the kitchen, surprise her with a hug, slit her throat from ear to ear, and then sit down and eat the meal she had cooked for him. But if the deal he made with Seth produced the result Fumio demanded, then using even scum like him was justified.

Hangar 23 was one of several hangars at Narita reserved for the exclusive use of Ministry of Transport and came under administrative control of Fumio's Civil Aviation Bureau. MOT records indicated it was vacant and unused so there was no reason for anyone to go there, but since the time Yoshida set it up as the place where Boris Petrevich and his two Russian assistants would work, he had driven himself there perhaps a hundred times. And even though Hangar 23 was located in an untraveled and secluded corner of Narita Airport, Yoshida worried the traffic would make someone curious.

Fumio felt at peace around planes and loved most the behemoth airliners like the 747, but his executive duties at the CAB were to be endured. They involved aviation, but nothing was like being out there on the tarmac looking up at the jetliners that were to him so beautiful, and climbing into the cockpit where he could experience the power that came with being at the controls of a machine that could lift four-hundred tons and transport them to some place thousands of miles away before it touched Earth again.

Fumio's most cherished memories of his father were of him in the military. He had a photo of him standing by the wing of a small airplane Fumio imagined was the one that carried his father and, Fumio hoped, many American soldiers to a fiery death. Back then Fumio had known only that his father was a pilot. It was many years later that he found a letter his father wrote to Fumio's mother on the last day of his life. Today his plane would be given enough fuel for a one-way trip. He was proud to have been selected by his leaders to fly it into the enemy. When all his bullets were spent and bombs released, he would still have one weapon left: Himself, as part of his plane. He would do it again and again for the defeat of the hated America if he could.

Fumio Yoshida had many times closed his eyes and imagined those last glorious seconds of his father's life. He had not dropped like a rock onto his target. He came in low, almost like he was landing, and took out a long swath of planes on the deck of a U.S. aircraft carrier. The burning planes. Every one of them filled with fuel. American sailors on deck, unable to escape below in time to avoid slow and painful death, many of them jumping into the Pacific Ocean to escape the flames and perishing there.

The screams for help. The joy, the pride his father must have felt in those moments before things went blank for him.

To Fumio, the Americans were the root cause of the war. His own hate stemmed from that. The Americans had claimed not only his father and mother, it had left his brother forever dependent on others, never to be free of health problems, never able to make decisions for his own life. Fumio sometimes had wondered if Jotaro, by some miracle given a few minutes of lucidity in which to consider his circumstances, would choose to continue the life determined for him even before he was born, or would he prefer death? Jotaro would never have that moment of contemplation, and Fumio had made the decision for him.

Fumio's responsibility to Jotaro had robbed him of a career of flying the world, perhaps as an airline pilot or in the military. Jotaro could never be left alone for more than a few hours during the day. But the positions Fumio held at CAB at least put him on the periphery. For a period of time he had direct responsibility for pilot certification standards and spent every possible moment analyzing and redesigning training manuals, configuring cockpits for better safety and revolutionizing flight simulators, the stationary virtual cockpits used to train and test pilots. Fumio Yoshida became recognized around the world as a leading authority in civil aviation training and safety.

He looked for every opportunity to fly, climbing out over Japan's snow-capped mountains to the north or above the silver ripples of the ocean, forgetting for those precious minutes about Jotaro and the responsibilities that would still be there for him when he returned that evening. He became certified on every type of aircraft used by the Japanese airlines and spent hundreds of hours in the simulators, often choosing to conduct the test sessions for pilots himself.

Fumio parked the motor pool car behind Hangar 23. He bounced out of the car and strode past the summer weeds that grew along the side of the hangar to the personnel door. Boris Petrevich sat in his makeshift office across the hangar. Yoshida stopped for a second before he crossed under the belly of the splendid Boeing 747-400 sitting in the hangar and looked up at it.

Dr. Boris Petrevich saw Yoshida coming and gathered up the Guido's Pizza boxes from the office floor and stuffed them into a trash can. Fumio had never been satisfied with the Russian's housekeeping habits and had directed him to shape up. How could the clear, precise knowledge of nuclear physics coexist with such slovenliness within the same mind?

"You are still on schedule?" Fumio demanded, scowling at the messy office.

Petrevich had imported two men he'd trained in Russia—Mikhail, a nuclear technician, and Ivan, an aeronautical engineer—to help him with the project. He'd asked Yoshida for local labor to do grunt work but Yoshida refused. Too risky, he'd said, thinking of his project's necessary secrecy. Petrevich managed to keep on schedule by working long hours. He and his crew did a lot of things he would have assigned to flunkies in his exalted position back at Kremlyov.

"I think so," he answered. "Even if something goes wrong we should meet the required schedule at the end."

Fumio Yoshida's eyes blazed as his body became rigid. "Give me your attention!" he barked, and waited for Petrevich to face him. "You will allow nothing to go wrong! Everything will be exactly as agreed, precisely on schedule. There will be no delay." Fumio did not wait for an answer and did a right face to leave, clicking his heels together as he'd done as an officer in the military, then abruptly stopped three steps away. "Anyone asking you questions?"

"Questions...?"

"Where you live. Why you are in Japan."

"*Nyet.*"

"Met anyone from Russia who knows you?"

The Russian stiffened and looked at the floor. "Nyet."

Fumio Yoshida's face was the look of death as he moved closer and put his finger in the Russian's face. "Do not lie to me, Petrevich," he screamed.

Petrevich had never forgiven himself for the way he allowed this little Jap bastard intimidate him. He backed away as much as he could in the small cubicle and said, "There is one slight possibility, Comrade. I saw a man I knew from Russia. Some sort of military officer then, but I am sure he is retired by now so I do not believe he is in Tokyo in any official capacity."

Fumio roared from some place deep inside his chest, "Where were you?"

Petrevich hesitated, then, "A bar."

"Your Moscow club again!" Yoshida snapped.

Petrevich said nothing. Yoshida kicked the trash can across the floor and paced around for a few seconds.

"You are not to be seen. You risk this project," he spewed.

"It will not happen again," Petrevich said.

Fumio turned to leave but then whirled around and fired a final rocket. "One other thing Petrevich. Never call me *comrade* again."

Petrevich reeled. It took all of his inner strength to overcome the impulse to go for Fumio then and there. Moments later, after Yoshida was gone, the Russian realized his men had witnessed his humiliation. To make it worse his hands trembled from unspent adrenaline. They saw what happened and now he would look weak to the aggressive Ivan. Boris Petrevich hated Yoshida now more than ever. *The little sawed-off Jap rooster.* That was his favorite description of Yoshida. He wouldn't care if he'd killed him except that so much money was at stake. Good thing he kept his T-33 under his pillow instead of in his pocket, he thought. The temptation might have been too great.

Now he had to calm Ivan, who could screw up the whole deal. Petrevich never liked Ivan much back in Russia but brought him in because of the skills he possessed. He was a brilliant young engineer seven years out of the university, but brash and resentful of authority.

Ivan had boarded Fumio Yoshida's train near the Ministry of Transport building after work one day and tailed him through the labyrinth of Tokyo subway tunnels and all the way to Yoshida's home. Once he saw where he lived he didn't know what he'd ever do about it, he told Petrevich later. It was part of knowing your enemy, and Ivan considered Yoshida just that.

As Ivan was about to leave the area and head back to the hangar that day, he'd seen Fumio Yoshida and another man emerge from his home. He decided to follow them and this time ended up at a bath house a few blocks away. "Looked like some sort of little retard that went with him to that swimming pool place," he told Petrevich then.

Petrevich had reacted in anger that day. "You're a fool, Ivan. He sees you, I have a lot of questions to answer." Petrevich had considered eliminating Ivan then, or maybe getting one of the Russians at the Moscow East who would do anything for money to do it for him, but Ivan was creative and Petrevich needed him. Like no other engineer Petrevich had ever seen, Ivan could design a nuke delivery system to satisfy the most demanding situation. This one wasn't so bad but it was unique. The job could be done best by Ivan, and Petrevich decided that day to keep him on the team but ordered him to stay away from Yoshida.

Petrevich gave himself a pat on the back for not exploding all over Yoshida. His *comrade* outburst was the straw that almost pushed him over the edge. Once he had the rest of the money Yoshida owed him maybe he'd let his impulses loose, but until then he would manage to control both himself and Ivan.

A far more worrisome problem to Petrevich was Aleksei Antonov, the Russian general he'd spotted at the Moscow East Social Club. He figured Antonov saw him too but he'd lied to Yoshida about it. Petrevich always knew that sooner or later someone would come. He could take no chances now. Antonov had to be dealt with.

Petrevich summoned the two Russians to his office. "No more trips to the Moscow East. Understand? We are almost finished here, anyway. And you, Ivan, if there is any more trouble, I will wrap you up in more chains than you can swim with and throw you in the ocean! Clear?" He was standing toe-to-toe with Ivan, venting his built-up rage when he noticed the Guido's Pizza boxes that scattered when Yoshida kicked the trash can. "And keep your trash out of my office."

That evening Petrevich left his makeshift living quarters at Hangar 23 without telling his men where he was going. Wearing a baseball cap and sunglasses, he sat at a corner table in deep discussion with another Russian at the Moscow East for an hour. He returned to Hangar 23 after midnight.

CHAPTER 13

THE SUN REFLECTING OFF the shimmering blue waters of the north Pacific woke Warfield. The captain announced the plane would be on the ground at Tokyo's Narita Airport in thirty minutes. After sixteen hours on the plane, Warfield was anxious to get out and stretch. Better yet, he'd go for a run if there were time.

He asked a flight attendant for something with caffeine and pulled both of General Antonov's e-mail messages up on his iPhone. In the first one, Antonov notified him he had new intelligence about their "common interest" and said he would contact him again when he had more information. That message was dated two days before Warfield left Washington to visit Macc in Arizona and he had missed it.

Now it was impossible to think of that trip without a flash of the reason he went. He had fixed everything that could be fixed. His condo mortgage was now in good standing again and he'd paid the other bills for which he'd been irresponsible. He drove to Ticcio's, owned up to the damage in the men's room and wrote Ticcio a check for double the repair cost even though Ticcio told him to forget it. And Fleming. Why had she even tolerated him? He'd ignored the lifelines she threw out to him, like everything else. On the evening of his return from Arizona they talked about the darkest episode of his life. He groped around for explanations—as much for himself as for Fleming—and Fleming told him the guy he was trying to explain was passing through and wouldn't be returning. "So don't look back any more," she said. He had felt tears on her cheek that night as they made love for the first time in months.

The next day after that he couldn't wait to start putting his condo back in shape. Fleming had cleaned the place and he spent his time finally unpacking the Lone Elm boxes and setting up his office. When he got around to checking his e-mail that day he found the two messages from General Antonov. The general said in the second one that he was in Tokyo and Warfield should join him there if he was interested.

If he was interested? Antonov knew something about this Russian who was a threat to humanity and who on a professional level had impacted Warfield's life. Catching up with this man was almost as important to Warfield as life itself.

As the plane began its final approach to Narita, Warfield reflected on the smaller and simpler American plane that flew over Japan some seventy years ago and introduced weapons of mass destruction to the world. He saluted the Japanese for overcoming the disastrous effects of World War II by way of intelligent economic policies and assistance from the United States. Now, Japan, an island smaller than California but with as much as half the population of the U.S., was a top-tier economic engine and America's solid ally in that part of the world.

Warfield had e-mailed Antonov his flight schedule and once inside the terminal he heard someone speak his name. The man in his late thirties introduced himself as Takao Komeito and said Antonov sent him. They weaved their way through the crowded concourse to a waiting limousine outside the terminal and after Komeito gave the driver instructions in Japanese, he turned to Warfield. "General Antonov speaks very well of you, Colonel Warfield."

"He'll get to know me better," Warfield said, wondering if an attempt at humor was appropriate.

Komeito stared at him. "Better hope not, Colonel."

"How so?"

"General doesn't like? He kill." Komeito kept a straight face for a second before breaking up. Warfield knew he could like the guy.

"You work with General Antonov?" Warfield asked.

"I worked for him when he traveled here on military business before he retired. I am employed at the Russian Embassy here. Unimportant job. Easy for me to take leave while general is in Tokyo."

Warfield nodded and asked the dapper Komeito, "So Antonov still receives official treatment?"

"Embassy is most hospitable to General Antonov even now. Highly respected."

"Where is he?"

"He is busy. If you please, you will check into hotel now and meet with General Antonov for dinner. I will be assisting you both, if okay with you."

Warfield nodded and asked Komeito how he would like to be addressed. "Komeito. Call me Komeito."

Warfield liked the way Komeito handled himself. Confident but unpretentious. He doubted if Komeito was as unimportant as he painted himself.

The hotel's name, East Island Winds, meant nothing to Warfield but its lobby was as grand as any Ritz-Carlton he'd seen. Komeito registered for Warfield and stayed by his side until he was in his room and Komeito was satisfied it met his satisfaction. Some of the staff seemed to know Komeito, and Warfield wondered if he was receiving V.I.P. treatment because of him, or maybe Antonov, or if it was hospitality typical of a fine Japanese hotel. "General Antonov wishes for you to meet him in Izumi Restaurant for dinner at seven this evening. May I say you will join him?"

Komeito said the restaurant was four blocks from the hotel and offered to pick him up but Warfield opted to walk.

After Komeito left, Warfield dressed in shorts and tee-shirt and went for a run, committing landmarks to memory at every turn. He saw no one else running in the streets and soon understood why. Vehicle and pedestrian traffic was dense, presenting an obstacle course. He ran twenty minutes out and turned back.

Warfield recognized Antonov standing in the bar. He hadn't changed much since they met years ago in Russia, although his leathery face reflected the hard Russian winters. Antonov was better than six-foot-three and looked even taller among the Japanese. Retirement agreed with him. Tan, fit looking, full head of graying hair. The Hawaiian shirt he wore under his blazer was anything but that of the stereotypical Russian military leader. Warfield was surprised when the general gathered him into a bear hug, then held him by his shoulders at arms' length and sized him up as he might have looked at a son he hadn't seen for a long time. The Russian would have gone unnoticed in any fancy restaurant in the U.S., his graying hair neatly trimmed and hanging softly at the top of his collar, shuttered eyes barely masking the harder days of the Cold War, neither a smile nor a frown on his face. A man, Warfield thought, who undoubtedly inspired trust and confidence in his leaders and followers from the past.

The crowded restaurant was full of chatter and the clanking of dishes. The warm smells of garlic and other tantalizing kitchen juices filled the air. The general signaled the maitre d', who seated them at a corner table that afforded privacy. Warfield hadn't noticed Komeito at the bar, but he showed up when they were being seated. "You've met Komeito, correct?" Antonov asked.

Antonov leaned back in his chair and asked about Warfield's flight, said he was glad he came and told a couple of Russian jokes. Warfield had not thought of Antonov as lighthearted and felt the jokes were meant to mislead anyone who might be observing. So he jumped in with a couple of stories of his own but allowed Antonov to set the pace. There was no room for two chiefs here and not only did Antonov outrank him, this was his show. In a technical way, rank made no difference. Both men were retired from the military and from different countries, but there was an understood protocol in such circumstances. Warfield liked Antonov and hoped he could trust him. The man made easy eye contact and had a comfortable air about him, and by contacting him as he did about Petrevich, Antonov had followed through on an informal agreement the two men made years earlier.

The first hour was light. Antonov in his gravelly voice told Warfield about his history with Komeito. Komeito had been his interpreter and aide on Antonov's trips to Japan over the years, and he knew how to get around obstacles. Warfield took that to mean Komeito had helpful official contacts and perhaps served as a bodyguard. Warfield explained his unofficial connection with the White House and Antonov wanted to know how it was to work there, and with President Cross, and contrasted it with his own experience in Moscow.

They talked about the changes in their countries' relationship, and the fact they could sit at dinner together. Antonov caught the waiter's eye and they ordered. Warfield and Komeito ordered sushi. Antonov was shy about ordering the raw delicacy but when Warfield cajoled him he threw up his hands, relenting.

Antonov then leaned in toward Warfield. "You are wondering why we are in Tokyo".

Warfield nodded.

"Our friend is here."

"Petrevich?"

"Boris Petrevich. Exactly."

Warfield took a second to digest it. So Petrevich's entry into Iraq was a red herring. That was believable. Petrevich—or his handler—knew Iraq was a destination no one would question and Warfield admonished himself now for not thinking outside the box. But Japan?

"Why?" he asked.

"I cannot answer that question yet," said Antonov. "Perhaps you and I will find out together tonight. But if you want to get involved in this, I must ask for a commitment from you."

"Which is?"

"That you will not involve your government agencies in this matter."

Warfield studied his drink. Without official U.S. involvement he and Antonov would be playing a dangerous game. The ramifications were unfathomable. And the responsibility would be theirs. Warfield had already tried to get the feds involved and failed and then the FBI blew the operation at the border. He hadn't forgotten where that left him. If he went to Cross now, the president would bring in national security advisor Otto Stern and Fullwood and Quinn, and that would make any swift action impossible. He'd be on his own.

He had no better alternative than Antonov's demand, and no choice if he wanted to be involved. He looked at Antonov and signaled his agreement.

Antonov looked him in the eye and nodded almost unnoticeably, sealing the contract. "There is a Russian men's gathering place here in Tokyo—Moscow East, they call it. Private nightclub. Outsiders not welcome—except for some female talent they bring in for entertainment. The regulars play Russian music, dance, gamble, drink, fool around with the women. You know the sort of hangout, Warfield. These men have their good times but it is a rough place located in the back room of a bar having the unlikely name of the Texas Saloon." Antonov's eyes smiled as if to say he'd been there a few times himself."

"On business, of course!"

Antonov nodded. "Mostly to watch for Boris Petrevich. Finally saw him. He saw me too, knows who I am—I saw the look in his eyes. Afterwards, Komeito and me, we followed him but lost him somewhere near the airport."

"How did you know he was in Tokyo?"

"Former KGB general I know. Garovsky. Retired now. I ran into him at a market in Moscow. Went for a drink. Conversation got around to the nukes impounded at various Russian sites and how vulnerable they were, how some of the physics boys had already tapped them. Give you one guess whose name came up in that conversation."

"Boris Petrevich," Warfield said.

"Right. And Garovsky told me he is in Tokyo."

"How long?"

"Year and a half now."

"Why didn't the SVR pursue him?" The SVR was Russia's central intelligence organization that took over most of the functions of the old KGB.

Antonov shook his head. "KGB was in shambles when the USSR dissolved, Colonel. Disorganized, broke, demoralized. Even after it became SVR there was more political infighting, and they had no money to operate with, like everything else in Russia. They couldn't protect the nuclear stockpile. Trying now to contain it but Russia has announced it will go it alone from here on without the help of your country. Nothing is guaranteed. You can thank Putin for that."

"Anything more about Petrevich?"

Antonov frowned. "A former big player at Arzamas-16, our nuclear research site."

Just as Abbas had said. Petrevich had worked at the great secret plant where the Russians sent their best engineering and physics graduates to design and build nuclear weapons. Russia's Los Alamos, and then some.

Antonov went on. "Petrevich is a dangerous man. A renegade all along, but a brilliant one. Our people had to put up with him because of his mind. He came up with one idea after another for getting ahead of you Americans, but when he was no longer a precious commodity to Moscow he received the same inadequate pension the commoners got. When things started picking up in the last few years and most of the scientists were making at least a few rubles, he was left out. He'd been high-handed during the Cold War, but when he was no longer essential the people he had offended didn't forget."

"Why did it take so long for this information to get to you?"

Antonov looked up in apparent wonder. "My contacts didn't know about it. I happened to pick it up in my conversation with my KGB friend. SVR forgot about Petrevich. They had more than they could do with plenty like him who had not yet found a way to do what Petrevich did. When Petrevich left Arzamas-16 he lived close to poverty. No family, no connections. No one noticed he had taken the nuclear materials with him. He knew how to go around the controls they had on the stuff. Covered his tracks very well."

"Is he alone here?"

"I do not think so. Two others may have joined him. I saw one big blond-haired boy with him at the Russian club. He fit the description of one of them. Little rough. Petrevich had trouble keeping him in line that night at Moscow East."

Damn Fullwood, Warfield thought. He could have prevented all of this. After a moment he asked Antonov, "You have a plan?"

The waiter cleared the table and Antonov pulled three cigars out of his pocket. "Cuban," he said. He smiled with his eyes and winked at Warfield as he offered them around.

"It's going to be more difficult now that Petrevich has seen me. Later tonight we may learn more."

"Tonight?"

"The Texas Saloon, entrance to the Moscow East." Antonov said he had talked with a prostitute named Romi, whom he'd met there. She had noticed the big man with blond hair in the Russian club. Saw him later in the Texas Saloon drunk, obnoxious, talking loud. She told Antonov he might learn more from the bartender at the Texas.

"A man of that description is noticed in Japan, you know," Antonov said.

Warfield nodded. "Like us."

Antonov released a cloud of blue smoke above the table.

"Yes, like us."

They looked at Komeito. He was laughing at them.

"What else did this Romi tell you?" Warfield asked Antonov.

"One other minor detail: The blond Russian kid, there in the Texas Saloon, threatened to kill his boss—his Japanese superior—at his bath house."

"She heard him say that?"

Antonov nodded. "The man's brother too. I don't know why the brother. Romi says the blond Russian called him retarded."

Warfield seemed skeptical. "How much credibility do you give the girl?"

Antonov shrugged. "You tell me. She also said he brags about building bombs for a living."

"We're getting warmer."

"And that the Russian and the bartender got into a hot argument."

Warfield blew a stream of cigar smoke. "Maybe vodka talk."

"Could be, yes. Let us ask the bartender what he thinks. Name is Tex."

"I suppose Petrevich will not return to the club," Warfield said.

"Not openly. Too smart for that. After seeing me there he will play it safe."

"You never saw the kid with blond hair again?" Warfield asked.

"No."

"He got a name yet?"

"No, but we will find him. His eyelids are tattooed."

Warfield couldn't keep from smiling. "That should help! We'll just catch him sleeping."

Antonov chuckled. "Snake on each eyelid. They look at each other. All coiled up, tongues leaping out like this." He pointed his index fingers at each other and wiggled them, and darted his tongue in and out. Warfield and Komeito laughed. This big Russian could be a clown.

"Know anything about this bath house?" Warfield asked.

"Romi knew it was called the Tomodachi Sento-yu. Took me there. I even got into the water to see what it was like. When she questioned the old man running the place for me and described Snake-eyes to him, he said he'd seen a man who fit the description outside the bath house a few days earlier looking the place over. Probably him."

Warfield nodded.

"It gets better," Antonov said. "We are talking with the super at the bath house when two men walk in together. Japanese. Something wrong with one of them. May be the retarded brother. Maybe not. Romi thinks the man we saw was a radiation victim."

"Radiation?"

Antonov nodded to Komeito to explain.

Komeito sat forward in his seat. "Romi suspect this because schools in Japan teach about it. When the bombs were dropped on Hiroshima and Nagasaki, radiation affected certain fetuses in the womb. Some very badly," Komeito said.

"And Romi thinks he might be one of them." Warfield said.

Antonov nodded. "After the pair left I got Romi to ask the old superintendent about them. They were brothers who had been coming there since he could remember. He did not know for sure but said the regulars there assumed the slow one was a radiation victim."

"So you think the retarded guy's brother is Snake-eyes' boss, the guy he threatened to nuke?" Warfield asked.

"Long shot, but I can't ignore it. It all fits with what Romi overheard."

Antonov excused himself and got up to go to the restroom and Komeito followed a comfortable distance behind. Some of the diners watched the tall *gaijin* cross the dining room toward an archway that led to the restrooms. Not even foreigners were often as large as Antonov.

Warfield leaned back and mulled Antonov's theory. To say it was a long shot would be the understatement of the day. What were the odds against Antonov and his prostitute running into Snake-eyes' boss and his brother there? But on the other hand, Antonov and Romi were at the right bath house—Romi claimed she overheard Snake-eyes call its name, the Tomodachi Sento, and the old attendant there had noticed someone who could have been Snake-eyes hanging around outside the bath house. And how many pairs of men fitting the description of the brothers could there be, at *any* bath house? Warfield conceded it was worth looking into. Besides, what else did they have to go on?

Warfield looked around at the wall murals and the décor. The Izumi was elegant by any standard. A vase of cut flowers sat in the center of each table and candles provided soft light. Japanese music played unobtrusively in the background. Every table was occupied and the clientele appeared to be well-heeled, belying the fact that Japan's economy had languished in the recent several years.

Warfield glanced at his watch. Antonov and Komeito had been gone for ten or twelve minutes now. When he looked toward the restrooms Komeito was walking toward him, almost running. Antonov was nowhere in sight.

By the time Komeito reached the table it was obvious something was wrong. He leaned over Warfield's shoulder.

"You must follow me, quickly, quickly!" His voice was quiet but demanding. When Warfield started asking questions Komeito was firm. "You must trust me and do as I say now. Do not delay!"

Warfield was stunned. "Where is Antonov?"

Komeito drew a breath through clenched teeth. "Warfield, you must comply this second. You are in danger." Komeito started toward the main entrance through the bar.

Warfield, his mind reeling, followed as Komeito routed his way through the tables, out the front door and to a black limousine sitting at the curb. It was Antonov's and Komeito rattled off instructions to the driver in rapid-fire Japanese as he and Warfield climbed in. Then he turned to Warfield, his eyes wide with terror. "Antonov is dead!"

Warfield was dumbfounded.

As the driver hurried away from the Izumi, Komeito spoke to someone in Japanese on his cell phone, listened for a moment, looked at his watch, and barked another mouthful of words. He lowered the privacy window that separated them from TK the driver and rattled off more Japanese.

There was a time to lead and a time to follow, and Warfield understood his role in the present situation. He was in a strange place, didn't speak the language, didn't know the city. Komeito did, and Warfield, believing Antonov trusted him, was inclined to follow, at least until the immediate crisis was over. But the obvious questions raced through his head all the same. If Antonov was dead, who killed him? Why? Was Komeito involved? Was it possible Warfield was the dupe in some kind of plot? In Warfield's business nothing was taken at face value. But don't jump to conclusions, he reminded himself. Observe, analyze, plan, *then* act. Every crevice of his mind searched for something he could grasp.

Sirens wailed in the distance as TK cut the car lights and pulled to a stop in the darkness of an alley at the back of a building. Warfield recognized the dimly lit logo on the delivery door as the East Island Winds Hotel where he checked in hours earlier. The hotel door opened but light rain had started to fall and the steam rising from the warm pavement made it difficult to make out the human figure silhouetted against the light inside. The car had not even stopped when Komeito jumped out, ran to the person at the door and got back in the car with a luggage bag. He told TK to go.

"If all right with you," Komeito said, "we go to my *gensanchi*. Safe there."

Warfield nodded. As they drove through the worst scramble of streets he could remember, the rain got heavier and the sounds of the sirens faded. TK had put distance between them and the Izumi—and Antonov's dead body. Warfield tried to imagine the scene at the restaurant and knew the police would learn of his involvement with Antonov. Someone at the restaurant would describe the Western-looking man sitting with the victim and the authorities would learn Antonov was connected with Komeito, and Komeito with Warfield: He was with Komeito at the hotel front desk when he checked in. Being caught up in a police investigation would mean his and Komeito's names and photos in the papers with Antonov's, and that could alert Petrevich.

Petrevich of course was Warfield's prime suspect in Antonov's death. Antonov was a threat to him and his project, whatever that was.

Komeito listened to news on the radio and told Warfield they were announcing the discovery of a man found dead in the restroom at the Izumi.

When they reached Komeito's home his face reflected the trauma of the last hour. Warfield wondered whether he himself looked as bad. He now demanded that Komeito explain what happened at the Izumi.

"First, Antonov waited outside the door while I checked out the toilet security. Opened all the stall doors. No one there, so Antonov goes in. I wait outside restroom for him. No one enters during that time. After he has been there too long I go in to check. Throat is cut. Head almost separated from body. Blood everywhere." Komeito shook his head as he recounted the scene.

"*God almighty!*" Warfield whispered.

"Hai! I cannot believe this has happened. It is my responsibility," Komeito said, looking at the floor.

Warfield was puzzled. "But you said you checked it out first. How did the killer get in there, Komeito?"

Komeito shook his head. "Door to supply closet is standing open when I go back in to check on Antonov. Killer must have waited inside closet with door locked, and when someone enters he checks to see if it is Antonov. Closet locked when I go in before Antonov."

"So the killer tracks Antonov there to the Izumi and waits for him in the supply closet, figuring Antonov is going to the john sooner or later. When he does, it's his waterloo."

Komeito shook his head. "Waterloo?"

"Means it was over for Antonov," Warfield said, "but how the hell did the killer exit? You were standing at the door."

"Window to outside. It is cranked open wide when I find Antonov."

Warfield thought for a second. "Why the stop behind the hotel?"

"The man at hotel works for me sometimes. Trustworthy. He went to the general's room and packed his things. That's what he brought to the door." Komeito gestured to the suitcase.

Warfield thought for a minute. "Tell me everything you and Antonov did before I got here."

Komeito spent ten minutes describing when, where and what. When he finished, Warfield asked about Romi.

"*Gaishou*, whore, as Antonov said. Took us to Tomodachi bath house. Antonov and Romi stayed there and Antonov sent me to meet you at airport. After I left you at hotel, I picked up Antonov and Romi at a bar near bath house."

"You know her, Komeito?"

"Only few days, with general."

Warfield opened Antonov's travel bag from the hotel. There were the usual—slacks, shirts, underwear, toiletries—but a couple of things caught his attention. A leather notebook contained a five-by-seven black and white photograph of a man. "What's this say?" Warfield said, referring to Cyrillic characters at the bottom of the photo.

"Ahh, Boris M. Petrevich. So now at least you know what your man looks like."

The other item of interest to Warfield was a note pad from the East Island Winds Hotel. Antonov, or someone, had penciled two sets of numbers on it.

"First one is a phone number," Komeito said.

The other was the number *8.6*, underlined twice. Komeito said it meant nothing to him.

"You will be staying in Tokyo?" Komeito asked, after they finished going through the bag.

Warfield nodded.

"I work with you if you want."

Of course Warfield wanted to keep him around. He wanted to keep an eye on him. No one was eliminated as a suspect in Antonov's death, at least not yet.

"Need a different car. Regular sedan that won't be noticed."

Komeito nodded.

"And check into a hotel. They'll start looking for us. I'll move to a different one under another name."

"Okay."

"You trust TK?"

"Yes. He drove for Antonov. Russian security clearance, like me."

"You got a private voice-mailbox?"

"Yes."

"Anybody else have access to it?"

"No one."

"Change the access code anyway. We'll use that to communicate. No direct calls between us. I'll need the phone number and code." Both men were lost in their own thoughts for a few seconds. Then Warfield said, "Now let's go to the Texas Saloon."

On the drive to the Texas, Warfield went over what he knew, and every detail of what Komeito had said. When they got to the bar TK parked about a block away and Komeito suggested he and TK go in alone, as the Japanese bartender would be less inclined to open up to an outsider.

Warfield vetoed that. He wanted to see the bartender himself. Komeito could go with him.

It was after midnight when they walked in. The lounge was rather deep but relatively narrow from side to side, having a hardwood-covered section of the floor to the left, which adjoined the bar and separated it from an L-shaped carpeted area with tables on the right side and to the rear. It was empty except for a Conway Twitty song pouring from the jukebox and cigarette smoke that lingered in the air. And the bartender.

"Too late. Bar is closed," the bartender said, without looking up from the cocktail glass he was washing.

Warfield had told Komeito to keep an eye on the back of the lounge and watch the door that connected to the Russian hangout in the rear. Warfield walked to the end of the long bar where the bartender was putting things in order to close for the night. *Tex-san* was sewn into the white shirt he was wearing, which was adorned with black pearl snaps instead of buttons. The Western hat he wore was too large for his face and despite his muscular build gave him a cartoon-like appearance.

"I said bar is closed." His English wasn't bad.

"How 'bout a beer? We'll make it quick." Warfield looked the place over. "Last time I was here it was crowded."

"It happens," Tex grunted, setting two drafts on the bar.

A set of steer horns hung above the back bar, and clusters of photos of cowboys in rodeo scenes covered the walls. A life-size cardboard cutout of a Japanese Marlboro Man stood near the end of the bar. The wood floor was finished to a high luster. Half way through his beer, Warfield made reference to a large blond-haired man he saw the last time he was in the place. He tried to sound casual. "Think he said something about an atomic bomb. Surprised anybody jokes about that here."

The bartender put down the glass he was cleaning and looked at Warfield. "Funny, *gaijin*. I don't remember seeing you here that night."

"You were probably busy."

Japanese don't always make direct eye contact but Tex leaned on the bar and lasered into Warfield's eyes. *"Kyomou!* You lie. I remember that night! Four people were here. Me, the drunk Russian, a woman and another man. You *not* here!" He sucked in a breath through yellow teeth and slammed both fists on the bar. "I do not know why you are here. Now leave!"

Warfield finished the last of the beer, pulled a bill out of his wallet and laid it on the bar. "Maybe you wouldn't mind giving me the name of that Russian before I go."

"If you have a message for him, write it down. I do not think it will be very healthy for you, so please do that."

"Note could get lost. I'll wait here for awhile and see if he comes in."

Tex erupted. "You don't understand, gaijin. Bar is closed!" Tex palmed a knife he used behind the bar. When he reached with his free hand to pick up Warfield's money, Warfield grabbed his arm with both hands and jerked him over the bar in a single motion. His hat and the knife flew free when Tex hit the floor. Warfield grabbed the knife and plunged it through the bartender's hand, pinning it to the wood floor. It was over in three seconds.

Tex's scream could have been heard back in the Moscow East where he may have had allies. Komeito stood guard at the connecting door while Warfield sat astraddle of Tex, his hand on his throat, as Tex answered his questions before passing out.

TK was waiting with the engine running. Warfield ordered him to drive to his hotel, and told Komeito Tex's pained revelations as they rode: Snake-eyes—Ivan was his name—comes there on some Saturday nights. Tex heard him say he followed his boss to the Tomodachi Sento one evening and that he threatened to nuke the bath house, as Romi had said. He also said Snake-eyes shoots off his mouth all the time and Tex never knew when he was serious. Then there was something about pizza.

He turned to Komeito. "Know about Guido's Pizza?"

"Hai. Guido's. All over city."

"Snake-eyes orders pizza brought to the Texas Saloon when he's there."

When they got back to the hotel vicinity, by then four hours after Antonov's murder, police cars and other emergency vehicles jammed the streets.

Komeito decided he should go to the police. He was known at the Izumi and it would look suspicious if he dropped out of sight. He could tell the truth and the police would not hold him since they knew and trusted him. He would say Warfield was a guest of Antonov's who remained at the dinner table the entire evening, and left the Izumi at Komeito's insistence in the interest of safety. If the police needed Warfield or him they would be available. Warfield agreed, and told Komeito to leave him a voicemail message when he left the police station.

Police officers and hotel staff stood together at each entrance to the East Island Winds. Warfield was asked to present identification and pulled out his Virginia driver's license and magnetic room key. "What's going on," he asked, showing mild interest.

They told him there had been some sort of disturbance a few blocks away. It would not be a problem at the hotel. Warfield was cleared to enter and another hotel employee waiting nearby escorted him to his room while telling him of a murder at the Izumi Restaurant. He didn't mention that the victim was a guest of the hotel.

Warfield packed his things in three minutes and took the elevator down. Security didn't seem to be concerned with anyone leaving the hotel and he walked out a side door onto the street. He glanced through the glass front and saw a police officer eyeing him. He was talking with the desk clerk and pointed in the direction of the door Warfield had used. Warfield picked up his pace and blended into the crowd.

He caught a cab to the Orient Pacifica Hotel miles away in an old section of the city and checked in under the alias Rolf Geering with a Zurich address. His credentials for the alias would pass if anyone became suspicious and investigated. He let himself into his room, which was a couple of stars below the one he checked out of, and once again reviewed everything leading up to Tokyo, all details of the evening, and what he'd gleaned from Antonov and Komeito. Petrevich had crossed the border into Iraq with bomb-grade uranium, which he already knew. Antonov saw Petrevich at the Russian club and believed two of his technicians from Arzamas-16 had joined him in Tokyo. There was Romi's report of the drunk Russian, Ivan, who goes to the Texas Saloon on Saturday nights and likes Guido's Pizza. Antonov's travel bag contained a photo of Petrevich, a note pad bearing the perplexing notation *8.6* and a telephone number (which he tried, but there was no answer.) There was reason to believe the retarded man at the Tomodachi was a victim of radiation. Probably Petrevich or someone connected with him had slashed Antonov's throat.

Warfield flipped on the TV and found an English-language local newscast. There was a short piece on a murder at the Izumi Restaurant, and interviews with the restaurant manager and their waiter. The victim's name had not been released but there were reports he was a high-ranking Russian official. Police knew little, they said. Reporters mentioned that a Takao Komeito may have been with the victim before he was murdered. Another man, a Westerner, was with him also. Police were looking for both.

Warfield had to avoid being picked up by the police if he was to have any hope of finding Petrevich.

It was four-thirty a.m. when he turned in. There was time for a couple hours of sleep and then he would call the telephone number found in Antonov's bag.

"Good morning. R-E-R-F."

"Mind telling me who I've reached?"

"R-E-R-F, sir," said a cheerful Japanese voice speaking English.

"Which means…?"

"This is the Hiroshima lab of Radiation Effects Research Foundation."

"Who's in charge?"

"Dr. Anderson."

"Connect me to Anderson."

A pause. "Dr. Anderson is not available. I can connect you with—"

"Tell Dr. Anderson Rolf Geering is on the phone?"

"I'm sorry, sir—"

"Say I'm from Washington. Official business."

"Please hold."

Half a minute later John Anderson got on the line and introduced himself. "Namiko tells me you're calling from Washington?"

"Rolf Geering, John. I work out of the White House but I'm in Tokyo this morning. I can use your help."

"About?"

"National security."

Anderson laughed. "Well, that's broad enough, but there are not many secrets here. About anything I can tell you is available to anyone for the asking. That is, when we have the time to pull it up. For you, I'll find the time. But for the record, I suppose the White House will vouch for you."

"Yep. Call there and ask for the president."

"Uh huh. I'll just wait and ask him tonight. He and the First Lady are coming over for dinner."

Warfield laughed.

"What can I do for you?"

"For starters, what is RERF?"

Anderson gave him the Cliff Notes version. The Radiation Effects Research Foundation was funded by Japan and the U.S. to study the effects of radiation released by the atomic bombs the Americans dropped on Hiroshima and Nagasaki. It was staffed by scientists from both countries. There was the Hiroshima center, where Anderson was located, and another in Nagasaki. Anderson managed more than forty scientists and their support staff. "What we do is research—primarily a continuing study of the effects of radiation on people who survived the bombs. Now what is it you need?"

"Not sure. Found your phone number in a dead man's hotel room here in Tokyo."

"*Really!*"

"There's no name with the number."

"So you want to find out if there's any connection between the victim and RERF."

"Right. Name's Antonov. Aleksei Antonov. Russian General, retired. Sound familiar?"

"No, but hold on. I'll get someone to check it out." Anderson put Warfield on hold and returned seconds later.

"Okay, what else?" Anderson asked.

"I spent the evening with Antonov before he was killed. He said something about retardation in fetuses. Radiation related. Tell me about that."

"Yes. The technical version or plain English?"

"Something in the middle."

"The risk posed to a mother's fetus at Hiroshima or Nagasaki was dependent on a couple of things. One is proximity to ground zero; as you would expect, closer equals more exposure and therefore more risk. The other major factor was fetus gestational age at the time of exposure.

"Never thought of this."

"Most people don't."

"You mentioned gestational age."

"Yeah, the age of the fetus when exposure took place. This is the more important factor in determining degree of retardation. Of fifteen-hundred or so cases, exactly twenty-five were classified as severely retarded. It turned out that these were prenatally exposed at developmental age eight weeks through twenty-five weeks."

"So an unborn child in, say, week thirty wasn't affected."

"Generally not much. But it varies."

Warfield thought of the grim events of August 6, 1945, when the first atom bomb was dropped on Hiroshima. He recalled some of the details from reading he'd done at the library in high school. The B-29 bomber famously nicknamed Enola Gay left Tinian Island in the western Pacific carrying the five-ton bomb containing uranium-235. Someone had mockingly named it *Little Boy.* The bomb detonated above the city and generated winds of almost a thousand miles an hour. The ground-level temperature rose to 7,000 degrees Fahrenheit. The heat and the wind pressure destroyed all structures and instantly killed every living being within a third of a mile of ground zero. Still more exposed people died before the end of the year; in all, close to a half-million people in Hiroshima and Nagasaki perished.

Warfield mulled over the grim description. "Tell me more about these kids."

"Most need only a little assistance if at all. But the severely retarded ones, they might have trouble carrying on a simple conversation with another kid, or adding six and four. Probably can't manage basic living skills, you know, like brushing their own teeth. Some are institutionalized or at least have intense home care by someone."

"And there are exactly twenty-five like that?"

"Yep."

Warfield said nothing, thinking.

After a moment, Anderson continued. "I could fax a summary of the official report to you. Only a few pages."

Warfield read the fax number to him off the hotel room key.

"You'll have it in a couple of minutes. Oh, by the way, Namiko tells me there's no record of an Antonov calling or visiting here."

Warfield got off the phone with Anderson and called Komeito's voicemail. Komeito had left a message that he was finished at the police station and would meet Warfield at eleven a.m. That was half an hour off, so Warfield called the hotel telephone operator and asked to have Anderson's fax delivered to his room as soon as it came in.

"Oh, it's printing now, Mr. Geering. I'll send it right up."

A bellman who appeared to be at least eighty showed up with the report and handed it to Warfield along with a *USA Today* newspaper that had been dropped at his door. Warfield threw the paper onto the bed and studied the RERF report. It contained a lot of dense detail and several graphs and charts. Anderson had circled the numbers he'd given Warfield on the phone.

Throughout Warfield's career, war victims of the enemy were statistics, but this report was about babies whose brains were damaged before they were born. *War is hell* was not just a cliché. He had never given the enemy a face, a life, a mother, a soul. Now he was holding a report about real people whose lives were ruined by war, innocent citizens of an aggressor country, which was no longer the enemy at all.

The second page of the report made reference to the radiation exposure dates, August 6 and August 9, 1945, when the bombs were dropped on the two cities. When Warfield finished reading, something nagged at him. He read it again and then ambled over to the window and peered down at the ant-size pedestrians on the street below, weaving in and out on the narrow sidewalks alongside what he decided were the least attractive buildings he'd seen anywhere. The structures in this part of Tokyo, northeast of the Imperial Palace in the central city, were older and more traditional, nothing like the modern buildings around the East Island Winds.

A sign mounted on the corner of the drab brick building across the street lazily gave the time, date and temperature, in slow rotation. Warfield watched as it displayed the time, *10:46;* the date, *8.5* and *27°C,* the temperature; over and over until the time inched up minute after minute and the temperature eventually increased by one degree.

He picked up the *USA Today* and sat down on the bed, still thinking about the information Anderson had sent him. The headline read, "Hiroshima Prepares to Pause." The story described the memorial service to be held tomorrow in that city, with similar silent observances all across Japan. Warfield stared at the words for a second, then jumped up and strode back to the window in two steps. The flashing sign! *The eve of Hiroshima, 8.5. Of course! Antonov's 8.6 notation referred to the day Hiroshima was bombed! August 6, 1945! That would be tomorrow!*

Warfield dialed John Anderson and while waiting for the receptionist to find him wondered if it would be possible to get anyone in Washington to act on the information he could present to them. He decided not. Even with the best of evidence, Fullwood would ignore him out of spite. How about the military establishment? The president? He could try them but out of caution they wouldn't take any action without their own independent intelligence to back them up and there was no time for that. *"My God,*

Warfield, you want to risk an international incident on the basis of speculative information?" they would say, and Warfield wondered whether he wouldn't say the same thing if the roles were reversed.

Warfield had always kept an ace in the hole but this time was different. No one sent him to Japan or even knew he was there, and if he went further he was setting himself up for no-telling-what violations of the law—both American and Japanese. But there was no return now. Something was going down tomorrow, August 6, a few hours away. With Boris Petrevich likely involved, that could not be good news.

Anderson got to the phone.

"Geering again. Need your help. Time's critical."

"Okay, shoot."

"Names of those twenty-five—the severe retardation cases. How fast can you get those to me?"

"Why didn't you ask for something hard, Geering. Those names are hidden away in a computer somewhere else. That's one thing that's kept confidential. They're given case numbers. It might take days to get names, even if I can get approval to do it."

"Can't wait."

"How about dates of birth, other stats? That help?"

Warfield thought for a moment. "Okay, birth dates. When can you have that for all twenty-five?"

"An hour, two at most."

"Good man. Need it in one. I'll call. Don't leave there until you hear from me."

Warfield had missed the meet with Komeito and went to the fallback they'd agreed on. A gray Toyota sedan cruised by and stopped a few feet beyond where he stood on the sidewalk. A window cracked open enough for Warfield to make out Komeito inside. He jumped in and told Komeito to go to the Tomodachi bath house.

Komeito asked what it was about.

"Later. What happened at the police station?"

"Went okay. They asked about the man who left the Izumi with me. I said you were at table all the time. Police know me through my job at the embassy and trust me but they want to talk to you anyway."

"They'll wait."

"Right. Now why Tomodachi?"

"Tomorrow is August sixth." He watched for Komeito's reaction.

Komeito looked at the car ceiling. "Ahhhh! Hiroshima, the 8.6 number."

"Exactly."

"And you think Petrevich is planning something for tomorrow." Komeito's eyes narrowed.

"*Someone* is. Petrevich is helping him carry it out. Too many things converge on the Tomodachi to dismiss them. Antonov's girlfriend told him she heard Snake-eyes Ivan mention a bath house. The bartender said Ivan followed his boss to the Tomodachi. The old man there saw Ivan casing the place. Ivan bragged he was gonna nuke it. Maybe drunk talk, maybe not."

"So you are going for Ivan's boss."

"We find him, we find Ivan. Then Ivan to Petrevich. I'll bet on it."

When TK stopped the car, Warfield never would have guessed it was the Tomodachi he was looking at. The area was run down, but the appearance of the sento was in sharp contrast to its surroundings. A red-tiled roof swept down in flowing lines to an upturned edge, and red ceramic tile that was still attractive despite fissures and faults covered the outside walls and paved the sidewalk. The place was a holdover from the old days when everyone went to a neighborhood bath house. Komeito told Warfield that traditional center-city sentos continued to scrape by on a dwindling clientele of students, the down-and-out, and traditional Japanese. Newer public baths included sauna, mineral baths, Jacuzzis, waterfalls, massage chairs, TV rooms and lounge areas to counter the dwindling flow of customers that resulted from modern in-home baths. Not so the Tomodachi.

Warfield and Komeito stepped inside the entryway to a wooden stand that served as the superintendent's station. The super was away and Warfield followed Komeito into the next room, which separated into men's and women's dressing rooms. Co-ed bathing had phased-out after the war. The moist, warm air caused Warfield's shirt to stick to his back. Komeito showed him inside the men's bath where two or three men soaked. Warfield was struck by a serene mural that covered one wall with a scene of blue sea dotted with islands and pleasure boats. Graceful trees covered the islands and gentle waves brushed a narrow white beach. Warfield made a mental note to return with Fleming when he could savor the Japanese culture.

The grayed superintendent came around the corner and took his place at the stand. Komeito asked him about two men who came there on a regular basis, one caring for the other who might be retarded. The old man shook his head at first and when Komeito persisted he glanced at Warfield and returned to his duties. Warfield got the message and went to the car.

Minutes later Komeito ran to the car and showed Warfield the notes he'd made inside. "The men *are* brothers. Fumio and Jotaro Yoshida. But that's all the old man would say."

Warfield shook his head. It wasn't enough.

Komeito smiled. "But when he went to check the water temperature, I found Yoshida's file. Lucky this place still works out of a shoebox instead of computers like the new ones."

"What else?"

"Birth dates. Fumio Yoshida, 17 September 1940. Jotaro, 3 November 1945."

Warfield considered the new information. Jotaro Yoshida was sounding more like the dependent brother Ivan spoke of. If his big brother turned out to be the boss Ivan talked about, he could lead them to Petrevich. Warfield turned to the notes he made from his conversation with Anderson. Fetuses in developmental weeks eight to twenty-five were the most affected. He went to the calendar in his iPhone and calculated backward from Jotaro's date of birth. Jotaro would have been conceived around 1 February, 1945. Warfield counted forward to week twenty-five. August sixth fell almost three weeks after the twenty-fifth week, outside the window of risk Anderson specified. His best lead yet *but Jotaro didn't fit the formula!*

It was a serious setback for Warfield. Minutes were slipping by and if Yoshida was not his man, he'd blown precious time trying to find him. August sixth drew closer by the minute and, if he was right, something Petrevich was doing was racing toward reality at this moment. If Jotaro's birth date didn't jibe with one of the kids in Anderson's records he would go in another direction. *Oh yeah? What direction is that?* he mumbled to himself as he dialed Anderson.

The receptionist said Anderson was having lunch but had told her to put Geering through to him if he called.

Seconds later, Anderson answered with a mouthful. "Rolf, I got birth dates, city and hospital for all twenty-five. Also got physicians' reports of the kids' conditions at birth for some of them. Listed by case number, no names. Want me to send this to you?"

"Tell me if one of those kids, the severe ones, has a birth date of November 3, 1945."

There was silence while Anderson checked the report. Seconds later he said, "How the hell you know that?"

Warfield's heart started again. "Tell me everything you've got on that one."

Anderson summarized as he ran through the report. "Male. DOB 3 November 45, hospital in Miyoshi—that's not far from Hiroshima. Weighed three pounds two ounces at birth and—"

"Hold on Anderson. That sounds low."

"It is, and according to these records he was born premature, five weeks."

Warfield looked at his notes. If the baby was premature, that meant the date of conception was later than the calculation he'd made by counting backwards from the birth date. By five weeks. *That put him perfectly inside the exposure risk window!*

"What's this guy like now?" Warfield hammered.

"According to his records, this kid—man, I should say—can't talk, can't read, can't write. He can't live alone. Mother died at childbirth, father in the war—kamikaze it says here. Government raised the kid in an orphanage but on 10 April, 1965, his older brother took him away. Would've been…nineteen then. Wish I could tell you more about him, where he lives, for example, but we don't have those files here."

Warfield didn't need to hear more. Anderson was talking about Jotaro Yoshida.

He thanked Anderson and started to hang up.

Anderson said, "Oh, here's something. A birthmark. Strawberry-like flat mark, size of a half-dollar, right side of his neck."

"Okay, John. Gotta go."

"See you at the White House next time I'm in Washington," Anderson said, laughing.

Warfield hung up and looked at Komeito, who had heard both ends of the conversation on the speaker phone. "He's our man," he told Komeito. "We've got to find him. Now. Tonight will be too late."

Komeito smiled again. "Did I tell you I got Yoshida's address?"

CHAPTER 14

THE STREET ADDRESS KOMEITO had for the Yoshidas was five blocks from Tomodachi Sento. TK knew the area, as he did many of the older sections of Tokyo, and five minutes later pointed out the Yoshida home. The modest houses sat close to the street on miniscule plots of ground. August in Tokyo was grueling, the hottest month there, but frequent showers made the landscaping more prominent than the houses it adorned. Cherry blossom and magnolia trees accented the Yoshida yard but, in contrast to others on the street, the Yoshidas' was a bit overgrown, as if it had missed more-recent grooming.

Komeito told TK to cruise by, make the block and come back around. On the second pass there was still no indication anyone was at home and TK pulled to the curb in front of the house and stopped. Warfield and Komeito went to the front door and knocked and when no one responded Warfield tried it and was surprised to find it unlocked. He looked back at TK and circled an index finger in the air, and TK drove off.

Inside, a hard-looking sofa and an étagère displaying a few ornaments and curios lined one wall of the drab front room, and a half-dozen books with faded covers lined the shelves of a corner bookcase. The two men listened for sounds of anyone who might be there.

Tatami mats covered the floor. Tatami mats, usually measuring three feet by six, served as the standard unit of measure used by the Japanese to describe room sizes. Modern Japanese homes often used Western-style flooring but the floors in older houses like Yoshida's were covered with the traditional mats, made of a rush straw core compressed down to a couple of inches thickness, with a soft layer of blond-colored reed on top. This picked up the scarce light that eked through Yoshida's drawn shades and gave even the darkened rooms a soft glow. The black trim that edged the mats showed some wear but the composition was soft and silent to walk on.

They continued to a small room furnished with a small bed, a straight chair, file cabinet, and small desk on which there was a stack of mail. The postmark was recent but the letters were unopened. Komeito began to thumb through them.

"Yoshida's place, all right," Komeito said, reading one of the envelopes. Warfield walked over and examined a grouping of framed photographs on one wall. Some were old and had a glossy black and white finish and others were more recent color prints. More than half of them pictured a Japanese man standing beside an airplane. Some of the planes had military markings and the man in the picture with them was dressed in military uniform.

More recent pictures showed the same man in civilian clothes, dwarfed by civilian aircraft. One of the photos included a second person, a smaller man, and Warfield recognized the house behind the two men as the Yoshida home he'd just entered. A picture in brown tones and dated 1951 hung above the desk. It showed four adult women and three rows of children, the front row sitting and the other two standing behind. Komeito read the Japanese caption at the bottom of the picture and told Warfield it was an orphanage group and that two of the names listed were Fumio Yoshida and Jotaro Yoshida.

Warfield opened the desk drawers and had Komeito read file labels to him. In the last one, there were only two files, labeled *Jotaro* and *Harvest*. Warfield told Komeito to check them out and began to explore the rest of the house. The kitchen was so spotless it might never have been used. The adjoining room was filled with children's toys and stuffed animals and a small TV in the corner. Everything seemed *too* neat, Warfield thought. He moved toward the next room, peeked in and after a second, froze. Someone was asleep on the futon. Warfield watched for several seconds for a sign the sleeper heard him. Tightly drawn shades made the room dark but he could make out a stain on the pillow. He leaned closer and realized it was blood. Dry. He touched the skin. It was cold. He shouted for Komeito.

Warfield moved the dead man's hair around until he found the hole where the bullet entered. He figured it was something as small as a twenty-two or twenty-five caliber since there was not much destruction and the bullet had not exited. There was very little blood and no signs of a struggle. Shot in his sleep. A *gentle* killing, Warfield thought, if there was such a thing.

Komeito jumped back when he saw the body.

Warfield pointed to the strawberry birthmark on the corpse's neck.

"Jotaro!"

"Let's go!" Warfield said.

As Komeito moved away he tripped over something under the edge of the bed. It was the body of a dog, shot in the back of the head.

As they hurried to leave, Komeito ran back to the bedroom to grab the files. He'd started reading them when Warfield called him to Jotaro's room and had seen enough to think they were relevant. They slipped their shoes on, and as Warfield started to open the door someone knocked.

They stood dead still as Warfield took a second to study the options. After a moment he motioned Komeito to go in front of him. "You're a real estate agent. Yoshida is selling his house and sent you here to look it over. Introduce me as a prospective buyer if you have to," he whispered.

Komeito opened the door and the woman bowed as she and Komeito exchanged greetings. They spoke for a moment and the woman bowed again and left. Warfield stayed out of sight.

TK returned after the woman left and, as they drove off, Komeito told Warfield the woman lived next door and was checking on things after seeing them enter the house. "Mrs. Tanaka will be a problem," he told Warfield.

Warfield acknowledged Komeito's concern and told him to direct TK to the Narita Airport area. Antonov had said he and Komeito followed Petrevich there before they lost him, and most of the photos on Yoshida's wall included planes. Petrevich and Fumio Yoshida were linked by Ivan and they would be near an airport. Narita was a good place to start.

Buildings old and new, large and small lined the route to the Narita area. Thirty-million inhabitants of what was considered greater Tokyo had to be *somewhere* and Warfield thought most of them were on the roads. The traffic was like the Beltway around Washington at rush hour on a bad day, but here you didn't get beyond it. Only the uninformed tourist would attempt to drive in this city.

After riding in silence for half an hour, Komeito said, "Getting worried, Warfield."

Warfield was jarred out of his thoughts. *"What?"*

"The murders. Antonov, now Jotaro. We near both. If Mrs. Tanaka goes in the Yoshida house and sees Jotaro dead—"

Warfield cut him off. "Komeito, there's nothing we can do about that. And tell TK to move it. It's not a funeral cortege."

Warfield continued combing his mind for answers. Minutes later he asked Komeito again the name of the pizza place Snake-eyes liked so much."

"Guido's. Guido's Pizza. Biggest pizza company in city."

"The lead we need is at the place he orders those Pizzas from."

Komeito nodded.

"How many of those Guido's here?"

"In Tokyo? Many stores." Komeito googled Guido's on his phone and shook his head. "Hundreds!"

Komeito located all the Guido's in the airport area on his phone as TK hurried toward Narita. Komeito called three of them and although none delivered to the airport area, an employee at the third call gave Komeito the addresses and phone numbers for several that may.

Twenty minutes later Komeito went into the first of them but no one there knew of a Russian customer. It was when they reached the third that their luck improved. As soon as Komeito mentioned the word *Russian*, Norio, the manager, smiled big. "Ivan! Hai! Borscht man. Calls us often. He is regular customer. Delivery boys like him. He jokes around with them. They are always talking about Ivan."

"Delivery address, please."

Norio's smile disappeared. "Privacy, you know."

Komeito pulled a laminated card from his wallet that identified him as an employee at the Russian embassy and handed it to Norio. The manager looked at it and frowned.

"Ivan in trouble?"

"Has to sign some official papers from the embassy. Tried mailing them but we must be using an incorrect address. Papers were returned. He'll be in trouble if I don't find him in time. May be sent back to Russia."

Norio opened the computer database. "It will be no problem in this circumstance. The computer will sort the customers by their type of pizza," Norio said. "You would get a thousand names if I put in cheese, but Ivan likes a special kind of pizza we make for him." He punched several keys on the keyboard and typed in *borscht*. One listing showed up on the screen. It was Ivan.

"That is Ivan's usual order. Borscht. And this is the information we have for him."

"Borscht?" Komeito repeated, frowning.

"Not really borscht. Ivan requested borscht, so we started keeping beets here. We slice the beets and bake them on top of regular sausage pizza." Norio shrugged. "Ivan is happy with that."

Komeito looked at the address on the computer screen. It was nothing more than a numbered aircraft hangar. "You deliver to hangar?" Komeito asked.

"Hai."

"Ever deliver to his home at night?"

"That's it. Can you believe it? He lives in that hangar—Hangar 23, it says here. Three men live there, the boys tell me. All Russians."

Komeito ran to the car to tell Warfield what he'd learned. While they were talking someone tapped on the car window. It was Norio and a younger man with the name *Aoki* on his Guido's shirt. Komeito lowered the window.

Norio bowed. "Excuse please. Aoki came to work his shift. Knows Ivan, delivers to him all the time. Can show you way to hangar." Aoki looked about twenty. He was above average height with jet-black hair cut short. He had a sincere smile.

"Hi," Aoki said in English.

Warfield asked what he knew about the hangar.

"Hangar 23? Well, that big plane in there, they work on it all the time. Mainly up under the open belly of it, you know, in the middle. They're working on something else at the other end of the building but I take the pizza right to a little office area and don't go down there. Think they're through with what they were doing. Last time I went there the plane was all back in one piece again."

"When were you there last?"

"Two or three days ago."

Komeito thanked Aoki and the manager and said they might need more information later.

Warfield and Komeito strategized for a minute at the car and went back into the pizza place to talk with Norio and Aoki again. Warfield asked for their help.

"I thought Ivan was not in trouble," Norio reminded Komeito.

"He may have some information that will help in an investigation." Komeito told Norio Warfield was from the FBI in Washington, cooperating with the Japanese government in an undercover investigation.

Norio looked at Aoki. They nodded to each other and then to Komeito and Warfield.

"Good," Warfield said. "We need to go to the hangar. Is it necessary to use the main airport entrance?"

"No. There is an entrance for service vehicles," Aoki said. The guards there know the Guido's car."

"Can you draw us a route to the hangar and a diagram of the inside?" Warfield asked.

Aoki nodded. "I will drive you there," he said, looking to Norio for approval.

Warfield shook his head.

"You can't get past the gate guards," Aoki said. "Even with the car, they will look for familiar faces. They don't ask for my I.D. any more but they stop the car and look inside. And Ivan, he knows me. He will freak if you walk in."

Warfield had no intention of walking in like that, but Aoki had a point. "We'll do it then. Komeito will go into the hangar with you to deliver the pizza and get the lay of everything. Say he's your boss, riding with you today. I'll stay out of sight in the car until you come out. Komeito and I will take it from there."

Aoki and Norio nodded.

Warfield said, "But you need a reason to go there. Ivan will wonder why you are there if he hasn't placed an order."

"I surprised him one time," Aoki said.

Komeito went to the car and gave TK instructions to follow them to the guard gate. He was to park there and wait. When Komeito got to the delivery car, Norio handed him a green and white Guido's Pizza shirt and hat to wear and two boxes of pizza. To save time, Norio had added beets to a sausage pizza already in the oven. Aoki got into the front with him and Warfield crawled into the back seat.

When they were close to the gate Warfield shrunk himself into the rear floor space and Komeito hid him with extra uniform shirts he found in the car.

When they reached the gate Aoki handed the guard a box of pizza. "Making me fat, Aoki," he said, patting his stomach. When the guard peered in at Komeito, Aoki said Komeito was new and the guard waved them through.

Hangar 23 was at the end of a service road in a remote corner of Narita about a mile from the service gate they'd used. Sprigs of grass that poked up through cracks in the pavement testified to the low volume of traffic in the area and Warfield saw no other buildings close enough to worry about. The only other cars he saw were on an expressway in the distance. As they approached the mammoth hangar Warfield ducked down behind the seat again.

The road went to the left just before the beginning of the tarmac and ran alongside a dense hedge that lined the outside hangar wall. Aoki slowed and followed the road to the back corner of the building. "I always park around the corner here," he said. A moment later they came into view of the parking area and Aoki stopped in the middle of the road.

"What's wrong?" Komeito asked.

"That car," he said, pointing. "Ivan said I should never stop if a government car is here." It was a dark blue sedan with an official-looking insignia on the door. Komeito told Warfield the insignia was Ministry of Transport.

"What happens if you do?"

"Not much, probably. He said his boss doesn't like outsiders coming here."

"What do you think, Warfield?"

"You two go in as planned," he said from the floor. "We'll talk when you come out."

Aoki drove on to the parking area and turned off the engine. Warfield reminded Komeito to memorize the layout inside.

The whine and whoosh of jet engines in the distance were the only sounds after they left the car. Warfield thought about the time, and remembered his slow-motion powerlessness as a kid when trying to run in a pool or the ocean. August sixth was approaching faster than he could get everything out of the way.

Aoki and Komeito walked to the personnel entrance beside the huge hangar door and Aoki froze in his tracks. *"Look!"* he shouted. "It's gone! The big plane is gone!" Aoki's voice echoed through the cavernous hangar. "The office over there, that's where I take the pizza," he said, nodding toward a chain-link enclosure at the center of the left wall. They ran across the floor in that direction. No one was in sight.

"What's going on here?" Aoki mumbled, when they reached the office area. The building was almost empty. Two computers sitting on a desk in the center of the area had been smashed and the hammer that did the damage lay nearby on the floor. Aoki stood with his hands on his hips and looked around. "That canvas there," he said, pointing to a big roll of tent cloth outside the office area, "it used to hang on the fence. Ivan said it was there to make the office more private." Aoki kicked at two old Guido's Pizza boxes lying on the floor next to an over-full trash can. "Everything's gone. The plane. Ivan, the other two. The big thing they were working on at the other end. What has happened?"

Komeito ran back to the car. "Warfield! There is no one inside."

As Warfield, Komeito and Aoki inspected the hangar together, Aoki pointed out the small enclosed area the Russians used as their living quarters and told them other details he knew from previous visits. In contrast to the disheveled office, the rest of the hangar—tools, machines, a supply of what appeared to be aircraft parts and the Russians' living quarters—was okay. Warfield finished looking around the makeshift dormitory room and was making a second pass through the office area when he spotted the edge of a notebook peeking out from beneath some papers on the cluttered desk. He flipped it open and saw the Cyrillic characters of the Russian language. He called to Komeito.

Komeito scanned the pages. "Boris Petrevich," he yelled. "This is Petrevich's notebook!" When he got to the third page, he shouted, "and Yoshida's listed here, his phone number, too!"

"Got 'im!" Warfield said, his eyes narrowing. "Let's get out of here!" He pocketed the notebook and hurried toward the car. Warfield told Aoki to take them back to the gate where TK was waiting. Aoki was confused by it all, but complied.

En route they saw several police cars, lights flashing, near the gate. It was hard to make out in the distance but it looked like they had surrounded a gray car. "Think it's TK," Komeito said.

"Find another way out of here but don't attract any attention!" Warfield ordered.

Seconds later they reached the road that led back to the service gate where they entered but Aoki turned left, away from the gate, and followed the access road around a hangar where the tarmac resumed, and to another gate half a mile from the first one but on the same street. There were no police cars. Warfield hid himself on the floor again. The security guard remained sitting in the kiosk and waved Aoki through.

Aoki turned left onto the street, away from the first gate. Warfield told him to drive to the nearest hotel.

Several blocks later Aoki wheeled into a high-rise Holiday Inn and stopped. Warfield put his hand on Aoki's shoulder and told him not to worry. "You've done nothing wrong."

As Warfield jumped out and ran toward the hotel, Aoki turned to Komeito for reassurance.

"What you have done is for good," Komeito said. "The police don't know the good actors from the bad ones in this case yet, but they will. And you will understand very soon also."

Komeito caught up with Warfield as he entered a side door of the hotel. Warfield told Komeito to call the number in Petrevich's notebook for Yoshida. "See what you can find out about him." Warfield looked at his watch. It was exactly six p.m. Saturday evening in Tokyo. In Washington, five o'clock Saturday morning, where it was already August sixth!

Komeito knew chances were slim anyone would answer if the number in Petrevich's notebook was to Yoshida's office, even though Saturday was a workday for many Japanese. The number rang for a long time and he was about to hang up when a woman answered in Japanese. "Vice-Minister's Office!" She was abrupt, and sounded angry.

"This Fumio Yoshida's number?"

"You know it is Vice-Minister Yoshida's office! And I know you are another reporter calling about his brother. Please do not call back. Good-bye."

So they had found the body. "No, wait! This is police."

"Police! Again?"

"Yes. I am Captain Iwamoto," Komeito said. "In charge of the investigation into Jotaro Yoshida's death. Any of my officers still there?"

"Two *were* here. That is why I am still here. They left a minute ago."

"We're having radio problems. Haven't talked with them since they left you. Mind repeating what you told them?"

"I told them the vice-minister cannot be reached at this time. They were rude, so I did *not* tell them that he is on a training flight. They asked questions that were none of their business."

It was an opportunity made for the moment and Komeito seized it. "Please tell me your name, *keishu.*"

"Mrs. Nakamura." Being called a lady seemed to calm her down.

"I am very sorry for their unforgivable rudeness, Mrs. Nakamura. I will speak with them, and I will see to it they apologize to you."

"You are a *jentoruman.* How can I help you?"

"Did you say the vice-minister is on a training flight?"

"Mr. Yoshida is responsible for pilot training standards and certification. Indirectly, I mean. He is a pilot and flies often, but his responsibilities include much more than that now."

"What is he flying?"

"Not sure. A Ministry plane."

"Why can't he be reached by radio?"

"We're trying now. For some reason he isn't responding. Couldn't have gone at a worse time. We are very upset about his brother. Have you found the two men who did it?"

She knew it was two men, so it had to be Mrs. Tanaka, the old lady next door to the Yoshida's, who called the police. He knew she would. "No, but we will get to the bottom of it soon."

"Minister Yoshida's brother was affected. The bomb, you know. He cared for him all these years. I feel very sorry for both of them," she said.

Komeito gave it a respectful moment before going on. She was close to the edge. "You didn't say where he is flying to on this training flight."

"Oh, to Los Angeles, in America. You can check with air traffic control for details. He always files a flight plan. Vice-Minister Yoshida is very particular about things like that."

"I was wondering if you would call air traffic control and ask for his flight plan, Mrs. Nakamura. You must know some people over there."

"Sure, Captain. We work with them all the time."

"I'll call you back. Five minutes long enough?"

"I think so."

"Oh…, Mrs. Nakamura, please do not discuss this matter with anyone but me for the time being. If anyone asks, you should say you have spoken with several police officers about it. It will not be necessary to mention our conversation."

She was silent for a moment. "You are keeping secrets from your officers?"

"Uh, not at all. It's just that you would have no way of knowing who you are speaking with on the phone. It could be the reporters falsely identifying themselves in order to get information from you."

"Oh, yes, of course. Glad you reminded me."

When Komeito called Mrs. Nakamura back she had all the flight plan details. He wrote them down and thanked her.

Komeito told Warfield everything Mrs. Nakamura had told him about Yoshida. His position at the Ministry of Transport, her job as his assistant. "He's in the air now and guess where he's going."

The hair on Warfield's arms stood on end when Komeito told him.

Komeito handed him the notes he'd made when talking with Mrs. Nakamura, including the flight plan. "He expects to be there at five a.m. Los Angeles time. Logged it as a training flight."

Warfield did the time conversion. *Yoshida's Los Angeles ETA was less than three hours away.* He barked instructions to Komeito to use his connections in Tokyo to get the Japanese authorities to Hangar 23 to look for nuclear traces. *"Now, Komeito!"*

Warfield had to call Cross but needed more information if he was going to convince him to act. He remembered the file Komeito checked at Yoshida's house and asked him about it. The Jotaro file.

Komeito thought for a moment. "Uh-oh. Left in Aoki's car."

"Did you read it, Komeito?"

"First page. Looks like a diary."

The file might give Warfield what he needed to sell Cross, but time was short. "Call Guido's and speak with Norio. Get him to bring it here ASAP."

"ASAP?"

"Means *now*, Komeito. In a pizza box to Rolf Geering at the concierge desk."

Warfield stood out of view and watched as Aoki dropped off the box less than ten minutes later. He'd told the concierge to expect it and gave her cash for the driver. She was all smiles when Warfield retrieved the box. He stuffed the Guido's delivery form into his pocket and hurried back to the telephone lobby, where Komeito was trying to reach the hazmat authorities, and took out the Jotaro file. "Translate this, Komeito, quickly!"

Warfield listened impatiently as Komeito read excerpts aloud, yet he needed every nuance of Yoshida's thoughts if he was going to move Cross. Fumio Yoshida had started the file diary-style when he was nine, recording his musings about his family's devastation. It included his earliest awareness something was wrong with Jotaro and identified the beginnings of Fumio's hatred for the Americans who caused it.

His desire to get revenge showed up when he was twelve, and he had thought out the framework for a plan before he was twenty. He drove the first stake in the ground by taking a job with the Ministry of Transport. Entry after entry in the diary of RERF's periodic evaluations of Jotaro's progress, or lack thereof, revealed Fumio's growing despair. His frustration and hatred grew unchecked.

Komeito read Yoshida's last entry, dated two years ago: "The Emperor in surrender (to the Americans at the end of World War II) did not speak for Fumio and Jotaro Yoshida, to whom the only acceptable alternative to victory is a fight to death. The instruments are now in place to achieve a modicum of justice for Jotaro and for other Japanese lives destroyed by the Americans."

Warfield was certain what was coming down and knew it was time to contact the president. But Cross hadn't seen what he had seen, been where he'd been these last few days and wouldn't buy it without a fight. The average wild-eyed conspiracy theorist would have more convincing evidence about his latest wacko extrapolation than Warfield had about Yoshida, and how many of those kooks even got beyond the three a.m. radio shows? To act on Warfield's combination of circumstances and facts, the president would have to immediately commit to a course of action that had serious or even irreversible consequences no matter whether Warfield was right or wrong.

If Warfield had a best, it was during a crisis. All his systems responded well. His pulse was steady, his thoughts clear. He had an ability to convince others with logic and reason. All these would be on the line now as he attempted to convince the President of the United States to take action on this. Time was again the enemy. Warfield went into a phone cubicle in the lobby wing and closed the door, which had a small rectangular slit for a window. At least there was privacy. He sat down and dialed the access number Cross gave him. It seemed so long ago.

"State your name and I.D. code," a live voice said seconds later.

"Cameron Warfield," he said, and gave him the code Cross had written for him.

The voice told Warfield to hold and as he waited he thought for the first time how he would put it to Cross. *That there was a madman in the air who was going to drop a nuclear bomb on the United States in two hours and so many minutes? How many disaster movies had done that? But he had to somehow convince the president this was real, that a Japanese madman had arranged for nukes and for someone to make them into a deliverable atomic bomb—remember Habur, Mr. President?—and that this man who was crazed by the bitter fruits of World War II was at this moment flying that bomb over the Pacific toward Los Angeles. He was aiming for revenge, and would get it on this, the day that would be the most symbolic for him: The anniversary of the first wartime nuke; the day Japan had realized raw defeat and humiliation at the hand of the United States. The day Jotaro's, their mother's and his fates were sealed. Oh, don't discount the role of the Russian, Petrevich; he's the crucial tool of the mastermind behind the plan and maybe it couldn't have been done without him, but the day would go to the creator of it all who had suffered in mind and body and soul every day, every minute, for more than half a century. Who had neither forgiven nor forgotten nor moved beyond. Who self-generated the fuel necessary for hate to survive for so long. Who allowed himself to become a perpetual victim until he was no less evil than the evil he imagined had destroyed his life.*

The voice was back on the line. "Connecting you with the president, Mr. Warfield."

A click, then, "Cam! Is that you?"

"Sorry to bother you, Mr. Pr—"

"Forget that! Where th' hell are you, anyway?" The president's voice was clear and alert and gave no hint he had just been awakened.

"Tokyo. And as you can imagine, it's an emergency."

"I should hope so. Haven't had a good crisis in hours."

"Wish I could say you'll like this one." Warfield took a breath, searching his brain for the best place to begin. "Look, sir, this call is either too early or it's too late. I take responsibility for that. But I'm holding a short fuse. Some of what I'm going tell you is speculation at this point, but it will prove out. I may have that proof at any moment."

"You have my attention. Talk to me!"

"It relates to the Turkey-Iraq border incident that got me in trouble with Fullwood."

"That Habur border gate, yeah."

"Few days ago in Washington I received a message from an army general I know in Russia from Soviet days. He retired after the Soviet breakup and started working to keep nuke materials out of the wrong hands."

"What's his name?"

Cross, as the former CIA director, could have known of him. "Aleksei Antonov."

"Nope."

"Well, Antonov notified me he'd located the Russian I tracked from Russia and then lost at Habur, and invited me to meet him in Tokyo."

"You didn't notify anyone here?"

"I've second-guessed myself about that a few times in the last few days. But I'm a Washington outsider now, certainly with Fullwood and the FBI. And on short notice, this wouldn't have been strong enough to arouse the NSC's attention. Not until now, at least."

"So where does it stand now that you've met this General Antonov?"

Warfield checked his watch. Precious seconds Cross would need later were slipping away but he was bringing the commander-in-chief up to date as fast as possible.

"The transfer of the uranium into Iraq was a red herring. The Russian smuggler, Petrevich, wanted us to think his destination was Iraq or somewhere in the Middle East. I fell for it, but he's here in Tokyo, or was. I will know soon whether the uranium was with him. I'm betting it was."

"*Was*, you say?"

"Yes, *was*. Let me give you the fast version. Time is critical and—"

"Go as fast as you want but I'm going to ask questions and I expect answers." Cross was snappish.

"Okay, ask them." Warfield's impatience bled through as well.

"How did Antonov know the Russian was in Japan?"

"Former KGB agent tipped him, said they suspected him before it happened but didn't pursue it, I think because of the turmoil they were in after the Cold War."

"Go on."

"So I met Antonov here in Tokyo two nights ago. He said Russia acknowledged a little late that uranium was missing from Arzamas-16, where Petrevich worked."

"*Arzamas-16!*" Cross was knowledgeable about the old Soviet nuclear center. "How much was missing?"

"More than we used on Hiroshima."

"You're certain Petrevich is in Tokyo?"

"General Antonov saw him at a Russian hangout here in Tokyo. And Petrevich saw Antonov. That's when Antonov contacted me. He knew from our history together that I was interested in this case."

"So is Antovov getting Russia involved?"

"Antonov's dead."

"*What?*"

"Somebody killed him in the john at the restaurant where I met him that night."

Cross took a second to respond. "What's your take on that?"

"Petrevich. He had reason to be worried about Antonov."

"And you got input from Antonov before he died?"

Warfield glanced at his watch and wished he had called Cross earlier. "Not enough. Antonov told me of this hunch he had, based on an observation he'd made. It seemed off the wall to me but I followed it up and that brings me to the present. I can't prove this yet, but I know it's fact: There's a madman here, a Japanese, who paid to get Petrevich and the uranium to Japan. Then Petrevich and two technicians he imported from Russia built a nuclear bomb and modified a 747 to deliver it."

"*Oh my God! Do you hear what you're saying, Cam?*"

"This lunatic filed a flight plan to L.A. and he's in the air *right now* flying a 747 with this bomb on board. Look, sir, I just left the hangar at Narita where the work was done. The 747 that was there is gone. Yoshida's office says he's on a training flight and everything looks routine to them, but I know it's not. The last bit of evidence I need is confirmation from a hazmat squad that there's radioactivity in the hangar where the modification of the 747 took place. They should be at the hangar by now. But you can't afford to wait another minute to at least put something in gear, Mr. President."

Cross groaned.

Warfield's tone and volume had risen to a level not acceptable in conversation with the President of the United States and he tried to rein it in. "With all respect, sir, this man Yoshida's the number two man at the Japanese Ministry of Transport. He's a pilot. He has access to airplanes and airport facilities. Set up shop in a hangar here at Narita. This 747's been undergoing modification in the hangar for a long time but it's gone now. That's the plane Yoshida is flying. He told his office he's on a training flight. That's what I would say if I'm doing what I think Yoshida's doing."

"How do you know the plane was undergoing modification?"

"There's this pizza boy. He's made regular deliveries to the Russians at the hangar for a while. He went there with me today."

Cross was silent for a second. "You're telling me all of this on the basis of some pizza boy's story, Cam?"

Warfield's frustration edged through again.

"*Hell* no. He's one part of the story, sir. Look, this Yoshida, he's a triple victim of Hiroshima. Father was a kamikaze pilot, mother died from radiation. Brother's retarded because of the bomb and Yoshida sacrificed his own life to take care of him all these years. Today I went to Yoshida's house and found the brother whose brain was fried at Hiroshima. He's got a fresh bullet hole in his head. I'm sure his older brother, our man Yoshida, killed him, knowing he's not going to be there to take care of him any more. And that's because he's going to kill himself today along with half of Los Angeles. It's revenge he's after, for what he sees as the price his family paid because of the United States. And you know today is August sixth."

Out of frustration, Warfield jerked the phone booth door tighter. He hoped Cross's silence meant he was yielding. "Mr. President, there's not time to convey to you everything that has gone into my thinking but I'm saying you don't have a choice here. You have *got* to act. I wish I'd called you sooner but I can't redo that now. I'll bet my life I'm right."

Cross was silent for a long moment. "When's he due in L.A., Cam?"

"Five a.m. L.A. time. Two hours from right now."

"Give me the details."

Warfield read off the 747's identification and the other information on the flight plan.

"Listen, I'm going to wake up some people but I can't do more until you tell me that hangar is radioactive. Anything else you can confirm will help. I may need some official word from Tokyo, as well. I'll be standing by."

After they hung up, Warfield sat in the phone booth for a moment and thought of the steps Cross would take. It was five-fifty-seven a.m. in Washington and he'd wake up his national security team. Plantar Scrubb chaired the Joint Chiefs of Staff at the Pentagon. He'd have the military on alert in less than half an hour. Air Force F-15s would patrol the waters off the West Coast. Yoshida's estimated time of arrival in Los Angeles would be confirmed. Otto Stern would notify State, Defense and others. Someone would call Paula in to take care of admin details. There was no time to lose. Yoshida's ETA in Los Angeles was two hours and three minutes away. Sooner than that: They couldn't wait until he was over the city to act.

Warfield understood the tight spot he'd put the president in. The national security apparatus and the military get a little out of sorts when they're thrown a juicy bone and then denied the pleasure of gnawing on it, but that wasn't the end of the world. Taking action on a false alarm based on a last-minute phone call from a retired army colonel playing unauthorized spy games in Tokyo would provide a lot of fodder to the press and Cross's political opponents; that was a little more serious. There was zero chance it wouldn't hit the newspapers and talk shows and trigger endless congressional investigations. Cross and his administration would be painted as inept, paranoid and trigger happy. But the worst scenario would be to fail to act in time on what turned out to be an actual threat that materialized into disaster. Those consequences were too horrible to imagine.

Komeito was on the phone in the booth across from Warfield with the door open. He caught Warfield's eye and gave him a thumbs down, meaning he hadn't reached the right authorities to check the hangar for radiation. Warfield couldn't believe the delay. As he started to emerge from his booth he noticed four or five police officers walking toward the phones from the hotel entrance. Other officers fanned out across the main lobby.

Warfield crumpled to the phone booth floor. He couldn't tell what was going on but he heard the officers yelling right outside his booth and Komeito trying to explain himself in Japanese. The police sounded demanding. Soon all the voices faded into the background. Warfield remained still. Less than a minute later several police officers returned and Warfield heard other phone booth doors opening and slamming shut. He didn't breathe. There were ten or so of the cubicles but they checked only a few and left again. Had they missed him? Did they leave this time?

He lay still for a full minute before rising to the small window to look out. No one was in sight, not even Komeito. Warfield weighed his options for a moment, which were of course limited by his inability to speak Japanese. He pulled out the Guido's receipt he'd stuffed into his pocket when Aoki delivered Yoshida's diary, dialed Guido's number and asked for Aoki. He was prepared to try his luck with Norio if Aoki wasn't there but that wasn't necessary. Aoki answered.

"It's Warfield, the American. I need your help. Very important. You willing?"

"Hai! Willing."

"Can you clear it with Norio, be away for a while?"

"Yes, no problem."

"Come to the Holiday Inn in the delivery car. I'll watch for you. Make it quick!"

CHAPTER 15

PLANTAR SCRUBB HAD SEEN his share of crises in the three years since he'd become chairman of the Joint Chiefs of Staff, and he always jotted a code in his daily journal when they first hit his desk. A letter *C* with a circle around it when he thought it would prove to be an actual crisis, and a *T* when he smelled political overreaction. While listening to the president explain this particular incident, Scrubb sketched the outline of a block letter T in the journal and shaded it in, which meant he expected he'd be able to keep his regular tee time at his golf club this afternoon. The last time he tallied the Cs and Ts he was batting .710, but that was just a game he played. He didn't make Joint Chiefs chairman by pre-judging the smoke signals.

It took him twenty minutes after Cross called to get from his home at Fort McNair to the Pentagon, and he used the time in the car to get things rolling as his driver zipped through Washington streets. By the time he got to his office he had spoken with Cross again and also received confirmation of this supposed madman's flight plan. Cross had that correct but it meant nothing. Every airliner in the sky filed a flight plan. And he couldn't just send fighters out and shoot this 747 out of the sky. At this point it was nothing more sinister than an official of Japan's civilian air transportation system making a training flight from Tokyo to Los Angeles. Talk about an international incident! Shoot down a plane like that even if there were no passengers on board and it's open season on every U.S. passenger plane flying over foreign lands. And it would test the U.S. relationship with Japan. Scrubb was going to use his head for awhile before he used his trigger finger.

A Cross aide called everyone and briefed them before they got to the White House. He also sent for Paula Newnan to keep track of things, and the others summoned their own aides. When everyone arrived in the clothes they found handy it looked more like a gathering for a camping trip than a group called together by the president of the United States to handle an international crisis.

Secretary of State Hollis Hill said he had someone trying to reach the Japanese and U.S. ambassadors, but as it was Saturday night in Tokyo response could be slow. "Don't know who we'll get. Maybe somebody at Ministry of Transport. If this Yoshida's a vice-minister, and it's him flying that 747, they can tell us *something*. I'm not convinced yet there's a crisis here. What's interesting about this, Mr. President, is that you got this call yourself. How did that happen?"

Cross was hesitant to answer. "Cam Warfield called me. He's been on it in Tokyo."

Earl Fullwood bolted out of his chair. *"Warfield?* Mr. Pres'dent, you have got to be kiddin'! Haven't you had enough of him? He's already screwed up FBI operations at least once. I don't put a dime's worth of credibility in anything he says. Warfield's nothin' but a glory-seeker, wants to make a name for himself. He's a has-been, and he knows it. And Senator Abercrombie's committee? You remember that! They shut down Warfield's Lone Elm operation after he interfered with us at the border crossin' from Turkey into Iraq. And since then, I think he's been hitting the bottle a little too much."

Cross looked away for a second, questioning his judgment in requesting Fullwood's presence. "Earl, I'm not interested in your views on Warfield. If you've got anything constructive to add, let's hear it."

YOSHIDA'S ESTIMATED TIME OF ARRIVAL MINUS NINETY-ONE MINUTES

Komeito was still missing. When Aoki got to the hotel Warfield hopped in and told him to drive to the Ministry of Transport building. Aoki had delivered pizza there and knew where it was, five minutes from the hotel. Warfield pulled out the notes Komeito had scribbled when he talked with Yoshida's office and read Mrs. Nakamura's name to Aoki. Luckily, Aoki vaguely remembered delivering pizza to her up in the Bureau of Civil Aviation offices. The main entrance to the building was locked but a security guard stood inside the atrium-like lobby. He smiled recognition of Aoki, carrying a large pizza box, and opened the door. They chatted for a moment before the guard asked Aoki who had ordered pizza so late on a Saturday.

"Mrs. Nakamura."

The guard didn't call her for confirmation and told Aoki to proceed. Warfield had slipped a Guido's shirt over his own and the guard looked him over as he followed Aoki but said nothing. Now Warfield hoped Nakamura was still in her office. She would at least know how to reach top MOT officials.

Mrs. Nakamura was sitting at her desk when Aoki and Warfield rushed in, startling her. As Warfield had instructed, Aoki now told her there was an extreme emergency and Yoshida's life was in danger, and that Warfield, an American working with Japanese officials, must speak with someone at the top of M.O.T. this moment. There was not time to go through proper channels. Warfield was impressed with Aoki's performance.

Nakamura was small and wiry. Her strong voice signaled self-confidence but she was hesitant now. She didn't know Aoki that well and this was too much to comprehend on top of the day she'd already been through. But Aoki convinced her that failure to comply could result in disaster. She said Minister of Transport Saito was working late in his office and took them there.

Saito spoke English well enough. He was volatile about the invasion of his office, by a pizza boy and a gaijin no less, and was further incensed by the accusation that one of his senior executives hatched such an impossible plot as Warfield painted. He told Warfield the activity in Hangar 23 was in preparation for a new airline coming to Narita and threatened to call security to have the men removed from his office, but Warfield convinced him that could delay things to the critical point and that he had nothing to lose by checking Warfield's story with a quick visit to Hangar 23.

Warfield had never talked more convincingly, or had such a degree of disaster pivoting on quick success. Saito reluctantly agreed to drive to the hangar and see the conditions firsthand but refused Warfield's demand to send someone there to check for radioactivity until he knew more. Saito, Warfield and Aoki climbed into the minister's official car and headed to Hangar 23. The flashing lights and crying siren seemed to announce Saito's mood, Warfield thought, rather than his belief that a problem existed.

ETA MINUS FIFTY-FOUR MINUTES

When Saito flew out of the car and paraded to the hangar's personnel door, Warfield knew the angry official was primarily interested in embarrassing him with the truth. Saito walked ten steps inside, stopped and looked around the hangar and up to the roof. His swagger melted. "Yoshida spent millions renovating this hangar," he said. "Where is it?"

Aoki pointed to where the big plane sat for so long and told Saito about the three Russians who worked there. He then led him to the office area and showed him the destroyed computers and other damage. While Saito tried to comprehend it all, Warfield checked behind the chain link fence, and there he stopped dead in his tracks. The tarp he'd seen rolled-up outside the office area when he was there earlier was now spread open. Two bodies lay entangled in the bloody fabric.

"*Saito!*" Warfield yelled, bending to check for a pulse. He and Aoki told Saito the tarp was rolled up earlier. The bodies might have been inside it then, but they weren't visible. Who had been there since?

Saito was in a fog, ignoring Warfield's demands that he call police and hazmat. He stood there for a moment and walked toward the partitioned corner where the Russians maintained their living quarters. He went in first with Warfield and Aoki behind him.

Warfield heard the shot before realizing anyone was hit. Blood sprayed from Saito's head, and a second shot came as the minister crumpled to the floor. Warfield dropped and wheeled around to pull Aoki down, but a bullet caught Warfield. He put his hand to the hot area at the side of his head.

"Get down, kid," were the last words he mumbled before everything faded into darkness.

Cross was fielding questions and suggestions in the Situation Room. Otto Stern said, "We could be faced with shooting the plane down before we have all the data. This is a no-win, Mr. President."

Cross knew that was true but a president who preceded him had faced that frightening possibility in the dark hours of 9/11. While they waited for news from Warfield or the ambassador, others in the White House kept an eye on Fox News and CNN. If word of this got out they might need to release a statement to assure the public.

Cross counted on Scrubb and Stern to weigh the incoming information he would use in making a final decision. Earl Fullwood realized he'd been sidelined. He picked up his attaché case and marched off, stopping at the door to glare for a moment at the president, who didn't seem to notice.

At the Pentagon, Plantar Scrubb huddled with the Joint Chiefs in the Pentagon room known as the Tank, reserved for use by the chiefs.

ETA MINUS FORTY-EIGHT MINUTES

Flying the 747-400 was as appropriate a way to spend the final hours of his life as Fumio Yoshida could imagine. Unlike the -400 series, earlier versions of the 747 couldn't be flown by one pilot alone. The 747-400 was by far the most magnificent airplane Yoshida had ever encountered. Several planes like the one Yoshida's father had flown to his death could be parked on each of its wings. There was more space inside the cabin than in a dozen houses like Yoshida's and it could carry more than five-hundred passengers if so configured. The tail was six stories tall and the plane could fly eight-thousand miles non-stop. Four Rolls Royce RB211-524G engines powered the plane Yoshida was flying and it could carry many times the weight of the bomb that now occupied it. Fumio Yoshida knew the specs by heart. His only regret in this whole plan of his was that it was necessary to sacrifice such a beautiful aircraft.

The fate of the Russians didn't bother Yoshida much. Ivan had worried him all along. Petrevich said he was critical to the project but in the end Ivan was Petrevich's undoing. Maybe Ivan never gave much thought to what he and Petrevich and Mikhail were building, or perhaps the reality of the ultimate purpose of their effort never hit him. Until now. Ivan couldn't have been blind to it all, but maybe he rationalized it would never happen. After all, he and Petrevich and their counterparts back in Russia built all those nuclear weapons, tens of thousands of them, and as far as Yoshida knew not one of them was ever used against other human beings.

But then hours ago something came over Ivan when it was time for he and Petrevich to show Yoshida the two simple procedures he would have to perform to release the bomb. Sure, there were more efficient ways to deliver nukes but Yoshida wanted to replicate the Hiroshima and Nagasaki attacks as closely as possible

Ivan had waited until after Petrevich explained it all to Yoshida. How to release the safety system that prevented unintended detonation; and how to arm the trigger that would detonate the bomb at the required time. Ivan then smiled and calmly informed Yoshida he had decided to sabotage the work they had done. It stalled Yoshida for a moment but he was not unprepared for such an occurrence. He fired the .25 from inside his pants pocket and hit Ivan twice in the chest at near point-blank proximity. Petrevich yelled out in a combination of surprise and terror but Yoshida had the gun on him and Mikhail before they could react.

Yoshida ordered Mikhail to bind Petrevich's hands behind his back and tie him to the chain link fence that bordered the hangar office. Perhaps anticipating death anyway, Mikhail swung around as he finished tying Petrevich. He had picked up a wrench and swung it at Yoshida's head. Yoshida was surprisingly agile. He dodged it and fired, hitting the Russian in front of his left ear; he fired a second shot into the back of his head after he fell. Then he leveled the pistol at Petrevich, who was cursing Yoshida with all of his breath, and fired his fifth bullet.

Petrevich's limp body slumped from the fence, to which Mikhail had tied his hands. Yoshida jammed the muzzle of the .25 to the bridge of Petrevich's nose and pulled the trigger again, but this time there was only a click. Then, another click. He threw the gun at Petrevich but the Russian's body was still. Yoshida had not planned to kill any of them but had no regrets. Nothing would undermine his mission.

He cut the rope that suspended Petrevich and thought about loading the bodies onto the plane but they were too heavy for him to manage. He retrieved the tent cloth Petrevich had put up around his office area and rolled all three men up in it. Someone would find the bodies in the next day or so but by then it would make no difference.

Fumio Yoshida checked the time. Forty minutes to go. He was at peace with what was about to happen but nevertheless a little jittery from the adrenaline his excitement had generated. He saw the silhouette of a plane in the distance. Was it another airliner, or had the U.S. authorities found him out somehow? He had thought about the possibility that his plan might be discovered in Tokyo before it was complete, in which case he would encounter the U.S. military, but it wasn't going to matter. They might buzz his plane and try to intimidate him but U.S. authorities wouldn't think of shooting down a Japanese airliner, at least until it clearly posed a threat to life and before they did a lot of checking with authorities in Japan, which would be difficult on Saturday night.

Even if they reached Saito, the proud and powerful Ministry chief would be so supportive of Yoshida that even the most paranoid American officials would falter. "Vice-Minister Yoshida is on a training flight to the United States," Saito would say. "He is a humble servant who has served with honor in the Ministry of Transport. He cares for his family and is a model Japanese citizen." Saito would continue, "It will be determined that Yoshida had no connection with the irregular circumstances discovered at Hangar 23." And finally, "Yoshida is at the top of his career. Just last week he and I worked together in preparation for the Oberon."

Yoshida felt an adrenaline rush as he began the first of the two procedures Petrevich had shown him. This was the best day of his life.

In the Situation Room, Stern and Hill spoke with other officials on the phones to bring them up to date. The assistant secretary of state called Hill to say he had spoken with the U.S. ambassador to Japan, who said the Japanese officials he'd reached so far had termed Warfield's report as not credible unless there was more evidence to go on.

Plantar Scrubb called from the Pentagon. "Traffic controllers say the 747's requesting priority permission to land at LAX. Low on fuel. Could be a ploy to get into the area. We've sent F-15s to intercept. They'll ride along with him for a few minutes but I can't wait much longer before we begin to divert him away from the mainland. If he's low on fuel that's a problem."

"What's the most likely scenario?" Otto Stern asked.

"Hell, I don't know that, Stern," Scrubb said, "but just in case that plane is carrying a nuke we will keep her away from the mainland. Need to do something in the next few minutes. What are we waiting on, Mr. President?"

"Warfield. I'm waiting for Warfield to confirm that there's radioactivity in the hangar. And I need something from Tokyo."

ETA MINUS THIRTY-TWO MINUTES

The first person Warfield saw when he opened his eyes was Komeito. Warfield had a crushing headache and a bandage of some kind covered most of his head. He looked at the blood on the hangar floor and wondered if it was his. Sirens wailed not too far away. He sat up and took a moment to reconstruct what had happened before he'd passed out, and remembered that police had taken Komeito away from the Holiday Inn.

Komeito hurriedly explained that the police who picked him up at the hotel were responding to a call from the old woman next door to Yoshida, Mrs. Tanaka. These cops didn't know Komeito and blew off his story about the hangar, but when they got to the police station Komeito contacted Russian Embassy officials, who vouched for him. He then told the officers what had happened and they called for a radioactivity check at the hangar and rushed there with Komeito.

Komeito told Warfield that he and the police officers heard four gunshots as they arrived at the hangar. They rushed inside and found Saito dead. Warfield's head was grazed and bleeding, but the bullet didn't penetrate his skull. Police called for an ambulance and Komeito had finished attending to Warfield's wound the best he could when he regained consciousness. The bleeding had stopped but the side of his head was swelling.

"Aoki was lucky. Said you pulled him out of the way. He is grateful," Komeito said.

"Grateful!" I shouldn't have had him here in the first place. Where is he?"

"Police took him away. Back to Guido's I think."

"Who did the shooting?" Warfield asked.

"Petrevich," Komeito said. "I recognized him from the photo in Antonov's bag. Looks like he shot himself after doing all the damage he could."

"What about radioactivity?"

"Hangar's hot, all right. I got it from the hazmat techs over there. We need to get out of here." Komeito called one of them over and he rattled off the details to Warfield.

Warfield looked at his watch. Yoshida was half an hour from Los Angeles. There in the hangar, someone had thrown a tarp over all four bodies—Mikhail, Ivan, Saito and Petrevich. Thirty or forty police officers, government officials, crime scene types and hazmat technicians buzzed around taking photos, collecting evidence, and some stood around talking. None of them were near Komeito and Warfield.

"Let's go," Warfield said. He was a little wobbly when he stood but managed to walk on his own.

No one seemed to notice the two men leave the hangar. Saito had left the keys in the MOT car and Komeito got behind the wheel. Warfield felt a strangeness about riding in Saito's car, whose life ended without notice after driving there only minutes ago. Life was without any guarantees.

Warfield tried to reach the White House on the cell phone but the connection was poor. He told Komeito to get him to the Holiday Inn as fast as possible.

ETA MINUS FIFTEEN MINUTES

Warfield's head throbbed with each step as he ran from the car to the hotel side entrance where the phone cubicles were located, just inside. When he reached the White House, Cross was on the phone with Scrubb at the Pentagon. He put Warfield and Scrubb on the speakerphone so everyone could hear.

"It's confirmed," Warfield said. "Geiger counters are jumping."

"You're there?"

"Was. Police and hazmat are there now. What's the status in Washington?"

Cross gave him a twenty-second rundown and said he still needed to speak with a high-level Japanese official. Warfield heard nothing that gave him any comfort.

"Got radio contact with the plane?" Warfield asked.

Scrubb told him they did.

"Look," Warfield said, "even if Tokyo acknowledges the radiation two minutes from now, they'll still be a long way from the bigger picture I'm telling you about, and you don't have time for that. If you get me a hookup with Yoshida on the plane, I can break him with what I know and you'll have the confirmation you need."

"Break him?" Otto Stern was alarmed. "That's what we need! A 747 pilot over Los Angeles having a nervous breakdown. *God, If I had only known—*"

Warfield was hot. "Listen, Stern, what choice do you have if you're not going to act until you have some kind of approval from Tokyo? Yoshida's a rigid man. Holds himself to unrealistic standards. If he learns he's made a couple of serious mistakes he'll fall apart. I can convince him that he did."

"We don't have time for psychotherapy, Warfield," Scrubb said.

Cross thought it over for a few seconds and went against the grain, as he often did. "Take thirty seconds to make a showing, Cam. If it looks good, we'll go a little longer. Make it count."

Otto Stern shook his head. "For the record, I strongly advise against it, Mr. President. You know Warfield was on a liquid diet for a while. How do you know his judgment is sound."

"I'll take that responsibility," Cross snapped.

Electronics technicians had been working on a radio hookup and within seconds Warfield was direct to Yoshida. Cross, Scrubb and the others in both the Sit Room and the Tank could hear both ends of the conversation. Yoshida could hear only Warfield.

ETA MINUS TWELVE MINUTES

Warfield identified himself and said, "Mr. Yoshida, I'm at Narita. Hangar 23," he lied, as he would continue to do in this conversation. "You're familiar with Hangar 23?"

English language was used by flight controllers and pilots on all international flights and although Yoshida had long ago studied and used the language enough to get by, he was not fluent. But this was no flight controller and he wasn't sure whether or not to respond.

Aside from giving the Americans any information that would cause him to fail, Yoshida no longer cared what anyone knew—American *or* Japanese. As the time for this mission closed in, he had begun to dream of receiving posthumous honors from a grateful nation, certainly his own generation, that had longed for an avenger against America. Jotaro's death would be seen as the granting of the long-awaited mercy that it was. Deceiving the Ministry of Transport would be recognized as a necessary means to a justifiable end.

But for a few more minutes it would be necessary to play the game, deny the glorious things he had done, continue the lie. Soon enough after his work was finished, the authorities would find the Jotaro file in the desk drawer in his bedroom, and then all of Tokyo, all of Hiroshima and Nagasaki, and all of Japan would know the truth: That Fumio Yoshida was not a demon who bombed innocent Americans, but a resourceful patriot who had evened the score somewhat, and that he had done it not only for himself and his family but for every Japanese citizen. So be confident. To admit anything at this point, so close to the goal, could result in failure. Nothing was going to stop him—not until he was over Los Angeles!

"I know twenty-three," Yoshida finally answered.

"Police found three men here, all shot. Traces of nuclear material all over. I know that you know all about that!" Warfield said.

"I do not."

"Mr. Yoshida, you should be aware something in your plan has gone wrong. It's about Petrevich."

Yoshida resisted the temptation. "So sorry. Do not know any Petrevich. We discuss when I get to Los Angeles. Cannot continue conversation now."

Warfield increased the intensity. "Petrevich deceived you, Yoshida. He was working with the Americans. We knew what you were planning from the time you hired Seth to get the materials and the know-how to duplicate the Hiroshima bomb. We're ready for you. You won't be able to carry out your plan. You'll die in vain and dishonor your name, your country. Even Jotaro."

Yoshida didn't want to believe what he was hearing, but this man knew too much to be dismissed. There was a note of shrillness in Yoshida's voice when he answered. "You are talking to Mr. Fumio Yoshida, Vice-Minister of Transport, Japan. You are mistaken. I do not know any Petrevich."

Warfield knew he had penetrated. "We paid Petrevich five million dollars, Yoshida. He was working for us! Instead of a nuclear bomb, you're carrying a piece of junk in the cargo bay of your plane that won't detonate. Minister Saito knows where the hangar renovation dollars went. And another thing you should know. Two of the men you shot in the hangar are dead, but Petrevich survived. He's laughing about pulling one on you. He'll be living in the U.S. now and Congress will likely award him a medal. You've made him a hero, Yoshida. He's made you a fool. Turn back to sea now. You can at least salvage your honor."

It was more than Yoshida could bear. Now his name would be reviled in Japan instead of glorified. He would die in shame, an object of ridicule. He began screaming, sobbing, cursing Petrevich, the Americans and the Japanese emperor who surrendered to end the war. "I will not turn back and further dishonor my father's name. I will kill many Americans when I fly into the ground. The bomb will not matter." Then there was only the sound of Yoshida sobbing.

That was the last transmission, but Cross had heard enough. He authorized Scrub to take all appropriate action.

Warfield was still on the phone. "Mr. President, you know it's only Yoshida who thinks he's not carrying a bomb."

"I got it, Warfield," Scrubb said.

"Let's get it done, Plantar," Cross said.

Yoshida shut off the radio. He saw the distant lights of Los Angeles through his tears. Maybe the city had escaped the fate of Hiroshima but Fumio Yoshida would not die in complete failure. If he went in low and slow he could take out a long swath of homes full of sleeping Americans before the 747 skidded to a stop and burst into flames. He would find an area where many houses were built close together. It would be very much like his father had done.

He thought of the second procedure required to arm the bomb, but remembered that was no longer important. *But wait! Why not do it?* Maybe the American on the radio was lying. There was no reason not to. Yoshida grabbed the notes he made when Petrevich instructed him on the procedures. He'd completed the first one earlier.

ETA MINUS NINE MINUTES

F-15 pilot Major John Raines had tailed the Japanese airliner as ordered for the last half hour but he hadn't been told why. Now the colonel on the radio told him to bring the 747 down.

"Sorry, sir. Repeat that transmission."

"Fire on the 747, Major Raines." The colonel repeated Yoshida's tail number and other identification.

"Sir, if I am hearing you correctly, only certain generals are authorized to give that order."

"Major, you have your orders. Carry them out."

There was a pause, then, "Sorry, sir. I respectfully take exception to that order."

The colonel repeated the order to the captain flying the other F-15 trailing Yoshida.

"I agree with Major Raines, sir."

Yoshida wondered why the F-15 at his wingtips were allowing him to go on. If they gave him a few more minutes....

ETA MINUS SEVEN MINUTES

In the Situation Room no one had moved. "Plantar, can you confirm that it's over?" Cross asked.

"That's a negative, sir. There's a delay. They're contacting the...the...the...*oh holy God, the F-15 pilots are refusing to shoot it down...there's some jockeying going on, just another few seconds—*"

"*We don't have seconds, General,*" Cross fired. "Where is the 747 now?"

"Too close for comfort, Garrison. We're doing what we can here. *They've got to get me voice contact with those F-15s!*"

ETA MINUS FIVE MINUTES

The F-15's had peeled away and Yoshida was more hopeful now that they were letting him go. Maybe Tokyo intervened and somehow caused a delay. He had almost completed the final arming procedure when the F-15s began firing. In the brief moment he had left, images of Jotaro filled his mind. His father skimming the carrier deck. Charred planes and American soldiers. The emperor's detestable surrender. His mother crying in pain. Those were the only things that ever mattered to Fumio Yoshida. And the last.

PART FOUR
Cam Warfield

CHAPTER 16

THE DOCTOR WHO DRESSED Warfield's head wound reminded him how close Tokyo came to being his last stop. He and Komeito met with the Japanese and U.S. authorities beginning Sunday night to fill them in on Antonov, Yoshida and the Russians, and by noon on Tuesday Warfield was released to leave the country.

In the first two days of their investigation, Japanese authorities had interviewed the U.S. Ambassador to Japan, Norio, Aoki, John Anderson, Antonov's prostitute Romi, Mrs. Nakamura, the old superintendent at the Tomodachi bath house, Mrs. Tanaka and Tex the bartender. Tex, wearing a bandage on his hand, threatened to file charges against Warfield for assault, but police, who by then had the bigger picture, said they would find reasons to arrest Tex if he persisted. He backed off.

After the authorities were through with Warfield, TK and Komeito drove him to his hotel. It would be their final ride together. Warfield told Komeito to stop at Guido's first. There, he took Aoki aside. "If I ever have a son, I want him to be as brave as you."

At the hotel, Komeito walked with Warfield to the lobby and they stood there sizing each other up for a silent moment. Komeito had earned Warfield's respect. They had navigated a treacherous, narrow channel in the last few days and without Komeito the outcome might have been different. Warfield stood in front of Komeito and grasped him by the shoulders. No words were needed.

Cross arranged for a U.S. Air Force plane to return Warfield to Washington. As it climbed out over the North Pacific on the sunny mid-afternoon, Warfield looked out the window at the same blue waters Fumio Yoshida had flown above days earlier. He and his disastrous cargo had been sent to the bottom of the Pacific forty miles from the California coast—less than five minutes away from the mainland at five-hundred miles per hour. The bomb didn't detonate and the Navy was determining the risk it posed and what needed to be done. Japan was cooperating.

Warfield had learned more about the 747 from the U.S. ambassador. The MOT had held it in lieu of payment of airport fees and other money owed to the Ministry by a struggling airline. The airline had bankrupted and Yoshida managed to sequester the plane by manipulating reports.

It was around three Wednesday afternoon when Warfield's plane landed at Andrews Air Force Base near Washington. Cross had called him en route and invited him to come to the White House when he arrived. "Nothing urgent," Cross said, so Warfield begged off until the next morning, but Cross went on to say the media reports were alarming the country and the world. Some speculated the Japanese government was behind Yoshida, and others wondered what dangers the submerged bomb posed at the bottom of the Pacific, yet so close to the mainland. Cross said he was addressing the nation at ten that night to quiet the rumors. When Warfield got off the plane at Andrews, a driver took him to Hardscrabble in an air force limousine reserved for VIPs.

Warfield saddled Spotlight and rode for a long while, returned to the house and took a steaming hot shower. When Fleming got home they drove to Ticcio's for dinner and Warfield found himself loosening up. He didn't say much about Tokyo and she didn't probe. They had a couple of beers, danced a little and joked around. Fleming ribbed Warfield about the night he got bent out of shape when she came in with another man who happened to be her brother. Warfield winced at the memory but was able to laugh with her.

They got back to Hardscrabble minutes before ten and Warfield remembered Cross's speech and flipped on the TV. Cross came on and assured the American people and the world that the Japanese airliner downing was an isolated incident orchestrated by a single, deranged civilian who happened to be Japanese. The Japanese government was never involved. The 747 was believed to be carrying a nuclear bomb but it was never activated and went intact to the bottom of the ocean far from land. The Navy was handling the situation. "Our defense systems worked as intended and there was never any risk to Americans," Cross said. Warfield raised an eyebrow at that comment but knew the president's words were carefully edited by Cross's advisors.

252

Cross finished his prepared statement and offered a personal comment. "In addition to our military, I want to express my personal appreciation for my advisors who stood with me when difficult decisions had to be made, and for retired Army Colonel Cameron Warfield, who uncovered this situation in Tokyo and played the key role in bringing it to a successful end."

Warfield couldn't believe his ears. For the first time he could remember, he was embarrassed. Fleming whooped and hollered and grabbed him around the neck. "My hero!" she hooted. "My man saved the world. You're famous, War Man."

"Hey, you act surprised!"

They were still laughing when Warfield's line rang. It was Cross. "Hope you didn't mind me blind-siding you."

"Don't tell anyone, but it was a case of being in the right place at the right time," Warfield said.

"Some wise man said luck dwells at the intersection of preparedness and opportunity," replied the president.

In the Oval Office the next morning, Cross told Warfield he'd done him a disservice by calling his name on national television. "Destroyed your anonymity."

Warfield laughed. "Yeah, had a few calls on my voicemail this morning. Friends, army buddies, people from my home town, including the mayor; he wants to do a parade or something. Macc Macclenny. CNN. NBC. Fox News. U.S. News & World Report. *Washington Post.* No Hollywood producers yet, and that's the call I stayed up all night waiting for."

Cross turned serious. "Look, Cam. I want you to stay on the job. There's plenty to do."

Warfield wasn't sure he wanted that and it showed on his face.

"Don't decide now," Cross said. "After you get through the debriefings take a few days off and then call me."

Later that morning Warfield listened to the tape made in the Sit Room during the last minutes before Yoshida was shot down. He played a certain passage several times and wrote something in his notebook. Then he met with representatives from several agencies of the intelligence community to give them the details of his time in Tokyo. Their congratulatory comments after the meeting reminded him that before now he wouldn't have gotten as much as a *hello* from most of them.

Later that day Warfield got a call from Abbas Mozedah in Paris. He razzed Warfield for being a glory seeker, then congratulated him. Warfield laughed it off.

"Got an update about Ms. Koronis," Abbas said. "Her brother Seth's long-time mistress Suri? She left him. Escaped, I should say. Seth's group's now calling her a traitor of God. We're sheltering her here in Paris. Suri's talking to us some."

Then he dropped a bombshell on Warfield. Suri claimed Ana Koronis didn't know about Seth's involvement in terrorism when she first went to stay with him after the deaths of her husband and son. After a few months, Suri clued Ana in. When Ana confronted her brother he acknowledged knowing about the terrorist abduction of her husband and son but tried to justify the attack to Ana, although he said he wasn't involved himself.

According to Suri, Ana was depressed and furious. Seth persisted, charging that without America, there would be no turmoil in the Middle East and innocents on both sides wouldn't have to die. Similar to the prosecutor's hypothetical scenario in Ana's trial, Seth told Ana she had a role to play in this war: Return to America, take advantage of her status and position and assist the cause from there. After all, this was her homeland he was fighting for.

But the similarity ended there. Suri said Ana stormed out of the room and returned to the U.S. days later.

Warfield was skeptical. "Did Seth know about her trial? That she's in prison now?"

"Suri says yes."

"He could have saved her from that if all this is true."

"He had no use for her after she rejected his agenda. This man has no warm blood, no humanity. He does not meet the definition of a human being, Cameron."

"Why did Suri leave him?"

"Afraid of him. Seth's brother-in-law Hassan was one of Seth's henchmen. You remember I told you Hassan believed Seth murdered his wife, who was Hassan's sister. Suri knew it could happen to her as well."

"Yes. You said Hassan was going to kill Seth when he knew for sure."

"Seth hasn't survived this long by chance. One of his bodyguards suckered Hassan into believing the bodyguard was going to betray Seth, so Hassan hooked up with him and told him of *his own* plan to kill Seth. Soon after that, Seth summoned Hassan to his headquarters on the pretense of a planning meeting. When Hassan sat down at the table, Seth stood up behind him and swung a machete like one of your baseball bats. Lopped his head off clean and had it stuffed and mounted. Suri says it hangs on the wall in the room where he meets with his associates as an example to would-be traitors."

Warfield shuddered at the image. After a moment, he said, "Could be a setup, Abbas, this story of Suri's."

"I was able to cross-check some of it after she asked us for protection. I think she is straight. We are trying to get all the information we can about Seth but she is going slow. She is afraid for her life. It comes out in bits and pieces. But I admit I cannot say with certainty she is truthful."

"Not much to go on and it won't get Ana out of prison. Even if Suri's telling the truth, how could you prove it?"

"Listen to this, Cameron. She speaks of a meeting that I think could have been related to Petrevich—his escape from Russia with the uranium. Seth had made his needs known to a CIA source he had been working with but that source fell out of sight."

"Hell, that could be Harvey Joplan!" Warfield said

"Maybe. When someone else came along instead of the CIA source he knew, Seth was skeptical and sent one of his men to meet with this replacement."

"When did it happen, this meeting?"

Abbas checked his notes. "April 22nd last year."

"Prior to Habur gate then, sure." Warfield thought about it. If the meeting actually was before Habur gate, it could've set up the Petrevich transfer. After Joplan was killed, and after prosecutors in Ana's trial presented evidence she had the opportunity and motivation to be Seth's accomplice, Warfield had stopped thinking in terms of another mole: He was then satisfied it was Ana who provided the CIA database to Seth. But if Suri's information was factual, maybe Ana was innocent. That led Warfield back to one of his earlier theories: That Joplan revealed the name of his contact to his killer, who could have been planted in the Atlanta prison by someone who knew there was profit in the information Joplan had agreed to tell the feds.

Warfield now believed there was a good probability the mole was still operating in Washington, but he wasn't quite ready to share this. Chances were too great that this American spy was in the intelligence loop and would be tipped off. "I'm coming over to meet with Suri," he said.

"I thought you would."

Four of Abbas's men met Warfield at Charles DeGaulle Airport and drove him to their headquarters in the rear of Abbas's engineering office. Abbas got in the van with them and they headed to the safe house where Suri was kept. Warfield and Abbas rode in the middle row of an old Dodge minivan with darkened windows. Three men in back and the rider at shotgun scanned the street with assault rifles in the ready position. Warfield thought at one point they were being tailed but Abbas told him it was his men.

The safe house was located in an alley, tucked between buildings that might have been candidates for demolition. The scent of garbage fueled by the August heat filled the air, and the broken concrete pavement, ever sunless, was blackened with permanent mildew and discoloration. Graffiti covered graffiti on the brick walls along the alley, and a blob of paint someone had applied long ago had begun to peel away, partially revealing a stenciled red swastika that was once meant to be out of sight forever. When they stopped, Abbas's men lined the short walk to the door where a muscular man bearing an assault rifle met them. He was Jalil, Abbas said, who had been at Habur.

There was not much more light inside the darkened house than in the alley. A bar took shape around to Warfield's right, and beyond that a pool table with suspended lights above, a grouping of sofas and chairs and a mantle and stone hearth. The place had been a lounge in earlier times. The marble floor was honed to a fine patina by generations of boot leather and was now dotted with Persian rugs. Blue cigarette smoke, only a little less pungent than the stale air it displaced, hung below the ceiling. Jalil and a dozen other armed men stood or sat but were anything but relaxed.

Suri was upstairs in a small windowless suite they had made for her. A fist-size opening had been chiseled through the brick wall, long ago if the aging grime around the hole was any indication, and no doubt by someone who could no longer bear the absence of light, or perhaps wanted a breath of fresh air. Suri's eyes reflected her level of caution when Abbas introduced Warfield. "He's a friend," Abbas told Suri in English. "He knows why you are here."

Warfield interpreted the slight change in her quivering lips as an attempted smile.

"You're doing all right, Suri?"

"Scared. Very scared," she said quietly. Her eyes searched his as if to judge whether he was a friend as billed. Just as Warfield had come to Paris so that he could read hers.

Warfield considered this woman for a moment. She might be frightened but she was strong. "Of Seth. Of course."

"He will send someone to kill me. I trust no one now."

"You're safe here, Suri."

She nodded. "Maybe."

They talked for two hours, Suri slowly growing less cautious and referring to a secret diary she had kept for dates and specifics. As Abbas had reported, Suri said Seth had sent one of his trusted lieutenants to meet with the American contact and assess the risk in dealing with him. They had met in Paris.

"Who was Seth's man who met with the American?" Warfield asked.

"Pierre?…Philippe?…one of those. I can't remember his name," Suri said.

When he felt he had all the information she had to give him, Warfield expressed his appreciation and told her she was safe with Abbas. On the way back to DeGaulle Warfield mulled over everything Suri had said, including the date of the meeting, April 22nd last year. When Warfield's plane was airborne he called Paula at the White House and asked her to get in touch with Judge Hartrampf from the Ana Koronis trial and request permission for him to meet alone with Ana. Someone in Justice could have arranged it but Warfield wasn't ready to involve Justice in this.

"When?"

"As soon as possible. After you get the judge's approval, set the meeting up for me."

"You're pretty confident Hartrampf will agree to it."

"You can do it. If it starts to look impossible, get the president involved. If anyone requires reasons, say I have new information about Ana."

Ana Koronis read the form a second time. Cameron Warfield had obtained approval from a judge to visit her. No reason was given but she knew it was no social call. Without Warfield's role in her ordeal, she might still be on the outside.

Even given Warfield's involvement, Ana had been surprised at her jury's verdict, but she had no doubt that ethnic prejudice played a role. A *big* role. She might have understood a guilty verdict if there had been some hard evidence for the prosecutor to point to, say, the tapes in the safe under her desk at the law firm. Those would have been hard for her to explain to a jury. But there was nothing like that. Everything prosecutor Harriman gave the jury was circumstantial except the testimony of Helen Swope, Austin Quinn's housekeeper, and that was one person's word against Ana's.

She thought of the first time she met Colonel Warfield. What was it now? Seven, eight years ago? The U.S. Ambassador to Greece, Spiro Koronis, had invited Ana's senior partner Roy Addler of her law firm to join him at a roast for Austin Quinn in Atlantic City. Addler and Ana were friends as well as law partners and he asked Ana to accompany him. She agreed, even though she would know no one at the table and wasn't particularly political. And it had been awkward at first, that night. Ana, Roy Addler and Warfield had been seated at the Spiro Koronis table long before their host arrived. The Ambassador finally showed up muttering apologies for his tardiness. Some diplomatic matter had come up as he was about to leave his room, he told them. Garrison Cross, the current president of the United States, who was head of CIA back then, was even later, muttering something about never having all the parts to his tux in one place.

Warfield was still in the army back then and Ana thought he was a friend of Cross's. At any rate, she remembered that Warfield saved the evening. She liked Addler but he could be as boring as watching paint dry, and Warfield made the time fly by with some wit and a couple of colorful war stories. Ana recalled that Frank Gallardi, the emcee for the event, and some of the others seated at the dais were late getting there, too. The whole thing was off schedule all evening and Gallardi was in a foul mood. But thanks to an abundance of food and booze—and, in Ana's case, Cam Warfield—no one seemed to mind.

Ana remembered trying to discreetly scope out the guests in the ballroom. She'd never been in the presence of so many important people. Just about every person who ever had his picture in the *Washington Post* was there. To top it off, then-president McNabb made a brief appearance.

When Quinn's friends, including Cross and Spiro Koronis, were finished stinging him with mock insults from the stage, he dropped by Spiro Koronis's table and talked with everyone for a minute or two. Quinn held Ana's eyes with his own during that brief meeting. Years later, after her marriage to Spiro and his death, Ana and Quinn began seeing each other.

Ana stared out the tiny window of her cell now and shook her head. She never could have guessed in a million years that three men she met that night—Spiro Koronis, Austin Quinn and Cameron Warfield—would in turn have such a major impact on her life.

And she was certain the Cam Warfield who was coming to visit her in jail would not be so full of good humor and cheer as on that night in Atlantic City. Neither was she.

Warfield had to drag himself out of bed after the Paris round-trip but felt better after a run and shower. He wasn't back up to five miles yet but increased his distance with each run. Paula had left a message on his voicemail that Judge Hartrampf approved a meeting with Ana, and she had arranged it for one o'clock that afternoon. The Bureau of Prisons still kept Ana Koronis at Alexandria Detention Center under a special arrangement pending availability of space at a suitable federal facility that housed females.

Warfield arrived at the ADC at twelve-forty that afternoon and was greeted by Aubrey Holden, the lieutenant he'd met when he had visited Joplan. As they walked to the interview room, Holden, now a captain, mentioned his brother again. "Tom's here in D.C. now, the FBI Building."

"Maybe I'll run into him one of these days."

Warfield didn't know Ana on any personal level, but he knew she wouldn't view him as a friend. Although he hadn't testified at her trial, Ana knew he had been the impetus for her ordeal. And when reporters contacted him after the trial, Warfield had voiced contempt for her. "Ana Koronis did what spies do. Get the trust of somebody that's got access to useful information and betray him. In Ana Koronis's case, she got to the director of CIA." Ana wouldn't have missed that on TV, and she wouldn't have forgotten it was Warfield who said it. He remembered how she stared at the jurors on the day of closing arguments and wondered if she was still as angry.

He was surprised at Ana's appearance. She was frail at her trial but looked strong now.

Ana interrupted when Warfield started to introduce himself.

"We've met." Ana looked straight at him but he read no emotion in her eyes.

"Yes, we have."

They weighed each other for a moment.

"Being treated okay?" he asked.

"They complicate my social life some, and the air in here smells a little personal at times, but otherwise it's not bad. But you're not here to check on my well-being."

"Ms. Koronis, an intelligence source contacted me with new information that might affect your case. I went to Paris to check it out. Maybe together we can make more sense out of it."

"When you say, *affect* my case, do you mean it could help me?"

"It's only a possibility."

Warfield read her forced smile as an indication she didn't believe a word he said.

"I've never had the feeling you were interested in improving my situation."

"It was never personal. Hoped you were not involved. Still do."

"Do you need to hear me say it? All right, *I didn't do it*! Now what do you want me to do?"

Warfield studied her for a moment, then said, "I met Suri." He watched for a sign of recognition.

"*Suri?* Yes, I knew her."

"She turned against Seth. She's on the run. A resistance group in Paris took her in and she's been talking."

Ana nodded.

"She involved in Seth's operations?" Warfield asked.

"I don't know. A girlfriend I think. Know why she left him?"

"Thought Seth was going to kill her. Suri said he'd murdered Hassan."

"*Hassan?* I suppose I shouldn't be surprised at anything in Seth's world, but how does all of this help me?"

"Suri told us your reaction when your brother told you what he wanted you to do for him."

Ana stared at Warfield.

He continued. "It's only a start, but with Suri we have someone backing your claim that you rejected Seth and left him when you learned what he was involved in."

Ana stood up and walked around the small room. The young lines on her forehead deepened. "Look, I'm not a criminal lawyer but I *am* a lawyer, and I know this information from the ex-girlfriend of an international terrorist is not going to get me out of here."

"As I said, it's a start."

"That all she told you?"

"She knew about a meeting in Paris. Thinks it was one of Seth's men and an American. The date was soon after we arrested Joplan, the CIA mole."

"What do you make of the meeting?"

"I think Joplan told somebody how to contact Seth, and—"

"And that *somebody* is the person who met with Seth's man?"

"Could be. Joplan's contact needed a nuclear scientist and nuke materials. That's what Joplan told me right before he was killed. The CIA has a list of post-Cold War Russians they consider security risks in that category. We know from your trial that Petrevich was on that list. Given the timing and other parts of the puzzle, it's not too far out to believe Petrevich and the uranium left Russia as a result of Joplan telling someone who his contact was."

"Someone who had access to that CIA file. A significant part of my trial."

"Right."

Both sat without speaking for a few seconds before Warfield stood up to leave. "If you don't mind me asking, I...I'm curious...the name Seth—"

Ana smiled a little. "I think he was around seventeen—it was near the time he left our family here in the States and moved to Iran—when he adopted the name after reading about Seth in Egyptian mythology. The name our parents gave him is Ali."

Back in her own quarters, Ana lay on her mattress pad and stared at the ceiling. She thought of Suri. *"Yes!"* she breathed.

Warfield sat in his car in the jail parking lot for twenty minutes, staring at nothing, mulling over the information he got from Suri and now from Ana. Ana Koronis was a cold number. To him at least. Was it because he tipped Joe Morgan about her, or was that her baseline?

He roughed out a timeline of events and made a few notes. It was time to play his best card. Risky because, while he had a few solid facts, he was shooting from the hip. He couldn't see the target well enough to take direct aim, but this card might draw the mole into the open.

Back on the expressway, he phoned Paula Newnan and thanked her for setting up the meeting.

"Glad to help, Cameo."

"Then you get another chance."

"Thanks, mouth. Okay, what is it now?"

"Need to meet with Fullwood, Stern and Quinn. Together."

"Any special time you'd like this. I'm sure they will cancel everything to make themselves available at your convenience."

"Same as always."

"I know. ASAP."

"Subject is national security. They'll ask."

"I'll see what I can do."

"And no substitutes."

"Substitutes?"

"Deputies won't do."

"Got it, Cameo."

Warfield started to sign off, then said, "Oh, yeah, Paula, whadda you know about mythology?"

"Excuse me?"

"Seth. There's a Seth in Egyptian mythology. Thought you might fill me in on him."

"Sorry, can't help with that one."

Paula arranged the meeting for noon the next day and reserved a small room at the White House. Warfield briefed Cross on his agenda for the meeting before going to the conference room, but told the president he wanted to meet with Fullwood and Quinn alone. Otto Stern had cancelled.

Quinn was first to congratulate Warfield on his handling of the Yoshida matter. Fullwood grunted something about it but whatever he said wasn't clear. Fullwood still held him in contempt.

Warfield opened by saying he wanted to give them information about Joplan's contact.

Fullwood couldn't wait. "Learned that at the Koronis trial, Kunnel. That why we're here? So you can remind us that the terrorist Seth recruited his sister to steal secrets from Austin's computer?"

"That's what the trial came up with and I agreed with it. But now...maybe not."

Quinn looked surprised. Fullwood, acrid still.

Warfield went on. "Seth's girlfriend has turned against him, run away. She's at a safe house in Paris now. I saw her two days ago."

Fullwood rolled his eyes and asked Warfield how he came by this information.

Warfield remembered detailing Abbas's history earlier but went over it again before returning to Suri. "She filled in gaps in what I already knew. Based on the information I have from all sources, here's where I think we stand. Joplan's contact was Seth. Seth had instructed Joplan to get the names of former Soviet scientists who were CIA-listed security risks. One of Seth's clients—Fumio Yoshida, of course, using Japan's money—wanted nuke materials and expertise. Yoshida agreed to pay Seth a few million dollars for it on delivery. Seth was going to use part of that money to pay Joplan if Joplan produced. Joplan knew how to signal Seth when he had the information, but before he got back to Seth the FBI snagged him. That was 6 April last year. After that date—while Joplan was on ice—*Buyer X*, I'll call him, got word to Seth that Joplan had been arrested. If Seth wanted the information he had requested from Joplan, he would have to deal with Buyer X."

"And what conclusion do you draw from that?" Quinn asked.

"That Buyer X learned how to reach Seth from Joplan himself."

"And how did he do that?" Quinn asked.

"After Joplan agreed to cooperate with us, Buyer X went in and downloaded from Joplan the information he needed in order to step in where Joplan left off."

"Why *after* he agreed to cooperate?" Fullwood said. "He could have told someone after he was arrested, but before he agreed to cooperate. Say, someone who was in on it with him."

"Joplan was a loner. I don't believe he had any partners to tell it to. And he refused to cooperate with us until some unlucky soul's balls showed up in his cell and he realized that in this new world of his they could have been his own."

"So, what're you saying, Warfield?" Fullwood asked with his usual scowl.

"Somebody who knew that Joplan agreed to cooperate with us—someone who also knew there was a lot of money at stake for the right information—got to Joplan there in prison and milked the Seth information out of him. Wouldn't have been too hard to do, given Joplan's state of mind following the Red Russell castration. Then X killed Joplan that night, or had him killed, so Joplan couldn't reveal anything to the FBI."

"Got any thoughts about who X is?" Quinn asked.

"Since Joplan received no official visitors after he agreed to cooperate, my theory is that Joplan's killer—our mole—was spawned at our meeting in the Oval Office, the meeting when I turned Joplan back over to the FBI."

Fullwood jumped out of his chair. "Wait up here, Warfield! You sayin' one of us clandestinely visited Joplan that night, got the name of his contact and killed him? You've gone around the corner for sure!"

"I'm saying no one except the few of us who were in the Oval Office that day knew Joplan was ready to give up the name of his contact and that his contact had deep pockets. My Buyer X learned this from one of us who was at that meeting."

"Who was present at that meeting?" Quinn asked.

"The three of us, Stern and the president. And Paula was there. But it wasn't X himself who debriefed Joplan and killed him. X put someone inside the prison to do it."

"And after that, X knew how to contact Seth. That your conspiracy theory, Kunnel?"

"Call it that if you want to. Seth's representative, some Frenchman, Suri thinks, met with Joplan's replacement in Paris on 22 April last year. Now jump ahead six weeks to 9 June. That's the date Boris Petrevich crossed the border from Turkey into Iraq. Whether he had the uranium at that time is irrelevant to this discussion. I think Petrevich was the name supplied to Seth by X. Petrevich and the uranium ended up in Japan and we know the rest of that story."

"What is the point here, Kunnel, in spinning this tale of yours?"

"The point is we still have an internal security problem and we're going to have more losses until we find it. Unless you can discredit what I laid out here, you can start looking for another mole. It wasn't Ana Koronis."

Earl Fullwood looked self-assured. With elbows on the table, cigar in hand, he said, "Kunnel, I believe even you would say this story of yours is based on a lot of speculation—the girlfriend of a terrorist, some dark spy-meetin' in Paris, a conveniently mysterious murder in a prison. We can't run around witch-huntin' because of your phlegmy hallucinations. Might as well be readin' tabloid newspapers and tarot cards. Pretty soon it'll be the man in the moon spyin' on us."

Warfield was at a loss as to why the director would refuse to consider the possibility of a mole.

Quinn asked, "Learn anything else on your Paris trip?"

"Few things I'm check—"

Fullwood cut Warfield off. "Quinn, you're askin' for more fairy tales. Save your breath. I don't know what's goin' on here. Warfield is guessin'. Like he did about that uranium, for example. There's not an ounce of proof that the Russian at Habur is the one in Japan. Warfield's tryin' to make hisself look good after his big fiasco there."

Fullwood crammed his cigar between his teeth and stood up to leave. "I got Bureau business to take care of."

There was a tap on the door and Cross walked in. "This just came in. Might be of interest to all of you." Cross placed a thick folder on the table. "It's a translation of Yoshida's diary."

That Jotaro file! Warfield wanted to jump up onto the table and dance. The authorities in Tokyo had kept it but Warfield requested a copy be sent to Cross. Incredible timing, and it might contain some information for Fullwood.

Warfield sat back as Fullwood and Quinn began going through it. As Cross was leaving, he caught Warfield's eye with a look that said everything Warfield had told him about Petrevich and Seth was there in the diary. That meant Fullwood's rhetoric would crash before his eyes.

Twenty minutes later Quinn looked over at Warfield. "In skimming this, Warfield, I see some support for your position, but I'm not convinced of another mole. And how much can you believe this girlfriend, Suri?"

Warfield fired back. "Are you two going to stick your head in the sand? Look at Rick Ames, CIA. Operated right under Stern's nose for ten years before he was caught. FBI's Robert Hanssen spied twenty years. Mohammed Atta and the other 9/11 World Trade Center terrorists hid in open view for two years right here in our country while they planned their destruction. Think of the terrorist attack on our consulate in Benghazi, Libya and the murder of our Ambassador Chris Stephens and three other Americans. Look at how many Americans died because of these people. And there's Habur crossing. There were warnings and signals in each one of those cases but nothing was done. No one wanted to believe it. Haven't we learned anything about being proactive?"

"If you knew so much about the Russian, why didn't you act before he moved the stuff?" Quinn asked.

Warfield wondered how many times he'd explained this and wasn't ready to talk about his conversations with Rachel Gilbert again. Now he was angry. "Look, it boils down to this. Either the CIA's source lied to the CIA, or somebody at CIA lied to the FBI, or somebody at FBI revised the intelligence that came from the CIA. Two out of three of those scenarios point to a mole. If you buy my theory that only a mole could have known how to contact Seth, it becomes pretty damn convincing that we've still got a mole. If you don't, then you convince me."

"You were saying you had other information?" Quinn asked.

Warfield decided to play that hollow carrot for what it was worth. "Yeah, from Ana, but nothing I'm going to talk about until I check into it."

Quinn seemed surprised. "Ana?"

"Saw her yesterday."

Quinn measured Warfield for a moment, then said, "She's all right I hope."

"She's fine," Warfield said dismissively.

Warfield was in his office later on when Paula called. "Cameo, Director Quinn called here, wants you to meet him at Langley."

"Yeah?" Warfield expected it. Had his theory caused some concern?

"Five this afternoon."

CHAPTER 17

WARFIELD DROVE PAST A six-foot-square sign on the side of the road that warned the unauthorized to keep going, fell into the turn lane and shot into the divided street that led inside the CIA campus. Another sign loomed there and a large and ominous armored personnel carrier with blackout windows stood at the corner poised to eradicate any problem. A guard shack manned by armed security personnel sat two-hundred yards inside the compound. The gate officer required I.D.

Always the same, Warfield thought. No credit for good behavior on earlier visits. He cleared the checkpoint and drove deeper into the woods to where the headquarters building hid far from the view of outsiders. For years the location of CIA was a guarded secret, and even now it was far more shielded from the public than was the White House, a more sensitive and symbolic target. In the midst of Washington city streets and public parks the White House compound was a sieve in comparison to the CIA base. The White House, icon of democracy and freedom, must not be seen as a fortress. The CIA had no such image to protect. Darkness and shadows were its stock in trade.

An armed officer inside the CIA headquarters building seemed to be expecting Warfield and led him to a parking garage where Quinn was already seated and waiting in his SUV. Quinn and Warfield sat alone in the rear of the vehicle, which was configured with a small round table and leather seats. A glass partition separated them from the driver. Quinn offered something to drink but Warfield declined. The driver maneuvered around barricades and tire-shredders along the road leading back to the public highway as Quinn initiated the conversation. "Just curious about Ana," he said. "Haven't seen her for a while."

Quinn was taking a swipe at the carrot Warfield had thrown out a few hours earlier at the White House. Warfield wanted to slap the table but reminded himself that Quinn's hyper curiosity proved nothing—yet.

"Frankly, Cam, I miss her. Thought you could clue me in. How is she?"

Warfield yielded no clue that he was beginning to suspect Quinn now. "Seems okay. I hadn't seen her since the trial. Actually looks healthier now."

"I got the impression you know more than you shared with Fullwood and me. I know how it is with Fullwood, so I thought you and I could talk."

Warfield shrugged. "Couple of things. Maybe insignificant, so I don't want to clutter the table with it at this point."

Quinn turned to look at him. "You're safe talking with me about it."

Warfield looked straight at Quinn. "I'm not discussing it with anyone. Not yet."

Quinn's eyes narrowed. "You know, Warfield, you're not only chasing shadows, you live in the shadows. You'll have everybody in Washington on a list of suspects. Could cause trouble for a lot of innocent people around here!"

Quinn hit the intercom button and told the driver to return to Langley. When he stopped to let Warfield out near his car, Quinn laid a finger on Warfield's shirt sleeve and looked at him for a second before speaking. "The president likes you, Warfield, but I've known Garrison a lot longer than you have. We played college ball together. Drank whiskey. Chased girls. Drove fast cars. Best man at each other's wedding. We were buddies then, and we've become more than that through the years. He appointed me to run the CIA, for example. Like brothers, Garrison and me."

Quinn squinted at Warfield for a long moment and tapped the finger. "But Garrison's a nice guy, sometimes too nice. He feels loyal to you because of what you've done for him, for the country. Doesn't want to seem ungrateful. But he wants you to back off of this mole hunt. You're making him look bad, putting him on the spot with Fullwood. Earl gets frustrated and chews that cigar but he's capable of running the FBI. If there's a mole, he'll find it. Finding moles, Colonel, that's an *FBI* function. The president knows Earl's got a big job to do, doesn't want him distracted by all this stuff coming from you. So find another undertaking for yourself. I urge it in the strongest terms." Quinn stopped for a moment, jabbed the finger and forced a pasty smile. "And don't be surprised if you get some sort of high-level appointment by the president one of these days."

Warfield jerked his arm away from Quinn and stepped out of the SUV. He knew better than to give himself any more time to react. Whether or not Quinn was passing on a message from Cross, the appointment-for-compliance insult was Quinn's alone. And Warfield didn't like it. He didn't like any of it. And he damn sure didn't like Quinn.

Warfield stood at the SUV door and looked in at Quinn. "Cross is a man. If he wants me off he'll tell me. Until then, Quinn, I go with his prior instructions." He slammed the door and went to his car.

The news headlines were airing on the radio when Warfield started his car. The recent calm in Israel was in jeopardy as violence broke out between the Israelis and Palestinians. President Cross was in California campaigning for congressional candidates in the upcoming November elections. Sports wise, the Redskins were three-point underdogs to the Cowboys in Cowboys Stadium Sunday. In the weather, Hurricane Veronica, which had threatened the East Coast for several days, was now expected to spare Wilmington, North Carolina, the most recent of coastal areas to evacuate as the hundred and ten mile per hour hurricane continued to defy forecasters' predictions of its path and strength.

Earl Fullwood stood with his hands stuffed inside his pockets looking out of his window in the J. Edgar Hoover FBI building, his unlit cigar wagging up and down as he unconsciously chewed on it. He was waiting for Rachel Gilbert to bring in an up-to-the-minute surveillance report on Cameron Warfield. When she arrived, Fullwood sat in the leather chair behind his desk, which rested on a carpeted platform two steps above the main floor. It was not unlike a judge's bench, in front of which Fullwood's visitors were forced, by design, to look up at him.

Fullwood learned from his father and his grandfather that women had their places, alright, and those places were the kitchen and the bedroom. They had no station in a man's world. He couldn't deny that Rachel Gilbert and women like her had made it through law school, some of them even excelling, but the last thing he wanted was one of them as his deputy director at the Bureau.

When he bowed to the political pressure to put a woman somewhere at the highest levels of the Bureau, he brought Rachel up but saw to it that she had no power. Despite her title, she was relegated to little more than a paralegal to manage his paperwork and deliver his orders to his lieutenants—the men who ran things, got the real work done. He consoled himself with the fact that he could point the finger at Rachel Gilbert when things blew up. And she would bear the burden if she had any hope for her future.

Rachel Gilbert took her seat in front of Fullwood's big desk as he peered down at her from the platform.

"So what've th' boys got on Warfield today?" he asked.

"Okay, first, he was at the White House with you and Quinn this morning."

"Well, thank you for that, Gilbert, you think I didn't see Warfield sittin' there across from me?"

"I, I was just—"

"Go on with the report. I don't have all day."

"Well, Warfield was at the White House until four-fifteen. No visitors. Then he drove to Langley and met with Quinn for twenty-two min—"

"*Whoa*, Gilbert! Did you say *Quinn* again?"

"Yes, sir."

"Well what th' hell was that about?"

Gilbert swallowed hard. "I don't know that, sir."

"Well, where'd they meet, Gilbert?" Fullwood half-stood out of his chair now as if he was about to lunge over the desk at her.

"In the Director's SUV. They just drove around. Twenty-two minutes to be exact."

"Well, tell me what was it about, Gilbert."

"We, uh, they were in Director Quinn's vehicle."

"You said that. So what?"

"We don't have the CIA director's vehicle bugged, sir."

Fullwood frowned and looked out the window. "Damn that Warfield," he mumbled. "He doesn't give up."

"What was that, sir?"

"Get Warfield off the mole hunt, Gilbert."

"I've told him before to stay out of Bureau business."

"Apparently that hasn't worked, Gilbert!"

"What would you like me to do. He works for the president, you know."

"But *we* don't, do we Gilbert? Your *tellin'* Warfield didn't get the job done, now did it? Hell, you're in the FBI now, Gilbert. Th' dep'ty director. If you can't figure out how to get rid of a problem like Warfield—"

Gilbert's throat lumped up. "Yes sir. I'll take care of it."

Back in her office, Rachel closed the door and propped her feet on her desk. During her years at the Bureau, she'd seen Fullwood become more and more impossible. He'd always been tough, but now he was unbearable. It seemed to be related to Warfield now. Fullwood spent most of his time worrying about his whereabouts and activities instead of directing the fight against terrorism and corruption. It was almost as if Fullwood himself had something to hide, Rachel thought.

She drew in a deep breath and swung around to her phone.

Warfield sat in his office at the White House staring into space. He had to find a way to look into the CIA director's whereabouts on the date Seth's man met the American in Paris. He didn't want to attract attention to Quinn or to himself. That could embarrass or even alienate his closest ally, President Cross, even if there was no truth to what Quinn had said about Cross in the car. Warfield couldn't care less about some high-level appointment, but he didn't want to scrap his name in Washington and in the intel community. He picked up the phone and punched in Paula Newnan's number.

"Well, it's Cameo again. What good fairy do I owe for all the attention I'm getting these days from my favorite eligible bachelor?"

"You always make things look better, Newnan."

"What's your problem now, Cameo?"

"Ah, no problem. Need to know where to find a little information."

"Like what?"

"How about a beer after work. I'll tell you then."

"Well-l-l-l, I think I'm supposed to say I'm busy, but this time I'll make an exception! May be the only way I'll ever get you away from that gorgeous Fleming DeGrande."

Paula walked the four blocks from the White House and had commandeered a table when Warfield arrived. Castrogiovanni's was noisy because of all the hard surfaces. Walls, floors, doors and the bar itself were finished in polished cherry veneers that bounced the sounds all around the room.

They both ordered a draft.

"My staff thought I was sick when I walked out at six," she said.

"Oughta take more time off."

"I'd probably spend it in some place like this. I like it here."

Warfield looked around. He'd been to Castro's a few times. Something about the place reminded him of Rawlings, Texas.

"The drug store in my home town, Trane's Pharmacy, we used to go there after ball practice, catch the girls hanging out at the soda fountain. Had a high tin ceiling like this place. We'd get a couple burgers, double fries, big shake, put quarters in the jukebox, flirt with the girls while we pigged out. Old man Trane would come around and turn down the music. As soon as he was back filling another prescription, we'd sneak behind that Wurlitzer and crank it up again."

"That's probably the least bad thing you did in those days."

Warfield chuckled.

He signaled the waitress to bring another round.

"Speaking of trouble, Cameo, wanna know about Seth? Your mythology question. I had a chance to look it up."

"Give it to me."

"Okay, he's got a long story, but the short version is Seth was a god in charge of storms, violence, disorder, unrest, usually drawn with slanting eyes, snout. A composite of various animals. If he wasn't sufficiently appeased by his people, so it goes, they were hit with violent sandstorms, something like that. Not a popular god."

Warfield didn't spend much time thinking about it. "Need some info, Paula. Who keeps track of the comings and goings of the wheels?"

"I get the president's itinerary, of course. Who are you talking about?"

"Quinn. I'd like to keep it quiet. Cross doesn't need to know."

"Quinn? You're snooping on the head snoop?" Paula laughed. "That's funny, Cameo." Then she frowned and said, "but it's also very dangerous."

"How about it? Can you help?"

"I get Quinn's itinerary if he's traveling with the president, or if they're going to be at the same place at the same time. That's not often."

"So if I gave you a certain date…"

"You haven't changed since those drugstore days, Cameo. Still pressing the envelope, except the stakes are a little higher these days. About all Mr. Trane could do was run you out."

Warfield nodded.

"Tell me the date and I'll check."

"Last year, 22 April."

"Have some work to do at the office tonight. After everyone leaves I'll see what I can find out. Call you first thing tomorrow."

"Tonight."

It was midnight and Fleming had gone to bed when his phone rang. Warfield answered in the great room. Paula said, "I know it's late, but I wanted to call you from home."

"What've you got?"

"Your man was at the New York Four Seasons Hotel on the night you asked about. Nothing unusual. According to the itinerary in the file, the president was there to address the U.N. He returned to Washington that day but your man stayed overnight. Looks like he was speaking at some committee meetings."

"How long did he stay?" Neither of them used Quinn's name.

"Checked in on the twenty-first, a Tuesday. Made a speech at eight the next morning, the twenty-second. Then another speech Thursday the twenty-third at noon. Checked out of the hotel that day."

"Thanks, Paula."

"No thanks necessary, Cameo. By the way, I heard that Fleming DeGrande has a contagious fatal disease. Wouldn't go near her."

"I'll check it out." Paula was a good-looking woman. Fortyish. Smart. Damn responsible. Worked all the time, which he figured was the reason she never remarried. After her husband died in a car accident years ago she seemed to turn all her energies to her work. She joked around with people she liked. She worked for Cross even before he entered the government sector and was the administrative standard of excellence by which others could evaluate themselves.

Warfield eased into bed and contoured himself to Fleming's nude body without waking her, and tuned in to her breathing pattern. It was slow and peaceful, strangely in sync with the old grandfather clock that stood at the end of the hallway outside the bedroom, ticking off the seconds with undisputed authority as if it were the Chief Clock over all others.

He stared into the darkness and thought about Quinn, relieved and at the same time disappointed. Quinn was in New York at the time of the Paris meeting. It wasn't that he hoped to find that the CIA chief led two lives, but it left Warfield back at the starting line. He had nothing. Quinn could be a bastard, but it was unimaginable that he was a traitor.

Warfield woke up tired the next morning. He'd dreamt he was a corporate accountant and couldn't make his books balance. The dream kept coming back around but the numbers never made sense: The computer-generated financial reports bore no resemblance to the input data and the reality of the financial status of the business.

The dream stayed with him all morning. He called Paula back. "Those records show whether my man had anybody with him on that New York trip?"

"You mean someone other than officials?"

"Right."

"They don't."

Helen Swope dabbed at her eyes and then her forehead with a lace-bordered white handkerchief. The Reverend Ebenezer Fuller sat beside her and gently squeezed her bony shoulder in his large hand. "You're doin' the right thing, Sister Helen. Don't you fret." His tone comforted her. Helen was Austin Quinn's once-a-week housekeeper during the time Ana was living there. She had testified at Ana's trial that she saw Ana sitting in front of Quinn's CIA computer terminal taking notes on several occasions.

Not long after the trial Helen began having headaches that kept getting worse. Her fingers took on a tremor and she lost from one-hundred-eighty down to ninety-five pounds. A tic developed that caused one corner of her mouth to spasm every few seconds. She hadn't worked in six months. Her doctors couldn't explain any of it.

A few weeks ago she confided in her minister, the Reverend Fuller, what she had done: She'd lied on the witness stand about Ana Koronis. And she knew her maladies were God's punishment. She didn't even know the name of the man who paid her the five thousand dollars to do it. Never saw him before the day he came to Quinn's house when she was working alone on a Saturday, her usual day, and sat down and talked with her about Ana and what Helen must say at the trial. He said he couldn't reveal to her all there was to know about the case, but justice could be served only if Ana was convicted and sent away. Helen would be doing a fine service to her country and even to her God, and the man didn't want her to think of herself as being anything other than patriotic.

Helen and Austin Quinn had never exchanged so much as a single glance about it, before or after the trial. She was certain he never knew it happened. She didn't know now any more than she knew at the trial about Ana's guilt or innocence, but she did know she had stood there in front of that judge and that jury and her God and she put her hand on that Bible and said she would tell the truth, and then she got on the witness stand and knowingly spoke lies.

Her attorney Filmore Dunstan sat across the desk and leaned on his left elbow, chin in hand, making notes on a legal pad with the other. He told Helen he didn't know how this was going to play out, but Helen made one thing very clear. She wanted to get it off her chest to the authorities. Come clean, whatever the consequences. Dunstan's secretary brought in the phone number he had asked her to find, but he had some questions for Helen before he placed the call.

"The man who talked to you that Saturday, Helen. He tell you how he knew you, or why he thought you'd be at Quinn's place that day?"

Helen shook her head.

"Would you recognize him if you saw him?"

"Doubt it. He wearin' a hat and he had on some real dark glasses all the time he talkin' to me."

"Anybody ever ask you those questions at the trial?"

"No sir."

Filmore Dunstan dialed the number for Joe Morgan, identified himself and asked Morgan if he remembered Helen Swope from the Koronis trial.

"How could I forget the key witness."

"She's sitting in my office. Has some information for you."

"Uh-oh."

"Yep."

"Something like a guilty conscience?"

"Yep. Could involve others, as well."

"She was put up to it?"

"Could be, but look, Helen wants to tell you all of this in person."

"I'm outta town next three days. How about my office Friday morning at ten."

"So, we meet again, Colonel Warfield," Ana said.

"Need a little more input."

She nodded blankly as she smoothed a wrinkle in her prison garb.

"You traveled with Quinn on official trips?"

"Sometimes."

Warfield looked at Ana for a moment, sitting there in her orange ADC jumpsuit, plain Jane, used to such a different life, another world. "Guess that was an ordeal. All the security around him, I mean."

"I was not unaccustomed to security, you know, married to the ambassador. But it can get to you."

"Ever able to get away from it, even for a short time?"

"Austin had many of the same security people for a long time. Sometimes he'd put on some sort of token disguise—hat, sunglasses, mustache even, when he was feeling a little frisky—and tell whoever was in charge of his security detail he didn't want them tagging along. I think they were pretty used to it."

"It happened often, then?"

"I think Austin left them guarding an empty room now and then. I don't know, didn't travel with him too much because of my work."

"How long would you stay out without security?"

"Sometimes we'd get a cab, go shopping, out to dinner, the theatre. Several hours, I guess."

Warfield put away his notes. "Speaking of Quinn, seen him lately?"

She smiled dismissively. "I'm...I'm sure he's been busy."

"You still...oh, sorry."

She shook her head. "It's okay. I still think of Austin. Nothing romantic. That was over before the trial, but I know the whole thing was hard on him, too."

"Saw him yesterday. He asked about you."

She nodded. "Wouldn't mind spending some time with him one day. You know, closure. Some old issues we never got to talk about."

Warfield mulled over the meeting as he headed back to Washington. Nothing incriminating about Quinn shaking his security detail now and then. Warfield figured he would do the same thing himself under the circumstances. But Warfield's bottom line was that he wasn't satisfied.

He dialed Paula. "Can you meet me at Castro's?"

"It'll have to be later, say, seven."

After Warfield left, Ana stood at the narrow window in her room at ADC. Birds were chirping, flying tree to tree, chasing each other around the compound, Ana thinking of their total freedom. She wondered how much longer before she was free. She was pleased at her progress with the colonel. And Suri. Suri had more of an impact on Warfield than Ana would have imagined.

Castrogiovanni's was a place you didn't worry about being overheard. The noise level took care of that.

Warfield asked Paula, "Can you find out who was on Quinn's security detail at a given time? That New York trip for example."

"Security Protective Service may have provided us a crew list. I can check."

"Before noon tomorrow?" Warfield pressed.

Paula groaned. "Gonna get me fired, Cameo."

When Warfield got to his office the next morning there was a voicemail from Joe Morgan, the U.S. attorney. "Only got a second before I catch my plane. The lawyer representing Helen Swope called. You remember Swope—the Koronis trial. Something on the little lady's mind. Impression is somebody helped her with her testimony, and now she's having a problem with it. Wants to talk. Meeting's Friday at ten. Knew you'd want to know."

Warfield hung up and mulled that little tidbit over for a moment. What a bombshell that would be. But until he learned more on Friday it would be a waste of time to speculate on it. Things like that came up frequently.

Paula walked in with a tan envelope containing the information he had asked her for, put it down with a smile and left. Warfield dumped the contents onto his desk. The agent in charge of Quinn's security on the New York trip had been Randall C. Coffman.

Warfield waited until evening to call. "Mr. Coffman, this is Cameron Warfield. I work in—"

"Uh, sure! That Japanese bomber, Yoshida, was it? That's you, right?"

Warfield acknowledged it was him. He told Coffman he needed information about one of his assignments.

"I'll try to help."

"Ever work for the CIA director?"

"Quinn?"

"Yes."

There was silence for a few moments, then, "Maybe we could meet."

"Breakfast tomorrow morning."

Warfield arrived first and chose a corner booth and watched the action behind the counter. At five-thirty in the morning Waffle Houses around the country are preparing the service workers of the world for the day with hot coffee, pecan waffles, bacon and eggs, grits and their favorite music on the jukebox. To Warfield, it was something to watch. The waitresses barking orders one after another and the cook keeping track in his head of every order in the house. Warfield wondered how they kept it straight.

Randall Coffman was thirty-one and had been with the Agency for nine years. Graduated fifth in his class at Spelman College in Atlanta with a major in government and minor in criminal science. He had been quarterback and senior-year captain of the football team and active in the Spelman chapter of SIP, Statesmanship in Politics. Coffman denied any interest in running for political office, but he'd always been awed by the vision of the founding fathers. Now he'd come to loathe the double-speak, the legal bribery and so many other examples of what he considered depravation and moral prostitution in Washington. Warfield had gleaned that information off Coffman's personal Web page after they talked on the phone last night and decided the guy was pretty gutsy to publish some parts of it.

At six-two and two-hundred pounds, Coffman was in good shape and well-groomed. He wore creased khakis and a navy knit shirt.

"Knew you from your pictures on TV," he said with a wide smile of healthy white teeth.

After a few minutes of sizing each other up and weighing the prospects of the Redskins at Dallas, Coffman beat Warfield to the point. "Quinn in trouble?" There wasn't much chance of a conversation being overheard in the Waffle House either.

Warfield shook his head. "Special project."

Coffman nodded and smiled. "I'm cool with that."

"You were on his security detail?"

Coffman nodded again.

"He leave you guys behind a lot?"

Coffman shrugged. "At times."

"And you protested."

"And how did you know that?"

"Tell me about it."

Coffman took a deep breath and exhaled. "I'd seen it happen now and then...before I was in a *position* to protest. It was okay with me before I was put in charge of his detail. At that time it wasn't my place to call him on it."

"Talk to Quinn about it when you became in charge?"

"First couple of times, no. It was an hour or two here and there. He'd say where he was going, we'd shadow him from a respectable distance, stay out of his way. I always knew where he was. No big deal."

"And then?"

Coffman looked out the window. His lips pulled tight and his eyes glassed over a little. "I'm telling you this because I'm still stinging from the transfer. And because I think I know the kind of guy you are. But I'll deny saying it so don't quote me...unless you're wired. You wired?" His facial expression said he was only half joking.

"We're on the same team, Randall."

"Quinn was in New York couple days. Just finished making a speech at a breakfast conference one morning. It was early, around eight. Said he had some private business to take care of and would be back in time for a meeting scheduled for noon the next day. I'm saying to myself, *the next day?* He didn't want a tail—nobody was to follow him. Told me to cover for him. That's more than twenty-four hours he's gonna be invisible. I figured he was visiting a lady friend, maybe, because of the sly little grin he gave me."

"You complied?"

Coffman nodded. "Big mistake. Murphy's Law or somebody's…you know, if something can go wrong, it will. Sure enough, my supervisor checks in with me. I lied to him. Told him Quinn was in his room, had the flu, didn't want to be disturbed for any reason." Coffman looked into his coffee mug. "You can't imagine how I hated myself for doing that."

"I think I can."

"So when Quinn came back the next morning I confronted him, respectfully. Told him I wouldn't be a party to that again. That turned out to be my last day on his security detail. At least he didn't fire me."

"Who knows about this?"

"The overnight? No one. Didn't even tell my supervisor. Quinn may have, I wouldn't know, but no one ever said another word to me about that night."

The waitress brought more coffee. The two men sat without speaking for a minute.

Then Warfield said, "You happen to remember the date?"

"*Remember!* It was the longest twenty-four hours of my life and I'll *never* forget it. The man whose life I was responsible for was out of touch. It was last year, April 22nd."

Warfield returned to his office perplexed. If all of this didn't cause him to wonder about Austin Quinn, it damn well did nothing to clear him. But that seemed to make Warfield more reluctant to believe it. Maybe he was afraid to learn it was Quinn. The CIA director might be arrogant, cocky, demanding, but it was unfathomable that he was disloyal to his country. Warfield found himself wanting to walk away from it, leave it where it was, let someone else find it out if it was true. But no man with an ounce of grit would let it lie.

He called the White House travel office and asked for flight schedules from New York to Paris. Someone named Tammy took his call.

"Most flights depart late afternoon or early evening from JFK and arrive in Paris the next morning, Paris time. That okay?"

"So if I need to leave New York around ten in the morning and be back by seven the following morning?"

"No, sir. That wouldn't be possible."

"One other question. Would those schedules have been different in April last year?"

"I'll have to check. Please hold." Two minutes later, she was back on the line and said none of the New York to Paris schedules had changed since then by more than an hour. "Anything else, sir?"

Warfield checked his notes. It looked like this cleared up any question of Quinn meeting with Seth in Paris on that night. He was relieved. "No, that's it."

Tammy caught Warfield before he hung up. "Oh, sir, I just thought of this: I don't suppose you want to consider the new Oberon. No one here ever uses it but I think it does meet your scheduling requirements."

The Oberon! Of course. "What's the schedule for the Oberon?" he asked.

"Depart New York JFK at ten o'clock a.m., arrive Charles DeGaulle seven-thirty that evening."

"Every day?"

"Seven days a week, sir."

"And return?"

"Leave DeGaulle at ten a.m. and arrive JFK at seven-forty-five a.m. same day as departure. Isn't that amazing?"

Warfield hung up after asking Tammy to repeat the Oberon schedule to be sure he heard it right. It *was* amazing, all right, and it meant Quinn could have completed his speech on the morning of 22 April, flown the Oberon to Paris to avoid leaving a trail flying on a government plane, met with Seth and returned to New York in time for a noon speech on the twenty-third. Again, not proof, *but it was possible.*

He called Paula and asked her to get the passenger lists for the Oberon on 22 and 23 April. That night he called Randy Coffman and they met at the Waffle House again. This time they sat in Warfield's car instead of going inside.

"What's up now, Colonel?"

"Ever know Quinn's aliases?"

Coffman chuckled. *"Mad dog!"* he said.

"Mad dog?"

"That's how I remembered the aliases. Melvin A. Davis and Donald O. Goodwin. He had credentials for both. Driver's licenses, credit cards, passports, Social Security numbers, home addresses. You know, the works. Using aliases isn't necessarily unusual, of course."

Next morning, Paula brought in the Oberon passenger lists. "I should get a medal for this one." She turned to leave and looked back. "Watch out for Veronica, Cameo."

Hurricane Veronica had strengthened overnight but was almost stationary seventy miles from land due east of Washington. Forecasters now believed she would begin to track to the north and west today, and had issued warnings for the coastal areas of Maryland, Delaware and New Jersey. The D.C. area was already soaked and torrential rain was expected to continue. The National Weather Service and Homeland Security were hyping the potential danger to not only coastal areas but far inland as well. It was possible that Veronica would prove to be the biggest and most devastating storm in U.S. records.

Warfield blew Paula a kiss and slashed open the envelope. There were two Davises on the twenty-second, but no Melvin. He flipped to the Gs and there his eyes froze. *Goodwin Donald O!* He thrashed through the names for 23 April and found the name there too. Warfield felt blood rushing to his head. Donald O. Goodwin flew the Oberon to Paris on 22 April and was back in New York at seven-forty-five on the morning of the twenty-third. Anyone taking those flights could have made the speeches Quinn made in New York on those two days.

Warfield drew a deep breath and stared at the ceiling. Ten minutes later he called Quinn's office and left a message with his assistant that he would be in his office at the White House until six that afternoon if Quinn wanted to talk about his trip to Paris last year on 22 April. Warfield knew it was about to get ugly.

CHAPTER 18

QUINN STOOD IN WARFIELD'S White House office doorway at five-fifty that afternoon. The director had a habit of fidgeting with the cuffs of his shirt until they peeked out beyond the end of his coat sleeves. He leaned against the door frame and looked down at Warfield seated behind his desk. "Had some other business here, Warfield, and remembered you invited me to drop by your office. What's on your mind?"

Warfield knew how the man must have felt about being there. The two were not in the same galaxy in terms of political power or prestige, nor had they ever been close enough in personal terms to set rank aside, yet Warfield had called the meeting. Quinn could have demanded an alternate setting or ignored Warfield's message altogether. By stopping at the doorway he at least remained on neutral ground, and he made a point of saying he was there because he had other business at the White House—not because of Warfield's call. Warfield knew better. The Paris reference had done its job.

"There are a couple of things I wanted to mention to you in private," Warfield said.

"Let's hear 'em."

Warfield had decided to get Quinn's reaction to the Swope news first.

"It's about Helen Swope."

"*Swope?* What about Helen Swope?"

"I got a call from Joe Morgan, the U.S. attorney. Said Swope's got a lawyer and plans to retract her testimony. Morgan thinks she may have been the target of tampering at Ana's trial." Warfield was careful to present this to Quinn neutrally.

"*Tampering!*" Quinn maintained a blank expression.

"Could mean a new trial for her. God only knows what else will come out of it. Morgan's meeting with Swope and her attorney tomorrow. If Swope is believable, Morgan plans to take it to Ana and Judge Hartrampf."

Quinn became pensive. After a period of silence, he said, "You also said something about Paris?"

Warfield nodded. "Yeah, the trip Donald O. Goodwin took to Paris last year. Twenty-second of April to be exact."

Quinn's cognition was subtle but Warfield caught it. After a couple of seconds, Quinn cocked his head again and said, "I travel a lot, Warfield. Sometimes to Paris, even. I lose track of places and dates but what the hell difference does it make to you, anyway? I don't answer to you or to anyone else. Snooping around on my travels part of your assignment? I don't get you, Warfield."

Warfield was calm. "Nothing like that, Austin. Came up in my mole hunt. Twenty-second April was the date of the Seth meeting."

"Screw you, Warfield, I was in New York when that..." Quinn stopped mid-sentence.

Warfield had him!

Quinn reddened, then turned his eyes down the hallway. After a few seconds, he stepped inside the room and closed the door. "Know why I came here, Warfield? I came here to put a stop to this. You can bet hell will go out of business before I ever explain one second of my time to you. Who do you think you are, you son of a bitch, looking over the shoulder of the director of central intelligence. Without Cross, you're a serial number buried in the hollows of an outdated army database somewhere, a farm boy come to town, a career army bootlick. I wonder how much brass you sucked up to on the way up—all the way up to colonel, too, huh Warfield? Couldn't quite climb that hill to general, could you? I advised you to get off this project of yours when we were in the car, but now it's you or me and I'll tell Cross that. Got any doubt about how that's going to turn out?"

Warfield didn't say anything. He maintained eye contact with Quinn, and waited.

Quinn finally spoke, having spent some of his emotion. With hoarse voice, he said, "I know it *looks* bad, Warfield, but it's certainly not that way. Who else knows about it?"

"No one at this moment. But that will change tomorrow."

"Why?"

"Like I said, Morgan wants to meet with Swope, her lawyer, and me. Then he'll see Ana."

"And you'll say what?"

"Put yourself in my shoes. What would you say?"

Quinn withdrew again. After a moment he leaned closer to Warfield, presented a strained smile and addressed him with newfound warmth. "Look, Cam, this Paris trip is nothing like you're suggesting, but if it gets out it'll be a problem—not only for me but for Cross, the administration. You and I go back too far for this to come between us. Those things I said a minute ago, I lost control, that was just my frustration boiling over. Don't hold that against me. We could work something out before you see Morgan tomorrow, just between us."

Warfield looked at Quinn. Groveling didn't become this man who was used to taking what he wanted without asking.

Warfield said quietly, "You know that's not an option, Austin."

"Goodwin?"

"Donald O. Goodwin, everything. All on the table when I meet Morgan tomorrow."

Quinn walked out. Only the swagger was missing.

Quinn's driver fought the storm all the way back to Langley. Hurricane Veronica continued to hover not far from land, dumping rain on D.C.— by the bathtubful, it seemed to Quinn. There was a chance she would blow right through the D.C. area once she cranked up forward movement, but now Veronica sat there building steam, taunting everyone within an incredible four-hundred miles of her center. Her winds had increased and the National Hurricane Center issued updates and warnings every few minutes.

Quinn checked his voicemail as soon as he got back to his office at Langley. He skipped half a dozen messages from members of Congress and two from his assistant, Angel Clawson. The one he listened to was from the attorney who represented Ana at her trial. He played it three times. "Mr. Quinn, uh, *Director* Quinn, Manny Upson here, Ana Koronis's attorney. I'd hoped to speak with you. That U.S. attorney Joe Morgan called me and it sounds like Helen Swope's going to retract her testimony. They're meeting tomorrow morning at Morgan's office. Swope and her attorney, a Filmore Dunstan. I thought you'd want to know because, well, I suppose because of Ana. Isn't this great news?"

Quinn filled a bar glass with Glenfiddich Scotch, sat on the sofa across from his desk and set his drink on the coffee table. The hairline crack in the glass top reminded him of the day Leonard Magliacci visited him. It was Magliacci who started this. Quinn had invited him to his office at CIA thinking he could intimidate him or buy him off with a few dollars but the guy was smarter than Quinn anticipated. When Quinn paid Magliacci in return for the incriminating contents of Magliacci's safe-deposit box, he buried them inside bags of cement from Home Depot for ballast and dumped them far out at sea, precluding any possibility they would ever be found.

The trees outside Quinn's window bowed to the wind as huge raindrops blasted the glass. The room lights were off, and by the time Quinn finished another Scotch the room was all but dark. The lights from the courtyard below beamed through the rills of water trailing down the window and created a bed of worms on the ceiling.

Quinn looked up at the squiggling lines for a minute and flipped on a lamp to make them disappear. He poured another Scotch, played Epson's message again, deleted it and looked up Judge Hartramph's private home number. The judge answered.

"Austin Quinn, Judge. Sorry to bother you."

"Austin? Well, it's all right. But is there a problem? You sound tired."

"No, I'm fine, Judge. Got a special request. Wanted to see if you'll approve a leave for Ana Koronis. I'd like to take her out of the ADC for a couple days."

Hartrampf paused before answering. "You're asking a lot, Austin. That's totally irregular."

Quinn told Hartrampf he would be responsible for Ana's return by Monday. He also said he'd get Cross to join in his request if that would make Hartrampf more comfortable with it. And he reminded the judge that Ana had not yet been placed in a federal prison. Taking her from the Alexandria jail would be less problematic.

Hartrampf agreed, but he didn't sound comfortable with it. He reminded Quinn that he'd be charged with responsibility for her. "I'll arrange it tomorrow morning."

"Uh, Judge, I was thinking of getting an early start—"

"Sure. I'll take care of it early for you, Austin."

Quinn hung up, watched the rain pound the window and thought about the close call he'd been in years ago at the Golden Touch in Atlantic

City, the night he'd murdered Karly Amarson in a fit of rage. The thought reminded him of an envelope he'd put in his personal floor safe. He took it out and looked at the photograph of Karly that he'd received at his office a couple of years ago in an envelope marked "PRIVATE AND CONFIDENTIAL TO AUSTIN QUINN." Someone had signed it "To Jag, from Karly" but there was no other inscription. Karly was long dead but it had shaken him. Fortunately, nothing had come of it since. Someone who'd known about Karly had sent it to him, but for what purpose? A sick joke, or was it Magliacci again with another blackmail scheme? It was a loose end that Quinn had never been able to dismiss.

Quinn turned to the phone and hit a speed-dial button.

"Biggers."

"There's a couple of problems."

"Okay."

"They gotta be fixed tonight."

Warfield left the White House after meeting with Quinn and drove to his condo. He left his car in the driveway while he ran in to get some clothes to take to Hardscrabble. The phone was ringing when he walked in. It was Fleming, still at her office, and she suggested they go out to dinner. To hell with the weather. She said she'd swing by Warfield's and pick him up.

Fleming got Warfield at his condo and drove them through the storm to Ticcio's. Ticcio seated them and sent over a bottle of wine. Warfield couldn't extricate himself from his thoughts and told Fleming some of his concerns without naming Quinn. After dinner Fleming suggested they drive to Hardscrabble instead of adding the trip back to Warfield's in the weather. She could drop him off at his place to get his car tomorrow morning.

Warfield couldn't sleep. It was as if he had left some important but unidentifiable duty undone. His restlessness woke Fleming and they talked for an hour while she massaged his neck and scalp. Her voice always soothed him. They finally fell asleep, their nude bodies intertwined, as the wind and rain pounded the windows.

Next morning, Warfield picked at a bowl of Cheerios while Fleming had coffee and an English muffin with honey. The rain continued and the century-old Hardscrabble house creaked and groaned to the tune of the wind. Veronica threshed schizophrenically offshore and continued to outfox forecasters, who had calculated the storm would have identified her prey by now. News on the kitchen radio said the maximum winds near the center were a hundred and twenty miles per hour this morning and showed signs of strengthening. The blow at Reagan National Airport was thirty-nine with gusts to fifty. Washington area schools and offices were prepared to act when necessary but for the moment it was business as usual.

Fleming studied Warfield as she sipped her coffee. "I know you, War Man. When you're this deep into something it's about to come to a head."

"I don't think I'm going to like it."

Driving rain and pockets of water on the road made driving to Warfield's condo torturous. When they were half a block from his condo, they saw the commotion around his place. Fire trucks and police cars were all over. As they drew nearer, Warfield could see that his condo was destroyed. He jumped out of the car before Fleming was completely stopped and ran through the yellow police ribbon to the nearest cop.

"What the hell happened here?" he yelled above the wind and rain.

"This your house?"

He started to say yes but caught himself. "Across the street," he nodded. He surveyed the damage to his home. The fire was almost out with help from the rain but the pungent smell of charred wood filled the air. Smoke from two of the tires on his car curled upward and disappeared into the rain. The roof of his condo had crumpled into the building and burned, and two of the brick-veneered side walls had collapsed. The windows in the two teetering walls that remained had blown outward, leaving ragged holes. His townhouse-style home stood separate from others and was the only one with much damage. Probably because of the rain.

Warfield the neighbor listened silently as the police and firefighters told him what they knew about the origin of the fire. The explosion occurred around four that morning. Fire crews first burst the door in to see if anyone was inside. Investigators said it appeared the fire resulted from explosives thrown through a window of the condo. The blast that followed ignited the car. Warfield now realized that CIA Director Austin Quinn, a man in a position to have unfathomable resources at his fingertips, was not going down without a fight.

What luck that he'd spent the night at Hardscrabble. He told Fleming to ditch her car, find the nearest cab and check into a hotel away from the city. She might be a target as well. "Don't go back to Hardscrabble. Call my voicemail once to let me know you're okay and don't say anything else. When they find out I'm alive they'll figure out how to pick up any calls. The only people I'm sure you can trust right now are Cross and Paula, but if Quinn or Fullwood already got to Cross, he may be slow to act."

"I'm going with you."

"No good. They find me, you don't need to be there. Besides, you've got patients waiting for you."

"But—"

"No time to argue, Fleming. Just be careful."

She pulled his head down to hers and nuzzled him for the second he remained still. "Take care of yourself."

Warfield left Fleming in her car and disappeared, caught a cab four blocks away, sent the driver through a maze of turns and got out ten minutes later. He gave the cabbie a twenty for the Redskins cap he was wearing and hurried through an alley to another street. He surveyed the area, jumped into another cab and took the Roosevelt bridge across the Potomac. He gave the driver random left and right turns until they got to Washington Circle, where traffic became frustratingly stop and go.

A weathered pickup truck loaded with tool boxes inched along on the cab's left. The sign on the door said, "Leroy's Anytime Plumbing Service." Warfield dropped some cash on the cab driver's front seat, checked all around, and jumped out of the taxi and into the truck.

The pickup driver was taken by such surprise that he almost rammed the car in front of him, but before Warfield knew it, he was staring at the end of a large blue semi-automatic pistol two inches from the bridge of his nose. Veins pulsed in the black man's muscular arms as he looked wide-eyed at Warfield. *"You crazy, man?"* he screamed.

Warfield threw his hands up. *"Listen, friend, listen. Listen! Someone's after me. I'm not here to hurt you."*

"You on the wrong end of this gun to hurt *me*, asshole!"

The driver studied Warfield for a moment and relaxed the pistol. "Who's after you, man?"

"Are you Leroy?" he asked, remembering the sign on the truck door.

"Hell yes, I am!"

"I'm Warfield. Keep going. I'll get out down the street. They won't bother you."

Leroy continued around the circle to K Street and drove east. "So what'd you do to 'em?"

"Plan to ask first chance I get."

Lines that radiated from the corners of Leroy's eyes tightened when he laughed. A four-by-six photo of Leroy standing in front of a modest white house with two women and four small children looked down at him from the sun visor.

"Yours?" Warfield said, hoping he could make Leroy less nervous. But he scanned every car for the threat he knew was looming.

"Those are my kids and my wife and my mama. I bought that house there too. *First one.* My wife Mona, well, I did some time and she hung on, then she put up with a lot more while I was getting this business going. Nights, days, weekends, whatever. She said I always put work before her and the kids, but it had to be that way. She's a good 'un."

"So business is good?" Warfield said, mechanically.

"Long time to get something up and going, make a little money, pay off the loans. Did it though. Me and the Lord and the bank, we're on real good terms now."

Leroy asked for directions as they approached Mt. Vernon Square.

"Go around to New York. I'll get out in a couple blocks." Warfield didn't want Leroy to get caught up in this.

After they were on New York, Leroy said, "They drivin' a black Mercedes?"

Somehow they recognized Warfield through the blinding rain when he looked around. The first shot bounced off a steel tool box in the back of the truck and echoed through the truck.

"God help us!" Leroy screamed.

"Zig-zag, Leroy! Back and forth, back and forth." Warfield grabbed Leroy's pistol from the seat.

Leroy swerved left into Fourth Street with the Mercedes right on him. When he turned left again onto Ridge the Mercedes pulled up beside the pickup. The rider in the right front seat took aim at Leroy with a sawed-off shotgun. Warfield saw his own barrage from Leroy's gun explode the shooter's chest but it was too late. *The contents of Leroy's head flew throughout the cab of the truck.* Warfield ran his hand across his own eyes to clear the blood away. The truck hit the curb and rolled to a stop against a utility pole.

Some of the shot from the sawed-off caught Warfield's shoulder, but he continued to fire until the three-fifty-seven was empty. He thought he caught the driver but he was shooting blind because of the blood and broken glass. Warfield looked at the man upon whom he had brought this tragedy. *God forgive me!* Half of his skull was missing. Blood, bone and brain tissue covered Warfield and everything inside of the truck. It was a scene Warfield wouldn't forget. As he started to jump out, he reached back and grabbed the photo off the visor and shoved it into his pocket.

Warfield heard sirens but now he trusted no one. Even if it were the D.C. police he would be detained and the FBI or CIA or whoever they sent after him would soon know they had him. As he ran several blocks north through the backyards of houses, he caught a glimpse of the Mercedes creeping along Fifth Street to his left.

Warfield came to an unbroken line of backyard fences across his path, turned right toward Fourth, navigated through the trees at full stride and came upon another five-foot chain-link fence. There was no way out except the way he entered. The German Shepherd claiming the yard came to attention, but Warfield's choices were limited. He gripped the steel top rail of the fence and threw his body over, bounded two long strides to the point where the taller wood fence that had blocked his path in the adjacent yard connected, and jumped back over the other chain link. It happened so fast that the snarling Shepherd was still sharpening his fangs when Warfield was out of reach again.

Warfield didn't see the mud hole until he'd leaped from the fence. It was six- or eight-feet across and a toy boat lay just out of the water next to a rubber duck. A water hose that had been used to fill the hole on a drier day ran from a faucet somewhere across the yard and disappeared into the hole. Warfield landed in the middle of it. It was deeper than he expected and he lost his footing. He scrambled to his knees and poked his head out. Mud dripped from his face as he made a quick reckoning. The dog in the next yard was having a heart attack. Warfield's only shot now was north, through the backyards of the houses that fronted on both Fourth and Fifth, and he needed to move before the frantic Shepherd drew a crowd.

The Mercedes had circled around and now stopped in the middle of Fourth, about a hundred feet east of Warfield. The shooter, a blur in the rain, emerged from the car and headed toward the barking dog. Warfield ducked back into the hole until his head was submerged, groped for the water hose, managed his Ka Bar pocket knife and sawed off a three-foot section of the hose. Still holding his breath, he inched the end of the short section of hose out of the water and into the edge of the grass, blew it clear, expelled as much of the muddy water from his mouth as he could and sealed his lips around the submerged end of the hose to make a snorkel.

Finally! As he began to breathe again, the shooter was trying to get a clue from the ballistic Shepherd in the adjacent yard as to the intruder's location. Then something else attracted his eye and he gave up on the dog. It was the hose! Warfield could make out the stubby shotgun hanging at the end of the man's arm as he moved around to the hose. When the shooter stepped into the edge of the mud hole, Warfield reached for an ankle and jerked. The shooter's arms flew up in an attempt to maintain balance and Warfield heard the gun fire.

Warfield figured he'd been shot but felt no new pain yet. The shooter was under the water with him now but had lost control of the shotgun. Warfield grabbed it and pressed the end of the barrel into the shooter's chest. When he cleared the mud from his eyes he saw that the gun was no longer necessary. Blood poured from what had been the shooter's neck. When he had accidentally fired the shotgun it had blown the front half of his head away.

Warfield threw the shotgun to the ground, disgusted, having lost the opportunity to find out from this goon who was behind the attack. As he expected, the man had no I.D. on him.

Other dogs were barking by then but Warfield didn't know whether they were yard dogs or if he were being hunted down. He was a threat now, to Quinn at least, and it had come to this. As unbelievable as it seemed, Warfield had been marked by the director of the CIA. Quinn's man or men thought he was at his condo because his car was parked in the driveway. When they realized they didn't get him, they went for him in the open, right on the street. Warfield had survived, but now an innocent man was dead, as well as this thug and the one he'd shot in the Mercedes.

The rain was heavier now and the wind stronger. The temperature was in the mid-sixties but Warfield was chilled from the rain and mud. He'd emptied Leroy's gun into the Mercedes and left it in the truck, and he had no shells for the shotgun. He kicked it into the mud hole. It was time to go, but he heard the police and emergency vehicles coming from the vicinity of Leroy's truck. He had to get out of there before they blocked off the area.

"Ready, Ms. Koronis?" Marybeth asked. Ana had made friends with the red-haired guard.

"He's here?"

"They called up for you. Excited?"

A crooked smile hit Ana's lips. "Don't exactly know how I feel, Marybeth, but I don't think it's bad." She took a last look in the mirror. Marybeth had sneaked her some drugstore makeup. She fidgeted with her hair.

"You're lookin' good, Ms. Koronis. Too bad it's raining, this bein' your first time out in a while. And you're not gonna believe that wind."

Minutes later Ana signed some papers at the desk of Captain Aubrey Holden and noticed Austin Quinn's signature was already on them. "Where is he?"

Holden nodded toward a deputy waiting outside his office. "Sergeant Brighton there will walk you down to the garage."

As they walked away, Holden said, "Don't forget to come back."

Ana wondered how many times Holden had used the line. Two floors down, Brighton led her across the basement to the black SUV. Quinn saw them coming and got out to greet her.

"Ana."

She smiled somewhat apprehensively. "Austin."

He pulled her to him. They embraced like siblings might, and talked for a few seconds as Brighton stood nearby. As soon as the SUV was off the jail premises she told Quinn she wanted to stop for a minute. The driver pulled over and Ana jumped out, raised her arms to the sky and turned her face to the driving rain. She stood like that for maybe thirty seconds before lowering her arms to shoulder level and winging like a graceful eagle exploring the skies. Her hair and clothes were soaked when she got back in. Raindrops ran down her cheeks, taking her new makeup with it.

Warfield's most urgent need was transportation out of the neighborhood. The Mercedes with the first dead gunman still inside was not an option. He slogged through the soaked yards several lots further north, somewhat obscured by the rain and low clouds, and spotted an old Ford Thunderbird in a driveway. He had it wired in seconds and drove north then east and then south again to avoid the intersection where Leroy's truck was sitting. Police hadn't blocked off all the streets yet and he made it out of the neighborhood without being stopped.

The T-bird began sputtering minutes later and Warfield wheeled into a motel parking lot and coasted around the end of the building to a secluded lot partially filled with run-down cars. The stained sign on the roof of the old building read, "Clean Rooms By The Hour." The round, seventyish woman behind the counter looked up at Warfield through eyes whose whites had long ago turned brown. She made no move to get out of her chair.

When Warfield pushed a soggy twenty-dollar bill across the worn Formica top she took a slow drag off the Camel cigarette she was smoking and surveyed the mud that covered him from top to bottom. At last she managed herself out of her chair, waddled to the counter and gave him a key stamped with the number 6, and a sheaf of ones she retrieved from her skirt as change.

It hit him that she was going to call the police as soon as he walked out. Dopers and hookers were the norm. Muddy and bloody hair and clothes were another thing. His eyes caught hers as he left the ones on the bar, figuring he was the first person to make eye-contact with her in years, and the only one who'd ever left a tip. Maybe she would think about it long enough for him to get out of there. All he needed were a few short minutes.

He'd lost his cell phone in the mud but found a pay phone nearby and dialed Paula Newnan's direct line. He'd spotted a Jiffy Lube oil change place down the street and told her to meet him there. "Soon as you can. Make it quick!"

When Warfield entered Room 6 the stale odors, dingy carpet and frayed bedspread reminded him of the quality of life experienced by those who were relegated to places like this. He took a shower, washed his clothes in the bathtub, wrung them out as much as possible and put them back on wet. Wet clothes would look normal on a day like today. He trotted along the back streets to the Jiffy Lube and was waiting when Paula arrived. They had the customer area to themselves.

"This better be good, Cameo. I don't usually come to this part of town without a gun. And I didn't need an oil change."

"Listen, Paula. They're trying to take me out. This has to be quick. I need—"

"*Take you...who? For what?*" she stage-whispered. Her eyes were saucer-size. "My God, you're putting too much heat on somebody!"

"Quinn. Or maybe he convinced Fullwood I'm a problem that needs solving. Fullwood wouldn't be hard to convince. Either way, I'm a target."

"*You think Quinn—*"

"Yes."

"You've seen them, these people who are trying to kill you?"

"They bombed my condo last night! When they realized I wasn't inside, they chased me down and tried to shoot me and they killed a Samaritan who was trying to help me. Somebody's going to pay for him if nothing else."

"Oh, God." Paula took a second to digest it all. "Out in the open? Come on, Cam, this can't be happening!"

"These guys weren't wearing coats and ties, Paula."

"Contractors."

"Exactly. Don't ever think the nice boys at Langley or the Hoover building are above using dirty knives to cut their meat with. They got 'em on speed dial."

Paula shook her head. "And what do I do?"

"I need your car. Catch a cab back to Hertz and rent something. We'll work it out later."

"That's easy—but wait a minute. You can go to Cross with this."

"What I've got on Quinn is too hot. And I can't prove anything yet. If Cross knew about it at this point he'd have a helluva dilemma."

"Where'll you go?"

"Don't know yet, but you haven't talked to me."

CHAPTER 19

WARFIELD HEADED NORTHEAST OUT of Washington, stopped at a mom and pop motel a few miles across the state line in Pennsylvania, registered under the name Pete Moore, avoiding even his aliases, and paid in cash. He'd jotted notes as he drove and now he looked them over from the perspective of a fugitive.

He called his voicemail and listened to a message Joe Morgan had left for Warfield at ten-forty that morning. Helen Swope hadn't shown up for the meeting. No word from Helen or Filmore Dunstan, her attorney. Morgan was afraid Helen had decided against changing her testimony, but maybe the weather delayed her. The second call was from Fleming. She was fine.

He looked out of his window as he waited for the final message to queue. It was almost dark at mid-afternoon. The wind howled through the trees and he wondered how they could bend so much without breaking.

The message played. It was a second call from Morgan, at noon. Warfield strained to hear the recording over the line static. Morgan was pumped this time and said Warfield was to call him immediately.

When Warfield dialed him back, the line crackled, making communication difficult.

"Glad it's you," Morgan said. "Veronica's about to run me out of my office, but listen to this, Warfield. Helen Swope was strangled to death in her bed last night."

Warfield was stunned.

"Her lawyer's dead too. Shot in the head as he—"

The line scratched and crackled before going dead. Warfield redialed and got a phone company recording that said phone lines were down in some D.C. areas due to winds from Veronica.

He hung up and put this news flash from Morgan into the equation. A few short hours earlier Warfield told Quinn that Helen Swope was going to tell Morgan this morning she had lied about Ana. Now both Helen and her attorney were dead—murdered. Warfield barely escaped the same fate—so

299

far. He stood there watching the rain fly sideways by the window as he tried to put it all together.

"Oh, God!...*Ana!*" Warfield mumbled. *Quinn was eliminating everyone who held keys to his history. Ana would have known Quinn aliased as Donald O. Goodwin and now she was going to die for knowing it.* She was not safe from Quinn even locked up in the ADC. Look at Joplan, for example.

He remembered meeting an officer Holden at the Alexandria Detention Center, where Ana was being held until they assigned her to a federal prison. He got the AT&T operator to try the line, hoping it was still in service.

"ADC." The line was noisy.

"Holden. Got a Holden there?"

"Captain Holden. One moment."

"Aubrey Holden."

"Holden, Cam Warfield."

"Colonel Warfield! Help you with something?"

"Ana Koronis! Everything okay with her?"

Holden laughed. "Pretty revved when I saw her few hours ago. I guess you know that the CIA guy, what's his name...Quinn? got her a pass for the weekend."

"She's with Quinn?" That was very bad news, but Warfield wasn't totally surprised.

"Yes, sir. I got an order to release her into Mr. Quinn's custody until Monday morning."

"Tell me that you know where they were going, Holden!"

"No idea, sir."

"You've got to find out, Holden. Now."

"I don't...well, hold a second. I'll see if anybody knows."

Holden was back a minute later. "Deputy Brighton here, he escorted Koronis to Mr. Quinn's car. Said Mr. Quinn told Ms. Koronis they were going to 'AC.' That mean Atlantic City, you think?"

"When did they leave?"

"This morning, right after eight."

Warfield hung up and ran through his options. It wouldn't be easy to stop Quinn. After all, *who in all of law enforcement had the will, the capacity—the thought that he could be a criminal—to apprehend the widely-known director of central intelligence?* Even Ana, in the dark about all of this, would laugh at the absurdity of it if anyone attempted to *save* her from Quinn. Cross was the only possibility, but Ana could be dead by the time it took Warfield to make the case to Cross that the man he loved like a brother was a traitor and a murderer. Even then, how much longer would it take Cross to assimilate the facts to the point of action?

Cross was not the answer. Warfield clicked on the motel room's vintage TV and stood there while the tubes warmed up. Under normal conditions, Atlantic City would be ninety minutes max from his motel, but the Weather Channel showed Veronica moving northward now, paralleling the coast with winds at speed of hundred and twenty. A spokesman from the National Hurricane Center couldn't say where or when she would turn westward to land, but the wind and rain would continue. Warfield knew it would only get worse as he drove closer to the coast.

He took I-95 north. The interstate was less prone to flood than the secondary roads he used earlier to avoid Quinn's thugs. It was three p.m. when he turned south at Philadelphia to take the Atlantic City Expressway. The weather had traffic crawling at a time when he needed to make speed. Quinn and Ana, hours ahead of him, had reached Atlantic City by now—if Holden was correct.

On the radio, the announcer said the New Jersey governor ordered the national guard to duty earlier in the day because of the threat from Veronica. The hurricane center broke in and said it now looked like the eye of the storm would hit a few miles down the coast from Atlantic City. Landfall should be around ten p.m. with winds near a hundred and thirty-five miles per hour. The accompanying storm surge could be as high as eighteen feet and would precede the eye of the storm by around five hours. Residents in Atlantic City and New Jersey coastal areas were ordered by the governor to evacuate.

That meant Warfield had two hours to get to the Golden Touch before the storm surge—evacuation or not. He was an hour from there in normal conditions but at the present rate he needed some luck. There were no cars going in his direction but he couldn't make out the roadway if he drove faster than forty.

The maximum storm surge occurs to the right of the center of the storm as it goes onto land, and it is that dome of water, pushed up at sea by the winds and low atmospheric pressure, that causes the most deaths and property destruction. Far out at sea, the water dome dissipates and causes no harm, but as the ocean floor rises to shore the water is forced up with it and rushes inland. Category four hurricanes, with winds up to one-fifty-five, hammer anything near the shore with giant waves and wreckage from other structures. The water action can undermine foundations and even topple buildings. Roofs, windows and doors become airborne. Low-lying areas are flooded. Deaths are common among people who can't get out of the way soon enough, or who say no to leaving their homes. Electric power is lost, which means stores and gasoline stations are down. The result is many deaths, billions of dollars in property destruction and total paralysis in the affected areas. Warfield flashed the thought of the Katrina victims and all the chaos in New Orleans afterward, and the more recent Sandy that devastated New Jersey and New York just months earlier.

Ten miles out of Philadelphia, flashing lights filled the roadway a hundred yards ahead of Warfield. He stopped on the shoulder and watched for a minute. State police were turning all Atlantic City-bound traffic back! Cars in the southbound expressway lanes sat in line on the exit ramp to cross the bridge over the highway and merge into northbound lanes that were already jammed with drivers escaping the coast. Military vehicles idled under the bridge and in the road beyond the police cars. National guardsmen in rain gear milled around, some directing traffic. Warfield knew other troops had the harder job of locating and convincing people to leave their homes.

Warfield surveyed the scene, pulled the Redskins cap down over his eyes, left Paula's car beside the road and jogged up the ramp to the crossover. A Humvee sat there with lights on, engine running and no driver. There were no soldiers nearby, as they were down at the expressway directing traffic. Warfield climbed in. Hummers were not new to him.

As he entered the ramp to the southbound lane toward Atlantic City, a soldier sitting beside the road in another Hummer threw up a hand in a casual gesture. Warfield waved back knowing recognition was not possible in this weather and moved onto the empty roadway south of the roadblock.

State troopers monitored the flow of traffic, moving at around thirty. Military vehicles roamed the side of the expressway and no one seemed to pay special notice to Warfield, just another guardsman on duty. He continued on the shoulder until he came to other idling military vehicles blocking the roadway and was forced to the ditch. Water rose to hood-level on the Hummer, but the Humvee was equipped with large-diameter wheels and a snorkel system that extended the air intake and exhaust above roof level enabling it to take the virtual river in stride until he could get back on the pavement.

Thirty-five was all Warfield could manage. Even if the wipers could handle the rain, he couldn't see beyond the front end of the Humvee. He was hoping almost against hope now that he could beat the storm surge. And what if Quinn and Ana weren't there? But he couldn't worry about that. There was no other place to look. Phones were out. Same for transportation. But Quinn *would* be there. It was human nature to go to a familiar place in times of crisis.

As Warfield approached the crest of a rise, a sea of car lights greeted him. Police vehicles, blue roof-mounted lights flashing, lined up across both sides of the expressway from fence-to-fence, and dead-still traffic lined up behind them as far as Warfield could see. There was no way around the roadblock. Warfield realized they were waiting for him, the idiot who had stolen the Humvee. He locked the doors, pulled to a stop near one of the state troopers who was flashing a light at him and lowered the window slightly.

At least fifty New Jersey state troopers and national guardsmen surrounded Warfield's Humvee. Some of the soldiers were talking among themselves and laughing at the absurdity of anyone stealing a Hummer, especially in this weather. Drivers who were lined up behind the row of police cars sat on their horns. A heavy state trooper captain with the name *Haygood* on his slicker focused a spotlight in Warfield's eyes. His right hand was concealed somewhere inside his raincoat. "Step down out of the vehicle, sir!" he shouted.

Ana was in the kitchen trying to pull together a meal from a few things she found in Quinn's personal suite at the Golden Touch. He hadn't anticipated that Atlantic City—and all food service at the Golden Touch—would be shut down before they arrived.

Quinn found himself with time on his hands. He'd put the five ten-milligram Valium tablets from his medicine cabinet into his shirt pocket and slipped the little .38 Smith & Wesson revolver from his bed table into the pocket of his slacks. He went over to the window to check on the storm again but the glass breathed in and out so much now that he feared it would break. He closed the heavy drapes so they might slow down any flying glass and poured himself another Glenfiddich. The main building power had gone off an hour earlier but his suite was connected to the auxiliary generators that came on in a power failure and ran the elevators and other critical areas of the Golden Touch.

He returned to the den where the TV was on. A crew filming from the eighth floor of another building along the coastline showed waves lapping over the Boardwalk, crashing into the casinos and ripping out sections of the famous walkway that Sandy hadn't already destroyed. His brow furrowed. Driving was no longer possible, but he hadn't lost hope.

He turned off the television and went to the kitchen. While Ana was looking for something in the fridge, he dropped the five blue Valium pills into her glass of Pinot Noir that sat on the bar.

"Who's the national guard officer in charge," Warfield said through the crack above the Hummer's window. He had to literally shout down to state patrol officer Captain Haygood to be heard over the weather and car horns.

"Military's not running this show, buddy. Get out of the truck!" Haygood shouted.

"Soon as I see the ranking military officer standing there." A couple of the soldiers started to take closer notice.

Haygood's hand began to move about inside the slicker. "You'll get out now, or we'll *take* you out."

Warfield closed the window. He didn't think the enraged trooper would go so far as to shoot him. Haygood consulted with his men and spoke into a radio. Minutes later additional troopers began arriving on the shoulder. The symphony of horns rivaled the noise of the storm. One of the soldiers grabbed his radio and started talking. Warfield looked at his watch. His chances of getting to the Golden Touch ahead of the storm surge diminished by the second. Even the Humvee had its limits.

The standoff went on for fifteen minutes, by which time at least a hundred troopers and national guardsmen had congregated, all standing around Warfield's Humvee in the rain and struggling at times to balance themselves against the gale. Another Humvee arrived on the shoulder and a general riding in the right seat got out and strode through the mass of troopers and guardsmen, who cleared a wide berth for him and threw their hands up in salute.

"What's the problem here?" The general stood at least six-four and had some meat on his bones. His voice had no trouble overcoming the sound of the weather and the cars.

Warfield saw the star on his collar and started to emerge, but Haygood began to vent to the general about the disruption Warfield had caused, the number of troopers he'd tied up for too many precious minutes, and only God could know how many lives he'd cost by shutting down the evacuation. This thief had refused his order to get out of the vehicle and was under arrest.

The general looked around at one of his own men. "Know anything about this, Sergeant O'Hare?"

"Yes, sir, sounds 'bout right. The dude apparently stole the Hummer up the road. When the troopers stopped him here, he refused to get out 'til he could talk to you."

The general looked up at Warfield and started to speak but Haygood started again. The general turned to him, saying, "Is this the biggest problem you got today, Haywood?"

"It's Hay*good*. You see all these cars sitting here? Hear those horns blowin'?"

The general looked at the cars. "Who stopped 'em?"

"I did," Haygood said. "Only way we could stop this thief."

"That'd be a little hard for me to understand, but I'll handle this man and you can take care of the traffic—unless you want us to take that over too."

The general looked up at Warfield. It was dark except for some light from the cars. "Well, I'm here, podnuh," the general boomed. "So let's see if you can get down and tell me why you borrowed this car of mine."

Warfield jumped down to the ground and pushed the Redskins cap back.

The general put a light on Warfield. *Warfield!...My God! That you? What the hell?* The general began laughing. "Casinos are all closed in Atlantic City, man!"

Warfield caught his face. *"Damn Right Donaldson?"*

"Damn right!" The two men fell into a bear hug with almost child-like glee, Warfield abandoning for the moment the gravity of his situation. Captain Haygood looked around at the other troopers in disbelief. Some looked away to conceal their amusement.

Haygood nodded to two of his men and took a step toward Warfield. "I'm taking this man in, General Donaldson. My jurisdiction."

Damn Right's huge black hand blocked the trooper. "Harwood, you'd prob'ly be speakin' Russian right now, wasn't for Warfield here. I loaned him this car, so there is no crime. Now you reckon you could just go back to helpin' those folks get away from the hurricane? Sounds like some of 'em are getting a little irate. I'll take care of Warfield, here."

Warfield and Daniel R. Donaldson paralleled each other through the military ranks and co-operated on missions more than once over the years. Donaldson had earned the nickname that matched his initials through his positive attitude and self-confidence: Anytime he was asked if he was certain about some plan he'd laid out, his answer was always *damn right*. Warfield had thrown a party for him when he retired from active duty three years ago and joined the guard.

But right now Warfield had no time for fraternization. "Danny, I can't tell you anything right now except that it's life-and-death important for me to get to Atlantic City. This storm's not helping. Can you get me there?"

Donaldson nodded. "Take Sergeant O'Hare with you. Go as far as you can in the Humvee. Can't put a chopper up in this, but we got a couple Triple-AV's there in Atlantic City. O'Hare can radio ahead and get one to meet y'all where the water gets too high for the Hummer. That oughta do it, Warfield. Now get the hell outta here."

Ought to do it was the understatement of the day, Warfield thought. The Advanced Amphibious Assault Vehicle had a forty-five-mile offshore range. It could span an eight-foot trench, walk over a three-foot vertical wall and handle eight-foot waves. The Marines used it transport troops ship-to-shore and to move them around on land.

As soon as they were on the road, Warfield used O'Hare's radio to check his voicemail. The sound quality was poor but he heard Holden's voice say it was urgent. Warfield called the number Holden left.

"It's Warfield, Holden."

"Don't know what it's about, but my brother Tom—FBI, you'll recall—I was on the phone with him after I spoke with you. He said he's got to talk to you before you see Mr. Quinn. I, I'm embarrassed, sir. Guess I said something to Tom about your call this morning. Know I should keep my mouth shut."

"Don't worry about it, Holden. Can you track him down while I hang on?"

Holden put Warfield on hold and came back on the line a minute later. "Tom's phone's out. I'll send a deputy over to his house and bring him here. Thirty minutes!"

Warfield said he'd call back to the jail in half an hour.

All expressway lanes were northbound now but Damn Right Donaldson had ordered his guard troops to create a rolling roadblock on the outside lane of the expressway ahead of Warfield and O'Hare. That allowed the Humvee to make a speed of about thirty until they reached the western edge of Atlantic City, where the AAAV met them. O'Hare left the Humvee and rode with the Triple-AV crew and Warfield to the Golden Touch. The city was vacated. Boats and debris floated in the streets. Dark traffic signals flapped from their cable supports like kite tails. Trees were uprooted or broken, lying in streets that were under four feet of water. Warfield had never seen it rain so hard.

The triple-AV driver Juan Gonzales stopped in front of the Golden Touch, the only structure between them and the edge of the churning ocean. A submerged landscape area preceded a set of steps that led above water level to a plaza bordered by a concrete balustrade. There was just enough space between the four foot diameter building support columns for the vehicle to get through. Gonzales said he could deliver Warfield to the escalator steps that ran from the plaza up to the lobby area, well above the swirling water. "You say the word, Colonel Warfield."

Warfield told Gonzales to wait while he checked back with Holden at ADC.

Captain Holden put his brother on the phone.

"It's Tom Holden, Colonel."

"Listen, Tom, I'm minutes away from seeing Quinn. What's this about?"

"I'm a little uncomfortable telling you this but you need to know, even if it backfires on me. It's not confirmed yet, still restricted to the very highest level and a handful of others at the Bureau. Not even the White House knows. Consequences are too great if it's leaked and then couldn't be confirmed. I have it only because I'm in charge of security for Fullwood's data bank."

Warfield looked at his watch. "Understood. Get to it."

"Ever hear of a Leonard Magliacci?"

Warfield listened for the next ten minutes without saying a word.

Warfield nodded and Gonzales ran the amphibian up the steps. Before Warfield jumped over to the dead escalator he asked O'Hare if there were any firearms on board. There were none. The evacuation was a domestic operation.

"How many flights you gotta go up?" O'Hare asked, as Warfield made the leap.

Warfield had heard Cross mention Quinn's suite. "Twelfth floor," he shouted back. He ran beyond the cavernous lobby, through a roomful of slot machines and past the Austin Quinn Ballroom, where he found a stairwell and took two steps at a time. The elevators were likely operating on emergency power but he couldn't risk being trapped in one. At the eleventh floor he took a minute to catch his breath and weigh the information Tom Holden had given him. He tried to imagine every scenario he might encounter at Quinn's, and how he would respond. His first objective was Ana's safety. Then Quinn.

Privately owned apartments occupied the twelfth floor of the Golden Touch. A couple of emergency red exit lights in the hall prevented total darkness. A sliver of light escaped under one of the room doors, frosting the hall carpet, and Warfield gambled that was Quinn's suite. He went back to the stairwell and removed the fire axe he'd seen mounted there and planned his arrival.

Warfield stood in front of Quinn's door and brought the axe down hard. It slammed through the lock and Warfield swooped low, rammed the door with his shoulder and rushed the room.

Quinn calmly stood there with a gun pointed at him.

"Well. I was getting concerned, Warfield," Quinn said. The cocky smile had returned. He waved Warfield to a chair with the pistol. "Almost thought the storm kept you away. You'll have to forgive me for underestimating you again."

Warfield's head was spinning. Quinn was *expecting* him? *Why? Did that mean Quinn used Ana to draw him there in case he survived the goons who tried to kill him? Was Ana complicit in Quinn's plot, or a victim?*

"Ana. Where is she, Quinn?"

"Ana's fine. Got a little sleepy after dinner. How about you, Colonel. Care for a drink? Or did you swear off after your…what would you call it? Your dark period?" Quinn put the .38 on the bar and kept an eye on Warfield as he poured a glass of Glenfiddich. Warfield noticed that he looked worse than when they met the day before.

"You kept up with me pretty well, Quinn, after Joplan," Warfield said, trying to buy time.

"Joplan. Now there's a subject, Warfield. We could talk about him all evening, couldn't we? Figured I'd have to deal with you when you told Fullwood and me you'd narrowed the Habur gate screw-up to three possibilities and that two of them pointed to a mole. Trying to smoke me out. I'd sold you short before then."

"What's the plan now?" Warfield kept his eyes peeled for an opportunity but Quinn never took his eyes off Warfield.

Quinn nodded toward the outside. "There's a dangerous storm out there. You take a risk when you don't evacuate. People get washed away. Some never found. I won't miss you. You've hounded me."

"You're the victim, is that it, Quinn, beginning with the girl's murder? What was her name? Karly?"

Quinn looked surprised. "Your sarcasm doesn't escape me, but it's true. I didn't intend to hurt Karly. Things got out of hand when she demanded money and I momentarily lost control."

"And Frank Gallardi bailed you out."

"How'd you get all this, Warfield?"

"So Gallardi was victim number two. How many in all? Karly. Gallardi. Joplan. Swope. Her lawyer. You tried me three times—the car blast, the condo, the chase this morning."

"You failed to include the gangster that dumped Karly's body. This Matty Fig. I should get the citizenship award for that one."

"Who does your dirty work, Quinn? If it's Pat Biggers, he will be the last one on your to-do list. Who'll take care of him?"

Quinn put his drink on a small desk across the room from Warfield and sat down behind it, all the while keeping the .38 trained on him. "You don't discourage easily. This is a fallback plan, me dealing with you myself, and I admit I don't like it. But you amaze me, Warfield. Where'd you get your information?"

"Ever hear of Leonard Magliacci?" Warfield was playing the card Tom Holden gave him minutes ago.

Quinn's face revealed his contempt for Magliacci. "Forgot to count that lowlife. He's dead—another good deed to my credit. Magliacci never accomplished anything in his life, then he goes snooping around after Frank's death, finds things from Karly's room that Gallardi kept in a safe, like an idiot. Then this Magliacci blackmails me."

"And the timing was perfect for you to take advantage of Joplan's contact, Seth."

"I never met with Seth, Warfield. Joplan's contact I met with was some Frenchie—Pierre, or something like that—in Paris. I didn't know he was fronting for a terrorist"

"Don't try to sell that, Quinn. What good could anybody trying to get the names of unstable Russian scientists be up to? Treason is treason. You knew what you were doing."

"You'd have done the same thing, Warfield. You can't say otherwise if you haven't been through what has happened to me."

"Give it up, Austin. You can do something positive with the rest of your life, even in prison. Start by clearing Ana. She'd be free if you hadn't bribed Helen Swope."

Quinn smiled. "So you think Ana…" He stopped mid-sentence.

"What about Ana?"

Quinn didn't answer.

Warfield had no intention of dying there but he had to stall until Quinn made a mistake—or Warfield created one.

Quinn said, "I'm happy to fill you in, Warfield, because I'm the last person you will ever speak with. What happened that night up in Karly's apartment is ancient history, an unfortunate situation. And the CIA list, it got into the wrong hands, okay, Warfield? And it's a big regret that…that…that what I did put the country at risk. But I've got too much life ahead, too many opportunities, to let mistakes I made years ago stop me. When I get past you and one or two other obstacles I'm back on track. I'm not an evil man! It's the circumstances. You for example. I warned you to stay out of this. And because of what you stirred up, more people got hurt. Like that lawyer of Ana's, Upson. And Morgan. None of this should have happened to me. I'm going to take my life back."

"Yeah, Quinn, you were walking through the park one Sunday morning on your way to church when hell opened up before you and pulled you in. You parlayed that night with Karly Amarson into a crime wave, and none of it's your fault. Kill me or not, your own ruination is sure to come."

"Wishful on your part, Warfield." Quinn hit the Scotch again.

Warfield played another Holden card. "But you're forgetting the inevitable. Magliacci's sealed your fate."

Quinn was smug. "Magliacci's dead. You know that."

"He left the FBI a little surprise."

Quinn stared at Warfield silently.

Warfield continued. "Few things in a safe deposit box, including photos of Karly's jewelry, a knife, other stuff covered with blood—"

Quinn laughed. "Good try, Warfield. Those things exist only in some Bureau file. They're on the bottom of the Atlantic. I put them there myself. Photos are nothing."

"—along with a letter from somebody named Maria Sanchez and—"

Quinn sneered. "Listen Warfield, that maid's letter might snag some Joe installing floor mats over at the Ford plant, but the threshold's high for a man at my level. You know that. Remember Bill Clinton? Magliacci's claim won't get beyond the tabloids."

"—and blood types," Warfield continued. "DNA from two different people on the things Magliacci sent to the feds."

DNA! This one registered with Quinn.

Why hadn't Quinn thought of that, Warfield wondered.

"Turn yourself in before it hits the news, Quinn. More killing will only make it worse. Even if you get away with it, you can't live with what you've done. Sooner or later it'll drive you mad. Everyone in the world will know what Austin Quinn is. You'll be a *Washington Post* headline today and a footnote in history books tomorrow, but not for the reasons you'd like."

Quinn kept switching the pistol from hand to hand and running his fingers through his hair. He was silent except for heavy breathing.

As Warfield pursued the surrender tack, Quinn became more agitated and less stable. Then he sat stone still for what seemed to Warfield like a lifetime, all the while looking straight into Warfield's eyes. Every nerve in Warfield's body stood on alert for the slightest opportunity to take him but Quinn kept the .38 leveled at his chest from the desktop.

The wind and rain lashed the windows. Quinn finally rose and directed Warfield to stand up. "Put your hands on that wall behind you and lean against it, Warfield. Don't turn around. I don't want to be looking at you when you die." He spoke quietly and without emotion.

During the interminable wait, Warfield had scanned the room in search of a weapon to use. The object he chose now as he faced the wall was an octagonal crystal clock the size of a baseball that sat on a table within reach. It would be dense enough to take a toll if Warfield could manage it. His plan was to snatch the clock, drop to the floor and laser it to the exact point where Quinn was standing—all in a seamless, light-speed move with enough force to disable Quinn momentarily or at least distract him long enough for Warfield to overpower him.

The plan wasn't ideal, but neither was Quinn at his best. He'd been drinking, and the Magliacci revelation—the DNA part, it seemed—had him reeling. On the other hand, Quinn had him one-zip in firearms, and his movements were erratic. What Warfield had to do first was pin down Quinn's exact location behind him. With luck he might nail him with the clock. If not, it should at least confuse him for the instant Warfield needed. Quinn shouted for him to lean against the wall. He complied, but not before he established the coordinates he needed. Warfield had thought he might have convinced Quinn his plan was doomed and to give it up but now it didn't look that way.

Warfield waited no longer. In a swift move, he swept up and fired the clock-missile to the predetermined point with all the force he could summon from the awkward position he was in, and folded into a low profile on the floor at the same moment. The clock left his hand even before he could see Quinn in his peripheral vision.

The clock hit the wall—*not Quinn. Quinn had anticipated it and moved, or Warfield was off-target. Where was Quinn now?* Warfield spun around, but Quinn was no longer standing there, and then Warfield heard the gun discharge. Warfield fell to the floor.

In the moments that followed, Warfield realized he wasn't hit but Quinn had disappeared. Then he heard groans coming from a pair of double doors beyond the point where Quinn stood seconds earlier. They were locked, but Warfield stood to the side and used the axe to break in. Austin Quinn lay stretched out on the bed, one hand over his stomach, the other dangling off the side. The .38 lay on the floor.

A moderate amount of blood seeped from the wound where the bullet entered Quinn's right temple. His face was white, his muscles twitched and his eyes were dull. Warfield found a weak pulse. He ran to another room and found Ana alive but in deep sleep. He couldn't rouse her. He bounded down the stairwell to the lobby, hoping to find a medical-emergency crew. The lobby was ankle deep in water now and no one was in sight. He ran to the top of the escalator, and through the rain saw a vehicle plowing through the water a few yards from the building. It turned out to be the AAAV heading toward the Golden Touch. When it got closer he made out Damn Right Donaldson with O'Hare and Gonzales. What a beautiful sight.

The AAAV stopped at the edge of the lobby. "Decided I better check on you, Warfield. You got more lives than a litter of cats, but one of these days you're gonna use 'em all up."

President Cross stood by his desk in the Oval Office and pressed the phone hard against his ear. He didn't believe he was hearing Warfield right. It was the static.

Warfield spoke louder and slower this time. "It's about Quinn. He shot himself, Mr. President!"

"*Quinn? My God!*"

"May not make it."

"*What...what happened?*"

The line improved a bit and Warfield took a minute to sketch out the scene. "I know this is a personal matter for you, sir, as well as political, but there are some urgent decisions."

Cross knew Warfield was right. The president had to deal with realities first, emotions later. "Give me the situation!"

"I'm with Quinn now in Atlantic City. General Donaldson with the guard here in Jersey, he's getting us to a trauma center."

"You stay with Austin until I get somebody there to manage information. It won't be quick, the weather as it is, but the press can't get there either. And Cam, don't talk to anyone."

"Tell me what you know, Cam," Cross said. It was Sunday afternoon in the Oval Office and the storm had subsided. Warfield had returned from Philadelphia that morning and showered at the White House before meeting with Cross. He hadn't yet been back to see the destruction at his own place.

He laid out both the hard and the circumstantial evidence: Quinn's Paris trip. Randall Coffman. The Donald O. Goodwin alias. Suri. Helen Swope. Quinn's warnings to back off. The attempts on Warfield's life. Quinn's revelations to Warfield in the moments before he shot himself.

Then Warfield went back to the beginning with what he'd learned from Tom Holden minutes before paying his visit to Quinn: Karly's murder, Gallardi's role after her death, Maria Sanchez's role and Magliacci's blackmail.

Warfield laid out his theory that Quinn, desperate for money to pay Magliacci, placed a confederate inside the Atlanta prison right after Warfield revealed in the Oval Office meeting that Joplan had a contact with deep pockets. This operative extracted the contact information from Joplan and killed him. Armed with that information, Quinn had Joplan's contact, Pierre, all to himself. Once Quinn and Pierre exchanged the CIA list and the money, Seth orchestrated the movement of Petrevich and the uranium from Moscow to Tokyo. The crossing into Iraq was a red herring that worked. It was easy to believe Petrevich's destination was the Middle East. Certainly anywhere other than Tokyo.

Cross was destroyed by it all and when Warfield finished he shook his head. "So Austin did this. I guess I never knew him."

"He used Ana to lure me to Atlantic City after his hired hands blew it here. By then, he'd killed off everyone who could trip him up but Ana and me. A handful of unsolved murders in Washington is a little blip on the screen, so nobody noticed they were related."

Cross positioned his chin on a steeple of his fingers. "When you told him the FBI had the stuff from Magliacci's safe-deposit box...that was the feather that brought the bridge down."

"The DNA. Nothing else phased him. I tried to convince him to turn himself in, but..."

Cross shook his head. "Proud man, Austin. Self-destruction was easier."

Warfield nodded. Maybe Quinn never really allowed himself to think about it before. Faced with certain exposure, it all came home. In those few minutes, he morphed from homicidal to suicidal.

Cross had been staring out the window into the Rose Garden. He turned back to Warfield. "Anything else right now, Cam? Guess I need to sit with this for awhile."

"Nothing that can't wait, sir." What Warfield needed was sleep. He'd been up since Friday morning.

Next morning in the Oval Office, Cross brought Warfield up to date on Quinn. Emergency surgery had kept him alive so far, but more operations would be necessary. He'd be moved to Johns Hopkins in Baltimore as soon as the doctors would allow it. Even if he survived, he was not expected to recover his mental faculties.

"So he'll never stand trial," said Cross. "In a way, this is worse for him than a trial. This whole damn mess, it's the hardest thing I've had to face here in the presidency. Anywhere."

Warfield nodded.

"Now I have to deal with the press," Cross said. "It'll look worse if we try to keep it quiet much longer. Congress will jump in the middle of it. CIA may as well put their operations files on all the billboards around town when Congress gets through wringing them out."

After a while, Cross looked at Warfield in resignation. "Anything else?"

"This may not be the best time."

"What is it?"

"Ana Koronis. She's gotta be dealt with." After Damn Right Donaldson delivered Warfield and Quinn to the hospital, his men took Ana to Philadelphia where they held her until federal marshals returned her to the ADC.

"This Helen Swope thing?"

"Right. Take what we know about Quinn, Swope's apparent false testimony plus what Suri told me, you get some serious doubt about Ana's guilt."

"She'll get a new trial after Quinn has been dealt with, when all his doings have been fleshed out. And she can use those facts for her defense."

Warfield nodded. "If Ana's innocent, and I think she probably is, she shouldn't have to wait around for the system to work, knowing what we know. You're talking a year, maybe more. Swope's dead, but at least Joe Morgan survived, and her minister is going to make it."

"What are you getting at?"

"Some kind of temporary release."

Cross thought about it for a moment. "Okay, go for it. But it's your baby, Cam. I can't help right now. Quinn's enough, on top of everything else. But you can use my name when you need to. I'll back you."

Warfield left the Oval Office knowing he would be tied up in FBI interviews, CIA debriefings and Congressional hearings for some time. Then he'd get Ana out of jail.

CHAPTER 20

ANA WALKED OUT OF the Alexandria Detention Center five weeks after Cross agreed to lend his weight to get her released.

It hadn't been easy. Warfield had to stretch Cross's offer of influence to the limit by authorizing Ana's lawyers to tell the judge and government attorneys the president would grant Ana a pardon if they didn't find a way to release her until she could get a new trial. With that, the prosecutors gave in and Judge Hartrampf agreed, but imposed a few restrictions. Her travels were limited to the D.C. area and she was required to report to Hartrampf's clerk every Monday morning.

The press got wind of the pardon threat and published it. Cross called Warfield. "She'd better be squeaky clean. Otherwise, you and I may as well go back to prison with her."

Ana's townhouse was worse than she expected. Water had intruded somehow and ruined a stretch of ceiling and two Persian rugs and permanently stained her wood floors. She spent her first day back arranging for repairs and a cleaning crew. To her relief, the lady who cleaned for her before she moved in with Quinn was still available, and someone was coming out to look at the water damage.

She couldn't stay there that night and checked into a Holiday Inn a few blocks away. After spending half an hour developing a list of things she had to do, she took a cab across the river the following morning to her old law office in Washington. The reception she got from her former partners was reserved. They sat in a small conference room with her and chatted about nothing for a few minutes, clearly avoiding her ordeal. They didn't object when she requested the contents from her safe. Her office hadn't been occupied since she left and she decided no one ever knew the safe was there.

After leaving the law office in another cab, Ana made three quick stops and returned to the hotel. There she made a phone call that took almost half an hour, ordered a Domino's pizza and spent the next few minutes soaking

317

in a hot shower, the first moments she had taken for herself since she was released. There'd be more of those later, she promised herself, but there was work to do first.

The next day, she took a taxi to the J. W. Marriott Hotel on Pennsylvania Avenue, where she browsed through one of the shops in the lobby for a few minutes. At two-fifty-five she walked over to the bank of phones built into the wall. Each phone had its own four-foot-by-four-foot enclosure with a privacy door. Several of the booths were available but Ana had waited until the second one from the left, of which she'd copied the phone number yesterday, became vacant. She sat down inside. It was two-fifty-seven in the afternoon.

She had gone through reliable channels last night to get a message to Seth. She gave him three phone numbers at various public locations in Washington, and listed the date and time she would be at each. She expected Seth to reach her at one of them. She waited in the phone booth until three-thirty. The phone didn't ring.

The next day was no better. She hung around a phone near a secluded waiting area at George Washington University hospital but the call never came.

On the third day, at the remaining location, the phone rang at two past ten in the morning.

"Yes," she said.

"Good. No names," Seth said. "And be brief."

She took a deep breath, one of relief, as if it were her first in days. "Of course."

"You are free now from that prison?" He sounded reserved.

"Gratefully so."

"Why do you call me now?"

"I think you can imagine."

"I do not dare to guess, Ana."

"I've paid a heavy price for something I did not do."

"Perhaps because of your Iranian roots."

"I would never have been convicted otherwise. My release has done nothing to ease my resentment."

"But you are free now."

"Temporarily at least, but that is not the point. I am damaged goods forever. I've tried to avoid bitterness but I'm afraid it has taken over my soul."

There was silence for a moment before Seth said, "Again, why do you call me?"

"I will say I am more sympathetic now to your, uh, activities."

"You have reversed your position about assisting me?"

"I believe I am ready for that, yes."

"I do not know you. I must be very careful."

Ana didn't say a word. She quietly hung up the phone and sat there for a minute, wondering whether she'd done the right thing. She was walking away when it rang again. It rang five times before she picked it up.

"We can take one step at a time," Seth said.

Ana was silent for a moment. "What do you want me to do?"

"Provide information to help set up a U.S. operation, but it must have great potential if it is to be of interest to me."

"I think you'll find the opportunities to your satisfaction. I have contacts."

"There are logistical problems."

"Travel?"

"It is more difficult now."

"I can make those arrangements for you."

Ana hung up and called to make a luncheon appointment with an old friend at the State Department, Tot Templeton. Tot worked as a mid-level manager at State in the section that had oversight responsibilities for passports and visas. Tot's section was one of Ana's biggest clients when she practiced law. And she was the only one of Ana's acquaintances who attended her trial.

Tot had worked for State for more than seventeen years and watched co-worker after co-worker, most of whom she considered to have skills inferior to her own, pass over her en route to positions that offered more responsibility and better pay. She had expressed her frustration about it to Ana more than once, and told Ana she was a lifesaver for listening to her. Tot also worked nights and weekends as a volunteer counselor at a legal aid office, where she had come to identify with a certain type of client: Those who felt they had been downtrodden by their employer. Given the Washington setting, those were often employees of the federal government. Tot became known as a more-than-sympathetic ear at legal aid, one who would go the extra mile, perhaps bend the rules if it meant justice for her clients.

At lunch Ana talked and Tot paid close attention. It was an hour past the time for Tot to return to work when they hugged warmly and parted.

Four weeks later, Seth breezed through customs at Reagan National and called the number Ana provided, gave her an address and told her to wait for him there. She would be watched and if anything looked suspicious he would not show and would call her later with new instructions.

The address was a safe house held by a group in line with Seth's causes. They were to call him when Ana arrived if everything looked okay. Seth stayed alive by being cautious. He trusted no one but himself and certainly not his Americanized sister, but her contacts and knowledge of Washington might mean the difference between success and failure. Nevertheless, he would tell her only what he needed her to know.

It was unusual for Seth to play such an active role in an operation. He was a broker for information, materials and expertise—as in the Petrevich operation. He was infrastructure, facilitator. The brains. But the opportunity to carry out a high-profile project himself in the capital of his most hated enemy was too great a temptation. It would enhance his reputation among other freedom fighters and pull in new money from sympathizers. It would be near impossible to better the high-water mark left in the United States by his brothers before him but this operation would serve to perpetuate the uncertainty the Americans had lived with for years now and kept them off balance.

Seth's war would be won a kill at a time. And where he and others like him had it over the rest of the world could be found in their values. Westerners didn't have the will to kill innocents. To Seth, all Americans were fair game.

Seth got to the safe house ten minutes after Ana. "You look the same," she said, tugging on his beard as they embraced.

"And you…still beautiful, my sister." After they made small talk for a minute Seth looked at his watch and turned to the business at hand.

"What is next for you?"

"I may be free for only a short while. I'll get a new trial and—"

"—and they will find a way to keep you in prison. You are among the enemy, Ana. They would not negotiate with your son and husband's captors to save them. You were born to Iranian parents and can never be accepted here. And our people will never give up our fight. We cannot beat America in a great war such as might have occurred between Russia and the United States but we can keep their people off balance, take a few at a time. They will come to wish for a decisive battle but there will never be one. We will choose the battlefields in America as we have done in the rest of the world. They will never know where the next one will be. Or when. We will choose our implements of war and we have loyalists who will be the vehicles of delivery. The imbeciles of the United States can never compete with an enemy who believes as fervently as we do, who are willing to die for our beliefs. They can never be prepared for us or find us for retaliation. We are nowhere and we are everywhere."

Seth went on. "To kill us would be to kill the women and children who harbor us. The Americans will allow their own to be killed rather than do that. We are a perfect war machine, Ana, because we have a perfect enemy. Someday the Great Satan will bow to us."

Seth paused. The veins in his muscular arms bulged as he looked at Ana. "The name Seth will be revered or feared the world around. Our parents would be proud of both of us."

Ana wiped a tear from her eye.

"I have heard of your Warfield. Is he a concern?"

"Warfield feels somewhat responsible for my conviction. He got me out of jail."

"You have a way with men."

"I don't wish to talk about that. Tell me what you need me to do."

"You can acquire the materials I will need without raising suspicion. And you may wish to suggest a target. I will consider your suggestion but it must have the potential for great destruction of life, disruption of orderly process and psychological impact. It will be better if it is part of the government."

Seth didn't want to spend any more time at the safe house. He gave Ana cash for the materials he needed, including a box-truck with a hydraulic lift that lowered from the back of the truck to the ground. She would use the truck to haul the supplies and Seth would use it later in his operation. Ana agreed to come up with a list of targets. They arranged for their next phone contact and left the safe house separately.

Three days later they met at a new place. Ana left the materials she had acquired for Seth in the truck, which she had parked in a remote area of a shopping center far from any structures where it might invite suspicion. When Seth asked for her suggested targets she named several. At the top of the list was the Justice Department, whom she told Seth was most responsible for her wrong conviction. Seth wanted to know the number of workers at each potential target, their level of importance in the government, the probable effect of their loss on the operations of government and on the psyche of the citizenry. Those were the criteria he'd use in selecting his target.

Seth found the truck. When he drove onto the street a gray Chevrolet Suburban was following him but it soon turned off. A black sedan took its place but it also went another direction. *Paranoia*, Seth thought. *I have been lucky too long and now I am getting paranoid.* He drove a circuitous route and an hour later ended up at his motel, an extended-stay type that provided maid service only on request. He drove the truck around to the rear of the building and backed it up to his ground-floor room. Over the next three hours he moved the supplies into the room, waiting between trips until no one was in the parking lot to see him.

Enabled by the credentials Ana had secured for him in the name of Ahmed Ahmed with the assistance of Tot Templeton, Seth landed a full-time job with D.C. Private Select Services, the firm that provided maintenance and repair for several federal facilities, including the Department of Justice building. The personal interview that preceded hiring wasn't easy. Seth's very presence created anxiety if not fear in anyone near him. That persona was legendary and he had never done anything to soften the impact. But he had to work up a non-threatening act so he would be hired by a prospective employer.

Ana had helped him with the employment application and told him to name Templeton at State as a reference. He received the security clearance DCPSS required within a week and they put him to work the next day.

Every night when he returned to his motel he worked on the bomb until two in the morning and got up at six to go to work. It took him thirty-three days to complete his masterpiece, working in his off-duty hours.

It was a Sunday night and the area at the rear of the motel was deserted and dark. He removed the door and plate glass window from his room and rigged a series of pulleys and rope. This mechanical assist made it possible for him to inch the bomb across the floor to the lift gate. He then raised the lift gate to the level of the truck floor and slid the explosive into the truck using the pulley system again. He leaned against the inside wall of the box truck for a moment while he caught his breath. He imagined the carnage, and wished for a moment he could share it with someone.

His plan wasn't original. The same thing had been done in the United States more than once. And this wouldn't come close to the eleventh of September achievement. But none of the previous operations were carried out by one man working alone. Fumio Yoshida, the Japanese he'd made arrangements for, worked only with Petrevich and his two underlings but failed. This time the credit would go to Seth. Unlike others, he would escape to strike again. He would be the force dominating the news now, the object of endless, exhausting, futile searches worldwide. The mention of his name would from this day forward create a quickening of the pulse. He would be the new symbol of justice in the Middle East, the icon of fear in America. The replacement symbol for bin Laden, who had lost his life because of complacency and carelessness.

Seth had studied structural design at the German university he attended and knew how and where to place explosives for greatest results. During his DCPSS service trips to the Justice building, he surreptitiously took photos and made sketches of the visible structural components in the basement. Soon he had enough data to determine where to park the box truck for maximum effectiveness. Partial devastation of the building was his minimum expectation but total collapse was not impossible. He'd observed and memorized the security procedures and the names of the guards who inspected the vehicles entering the Justice compound. He involved Ana as little as possible and never told her he had selected the Justice building, or when the attack would take place, consistent with the extreme caution that had kept him alive for so long.

* * *

On the long-prepared-for Monday morning, Seth was awakened by his iPhone alarm after an hour of sleep. He'd killed the lights around three-thirty that morning when he was sure the bomb and his plan were firmly in place, but his mind ran wild with thoughts of the excitement that awaited him. Now he shaved his face clean and put on a fresh DCPSS khaki shirt and inspected himself in the mirror. He wore a plain white tee shirt under his uniform shirt.

He had just one more thing to do. When he was two blocks from the Justice Department building he stopped in a loading zone, left the engine running, unlocked the cargo door of the truck, raised it enough to slide under and set the timer for ten minutes. As he started to jump down he thought of the traffic, or maybe a delay at the guard station before he was cleared to drive under the building. Seconds clicked away as he stood there debating with himself. On the other hand he didn't want to allow time for the bomb to be discovered and disarmed after he parked the truck in place. He reset the timer to thirteen minutes and synchronized his wristwatch so he could monitor the countdown precisely. Seconds were critical. He jammed the large padlock shut.

Now back in the flow of traffic, he rehearsed everything one last time: *What to say to the security guard. Exactly where to leave the truck. His escape route. And don't attract attention by running.* He patted the Uzi under his right thigh. He wouldn't need it after he got inside and would leave it in the truck with documentation showing his real name, Seth, by which the intelligence agencies of the world knew him, before walking away and disappearing from the building. The adrenaline was flowing. If it wasn't already famous enough, the name Seth would soon be cemented among the most feared and despised names in the world. But among his brothers he would be proudly spoken of in the most revered terms.

He was a little relieved when he saw that the guard at the delivery entrance this morning was one he recognized. Their schedules changed from time to time. Seth's truck was third in line and he'd already used up almost eight of his thirteen minutes. He had five minutes to clear the checkpoint, park the truck and get out of the building. Perfect. When he got to the gatepost he told the guard, "The company truck got a broken axle, Larry. I must use this rental until repairs are made." He was confident Larry would pass him through as usual without inspecting his cargo.

Larry nodded his understanding. "Gotta put her in the computer, though, Ahmed. It'll be just a minute. *Hey! You shaved your beard!*"

"Yeah, my girlfriend, she wanted me to."

Seth drummed his watch. Three minutes and two seconds to go. He glanced at the hydraulic concrete barrier ahead of him that would recede into the floor when he was cleared for entry.

At a minute and thirty seconds, Seth looked over to see if Larry was almost finished checking him in, and something moving in the truck's mirror caught his eye. *Black helmets. Black uniforms! Assault weapons!* He spun his head around to the other mirror. There too! Larry had disappeared.

Seth jumped out and wildly sprayed his Uzi as he ran. He was two steps from the truck when his right leg collapsed in burning pain, then something ripped through his neck and he stumbled to the ground. As light faded from his eyes he knew he was dying, but at least the bomb would blow before anyone could disarm it. His name would mean something to the world forever.

It was mid-morning when a direct line to Cross rang in the Oval Office. "Yes?"

"Warfield."

"How did it go?"

"It's over. Two FBI agents are wounded but they'll be okay. Had emergency medical standing by."

"The bomb..."

"Eight seconds to spare."

"Seth?"

"Under heavy guard at a hospital. Took a couple hits. He'll live, though."

"And your Ms. Koronis?"

"FBI's picking her up now. I think they had an agent in every tree on her block for the last month."

"I want her brought here."

"To the White House?"

"Right here to the Oval Office. I want you here, too, Cam."

"Yes, sir."

Warfield was sitting with Cross in the Oval Office when Paula buzzed and said the FBI had arrived with Ana.

"Send her in."

"Alone, sir?"

"The agents can wait at the door."

Paula ushered Ana inside the great office. She caught Warfield with a glance and arced her eyebrows over an eye-roll on her way out.

Cross rose, walked around his desk and waited for a moment as Ana tried to pull herself together. "Ms. Koronis, I don't know where to begin what I have to say to you."

"I, I, uh, please excuse my appearance," she said. "I had no idea I'd be coming here. It's been…"

"I know. I know," Cross said, putting his arm around her shoulder. "I'm very sorry for what has happened. I wish it could have been different. But I must tell you the United States, and I'm speaking for myself personally as well, we owe you. We owe you an apology for the time you spent in prison. For robbing you of your good name, your freedom. The anguish you've suffered. And we owe you our gratitude for the service you provided in bringing Seth down. The tapes. The risk you took."

"The tapes? *You've* heard the tapes?"

"Read the transcripts. Cam brought them in yesterday. The phone taps. The wires you wore at the safe house. You're good."

"He's my own flesh and blood." She'd lost her composure and was crying softly. "It wasn't easy to, to…but I couldn't have lived with myself unless I at least tried."

"It had to be tough," Cross said.

Ana nodded and dabbed her eyes. "Cam Warfield made it possible. Without his planning, I don't know…I couldn't have pulled it off."

"Now tell me what I can do for you," Cross said.

She was thoughtful for a long moment. "My life," she said. "All I want is to get my life back. I have to do that for myself."

* * *

When Ana left, Warfield shook his head. "She's taken some hits. Prison. Austin. Her brother."

"Austin. Biggest disappointment of my life, too. We were like brothers."

"He's paying the price now," Warfield said.

The following Saturday evening Warfield and Fleming DeGrande picked Ana up at her townhouse and the three of them went out to dinner. They had avoided being seen together during the operation. They were into their second drink when Fleming asked the obvious question.

"What now, Ana, now that you're beyond this, uh, *detour?*"

"I'm going to organize myself to start writing my book."

"You're doing a book about all of this?" Warfield said, his eyebrows rising. "I see it now. Guess who's going to be the bad guy," he said, smiling.

"Cam, you know I don't blame you for what happened. Forget that. But I'm not writing about this mess, anyway. I've been planning this thriller for years and I'm not putting it off any longer. I've saved up enough international intrigue from my legal work for State to do a dozen spy novels. Austin gave me a lot more stuff, talking about operations at the Agency. I made notes from time to time and put them in a safe at the office—at least until my trial. Wasn't sure what to expect when I picked them up, but nothing had been touched."

Warfield said, only half-jokingly, "It could get you another trip to the courthouse."

"Don't worry. No one will recognize the source material when I get through mixing everything up and changing the names."

CHAPTER 21

AFTER THE SHOOT-OUT AT Justice, the press began to look at the sordid mini-dramas that led up to it. Someone was leaking information to reporters and most of it was accurate. Although Warfield disliked leaks and the fact that nothing could ever be kept private in Washington, he was not unhappy about this one. To *Washington Post* reporter Bob Roberts, Quinn became a personal crusade. He began his research as far back as Quinn's work on the New Jersey gambling legislation and his political success that followed. He reconstructed the evening of Quinn's roast and Karly Amarson's murder, only some of which was speculation on his part.

When Roberts reported the deal Fullwood made with Senator Abercrombie the Senate launched an investigation, and by the time it got under way, the General Services Administration notified Abercrombie's real estate firm, as landlord for the FBI office in Taylorville, that it was terminating the lease.

The GSA fired its man who had conspired with Abercrombie and the FBI arrested him. Abercrombie received the bad news about the lease cancellation from his sister, who called him at his office in Washington late one afternoon. She also told him the banks were initiating foreclosure proceedings. Abercrombie's staffers found him dead in his office the next morning. There was no note. At first it was reported as a heart attack but the autopsy revealed an extreme overdose of Seconal.

Fullwood continued his denials right up to the beginning of the Senate hearing, when he was asked whether he and Abercrombie ever had a conversation in which the Senate's termination of Lone Elm and the FBI's leasing of office space from Abercrombie were linked in any way.

"*Hell, no!*" Fullwood yelled.

Then the committee attorney played a video which an FBI agent identified as one found in Abercrombie's office after his death. The conversation between Fullwood and Abercrombie was played for the committee, and for the world on C-SPAN.

Fullwood's lawyer requested a recess. Before the hearing resumed the next morning, the lawyer met with the committee chairman and counsel and told them Fullwood was going to submit his resignation to President Cross that day. But if Fullwood thought that would end it he was mistaken. He left Washington in disgrace and returned to his home state, where the next Wednesday federal marshals arrested him at noon at his home. When they marched him out the front door, remote-broadcast trucks from the national and local networks lined the street. A federal grand jury indicted him a week later.

Warfield arranged a memorial service for Leroy Mitchell, the plumbing contractor for whose death he felt responsible. Reporter Roberts was there. He drew on the irony of Leroy's wife's attempt to comfort Warfield in his anguish over Leroy's death. Warfield put an envelope in her hand when he left the service that day. When Mona opened it, the crinkled photo Warfield had taken from Leroy's truck was inside with a heartfelt letter from Warfield.

Congress soon after passed legislation that recognized Leroy Mitchell for his service to the United States and awarded his widow one million dollars.

Within a couple of months after Austin Quinn shot himself, the cable news shows removed the sensational *Breaking News* graphics that had used up the lower third of the screen, but even then the 24/7 interviews showed no signs of slacking off. News anchors created endless phrasings of the same questions and the Pentagon brass, politicians, nuclear scientists and psychologists appearing with them looked for different ways to answer. It was as if the two groups, the questioners and the answerers, existed for the sole purpose of supporting each other.

Ana tried to shut it all out—the endless rhetoric, the re-living of it all, the if-onlys—but she wasn't there yet. She had run the emotional gamut from denial to grief to acceptance of her fate. Now she was free again and in the process of reclaiming her life. She needed the closure that only facing Quinn could bring. She'd asked Warfield to go with her.

"You can see him now," the desk attendant said. As she and Warfield followed the white-haired assistant down the echoing hallway, Ana thought of the hospital where she had her tonsils out when she was ten—the plaster walls, the white fish-bowl light globes hanging by a wire from the high ceilings, the small once-white tile hexagons that covered the floor. But there the similarities ended. In this place was a potpourri of odors that was more of death than of life. The air was still. The few staff people around didn't seem to have anything to do next.

The hall widened into a circular sitting area that was vacant except for a man in a wheelchair. A black and white television mounted on the wall ran an old Seinfeld show, its contemporary flavor in stark contrast to the place. The man in the wheelchair gave no indication he knew anyone had joined him. Or that the television was on.

"We told him you were coming but you never know what he understands. You all want me to roll his chair out into the yard?" the attendant asked.

Ana and Warfield glanced at each other as they came to realize this was the man they had come to see. Ana touched the fingers of her right hand to her lips and drew an audible breath. She wanted to excuse herself. *There's been a mistake. Please forgive me.* But there was enough left of the man she'd known, even with this white hair, the black-ringed eye-sockets, that she couldn't deny him. She couldn't just walk away.

"Yes. Yes, please."

In the courtyard, Warfield remained standing and Ana sat at the lawn table across from Quinn's wheelchair. The vacant eyes that rose to meet hers may have flickered recognition but she couldn't be sure. His hair didn't completely hide the scars and pink flesh left from the gunshot wound and surgery. A thread of drool had stained the white tunic he wore. His left hand, knotted into a misshapen fist, lay still, dead, as if an attendant had brought it out and placed it there. Quinn's eyes drifted to the hand, perhaps, Ana thought, to question why it failed to reach out as he willed it to. Ana had to force herself to look at this once-proud man who had been her lover; who only a short time ago sat at the table with the world's most powerful.

Sooner than she had planned to leave, Ana knew she could stay no longer. There had been so many victims, so much waste since that black day in Atlantic City when it all began, long before she even knew Quinn. Now here she sat before the man responsible. He had betrayed everything precious and loved and held sacred by those who believed in him. She looked once again into the empty eyes and wondered whether the bullet spared any of the brain cells that accounted for memory.

She rose and squeezed his hand in hers, and after a few moments nodded to Warfield. As they walked away she knew she would never return. Warfield glanced back at Quinn as they left, and was almost certain he'd seen Quinn looking directly at him before turning his eyes away.

Months after Seth's capture, in the spring when cherry blossoms defined the Washington landscape, Warfield watched from the front row of the courtroom with Joe Morgan as Seth stood before the United States District Judge James Piller for sentencing, a ragged scar on Seth's neck showing above his shirt collar. The jury had earlier found him guilty on all of the many counts against him and found for the death penalty. The judge could elect to reduce the sentence to life without parole and Seth's attorneys had fervently pleaded for that.

The court had appointed lawyers of Middle Eastern heritage for Seth to avoid any appearance of prejudice by his attorneys. Warfield figured they had coached Seth on respectful behavior before the court, especially now at sentencing.

"Anything you would like to say to the court before sentencing?" Judge Piller asked Seth, standing between his attorneys before the bench.

Seth had shown no emotion throughout his trial, including when the jury verdicts were read. Now, his hands and feet shackled, Seth stared at the judge with contempt, his head tilted back, his eyes piercing the judge's. "America is nothing," he sneered. "This court is nothing. Your jury is nothing. You have no authority over me. Proceed at your own risk. Any punishment I receive, you and your United States will receive one-hundredfold."

Seth then cleared his throat and spat on the polished mahogany front of the bench without ever taking his eyes off the judge. When the bailiffs threw him to the floor he bit one of them before they got him under control.

Judge Piller, himself shaken, gaveled the alarmed spectators in the courtroom to silence and declared a recess until eight o'clock the next morning.

Seth's attorneys looked at each other in dismay. There was no chance now that the judge would reduce the sentence.

That evening, Warfield called Joe Morgan at home.

"Some show today," Warfield said.

"Can you believe that scum bag? At least he's cinched the death sentence."

"I was thinking about that. You got any pull with the judge?"

"No pull. But I can talk to him. Something in mind?"

"Maybe you should get Judge Piller to consider life without parole."

Morgan seemed stunned. *"You get some sort of brain virus while you were in Tokyo, Warfield?"*

"No, listen…"

They spoke for a few more minutes and said goodnight.

The following morning, Seth stood before the bench in something resembling a straightjacket that bound his upper body. His feet were in chains and a heavy mask covered his mouth and nose.

Piller looked at Seth and cleared his throat. "In my thirty-one years on the bench, I don't remember anyone for whom the death sentence was more appropriate. The evidence presented in this court demonstrates your unsuitability, indeed abject incapacity, to live in harmony with the human race. You are a disgrace to humanity. Your behavior before this court has done nothing to improve my view of that."

Seth's lawyers stared at the floor. They knew what was coming.

Then Judge Piller handed down life without parole. Seth's lawyers looked at each other in disbelief. Warfield gave Joe Morgan a jab in the ribs.

That night Warfield called LaRez Sanazaro in Las Vegas to request a favor.

Ten days after sentencing, Seth sat alone at the table in the mess hall. It was his second day since arriving at the Atlanta Federal Penitentiary and completing orientation. What caught his eye was the way the other inmates moved out of the way of an older man he noticed trudging across the mess hall.

The old man sat down across from Seth without looking at him and was joined seconds later by a man with a balcony-like forehead that hid his eyes. Soon, a somewhat fragile, studious-looking man sat beside Seth.

Seth finished eating and was about to leave when Doyle Riley spoke.

"Seth. Right?"

Seth glared at Riley without answering, surely wondering how this man knew his name.

Riley nodded toward Cosmo. "My client, Cosmo here, he welcomes you to Atlanta."

On a warm evening in June, Fleming and Warfield went to the home of Ana Koronis for dinner, it being her turn to host. Fleming noticed several travel magazines on the coffee table. "Going somewhere?" she asked Ana.

"Some sort of getaway, to give my writing a kick start. Haven't decided where to."

Fleming jumped. "War Man, she's going with *us!*" she said, then turned to Ana. "We're going to the Grand Canyon. Got a friend who hosts tours on the Colorado River."

They spent much of the evening talking about the Canyon and pulling descriptions out of Warfield. By the time it ended Ana had agreed to go with them.

Warfield gazed out the window of the Boeing 757 airliner at the jagged crests of the Rocky Mountains in the distance. Ana Koronis got up to go to the lavatory.

Fleming looked at Warfield. "Okay, War Man. You're too serious. You're wondering why Cross told you to see him when you get back. Well, you're not back yet. You just left! So quit thinking about it."

"Taking up mind reading now, are you?"

"Exactly! You're thinking of the CIA job that's become vacant."

Warfield hadn't thought of that, but he wouldn't take CIA if Cross offered it to him. *Would he?"*

CHAPTER 22

Two Years Later

PATRICIA ADAMS STOOD AT her desk in the Chrysler Building on Lexington Avenue in Manhattan as an early winter snow fell silently outside her window. Since her first visit to the city she had loved the old Art Deco skyscraper she was now standing in and vowed that someday she would have an office there. That had been almost nine years ago, and three years ago she had fulfilled her pledge after years of growing her escort business—now sporting more than a hundred beautiful women suitable for all occasions to the well-heeled men who comprised her clientele. The early years, working out of a large old house in Brooklyn, had been rough, but hard work and perseverance had paid off, and here she was now. Patricia not infrequently made the society pages and was no stranger to the mayor, law enforcement agencies including the NYPD and FBI, and other ranking officials, her profession of social disrepute seeming to matter to no one, and in fact they often found her to be a valuable ally because of her connections. Her business savvy, professionalism, stunning beauty, and cheerful personality had made it all possible.

Of course, obligatory was keeping up with all that went on in her town by reading the *New York Times* and *Wall Street Journal* that were delivered to her offices every morning. Always of primary interest were articles involving high-profile officials and others who might be her clients, as any publicized association between some Fortune 500 executive charged with a white-collar crime and her girls could not only frighten away some of her other clients but also test her valuable connections. An article of interest in today's *Times* caught her eye: "Former CIA Director Seeks Release." The story went on to say that Austin Quinn, a former director of the Central Intelligence Agency, who had been held in a mental rehabilitation center for the past three years after a failed attempt to take his life by a gunshot to his head, had recently been declared competent to stand trial for the crime of

335

selling official secrets to a foreign government. The *Times* had interviewed a sampling of defense attorneys who agreed that the U.S. Government had no chance of conviction in this case due to the statute of limitations, but government prosecutors said they had found a way around that. A hearing on the matter had been scheduled. Patricia clipped the article and added it to a thick yellow file folder in her desk.

Patricia opened a floor safe inside her utility room, pulled out a large envelope and placed its contents on her desk, and retrieved the letter from old Doc Rivera, whom she—then Karly Amarson—had called the night Austin Quinn had stabbed her in the chest nine years earlier. Doc came to her apartment within minutes that night, stopped her bleeding and secretly rushed her, near death, to the emergency room at Charity Hospital in Atlantic City and admitted her as Patricia Adams. He stuck with her as she recovered over the next few days and they talked about a plan for her. The doctors said it was a miracle that no permanent harm came directly from the knife wound; the real risk was that she would have bled to death had Doc Rivera not acted so quickly. It was too dangerous for Karly to stay in Atlantic City, and they decided in the interest of absolute secrecy to not even let Frank Gallardi know she was alive. Karly, now Patricia Adams, then left Atlantic City for good and headed to New York to start her new life.

Now she opened the letter from Doc and read it again:

My Dearest Karly,

You no doubt know by now that Frank was murdered a few nights ago. Nothing is clear at this point but I confiscated his diary from his office before the police got there. I did so because Frank had asked me at lunch one day shortly before his death if I knew Patrick Biggers. Of course I said I do. Biggers is a rather mysterious character who once worked for Austin Quinn. Nothing more was said about him that day, but when I got the horrible news that Frank was killed my mind jumped back to that conversation. I figured there might be a clue in his private and personal daily writings as to why Frank asked me about Biggers. I'm sending you the diary in the belief that you will find that there is.

I've broken the law of course by taking Frank's diary, thus destroying evidence, but I figure there is more potential harm to you if the police get it than there is benefit to them toward finding his killer. Frank is dead. I want you to stay alive. And my guess is that justice will be served in either case. As for me, I am old and don't worry about consequences too much any more. You are my only family.

You have my love and best wishes.
Doc

Karly's eyes glassed over. Doc had saved her life. He had been a father to her and she had been one of only a handful of people who attended Doc's final services. She wished he could know what was going to become of his letter.

Austin Quinn remembered little of the time he spent with Cam Warfield in his Golden Touch suite four years earlier. He just knew he should have killed the bastard instead of succumbing to sudden remorse. The pressure he was under after Warfield had confronted him that day at the White House had driven him to hasty and unwise choices. Had Quinn not been drinking Warfield would be dead and Quinn would not have been so depressed and unnerved that he lost focus and shot himself. He had begun to regain his mind after awhile in rehab but had kept that fact to himself. On the advice of his lawyers Quinn had resisted any testing for the state of his recovery of mental faculties because of the well-founded fear that the government would take him to trial if it found him competent. Life in the rehab center was not bad. It had some of the comforts of home and he had a private room and essentially the liberty to move about the building and even the hundred-acre campus. There were tennis courts and other sports activities for those who had fared well, and he enjoyed long walks and casual association with some of the staff at times. He was certainly not free but voluntarily subjecting himself to testing that would lead to his being found competent and going to trial on the espionage charges was a huge gamble: It would not be a good trade to be found guilty at trial and sent to prison where life would be much worse than here, possibly for the rest of his life. However, his appeals attorney, Oscar Frye, was very forceful in encouraging him to take the chance. He explained the applicable statutes and case law, and acquittal was a slam dunk in his opinion. Frye even said he half-expected the judge to dismiss the charges before the trial began. And no one had ever brought charges of murder and he didn't expect them to. Even though there was no time limit on a murder conviction, he was certain he'd eliminated any possible witnesses long ago.

When he allowed his lawyer to go ahead with a petition to release him from rehab and return his life to him, newspapers revived the Quinn story and began to speculate. Some editorialized that he was a traitor and should never be freed. Most conceded however that there was little likelihood that he would even be tried.

On the first day of the hearing the courtroom was packed. Law students had come from schools all over the country. The CIA, State Department, FBI, and White House were abundantly represented. The requisite number of seats was reserved for the press and the few remaining were occupied by the curious. Conspicuously absent were members of Quinn's family. Patrick Biggers, possibly the only living connection to Quinn's past, was seated in the third row behind the defense table.

Judge Melvin T. Willingham called the court to order and asked if the parties were prepared to proceed, which Quinn's attorney Frye and the federal prosecutor Erwin Hollis affirmed. Judge Willingham then asked if either party had anything to add to the briefs they had submitted to the court. Oscar Frye said he stood by his argument. His client, Austin Quinn, former Director of the Central Intelligence Agency, should be set free.

"Yes, well, Mr. Frye, I'm inclined to agree with you. Does the prosecution have anything to add that might persuade me to let the trial proceed?"

Prosecutor Erwin Hollis had married this case, and it was of intense interest to him. He believed that Austin Quinn was responsible for a series of murders directly related to the case at hand, that of espionage. But Quinn was almost certain to avoid any charges for those murders as no witnesses had ever come forward. The killings could not even be mentioned in this case. The young, idealistic prosecutor, despite realizing the system was working as intended, feared he would lose all faith in the law if Quinn got out of this. Now, thankful for this last glimmer of hope offered by Judge Willingham, he spent the next twenty minutes trying to convince him, fighting against a decision about to go the wrong way. In conclusion, he said, "Your Honor, the defendant Mr. Quinn, serving in one of the most important agencies in our government, entrusted with the nation's most valuable secrets, betrayed his country and all who had placed their confidence in him. It will be a sad commentary on our system, an open invitation to any and all who might be tempted to do us harm, if he is allowed to go unscathed in this matter."

Following a fifteen minute recess the judge returned to the bench and announced his decision: There would be no trial due to the statute of limitations. Therefore, the documentation he had presented from professionals declaring him competent practically forced Judge Willingham to release him. Austin Quinn was free to leave! Paperwork releasing him from the rehab facility could be handled without his presence. Judge Willingham angrily banged his gavel when the courtroom erupted in groans that clearly indicated dissatisfaction with the decision. There was not likely a soul present who did not remember the case from four years earlier when it all came out. This friend of then President Cross and possible future presidential candidate had all but certainly sold national secrets to foreign agents and ordered a series of killings. Now he would go free.

Austin Quinn had leapt out of his chair with a whoop and thrown his hands into the air! He hugged Frye and followed those in the courtroom out into the hallway of the old courthouse, whose marble floor showed the wear of fifty years of trials. Quinn thanked his lawyer, joined Patrick Biggers, and was headed for an elevator when a beautiful woman, fortyish, veered into his path. His attention was drawn to her striking green eyes as he started to maneuver around her in the crowded hallway and, thinking she looked familiar, looked again.

He froze: *My God! No! No! No!*

"Hello, Jag!" Karly said with a wry smile. Except that now she was Patricia Adams.

Four men in suits standing nearby quickly approached, presented FBI identification, separated Quinn and Biggers, and began handcuffing each of them as one of the agents told them they were under arrest on multiple counts of murder." The president had asked the FBI to find a way to make Quinn's a *federal* case, as, unlike in most states, there would be no parole. Oscar Frye, the son of a close friend of President Cross, having met with Cross and Warfield, agreed that justice would be best served if he could get Austin Quinn declared competent.

Quinn could only stare at Karly, this *ghost*, in utter disbelief and confusion for a long moment but soon he looked resigned, dropping his chin to his chest in despair. He had listened to his attorney and lost his last and only chance—and traded the relative comfort of his rehab facility for a six-by-eight cell in the federal penitentiary—likely for the rest of his life.

A month after his arrest, Patrick Biggers' lawyer went to the United States Attorney prosecuting his case and proffered a deal. Biggers could fill in unanswered questions about Quinn in exchange for leniency. It took weeks but they worked it out.

At Quinn's trial, Biggers testified under oath that he'd accepted money from Quinn to arrange all of the murders in Atlantic City beginning with Gallardi, the killings in Washington, and the attempts on Warfield's life. He had also gone to Quinn's house before Ana Koronis' trial and bribed Helen Swope to lie. In the end Quinn was spared the death penalty but sentenced to life in a federal maximum security facility, where there would be no parole.

Five months later, Biggers stood before the same federal judge who had sentenced Quinn. The prosecution explained his cooperation in Quinn's case. He was sentenced to thirty years in a federal penitentiary. Both Quinn and Biggers were sure to receive additional state charges.

Karly Amarson waited in the hallway outside the courtroom for another spectator to emerge. She'd never formally met Cameron Warfield but had been in the courtroom on the day he testified in Quinn's and Biggers' trials. Now she stopped him and introduced herself. He of course knew who she was. "I admire you, Colonel Warfield, for your perseverance. Quinn and Biggers would be free men otherwise. I just want to say 'thank you.'"

Warfield smiled, and introduced her to Fleming DeGrande and to Ana Koronis, who were standing nearby. The women chit-chatted for a moment while Warfield found Quinn's attorney Oscar Frye and shook his hand. The two men looked each other in the eye and nodded almost imperceptibly.

Back in New York, Karly Amarson—Patricia Adams now and forever more—opened her safe, pulled out a worn yellow file folder, thumbed the contents as she absently stared out of the window overlooking the

Manhattan skyline, and placed it in the shred file. Karly Amarson was no longer.

About Nick B. Ganaway

Nick Ganaway loves the likes of thrillers written by of Daniel Silva, John Grisham, Michael Connelly, Ben Macintyre, David Baldacci, Don Winslow, Ken Follett, Vince Flynn, Nelson DeMille and many others, as well as true accounts of military special operations. Nick hopes you enjoy reading *To Free A Spy*, his first novel, as much as he loved researching and writing it. Nick lives in Dunwoody, GA, and has three loving children and five beautiful grandchildren.

ABOUT 'TO FREE A SPY'

I have long been an avid reader of thrillers and spent three years studying the art of writing as taught by many accomplished writers and writing experts, researching background for *To Free A Spy*, and writing, rewriting and changing every word until they refused to be changed any more!

The Tokyo segment was especially interesting to research and write, including direct communication with the very cooperative Radiation Effects Research Foundation in Minami-ku, Hiroshima in Japan. My uninvited exploration of the CIA campus in Langley, VA, was not exactly welcomed with open arms by security officers at the entrance guardpost, who questioned my intentions and my sanity for having ignored the large warning sign and armored vehicle outside the campus entrance and gave me clear orders where to wait for a reception "committee," who approached our car armed and outfitted in black gear. My wife and I were all but fingerprinted (as she reminded through clenched teeth that "I told you so") and advised we were forevermore in the CIA database—and not the one for Christmas cards! Nevertheless, followup phone calls were very productive. In stark contrast to Langley (and a little worrisome,) the White House compound in Washington would appear to be as vulnerable as it is visible, separated from the public only by a fence of (apparently) decorative metal pickets, and guardposts at entrance gates. I'm assured however that there are ample but unseen defenses.

One can never see all that Washington has to offer and it is always a great experience, but the Alexandria Detention Center, where my characters Ana Koronis and Harvey Joplan are housed for a time, is not likely one frequently visited (voluntarily.) Although the modern mid-rise orange-brick structure could easily be mistaken for just another office building a visit to the campus and inside the reception area reveals its serious personality. Although a county facility, the ADC houses often-high profile federal detainees as they progress through the court system.

Visiting and melding into the rolling northern Virginia countryside in and near Middleburg in Loudoun County, just an hour's drive outside D.C., kept us thinking how great it must be to live there in horse country, so close to the Capital yet a world apart, which is why my character Fleming DeGrande's ranch and home are situated nearby. We spent a delightful couple of days becoming acquainted with Middleburg, its art shops, restaurants, B&Bs, welcoming townspeople and lovely countryside.

A fun venue of a completely different world was Atlantic City, with its defining casinos, fun-loving throngs on its famous Boardwalk, weekend gamblers and high-rollers, gold-laden pawn shops and all the trappings of a casino town. All of course at the edge of the ocean.

Writing *To Free A Spy* has been a wonderful experience, and if you enjoy reading it that will be the icing on my cake!

ACKNOWLEDGEMENTS

I'm grateful beyond words to my late bride Lee Ganaway for her tireless reading, critiquing and support during the early stages of this book; to Julie Ganaway Blanchard for her valuable comments about contemporary fashion and style and her assistance in social media marketing; to Ginger Ganaway Smith for social media exposure of *Spy* and to Ginger and to John Ganaway for their unfailing enthusiasm and encouragement. To each of you, know that you have my undying love.

I greatly appreciate Tim C. Taylor for his excellent editorial and formatting services, his marketing effort far beyond what I could have done myself, his expert publishing counsel, and his book, "Format Your Print Book With Createspace." Tim is a business associate whom I have come to count as a friend.

I want to thank the Radiation Effects Research Foundation in Hiroshima for answering my endless questions and providing me with related RERF publications.

I also want to express my appreciation to the Central Intelligence Agency in Langley for responding to those of my questions that they could answer and for their gracious way of saying "no" when that had to be the response. I'm an avid fan of the Agency.

My thanks to my many other friends and family members who throughout the course of this project have generously encouraged me, read for me and offered valuable suggestions and ideas.

I am indebted to each member of this team, without whom *To Free a Spy* would still be just an idea. All errors belong to me.

APR X 2015

Made in the USA
Charleston, SC
12 February 2015